The Glorious Heresies

Lisa McInerney

JOHN MURRAY

First published in Great Britain in 2015 by John Murray (Publishers)
An Hachette UK Company

1

A CIP catalogue record for this title is available from the British Library

Hardback ISBN 978-1-444-79885-2
Trade Paperback ISBN 978-1-444-79886-9
Ebook ISBN 978-1-444-79887-6

Typeset in Sabon MT by Hewer Text UK Ltd, Edinburgh
Printed and bound by Clays Ltd, St Ives plc

John Murray policy is to use papers that are natural, renewable and recyclable
products and made from wood grown in sustainable forests. The logging and
manufacturing processes are expected to conform to the environmental regulations of the country of origin.

John Murray (Publishers)
338 Euston Road
London NW1 3BH

www.johnmurray.co.uk

This, like everything else, is for John

The Dead Man

I

He left the boy outside its own front door. Farewell to it, and good luck to it. He wasn't going to feed it anymore; from here on in it would be squared shoulders and jaws, and strong arms and best feet forward. He left the boy a pile of mangled, skinny limbs and stepped through the door a newborn man, stinging a little in the sights of the sprite guiding his metamorphosis. Karine D'Arcy was her name. She was fifteen and a bit and had been in his class for the past three years. Outside of school she consistently outclassed him, and yet here she was, standing in his hall on a Monday lunchtime. And so the boy had to go, what was left of him, what hadn't been flayed away by her hands and her kisses.

'You're sure your dad won't come home?' she said.

'He won't,' he said, though his father was a law unto himself and couldn't be trusted to follow reason. This morning he'd warned that he'd be out and about, so the kids would have to make their own dinner, though he'd be back later, trailing divilment and, knowing the kindness of the pit, a foul temper.

'What if he does, though?'

He took his hand from hers and slipped it round her waist.

'I don't know,' he said. Oh, the truth was raw, as raw as you could get, unrehearsed words from a brand-new throat.

He was fifteen, only just. If she'd asked him the same question back before they'd crossed this threshold he would have answered according to fifteen years' build-up of boyish bravado, but now that everything had changed he couldn't remember how to showboat.

'It'll be my fault anyway,' he said. 'Not yours.'

They were supposed to be in school, and even his dad would know it. If he came home now, *if*, all lopsided with defeat, the worse for wear because of drink, or poker or whatever the fuck, it'd still take him only a moment to figure out that his son was on the lang, and for one reason only.

'Here it'd be yours,' she said. 'But what if he told my mam and dad?'

'He wouldn't.' It was as certain as the floor beneath them. His father was many things, but none of them responsible. Or bold. Or righteous.

'Are you sure?'

'The only people my dad talks to live here,' he said. 'No one else would have him.'

'So what do we do now?'

The name of this brave new man, still stinging from the possibilities whipping his flesh and pushing down on his shoulders, was Ryan. In truth, his adult form wasn't all that different to the gawky corpse he'd left outside; he was still black-haired and pale-skinned and ink-eyed. 'You look like you're *possessed*,' shivered one of the girls who'd gotten close enough to judge; she then declared her intent to try sucking the demon out through his tongue. He was stretching these past few months. *Too slow, too steady*, his nonna had sighed, the last time she'd perused his Facebook photos. She was adamant he'd never hit six feet. His mother was four years dead and his father was a wreck who slept as often on the couch as he did in his own bed. Ryan was the oldest of the wreck's children. He tiptoed around his father and made up for it around everyone else.

Something didn't fit about that. Of course, men of any age were entitled to flake around the place giving digs to anyone who looked like they might slight them, and that was certainly how the wreck behaved: hollow but for hot, cheap rage, dancing between glory and drying-out sessions in miserable rehab centres a million miles from anywhere. Even when Ryan dredged up the frenzies required by teachers' scorn or challenges thrown down by bigger kids, he knew there was something very empty in the way the lot of them encouraged him to fight. He'd been on the lookout for something to dare him to get out of bed in the morning, but he'd never thought it could have been her.

She was part of that group of girls who wore their skirts the shortest and who commandeered the radiator perches before every class and who could glide between impertinence and saccharine familiarity with teachers. He'd never thought she would look at him as anything but a scrapper, though he'd been asking her to, silently, behind his closed mouth and downturned eyes, for *fucking years*.

Three weeks before, on the night of his birthday, she had let him kiss her.

He'd been in one of his friends' cars – they were older than him, contemporaries of his sixteen-year-old cousin Joseph, who knew enough about Ryan to excuse his age – when he'd spotted her standing outside the doors of the community centre disco, laughing and trembling in a long black top and white shorts. He'd leant up from the back seat and called her from the passenger window, and he didn't even have to coax to get her clambering in beside him. Dumb luck that she was in the mood for a spin. And yet, a leap in his chest that tempted him to believe that maybe it was more again: dumb luck and trust. She trusted him. She – Jesus! – *liked* him.

They'd gone gatting. There were a couple of cans and a couple of joints and a cold, fair wind that brought her closer to his side. When he'd realised he couldn't medicate the nerves, he'd owned up to how he felt about her by chancing a hand left on the small of her back, counting to twenty or thirty or eighty before accepting she wasn't going to move away, taking her hand to steady his own and then finally, finally, over the great distance of thirty centimetres, he caught her mouth on his and kissed her.

In the days that followed they had covered miles of new ground and decided to chance making a go of it. They had gone to the pictures, they had eaten ice cream, they had meandered at the end of each meeting back to her road, holding hands. And lest they laid foundations too wholesome, they had found quiet spaces and dark corners in which to crumble that friendship, his palms recording the difference between the skin on her waist and on her breasts, his body pushing against hers so he could remember how her every hollow fit him.

Now, in his hall on a Monday lunchtime, he answered with a question.

'What do you want to do?'

She stepped into the sitting room and spun on one foot, taking it all in. He didn't need to stick his head through the frame to know that the view was found wanting. His father's ineptitude had preserved the place as a museum to his mother's homemaking skills, and she had been as effective with clutter as the wind was with blades of grass.

'I've never been in your house,' she said. 'It's weird.'

She meant her presence in it, and not the house itself. Though she wouldn't have been far wrong; it was weird. It was a three-bedroom terrace so cavernous without his mother he could barely stand it. It echoed shit he didn't want to think about in chasms that shouldn't have been there. It was a roof over his head. It was a fire hazard, in that he thought sometimes he could douse it in fuel and take a match to it and watch it take the night sky with it.

She knew the score. He'd admitted his circumstances in a brave move only a couple of days before, terrified that she'd lose it and dump him, and yet desperate to tell her that not every rumour about his father was true. On the back steps of the school, curled together on cold concrete, he'd confessed that yeah, he clashed with his dad, but no, not in the way that some of the more spiteful storytellers hinted at. *He's an eejit, girl, there's only the weight in him to stay upright when he's saturated, but he's not . . . He's . . . I've heard shit that people have said but he's not warped, girl. He's just . . . fucking . . . I don't know.*

She hadn't run off and she hadn't told anyone. It was both a load off and the worst play he could have made, for it cemented his place on his belly on the ground in front of her. On one hand he didn't mind because he knew she was better than him – she was whip-smart and as beautiful as morning and each time he saw her he felt with dizzying clarity the blood in his veins and the air in his lungs and his heart beating strong in his chest – but then it pissed him off that he couldn't approach her on his own two feet. That he was no more upright now than his father. That uselessness was hereditary.

There was no anger now, though. He had left it outside the front door with his wilting remains.

She held out her hand for his.

'You gonna play for me?'

His mam's piano stood by the wall, behind the door. It could just as easily have been his. He'd put the hours in, while she fought with his dad or threatened great career changes or fought with the neighbours or threatened to gather him and his siblings and stalk back to her parents. She used to pop him onto the piano stool whenever she needed space to indulge her cranky fancies, and in so doing had left him with ambidexterity and the ability to read sheet music. Not many people knew that about him, because they'd never have guessed.

He could play for Karine D'Arcy, if he wanted to. Some classical piece he could pretend was more than just a practice exercise, or maybe one of the pop songs his mother had taught him when she was finding sporadic employment with wedding bands and singing in hotel lobbies during shitty little arts festivals. It might even work. Karine might be so overwhelmed that she might take all her clothes off and let him fuck her right there on the sitting-room floor.

Something empty about that fantasy, too. The reality is that she was here in his house on a Monday lunchtime, a million zillion years from morphing into a horny stripper. That's what he had to deal with: Karine D'Arcy really-really being here.

He didn't want to play for her. Anticipation would make knuckles of his fingertips.

'I might do later,' he said.

'Later?'

He might have looked deep into her eyes and crooned *Yeah,*

later, if he'd had more time to get used to his new frame. Instead he smiled and looked away and muddled together *Later* and *After* in his head. *I might do After. We have this whole house to ourselves to make better.* There was going to be an After. He knew it.

She walked past him and out into the kitchen, and looked out the back window at the garden and its dock-leafed lawn laid out between stubby walls of concrete block. She flexed her hands against the sink, and pushed back her shoulders as she stretched onto tiptoes.

'It's weird,' she said again. 'To have never been in this house until now. You and me have been friends for so long, like.'

It had been an anxious kind of friendship. There were school projects and parties and play-fighting and one time a real fight during which he had accused her of only hanging out with him to get access to those parties. It was during that outburst of impotent temper, between off-white walls in a wide school corridor, that he realised their closeness amounted to years of her dragging him along like a piece of broken rock in a comet's tail.

It hit him like a midwife's slap that if it wasn't for his house being so cavernous, if it wasn't for his dad traipsing the city looking for cheap drink and indifferent company, if it wasn't for the fact that scrappers cared little for mitching off school, she wouldn't be here with him now, offering him the possibility of removing the burden of friendship and at least some of his clothes. Karine D'Arcy looked back at him with one hand on the draining board, rearranging the kitchen by way of chemical reaction, bleak snapshots fizzling against her butter-blonde hair and popping like soap bubbles against the hem of her grey school skirt. The house looked different with her here, on his side. She didn't know the history in every room and every jagged edge. The bottom step of the stairs. The coffee table that was always there, just so, to trip him up whenever he was shoved into the front room. The kitchen wall, the spot by the back door, where he'd watched the light switch from an inch away with one cheek pressed against eggshell blue and his dad's weight condensed into a hand flat on his left temple trying to push him right through the plaster.

'You're beautiful,' he told her, and she laughed and blinked and said, 'God, where did that come from?'

'You are,' he said. 'What are you doing here?'

She nestled against his neck. *Missing Geography*, she might have said. But she didn't say anything and the longer her silence went on the closer they got to the stairs, to his bed, to whatever came after that.

He hated his bedroom marginally less than he hated the rest of the house. He shared it with his brothers Cian and Cathal, who were messier than he was. The space was laid out in a Venn diagram; no matter how loudly he roared or how gingerly he protected what was his from what was theirs, they always managed to arrange an overlap. She sat on his bed – gratifying that she knew which was his – and he kicked his way around the floor, sending Dinky cars and Lego and inside-out pyjama bottoms under beds and into corners.

She was sitting on her hands and so when they kissed it was as if they'd never kissed before and weren't entirely sure whether they'd like it. The second one was better. She reached to cradle his face. The side of her finger brushed against the back of his ear. He pushed her school jumper over her breasts and when she pulled back to take it off he copied her.

'Maybe,' she said, three buttons down, 'like, we should close out the door. Just in case.'

'I could pull one of the beds in front of it?'

'Yeah.'

He pulled the curtains too. They lay on his bed and held each other, and kissed, and more clothes came off, and all the way along he kept thinking that she was going to withdraw her approval, that his hands would betray him here as he worried they would on the piano keys.

She didn't. She kissed him back and pressed against him and helped him. And he wondered, if he could do this with her in every room would it sanctify the place, exorcise it of the echoes of words spat and each jarring thump recorded against each solid surface?

He wondered if he should stop wondering, when a wandering mind was heresy.

'Just be careful,' she whispered. 'Oh please, Ryan, be careful.'

She clasped her hands around his neck and he found his right hand on her left knee, gently pushing out and oh fuck, that was it, he was totally done for.

Cork City isn't going to notice the first brave steps of a resolute little man. The city runs on the macro: traffic jams, All-Ireland finals, drug busts, general elections. Shit to complain about: the economy, the Dáil, whatever shaving of Ireland's integrity they were auctioning off to mainland Europe this week.

But Monday lunchtime was the whole world to one new man, and probably a thousand more besides, people who spent those couple of hours getting promotions or pregnancy tests or keys to their brand-new second-hand cars. There were people dying, too. That's the way of the city: one new man to take the place of another, bleeding out on a polished kitchen floor.

Maureen had just killed a man.

She didn't mean to do it. She'd barely need to prove that, she thought; no one would look at a fifty-nine-year-old slip of a whip like her and see a killer. When you saw them on the telly, the broken ones who tore asunder all around them, they always looked a bit off. Too much attention from handsy uncles, too few green vegetables. Faces like bags of triangles and eyes like buttons on sticks. Pass one on the street and you'd be straight into the Gardaí, suggesting that they tail the lurching loon if they were looking for a promotion to bring home to the mammy in Ballygobackwards. Well, not Maureen. Her face had a habit of sliding into a scowl between intentional expressions, but looking like a string of piss wasn't enough to have Gardaí probing your perversions. There'd have been no scandals in the Church at all, she thought, if the Gardaí had ever had minds honed so.

She looked at the man face-down on the tiles. There was blood under him. It gunged into the grout. It'd need wire wool.

Bicarbonate of soda. Bleach. Probably something stronger; she wasn't an expert. She didn't usually go around on cat feet surprising intruders with blunt force trauma. This was a first for her.

She was shit at cleaning, too. Homemaking skills were for good girls and it was forty years since anyone had told her she was one of them.

He was definitely dead, whoever he was. He wore a once-black jumper and a pair of shiny tracksuit bottoms. The back of his head was cracked and his hair matted, but it had been foxy before that. A tall man, a skinny rake, another string of piss, now departed. She hadn't gotten a look at his face before she flaked him with the Holy Stone and she couldn't bring herself to turn him over. It'd be like turning a chop on a grill, the thought of which turned her stomach. She'd hardly eat now. What if his eyes were still open?

There was no question of ringing for the guards. She did think – her face by now halfway to her ankles – that it might be jolly to ring for a priest, just to see how God and his bandits felt about it. Maybe they'd try to clean the kitchen floor by blessing it, *by the power vested in me*. But she didn't think she'd be able for inviting one of them fellas over the threshold. Two invasions in a day? She didn't have the bleach.

She turned from the dead man to pick up her phone.

Jimmy had drawn priests down upon her like seagulls to the bridge in bad weather. He was sin, poor thing, conceived in it and then the mark of it, growing like all bad secrets until he stretched her into a shape no one could shut their eyes to.

If she'd been born a decade earlier, she reckoned giving birth out of wedlock would have landed her a life sentence scrubbing linens in a chemical haze, hard labour twice over to placate women of God and feather their nests. But there was enough space in the seventies to allow her room to turn on her heel and head for England, where she was, on and off, until the terrible deed she'd named James tracked her down again with his own burden to show her.

Some women had illegitimate babies who grew up to be

2

The man on the street, the scut in the back corner of the pub, and the burnt-out girl on the quay all said the same: it was better to run alongside Jimmy Phelan than have him run over you. In short pants he was king of the terrace; in an Iron Maiden T-shirt he was Merchant General of the catchment area. He'd sold fags and dope and cans of lager, and then heroin and women and munitions. He'd won over and killed cops and robbers both. He'd been married. He'd attended parent-teacher meetings. He'd done deals and time and half the world twice over. There wasn't much left that Jimmy Phelan hadn't had a good go of and yet it was only very recently he'd owned up to the notion that inside him was a void kept raw and weeping for want of a family tree. It turned out, though, that Jimmy Phelan's eyes were bigger than his belly, and that applied to anything he had a yearning for: imported flesh, Cognac, his long-lost mother.

The bint had only gone and killed someone. He supposed it was appropriate carry-on for the block he was chipped from, but it didn't make it any less of an arseache. Jimmy liked to leave himself room for manoeuvre in his diary, but 'Clean up after your mother offs someone' was a much more significant task than he'd ever have thought to factor in.

He had set aside an apartment by the river for Maureen's use. With his being such a captain of industry, it had never been the plan to have her living with him, even if it hadn't turned out that she was crazier than a dustbin fox. It hadn't really been the plan to bring her home in the first place – all he'd aimed for was to track her down and give her the lowdown on her grandchildren

– but he'd had to re-strategise when he'd found her living amongst shuffling addicts and weird bachelors in a London tenement. He'd heard enough nationalist rants to know that leaving an Irish person in poverty in England was leaving them behind enemy lines, and it had been well within his capacity to take her home. She'd dug her heels in, but there was no one who could draw away from Jimmy Phelan's insistence, no matter how much pride or how many limbs they looked set to lose.

He'd bought the building for a song because a bunch of Vietnamese had been using it as a grow house and the guards had left it with more holes in the walls than there were cunts down in Crosser. If there had been any Vietnamese left he might have sold it back to them, on the 'lightning strikes' adage, but they'd gathered their skirts and scurried down to Waterford, or so he'd heard, so he'd used it as a brothel for a while, and might do again once he found somewhere less draughty to store his mother. He'd left her in the ground-floor flat, convalescing from her emigration, and had a few part-time part-tradesmen making structural improvements to the floors above, but he'd thought it had been secure. Maybe susceptible to punters lost and roaming, but she'd been under strict instructions not to open the door to anyone, and it had been a while since they'd begun redirecting appointments to the newer venue.

So how Maureen had managed to kill an intruder was beyond him. How did the weasel get in? Had the Vietnamese forgotten him? Had the guards not noticed him tucked away in the attic? Was he a john whose longtime kink was climbing in through skylights?

Whoever he was, he was dead now, and it turned out he probably wouldn't have been an open casket job even if he'd reached his natural expiration date. In fact, looking at him, he'd clearly been in the process of hurrying that along.

'What the fuck did you do to him?' Jimmy asked Maureen, as she sat at the kitchen table making faces at her cigarette. She was a dour little thing. Lacking height himself, he'd resorted to growing outwards to achieve the bulk demanded by his vocation. Even now at forty he was mostly muscle, softened only very lately by a languid habit of eating out and drinking well. Maureen was whittled straight and had a glare just as pointed. They didn't look alike.

'Belted him,' she said. 'With the Holy Stone. I wasn't giving up the upper hand on the off-chance he was Santy Claus.'

'What Holy Stone?'

She gestured towards the sink.

For every Renaissance masterpiece there were a million geegaws cobbled together from the scrapheap, and this was awful even by that standard. A flat rock, about a fistful, painted gold and mounted on polished wood, with a picture of the Virgin Mary holding Chubby Toddler Jesus printed on one side in bright Celtic colours, and the bloody essences of the dead man on the kitchen floor smeared and knotted on top.

'Where the fuck did you get this?' If it wasn't for the fact it was mounted on that plinth, he'd have assumed some opportunistic crackpot had painted it for a car boot sale. He turned it over in his hand. The Blessed Virgin stared guzz-eyed back at him.

'I've had that a long time.'

'I didn't take you for a Holy Josephine.'

'You wouldn't want to, because I'm not.'

'You just collect bulky religious souvenirs to use as murder weapons, is it? No one ever suspects the heavy hand of the Lord. *Repent, repent, or Jesus might take the head off yeh!* How did you even swing this thing, Maureen? Did you take a run at him from the front door?'

'The Lord works in mysterious ways,' she said.

'I know a few lords like that all right.' He ran the Holy Stone under the tap and looked back at the dead man. 'You have no idea what he wanted?'

'Isn't it funny; I didn't think to ask.'

The body was weedy, its clothes shabby, even before the chap's blood had glued them to his frame. He had nothing in his pockets but a balled-up tissue and two-fifty in coins.

'Some junkie, maybe, looking for cash. I don't know the face.

He looks Irish. Or maybe a Sasanach. Rooted down in West Cork with the rest of the chin-wobblers.'

She sniffed. 'Dirty tramp. Robbing all around them. I'm just the type they target.'

'He's no one I know. And if he had any local knowledge at all he wouldn't have dared come near this house.'

He tossed the Holy Stone from one hand to the other. 'Dame Maureen, in the kitchen, with the rock o' Knock. We'll get rid of him for you.'

'The floor will need scrubbing.'

'And someone to clean the floor.'

'The grout will need replacing.'

'We'll get you a new floor, then.'

'You'll get me out of here. Who'd want to stay in a place a man died?'

'Oh, you'd want to watch out for vengeful spirits. He'll be in every mirror now, Maureen. He'll be coming up at you from the floor when you're trying to make the tay.'

'You can grin all you like, boy,' she said, 'but it's not right to leave a woman alone in a house like this.'

'It's you who made it like this,' he said. 'But point taken. I'll get you a cat.'

She threw daggers.

'First thing's first,' he said. 'I'll hire some hands. After that we'll look at living arrangements. I have nowhere else for you at the moment. I'll figure something out, but it won't be tonight.'

'It will. I'm not staying here.'

'You are until I find somewhere else for you.'

'I'm not. I'll sit outside for the night.'

'And you'll freeze and then there'll be two corpses and I tell you what, girl, I've only the patience for digging one grave.'

'You should have left me in London,' she said. 'Poor interest you have in me, at the end of the day.'

'That's right, Maureen. Poor interest. That's why it's me standing here, being fucking munificent with my fingerprints, instead of the state pathologist and Anglesea Street's finest.'

‘I’m not staying here,’ she said.

‘First thing’s first, I said. Will you stay here till I get back? Will you at least do that much for me?’

She tipped ash onto the tabletop. ‘I’m not staying here with a corpse.’

‘And whose fault is it that he’s a corpse?’

‘I don’t know yet,’ she said.

He met the challenge and it went right through him.

‘Fine,’ he said. ‘Fine. Come on. Sure Deirdre’ll be thrilled to see you.’

Maureen wasn’t officially living in Jimmy Phelan’s building. The building didn’t officially belong to Jimmy Phelan. Even so, he didn’t want to use his nearest and dearest men for this job. There was something off about the whole thing. He wasn’t convinced that the foxy-haired intruder was just some gowl hunting desperately for spare change. Jimmy Phelan trusted his gut, and now he felt it howling.

The job had to be done. There was a body on his mother’s kitchen floor, and it wasn’t going to get up and leave of its own accord. Ordinarily he’d have swiftly handpicked a few decent sorts – at the very least his right-hand man Dougan, whose brutish dexterity and wicked sense of humour would be just right for the occasion – but that would suggest that he had a designated clean-up crew, and he couldn’t be sure how Maureen would take it.

Or how Dougan and the boys would take her. They knew scraps of the story: that he had tracked down his birth mother and brought her home. They didn’t know she was such an odd fish as to be capable of impromptu executions. Their respect for him, and for his lineage, could well be mangled by news of her little rampage. He bristled at the thought of it. He was sore where he’d grafted on this brand-new past.

Deirdre Allen was as stubborn as she was tough, which may have sounded like an admirable mix, but as far as Jimmy could tell it simply meant she was too stupid to know when she was wrong and too slow to notice the consequences. She was still dyeing her hair jet-black, still smoking twenty a day, still insisting that if he funded her expedition into real estate, he'd get his money back and doubled again. Still thinking there was opportunity on the right side of the euro. Still believing the recession was a sag in Ireland's fabric, stretched as far as it could go and on the point of bouncing upwards.

That pig-headedness was what had taken her so long to leave him. She had sailed through nearly a decade of his debasing their marital vows before she'd run aground. He hadn't made a habit of affairs; there were plenty of girls he could fuck without having to fork out for extras. Even so, there were so many all-nighters, so many week-long absences that any other woman would have read the warnings. By the time Deirdre noticed, it was much too late to draw boundaries. Jimmy gave her the house and wondered if one day she'd chalk their collaborative fuck-up down to experience. For now, she still laid claim to the title of Jimmy Phelan's Wife. She didn't want him in her bed anymore, but she was too stubborn and too tough to give up what she thought were the perks of his infamy.

'I want to get the kids a piano,' she said, dispatching a cup of tea in Maureen's general direction, wrinkling her nose. She hadn't asked how Maureen took her tea, but Deirdre had long assumed, incorrectly, that she had a knack for hostessing. 'I've always regretted not learning an instrument. I don't want them saying the same thing in ten years' time.'

'Are you having me on, girl? They'd have no more interest in learning the piano than they did in anything else you demanded I foist on them. It's you who wants the piano. A front-room centrepiece. Something to rest a vase on.'

'You can be a very thick man, Jimmy.'

'Maybe it's because I never learned to tickle the ivories. There's no art in me.'

'You'd deny your children the opportunity to learn a skill so? Just because there's a chance they might not stick with it? Is it depressed you are, or just plain mean?'

Maureen took her mug and walked out onto the back decking.

'Ah, she's thrilled you found her,' sneered Deirdre.

'I'm glad you know her so well, girl, because she's staying here with you tonight.'

'What?'

'The flat's getting cleaned. Industrial shit. No way can I have her stay there overnight, and I have too much on to offer her my bed. Long and short of it: you're stuck with her till tomorrow.'

'I am in me shit, Jimmy,' she hissed. 'You can't leave that loon here.'

'You've got a spare room. And she's been wanting to spend more time with her grandchildren. At least until she starts knowing them from the next pair of spoiled brats.'

'The cheek of you, boy. That woman, wherever you found her, might have ties to you but she doesn't to *my* children.'

'That's a failure of the most basic concept of human biology, Deirdre.'

'You know what I mean, Jimmy. There's a lot more to family than . . .' She waved a hand and grimaced. 'Fluids. Genetics. Whatever you want to call it.'

Maureen wasn't moving but to bring cigarette to mouth. She stared out across the lawn, serene as a cud-chewing cow. Just the right demeanour for the city's newest reaper: taking the scythe in her stride. Jimmy hadn't met many new murderers who weren't bent double by the aftermath, who didn't puke on their shoes as an epilogue.

'Well look, I'll tell you what I'll do,' he said to Deirdre. 'I'll find you a piano and you can honky-tonk your musical regrets away to your heart's content. I won't even ask why Ellie and Conor's fingers are still pudgy as pigs' trotters in a year's time. And all you have to do is mind my mammy for the night.'

'Ah, in fairness, Jimmy . . .'

'You should try talking to her. She's got your children's history knotted up inside that wizened head of hers. She's got Ireland's history in there. She's a very interesting woman.'

'A bit too interesting. Don't you think I've had it up to here with how interesting you can be?'

‘A piano for sanctuary,’ he said. ‘You’d deny your children the opportunity to learn a skill just because there’s a chance my dear mum will leave smudges on your furniture? Don’t be plain mean, Deirdre. Aren’t you better than me and my ancestry?’

He went out onto the deck and closed the door behind him.

‘You’re to stay with Deirdre tonight, Maureen. Say nothing about yer manno. We’ll have him scooped up and out in no time. Who knows, you might even fall in love with the new floor.’

‘I won’t go back there,’ she said. ‘It’s not safe.’

‘Yeah. Well. We’ll talk about it after.’

He took care of some chores after leaving Maureen in the reluctant hands of the daughter-in-law she’d missed out on, but as day stretched into evening there was still a human sacrifice on his mother’s kitchen floor, one with a dent in the back of its head made by Ireland’s ignorance of fine art and penchant for cut-price religious iconography.

He wondered where Maureen had gotten the Holy Stone. Had someone pressed it on her when she was reeling from childbirth? Had they assumed that even that crude image of the world’s ultimate single mother would provide solace in hard times? Were they just blind, deaf and dumb to style?

Jimmy Phelan was raised by his grandparents, not unwillingly, but awkwardly nevertheless. They brought him to Knock once and offered him up to the wall once favoured by apparitions as a living paradigm of their piety. He’d been very bored, but afterwards they’d taken a jaunt through the town and he remembered gift shop after gift shop, gift shops as far as an eight-year-old eye could see, stocked to the rafters with baubles. Rows of Virgin Mary barometers; her fuzzy cloak would change colour depending on the weather, which was very miraculous. Toy cameras with preloaded images of the shrine; you clicked through them, holding the flimsy yokey up to the light. And so many sticks of rock. You could have built a whole other shrine out of sticks of rock.

Maureen’s Holy Stone wouldn’t have looked far out of place. Maybe his grandparents had purchased it. Maybe it was his speeding around this wonderland of faith-based kitsch, jacked up on neon-pink rock and too many bags of Taytos, that advised them of its relevance.

And so supposing the Holy Stone symbolised something to Maureen. Repentance. Humility. New beginnings. Supposing smashing it off the skull of an intruder set her back forty years. How much healing did a fallen woman require, if she had the whole of Ireland's fucked up psyche weighing her down to purgatory?

Evening was drawing in and there was a corpse drawing flies back in the flat, and no one yet nominated to move it.

He stopped at a Centra and bought himself a sausage sandwich and a coffee, and sat in his car to eat and think.

It felt wrong to be hiding from Dougan the source of a problem the man would have to fix. Jimmy wasn't used to this kind of isolation. His mother – the woman he tentatively thought of as his mother, as a rickety leg-up to understanding the blood that ran in his veins – had fucked up, and for once in his life, Jimmy felt a weak spot.

He was mulling this over when he spotted someone, ten feet away from his car. The figure was vaguely familiar. A dark, tousled head bent over an outstretched palm, opposite fingers picking through coins as one would for a parking meter. Thickset running thin, in a navy hoodie and blue jeans that had both been through the wash ten-too-many times. Jimmy balled up the sandwich wrapper, stuck it in his empty coffee cup, and stepped out of the car. Between the bin and his mark, he chanced, 'Cusack?'

The other looked up. It was him all right. More than a few years older, though Jimmy would have sworn it had been only months since they last spoke.

'J.P., boy,' he said, still with his palm out.

'Cusack. You're looking well.'

It was a disingenuous greeting but the only alternative was the most brutal honesty. *The absolute state a' yeh, Cusack! If there's a whore you've been visiting, it might be worth sprinkling her with holy water and commanding her back to the fiery depths, because you look like someone's tapped you for fluids.*

The desiccated accepted the salutation with a mournful nod.

'It's been a while,' said Jimmy.

'I suppose it has.' His voice was thick. Drunk? It looked more possible than anything else that had demanded his analysis today.

Back when Jimmy was in Iron Maiden T-shirts, Tony Cusack had been the useful kind of scamp, eager to prove he could hang around with the big boys by virtue of his keen eye and malleable morals. He'd been Jimmy's messenger when he was small enough to be fleet, but as he got bigger they'd drink together, or get stoned, and shoot the breeze about easy women and anarchy. When Jimmy was twenty-four, a coagulation of bad luck convinced him to head to London for a while, where he could carry on as before only with a shiny coat of anonymity, and, having fuck all else to do, Cusack had gone with him.

London had been good to Jimmy. It had given him cause to aim high. London had been good too to Tony, in its own way. He'd met a beour, impregnated her and brought her home with him, instead of staying put where the sun was shining.

His path had seldom crossed Jimmy's since. Christmases, here and there, they'd spotted each other in pubs. Jimmy had been known to send over a drink, but he'd taken care not to be too inviting. The charming laziness that had once defined Tony Cusack had morphed into dusty apathy; as a thirtysomething he was clumsy and morose, taxidermy reanimated. It was no secret that Cusack had pissed away what good London had given him. Even while his wife – had he even married her? – had been around, he had been steadily eroding his liver and the goodwill of every vintner in the city.

There wasn't much Jimmy didn't know about the city's vintners. Or its moneylenders, or dealers, or bookies. Cusack didn't have a reputation, as such, for that would be assuming that people bothered thinking about him, but if his demeanour didn't warn off investors then there were plenty of people able to cure their myopia.

Jimmy Phelan had a reputation. Tony Cusack had more of a stench. Forlorn and forgotten, cast out . . .

Perversely, that made him a good man for secrets, for who'd believe him if he talked? Who'd even listen to him?

'Are you busy? Jimmy asked, though he'd already anticipated the answer, and had already settled on the bribe.

Cusack wasn't busy. He wasn't a man used to being busy, and took the detour as a short holiday from whatever freeform tedium was routine to him. Jimmy gave him the bones of the brief – frightened woman, dead burglar, no suitable hands to complete the deed – and Cusack flinched, and puffed out his cheeks as if he was considering bolting, but Jimmy was OK with that. Fear was a quality he looked for in part-timers, though it was strange to encourage that attribute in a man he might once have called his friend, back, way back, when Jimmy had neither mother nor need for one.

When they got to the flat Cusack needed a minute on his haunches with his back turned, but after the rebellion inside him had been quashed, he dutifully found a ratty carpet on one of the upper floors, pulled up as part of the redecoration project, and helped Jimmy roll the dead man like a cigar. The tradesmen had left behind some cleaning tools; Jimmy and Tony scrubbed up as best they could, given the length of time the stranger had had to tattoo the floor. Maureen was right; they'd need to lay a new one. There was more to this job than the lick of a mop.

'How are you with tiling?' Jimmy asked.

'I did the bathroom of my own gaff,' said Tony. He'd sobered up, of course. 'Floor to ceiling. Put down tiles in the kitchen too, but that was a while ago.'

'Do a job here for me and I'll give you a few bob. I don't want to have to bring anyone else in on this now. What are you at tomorrow?'

'Nothing.'

'I'd a feeling you'd say that.'

In the absence of another vehicle, Jimmy drove his Volvo around to the back gate, at one end of a weathered brick alley garlanded deliberately with creepers and weeds. They flattened the back seat and laid the carpet cigar on a diagonal line: what once had been a breathing, thinking head to the back of the passenger seat, what once had been trespassing feet to the opposite corner. They arranged empty paint cans and a ladder on one side, and on the other the double-bagged rags and brushes they'd used to clean up the blood.

Jimmy handed Tony a set of keys and notes enough to buy tiles and bleach.

'You've a car?'

'I do,' said Tony.

'Go with quarry tiles.' And then, because custom suggested, he said, 'What have you been up to anyway, Cusack? You're not working?'

'Here and there. Best anyone can manage now, I think.'

'You're probably right, boy. Even this is a one-off; I have more than enough mouths to feed.'

'I know that.' Tony shifted his weight. 'I know that, boy.'

'Speaking of mouths, how many little Cusacks are there?'

There was a ghost of a smile; it set on and escaped Tony's mouth in a snap second. It was the first time in a long time Jimmy had noticed something approximating life in the old dog.

'Six.'

'Six? You'd want to tie a knot in it.'

Six made leverage plenty.

They stood by the back of the car, still enough to let birds continue their evening rituals in the greenery around them, flitting in and out of bushes, darting shadows moving on walls the height-and-a-half of Jimmy.

'There's one job I'll have coming up,' said Jimmy. 'Nothing big and certainly nothing worth what I'll pay you, but you've done me a turn today. I'll be getting my hands on a piano sooner or later. The ex is looking for one for the kids. If you're around you can help move it in.'

'What kind of piano?'

'Worried for your back, are you? Not one of them long ones, if that's what you mean.'

'No, I mean what kind are you looking for? I have one I'm trying to get shot of.'

'You? Where'd you get your grabbies on a piano, boy?'

Tony clucked and shook his head. 'Not like that,' he said. 'I own one. It's a few years old but it was bought new. It's a beauty, but all it's doing in my gaff is taking up space.'

'Is that the kind of thing that has to go, Cusack, when a man's got six kids?'

Tony shrugged. 'I can't play,' he said, though it sounded petulant, a tone not right for business deals, even on a day when reason had made way for blood, ties and tide.

Before they locked up Jimmy retrieved the Holy Stone and laid it carefully on the rolled-up shape of his mother's second greatest mistake.

Big Words, Little Man

'I'm just saying,' she says, 'that it's weird, like, that you can be so distant with someone you're actually in a proper relationship with.'

God though, tell you what but she's fucking beautiful when she's pissed off, even if it's pissed off with me. She's gone pink-cheeked and her eyes are flashing hazel to black and she's even standing with her arms folded and her chin sticking out. And all around her you get people moving from here to there in the school yard like dancers in formation, like snowflakes in the sky, like shitty little bangers around a falling star.

She's all like 'My friends think it's mean' and 'My friends say it's a really bad sign' and it's not like I'm whipped or nothing but what her friends think means a fuck of a lot more to me than she knows because you know the way ould dolls are, it's all fucking crowdsourced. But I go, 'Look, it shouldn't matter what your friends think, it should matter only what you think,' and she goes, 'Well it is *about what I think, Ryan, and I think it's awful because I've done everything for you, you know?' By 'everything' she means she's let me fuck her and she's not even being over the top with that; it was everything, it was the whole world. She doesn't know that though. She only says 'everything' because she doesn't want every Tom, Dick and Harry hearing her say the word 'sex' coz you don't get away with words like that in the middle of the yard in the middle of lunchtime with every kid in this school sporting lugs the size of Leitrim. Which is funny because what she's pushing me to say is a whole lot bigger.*

I say, 'You know how I feel about you, though.'

She says, 'How would I know it?'

I say, 'Coz don't I show you?'

And she says, 'Eh, the only thing I see shown is how much I let you get away with and what if it's all for nothing, like?'

And I smile and she goes, 'It's not funny, Ryan!' and looks like she might cry, and the thing is I know exactly what to do and I want to do it, believe me, I'm gagging to, only sometimes you have the right words in your mouth in the right order but it's such a big thing and a big fright that you're not sure if you can open up wide enough to get it out.

She says, 'Coz this is such *a big deal, Ryan,' and looks away and shakes her head. 'And if you don't, well, it just means I'm stupid for letting you after only a couple of weeks. And I wouldn't ever again then.'*

'That's not the way it is,' I tell her.

'What way is it?'

I get all mortified and look at the tarmac between my feet and she says, 'Oh my God. Fine so,' and turns away and I know she doesn't realise what a weird thing this is for me, because this isn't shit I've heard or said since I was a small fella, and I wince and she gets further away from me and I call, 'Hey, D'Arcy,' and she turns around, blazing, and I shrug and say, 'I loves yeh,' and the whole yard reels with her and shouts Oooooh! *and I go bright. Fucking. Red.*

But she smiles, and brings her hand to her mouth and gives me the eyes, because she knows there's no way I would have made a total gobshite of myself in front of everyone if I didn't totally mean it.

3

Georgie met Robbie when she was fifteen and he was twenty-two. He admitted to twenty-two; she admitted to nothing, not age nor origin nor the fact that she didn't have a fucking clue what she was doing. She was a runaway and he was wandering, and it happened that they found each other.

She lost him abruptly one April week, six years later. She couldn't say what day because there were often absences. She'd be working or he'd be climbing a wall somewhere, trying to come down before he fell down. So she didn't panic when she arrived home one day and he wasn't there, or start chewing her nails when he didn't pick up his mobile; he lost phones in perpetuity, sometimes quite intentionally. She phoned around the few friends they had but no one had seen him. On the third day she started to worry.

Georgie, small-town wild child and intermittent claustrophobic, self-styled, was into drugs well before she met Robbie. She wouldn't have met him at all if it wasn't for that shared interest: they kept bumping into each other on the same couches, doing the same drugs to the same end. He had sea-grey eyes and hair the colour of a muted sunset. Coasting on borrowed intelligence, they spoke about all manner of insubstantialities.

At one party, he told her that he had a room in a flat, and that she could sleep there, if she wanted.

'It's only a mattress on the floor,' he said. 'But it's better than couch-surfing or . . .' He blinked. '. . . moving from party to party, if you know what I mean.'

She went with him and twenty minutes later lay staring at the flaking wood on the inside of a white sash window, wincing as he shoved and stuck inside her, an invasion she'd sanctioned because she was spiralling and indebted. That was how Georgie lost her virginity: in a negotiation for mattress space.

After that he produced some more coke.

'You can stay as long as you like,' he said. 'I mean . . . that was really good of you.'

'No problem,' she replied.

His dick looked smaller than it had any right to feel when it had been inside her. He handed her his T-shirt and she bunched it between her legs.

She did another line and when she straightened up she noticed he was staring at her tits, gawping, like he hadn't seen a naked girl in years.

'No, it was really, really good of you,' he said.

Silence for a moment, and then, 'Do you like me?'

'Yeah. Course I do.'

He didn't believe her. 'I like you,' he said. 'Have done, too. For ages. You can stay as long as you like. I mean it.'

You can stay for six years, he could have said, and Georgie would have believed his offer but not in her ability to put up with him for that long. But that was it, wasn't it? You don't know your own strength till you need it.

Outside of their appetite for inebriation, Georgie and Robbie had little to hold them together, and there were more photogenic couples. He looked jointed enough to be folded away when not in use, and it wasn't often anyone had use for him. She was short and freckled, prone to weight where it wasn't wanted. The size of her breasts had made her barrel-like in her school jumper; ould fellas had breathed rough suggestions when they passed her on the street.

First she told Robbie that she'd moved to the city after her Leaving Cert to party. The longer she slept on his mattress, the heavier the lie felt, until she was too exhausted by its heft to be comfortable under it. She told him when she was sure he wouldn't baulk: she was fifteen and she'd run away but no one was looking for her because she'd told her parents she was just fine. Rang them every fortnight, actually, and evidently the guards weren't interested in tracking down a girl who was doing just fine. She was still here to party, she insisted.

Robbie took it exactly as she'd predicted. He scratched the back of his neck and puffed his cheeks out. 'Whoa,' he said, and reached no further than that. By then it was too late for him to demur, even if he had the guts for it. He had already walked her into an agreement with the guy he rented the room from; the landlord fucked her, now and then, in part-payment for another month of indoor binges and insubstantialities.

After that it was their dealer, and then a night's worth of punters around the back of the college while Robbie patrolled and parleyed, maybe once a week, maybe more than that. And Robbie, of course, though that was for free.

Birthdays passed, coke passed, crises passed. He patched her up when she needed it, she put her body against his debts when he needed it. She got pregnant but it didn't work out. Later, maybe. In the interim they stopped going to parties. They sat in, where he suffered death after death on his Xbox, and she sank into novels about dogged detectives and murderers who hid in plain sight.

She went to work indoors, at his insistence. Maybe he was just ridding himself of the responsibility of minding her, but he swore it was because the men who bought her in brothels would be less worrisome than the ones who trawled the streets.

He was wrong.

Up to that point she'd defined her time with Robbie in lively terms: *fighting*, *fucking*, *breathing*, *being*. After that point she was mostly concerned with death. The men who prearranged their time ensured that she was aware, every moment, of how many moments she might have left. By and large they were vicious, much more so than the last-minute trawlers. Maybe it was that these punters had time to stew in their contempt; it was often bubbling over by the time they got to their ordained girl. When she wasn't working she took solace in serial killers, and watched

Robbie bleed out on the TV screen a hundred times a day, until at last the irony started to sting.

One Sunday she got Robbie to borrow a car and drive her to her parents' house, where she waited, parked up the hill, until they'd gone to Mass.

Between brown walls, behind windows too close to sagging trees, underneath the tick-tock of wall clocks in sync, Georgie took in the scent of marrowfat peas and wet clay. She knew now how much worse things could be, and yet she still felt it: the hours lost and opportunities turned stale in the country air, the feeling that if she didn't get up and march out she'd grow roots down through the thin carpet, down through the foundations, down into the soil, the dirt, the rock, and trap herself there until her brain turned to jelly and thick hairs sprouted on her chin. Her parents were born of the land and stalled by the land, and Georgie was an alien. She'd taken off because there didn't seem to be any other way to go. Similarly, there was no way back now.

She stole one of her father's shirts from the back of the wardrobe and from the bedroom windowsill her mother's scapular. Because Home was something denied to her, she took only what bits of it wouldn't be missed. They served as bittersweet reminders of how badly she'd fucked up.

After that, every time she went to work she wound the scapular around the handle of the bedside table drawer. She eyed it as if to challenge it to produce salvation. Bleed out an angry Jesus. Call forth the wrath of his da.

These ecstasies kept her preoccupied, and it was a rare punter who noticed. Punters weren't equipped to notice such things, though they were clear-eyed enough when it came to her worldly being. Lack of enthusiasm for their libido usually provoked punishment in the form of thrusting hips or fists clenched around her hair, but sometimes they'd be passive aggressive and only take it out on her afterwards, sitting prim in front of their laptops, typing her into a hiding.

She'd a face on her like a slapped arse and an arse on her like a bag of Doritos . . .

The brothel moved to a new premises about a month before Robbie disappeared, and when the men came with the furniture the bedside table and its scapular was missing, and Georgie was too mortified by the shape of her sentimentality that she said nothing, except deep into Robbie's shoulder back in their flat.

So it wasn't that she feared that Robbie might be dead, because his death was the first logical conclusion. He wouldn't have run away because he had no one left to run to; they were, in all sorts of ways, the last two people on earth.

She looked for his corpse with determined detachment. If she found him bloodied or bloated that'd be something to deal with, but right now all she needed to do was her duty. She hunted for him. Alleyways, doorways, up the ways, down the ways. Nothing. It was like he'd been plucked out of existence, the way you'd flick a crumb off your shirt.

She reported him missing, and the guard taking her statement leaned back with his biro tapping out a march on the fleshy bit between his thumb and first finger, and stared as if she'd invented Robbie from scraps of punters and a fever-dream of wishful thinking. He sent her on her way with undisguised disgust and a flimsy promise to keep her updated.

If there had been a body, her grief wouldn't have felt so formless. As it was, the fact that Robbie had been there one day and gone the next, leaving behind nothing but second-hand jumpers and foodstuffs she didn't like, left her suspended between mourning and wired impatience. He was there, then he was gone, and wherever he'd gone to he'd taken six years of Georgie with him.

The practicalities inherent in suddenly finding herself independent were many and unfortunate. She could support herself – there was money in prostitution, not a huge amount, but enough to make up the rent and keep her smashed – but . . . Well, there had been things she hadn't had to worry about when Robbie was around. Like he'd make sure the heating was on, or he'd go do the various errands that kept the coke and smoke topped up, or whatever. And now there were all of these *whatevers* and Georgie without the wherewithal to get through them.

Maybe I'm depressed, she wondered, idly, as she stood in the shower, thirty minutes at a time and sometimes noticing at the end that she was still in her knickers or that she'd forgotten to take her hair down. What little peace she had made with her circumstances when he was around to encourage it disappeared. She supposed the sudden six-year gap was making her sick. She was sick of the brothel and sick of the pimp and neither the promise of a roof over her head nor having someone to handle her appointments was doing it for her.

She could have just walked out, but that would have created more problems than it solved; the pimp could have had her for loss of earnings and might have insisted she stay on to work off debts he'd conjured out of bloated waffle. Instead she drank her way out. Punters arrived for appointments and she belched her disapproval at them, which they tried to pound out of her. Then the pimp tried to beat it out of her. He tried to hammer her straight, when being hammered was her problem. He wasn't a very smart man, in fairness. He was running the brothel for someone else, which was all in all a pretty stupid career move.

A few days of belching and beatings and Georgie was out on her ear. She went home and cleaned herself up and was back on the streets the next day. Sure, she had to worry now about the guards, but that seemed very much the lesser of two evils, especially when she could point out to them that they should have been searching for Robbie, and not stunting her earnings by booking her for solicitation or taking blowjob bribes in a back street off the quay. Oh yeah, a man was a man, when he was there.

And so that led her, in the week after her gin-soaked dismissal, to search for another kind of man.

Georgie had felt Tara Duane was a construct from the first day she'd met her, though of a positive sort, back then, a slice of luck given form by some propitious celestial alignment. Tara had found her around the back of the college, pockmarked by pebbledash and bad weather. She'd brought her a sandwich and a coffee and, later on, a vodka in one of the pubs off Oliver Plunkett Street; Georgie couldn't remember which. Sixteen years old and getting into cars with married men, and yet Cork City remained a mystery, the expanse of it forbidden to people like her, a soirée to which she held no invitation.

Tara swore she'd done her time in sex work, and that after having brazened out her trials she felt it her duty to offer support to the girls still involved in the trade. Winningly she implied she understood better than anyone the circumstances pinning Georgie down. It quickly became apparent that being pinned down was, in Tara's opinion, nothing to be ashamed of in these recessionary times. Ireland in a tailspin? Who could blame the girls on the street for their choices! Georgie didn't remember making a choice and she felt uncomfortable having it so neatly abridged by this uninvited proponent, if it was there at all.

As a rule the other girls in the trade were as supportive as they had room to be. The oldest women – the ones too far gone with booze or smack to operate on anything but instinct – were best avoided. They had quicker fists than a cast eye would assume. But, in general, Georgie found she had little to fear from her peers, and that there were times when it was wisest to trust them, and when more than one of them told her she was better off ignoring the wandering affections of Tara Duane, she listened.

The more she listened, the more cracks appeared on that alabaster mug. Tara always knew where the pimps and the dealers were, which knocking shops were looking for staff, who was facilitating the cam work. Some of the girls whispered that she was the city's most devious madam, taking pay from all manner of third parties as she spun the streets. Georgie wasn't sure Tara was practical enough to be a madam. Instead she wondered if she wasn't just a creep, feigning aid like she feigned smiles.

The activism Tara Duane purported to fill her time with usually amounted to handing out home-made sandwiches to the destitute. So it was tonight. Georgie spotted her on the opposite end of the quay, filling plastic cups for a couple of the old junkies from a flask out of the boot of her car.

It was just after ten, and between the street lights and the river, damp shadows ran up Georgie's limbs and pressed springtime chills against her chest; every breath was a gasper.

Tara noticed her from fifty yards away, and broke into one of her cracked-mirror smiles as soon as she was sure Georgie was close enough to get the full-frontal benefit.

'Georgie! Hey, girl, how are you? I haven't seen you in so long; what have you been up to, hon?'

Georgie said, 'I need a dealer.'

Tara pursed her lips and tried out a couple of different faces until she settled on one approaching concern, but the flickers of the sides of her eyes, and the twisting to-and-fro of her lips, betrayed the connections whirring through her head. She pulled her ponytail tighter. 'Well, you know I wouldn't condone it, Georgie. I mean God knows you have enough on your plate.'

'My plate's swept clean,' Georgie said. 'That's the problem, Tara.'

Hmm. 'Would Robbie not know someone?'

'Robbie's not home yet.' She felt that one. Unexpected, a pang in her abdomen like a knifepoint, or the warning signs of a life about to be lost on a public bathroom floor.

Tara made another face.

'Not yet?' she sighed. 'Oh, poor Robbie. I hope he's OK, girl, I really do. I mean even if he'd left you; to know is to heal, pet.'

Georgie pulled her jacket across her belly. 'Yeah,' she said. 'In the meantime, though . . .'

'A dealer,' said Tara, thoughtfully. 'Of course, I don't like to enable it.'

'Oh sure yeah. You don't partake at all, do you, Tara?'

Stern now, Tara said, 'Well, there's a difference between a smoke and the class As, Georgie.'

'Who said I'm after class As?'

'I'm not insinuating anything. Just history, Georgie, you know yourself. What about . . .' She lowered her voice, though the old junkies had shuffled on, and there was no one to hear them. 'Work? Would they not provide?'

'I'm not working there anymore, Tara. I thought you'd have heard?'

Of course she would have heard. Tara Duane heard everything. She knew the city like a spectre of many hundreds of years, even though she couldn't have been more than thirty-five; she wafted into lives, poking and prodding, and listening, mostly listening. Maybe the toll due for a coffee was a rumour and a sandwich cost a story half verified. Maybe she did relief work around the city's brothels – not in the bedrooms, but answering their phones, keeping the doors locked, washing the towels, peeping through keyholes . . .

Maybe she had lovers in the criminal fraternity, though Georgie wondered who'd have her. She was wraith-like in stature, with long, pale hair and eyes wide as open graves. And the forged sincerity. Couldn't you just see it? Tara Duane's tongue circling some gangster's distended cock, imbibing his rage and the shapes he threw at the city from his back, his massive belly rising and falling against her forehead as he blathered all his secrets into her ears. Maybe they passed her around like a virus, and that's how she harvested specifics and conjecture both.

'Have you moved on?' Tara frowned, and then smiled widely and suddenly like she'd possessed another woman's face. 'Would you like a coffee?'

'I'm grand for coffee. And yeah. Moved on. Back on the street.'

'That's very dangerous,' said Tara, who had started to pour a coffee anyway. 'You know you're better off indoors. Clean, no Gardaí, vetted clients . . .'

Georgie took the coffee. 'That doesn't always work out as it should,' she said, carefully.

'Were you drinking?' asked Tara. Her face had turned solemn.

'And how would you know that?' Georgie said.

'I don't know that. At least I didn't.'

'Ah no,' said Georgie. 'Lucky guess.'

'I might have heard something,' Tara conceded.

'Have you heard, then, where I can find a dealer who's not up to his bollocks in the same swamp I was just fucked out of?'

'All right,' said Tara. 'I might know someone who'd suit. A young fella. We're close, so he'll look after you if I tell him to.'

This delivered with a sickening simper, an invitation to empathise that was ill-advised but unchecked; Tara was too pleased with herself. She might well take lovers from the criminal fraternity but rumour had it that she preferred younger men, and eyewitnesses suggested the effect intensified with every lay. Certainly she didn't discriminate between genders when it came to extolling the benefits of sex work. Georgie had been on the game for six years and in that time she'd learned plenty about the stranger tastes men developed. She had theories: that sex was everywhere, and so what was once titillating was now everyday and so men required boosters personal to them. Or that the entitlement natural to purchase of service made them savage with unchecked lust. Or that they'd all been diddled by priests. Whatever the reason, she'd seen plenty outside the remit of the freakiest girlfriend, but even so, she couldn't get her head around a young fella wanting to get close to Tara Duane, no matter how overpowering his MILF fantasies. The woman wore hunger like a second skin.

'You know young fellas,' Tara went on. 'They can be so very keen.'

'Yeah,' Georgie said, weakly. 'Take what you can get.'

'What's that mean?'

She was frowning. Georgie shook her head.

'That came out wrong,' she said. 'I didn't mean you'd have to take what you were given, only, like, seizing opportunities or whatever.'

Tara relaxed. She gestured for Georgie's mobile and entered a number.

'Be gentle with him,' she said. And though the joke begat a smirk, Georgie flinched, and felt unease swell and break from her belly to the hot points at the back of her ears and the fine tips of the hair on her arms.

*

See, people are afraid of dealers. Prostitutes are objectionable; you wouldn't want them tottering in their knee-highs for trade on your street. But dealers? Oh no. Abject terror, then. Dealers have guns and vendettas. They might target your children and kick down your door.

Georgie couldn't deny that there was some validity in that, though she wasn't afraid of the merchants, not as a general breed. Some of them were too keen to get into other forms of capitalism and looked working girls up and down the way you would a horse at a town fair. They were obvious as landslides and a clever girl kept her distance. Most of them, though, were but a slightly sharper edge on pathetic. A lot of them stocked up only to feed their habits, and lost a little up their noses and into their veins with each transaction, buying their way into slavery.

The smart ones fell somewhere between both categories; their efforts at expansion stayed within the realms of pills and powder, and their noses remained intact. When Georgie had worked indoors, there hadn't been a shortage of inlets for numbing substances, all but essential when you were fucked for a living. Otherwise it had been Robbie's responsibility, and he had hooked into the same network in recent months. Breaking away from brothel employment didn't mean that she was forbidden to tap her sources for coke, but there were within that network people that she never wanted to see again for the rest of her life.

Tara Duane's own dealer was not the ideal. Georgie went down to the corner and asked a couple of the other girls for contacts, but the market they frequented was practically a monopoly, and every avenue led Georgie back to ground she'd walked before.

Eventually it came to an impasse, so she buried Tara's smirk, and dialled.

'Yeah?'

'Hey. I got this number from a friend of yours. I'm looking for a bit; can you help?'

'What friend?'

'A girl named Tara.'

'Tara who?'

Obviously this one had little regard for the lugs of the law. Georgie hesitated. 'Tara Duane.'

'Oh,' he said. And there was a pause and then, 'I dunno. Where are you?'

'In town.'

'Coz I'm not.'

'I can go to you if needs be but "needs be" right now is a need-to-know,' she said.

'That's fucking poetry,' he said. 'You're lucky I'm stoned. All right. What is it you're after?'

In the lull between placing her order and making the collection, she managed to turn over a couple of punters, one fearful and unfit and sweating like a pig because of both, the other after a blowjob which failed to cure his boredom. That gave her enough to pay for what she wanted from the merchant, but not enough to go home on. Provided he was a decent skin who wasn't about to rip her off with ground up aspirin wrapped in tinfoil – and who knew what kind of person she was foisting upon herself on Tara Duane's recommendation – she would at least get a bump before getting herself back out there. Maybe conjure the scapular from behind closed eyes, and hope she didn't gush blood onto the client's neck.

It's stigmata, baby. I just blew my lord.

She didn't see him at first. She got back to the end of the quay and he was a little ways in behind a parked car, sitting on a bollard. He made her jump and she really hated that.

'You Georgie?' he said.

'Jesus.'

'Naw,' he said. 'Not even close. Ryan.'

He was sitting with his legs insolently stretched, but his shoulders were hunched and his hands deep into his pockets. He was feeling the cold. No wonder; he was wearing a school uniform, no jacket, just a thin maroon V-neck over a grey shirt it wouldn't have become him to button up.

4

First it occurred to Tony Cusack that he needed to track down Robbie O'Donovan's family and tell them that the poor divil was dead. Then it occurred to him that behaving anywhere approximating worthy would only land him in a hell of his own making. There'd be guards. The plaintive wailing of sisters and mothers. Above all there'd be Jimmy Phelan. Above all, looming like Godzilla, with a face on him like an old quarry.

Tony hadn't had much regard for Robbie when he was alive, but then it was rare Tony attracted the kind of company that demanded or deserved it. Robbie used to drink in the same local. Another daytime guzzler, he'd come in with his betting slips and a *Star* folded under his arm and his mobile phone, and he'd sit at the bar, looking up at the telly, and down at his slips, and then to the paper and then to his phone. Not much of a conversationalist, even when steaming, but Tony had never been concerned with that. He knew of him more than he knew him, even with hours spent on parallel stools, drinking in sync in the afternoon hum.

Finding the craitur all caved in on the floor of Jimmy Phelan's flat, though, had turned Tony's gut inside out. There was, of course, the ugliness of it, in a practical sense. Smashed egg physics, enough to turn all the stomachs of a cow. Then there was the fact that Tony knew the bloke, and that he hadn't expected to, and that he needed to yank tight his instincts in front of J.P. before that recognition gushed right out of him and all over the floor. That was physically exerting; Tony wasn't cut out to be an actor.

But more than that again. There was something of sickly camaraderie between Tony Cusack and the faces he saw, blurred and blubbering, haloed around him on a daily basis. Robbie O'Donovan got it on the back of the head and Robbie O'Donovan wasn't all that different to him. And what was the difference, really, if a man was going to meet a sticky end? The universe didn't care whether he was a gangly ginger or a dusty-haired chunk, if it was in the mood for killing off wasters. Fuck, like. It could have been him. It could have been any of them.

And if it had been him, would he not want his mother to know about it?

He'd gone home from the clean-up with a roll of J.P.'s money in his pocket and a headache that started somewhere below his shoulders and pulled a hood of churning colours down over his eyes. Sat in the kitchen with a bottle of Jameson and an empty glass. He'd wanted the drink, but it had taken him time and effort to get the whiskey from the bottle to the glass and then from the glass past his teeth. A few hours in the company of a corpse would do that to a man still living. And that state was hardly guaranteed, with his having duped J.P. into thinking he didn't know who the dead man was.

Maybe he should have told him. Maybe it would have worked out. *Eh, Jimmy boy, I know this feen.*

And maybe J.P. would have taken it as an invitation to drive Tony's head back into his shoulders. You don't go around telling wrought-iron hard men that you know who they've been offing. Otherwise they go around wearing your skin as a cravat.

It was such an insignificant thing, when he thought about it. He knew a guy, and he neglected to disclose it. That's all. A small fucking thing to be in fear of your life over. Forget to move your tongue and suddenly you're driven to drink with piddle dribbling down your trouser leg at your kitchen table.

He dragged himself between each conclusion for days stretching into weeks: read the death notice on the O'Donovan doorstep, or bend under Jimmy's shadow and wait for the guilt to wither. He was harsher with the kids because of it. Everything they did wrecked his head. He hid in the kitchen when they were watching TV, in his bedroom when they were eating, in the pub when he could afford it. He went over his potential revelation from various angles, and from each perspective it ended badly – with O'Donovan's family riotously questioning and him at a gaping loss.

Missus O'Donovan? I'm sorry to catch you unawares . . . Poor bitch. . . . *but your son is dead as a fucking dodo.*

And how would you know that, you bedraggled old fuck?

Cue J.P. screeching in just as the guards finished their questioning and blowing him out of this life and into the next, as if Tony Cusack's existence held only the durability of plastic sheeting stretched tight on an old door frame.

Tony and Maria had gotten married as a postscript; sure weren't they already bound together by offspring and his parents' disapproval? Maria had mentioned it as something that ought to be done at some stage after they got the keys to the house. Tile the bathroom. Adopt a puppy. Get hitched, I suppose, in fairness like.

He brought her home to Naples so that they could say their vows. The reception was held on the terrace of a restaurant chosen, decorated and, more importantly, paid for by her parents. He hadn't a clue what any of them were saying but they looked relatively jolly. Keen to provide an alternative to the Italians' frolics, his parents had spent the day wrinkling their noses as if, roused by foreign tradition, each of their new in-laws had lined up to cordially shit on the cake.

It got to him; first that the Irish party was so scrubby-thin, and then that it was in such foul form. The language barrier wasn't helping. Nor was Maria, floating around the place as Princess Mammy, a toddler under each arm while her décolletage was muddied with sugary thumbprints and white chocolate. She let the Italians monopolise the baby talk and kept her tanned back to her old enemy, her new mother-in-law, who sat sipping her G&T, scowling, sour, making a holy show of him right there on the edge of the dance floor.

Maria put down their small fella to adjust her neckline and

Tony scooped him up again, walked with him to the bar, and bought a Nastro Azzurro and a Coke.

'You having fun, Rocky?'

His son looked at him with the dopey, Disney-brown eyes the Italians had tried to claim credit for, and Tony pressed his lips against the curls on his little forehead and said, 'Coz I'm fucking not.'

He cowered between choices until the decision was made for him.

It was midday on a Thursday, some Thursdays after the deed. He'd been on the go since seven, and not for entirely wholesome reasons; the ugly favour he'd done Phelan had left him with episodic insomnia and an unwelcome tendency to rise early. This morning there had been copybooks to locate, shoelaces to tie, slices of toast to butter, teenagers to bellow out of bed. Once the brood had loped off to school he'd tidied away the topmost stratum of jumble, put on the first of two loads of washing, and made his way to the supermarket for milk, bread and whiskey. He was on his way home again when his mobile rang.

The thing with Cork having been built on a slope was the further out you got from the hub, the better the views were. Tony put the bag of groceries on the footpath and reached into his jeans pocket for the phone. Below him, his city spread in soft mounds and hollows, like a duvet dropped into a well.

The breeze and the elevation made the city feel emptier than it had the right to feign. Less than a mile further out the estates would lose to green fields and hedgerows; it was calm here, as if the residents had flowed sleepily down the hill to pool in the streets around the Lee. Else they were indoors drinking tea and quietly dying. Tony leaned on a dustbin sporting three of the same sticker: a guide in aggressive bold letters to rejecting the authority of the Irish courts and the banks they slyly served. Not for the first time, he was glad he'd never bought a house. The country had gone to shit and the desperate were growing mad.

When he turned his phone over in his hand there was J.P.'s

number, fresh in his contact list from their collaboration, bright and brash on the screen.

Tony Cusack felt a bolt of fear shoot down his throat and out his arse.

He hit the answer button.

'Are you busy, Cusack?'

'No,' Tony said. 'No, boy. No, I'm not.'

There was a gap, as J.P. considered the triplicated guarantee and Tony caught his tongue between his teeth.

'D'you remember that tiling job you did for me?' J.P. said.

'I do.'

'You're going to have to redo it.'

At the end of the quay, where the river curved and the traffic quietened and the grand Georgian facades were smudged and flaking and tagged black and blue in unsure, ugly hands, stood the house in which Tony was expected to replicate his own hard work.

He knocked and the door was opened by an ould wan, about his mother's age, dressed like a chilblained scarecrow with a face that would have reversed the course of the Grand National.

'You're Tony?' she asked.

'Yeah. I understand there's a problem with the floor?'

'I bet you do,' she said. 'You understand more than you're letting on.'

She stalked down the hall, and Tony picked his way after her like he was stepping around landmines, which, fuck it, he might as well have been, considering she was capable of knocking the stuffing out of him.

He watched her narrow back for signs of pole-shift. Fuck, he watched her narrow back for signs of brutality of any depth, for how could a pisawn the size and shape of a bog wisp kill someone? And how then could a stout man of thirty-seven, a father of six with the courage to roll up a corpse in a carpet, feel afraid of her?

He followed her into the kitchen and she gestured at the tiles with a floppy wrist and a childish lip.

She'd made a mosaic out of them. The squares he'd put down

in rows neater than any he'd thought his own home worthy of had been scattered in overlapping clumps, broken into shards, maybe by a hammer, maybe by the same force that had smashed Robbie O'Donovan's head like a jam jar.

'Holy fuck,' he said.

She sniffed.

He didn't want to ask. Afraid of the answer, maybe, but something beyond that too, basic as the gawks rising in his throat; he didn't want to acknowledge the presence of this ghoul in a cardie. In this space occupied by just the pair of them he felt his body seize up; first his neck, then the backs of his arms, then his waist. Like the horror-movie victim who'd just noticed the shadow at his elbow.

'What did you do?' The arse of the question formed a tuck in his throat; he swallowed, but it bobbed there, and grew.

'Ha?' she said.

He coughed.

'What did you do?'

'I told him I wasn't staying here. And his answer is to throw down a new floor and tell me that makes a new house?'

He didn't know what to say so he let her statement hang there, counted solemn breaths and said, 'D'you have black bags, or . . .'

She produced a roll of flimsy bin liners.

'That won't do,' he said. 'I'll look upstairs.'

He left her by her protest piece and hastened to the next floor. He went from room to room – shells of rooms now, bare floorboards and stripped-down walls. The floor echoed under each footfall. Here, he was alone. Downstairs, everything was wrong. The pall of the act and its cover-up. The little lady with the violent streak.

The fresh air of Cork spread out before him seemed a long way back now. Tony paused for breath and wiped his hands off his thighs.

One of the rooms had been set aside as a store for the workmen's rubble. Tony spotted a dustpan and brush with a roll of bin bags on top of an old bedside table.

He moved to the window and looked down to the street. J.P. had phoned in his orders over an hour ago. He was surely on the way over.

Outside, the Lee lay still and glistened green.

Tony turned his back to the river and looked at the piled furniture.

There was something knotted around the handle of the bedside table from which he'd plucked the clean-up tools. He ran his fingers over it. Fabric. Like a shoelace, only with square cloth tags bound up in it at intervals.

He unwound it from the handle for want of something else to do.

Tony made a home with Maria once they were given four walls to contain it, and he spread out and grew older around the clutter of a life lived in sweeping strokes and splash damage. One night, and one fight too many, she drove away from it all, cursing it loud enough for the whole terrace to hear, leaving Tony on their landing with the colour rushing to his stinging left cheek.

Her insistence on cultivating an independent social life and his disdain of the dawn-to-dusk jobs both their mothers claimed suitable for him were pretty stupid things to fight about, but Tony and Maria could draw a fight from nothing, if they were drunk enough. She had a bottle of red wine in her and blood stoked to madness, and all he could do was wait for the Gardaí to show up on his doorstep with their caps off. Didn't stop him hoping, though. That she'd swing awkwardly into the driveway – taking the gate with it if she liked, he didn't care – and hammer an aria up the stairs. Or that she'd phone him from a ditch, bruised but breathing. But she didn't. She drove from home right into the grave, with the shadow of his hands on the steering wheel.

The Gardaí sat with him at the kitchen table. His oldest son, eleven then and the soft curls well gone from his forehead, appeared at the door with wide-eyed gumption and Tony snapped 'Get out' at him, and then, when the lad didn't move, 'Get out!' again, having risen to his feet, and Jesus Christ but he regretted that afterwards. You can't blame yourself for your reactions when you're in a state; he knew that. But if he could have gone back to that moment for another shot at it he would have held his arms out and cradled the young fella and maybe stopped the whole thing going to shit from there on in.

'What's that?'

Tony stepped backwards, catching a toe off its opposite heel and snagging the end of the brown material as it came with him. The woman strode towards him. She held out her hand.

'What?'

'The yoke you're after ripping off that small table. Let me see.'

'It's nothing,' he said, and held it over her palm. 'Just a thing. I don't know what kind of thing.'

'It's a scapular,' she said. 'A churchy yoke. See? The Virgin Mary there, looking out at you . . .'

'What's she looking at me for?' he said, and put his hands in his pockets and the ould wan stared at him and said, 'It was an accident, you know.'

'What?'

She said, 'What happened here.'

'Oh.' She was no mind reader.

'I see you looking at me like I might crack you open too, but I'm telling you, 'twasn't the way I'd planned to spend my morning.'

'Course not,' he muttered.

'Maureen is my name,' she said.

'Oh. Yeah. Tony.'

'Tony what?'

'Cusack.'

'And which Cusack are you?'

There wasn't exactly a rake of Cusacks in Cork. 'Up Mayfield.'

'John,' she said. 'And Noreen. And you're the only boy. Ah, I know you now.'

A knack for geographical pinpointing was, at least, an expected trait in an ould wan.

'It wasn't intentional,' she said. 'I'm living alone, you know.

What would you do, if you're half the size of the fridge and there's a fella in front of it as wide as he's tall?'

'A skinny yoke, wasn't he?' Tony said, weakly.

She sniffed again. 'Sure perspective is the first to go when your arse is against the wall.'

She bunched the scapular into one of her pockets.

'Was it yours?' Tony asked.

'Indeed it was not.'

'Funny thing to find here,' he said. 'What did you call it? A scalpula?'

'A scapular. Why is it a funny thing to find here?'

It occurred to him that it probably wasn't the ex-madam he was talking to.

'No reason,' he said.

She frowned.

'No,' she said, 'why is it a funny thing to find here, Tony Cusack? Because it's a holy thing and there's something wrong in this building, is it? Because a man died, and artefacts of God no longer belong? Is that your line of thinking, is it?'

'No. Not at all,' he said, though the sound came out as *No, not that tat all*. 'Just . . . y'know, workmen aren't known for taking prayer breaks.'

'That's not what you were getting at,' she said. 'You think I've sullied the place.'

'I don't.'

'That's what it is.'

'It's not.'

'You think I've blood on my hands.'

He seized the dustpan and brush and made to walk out of the room, but she caught his left arm and hung on, weight in her now like a bag of coal and his head suddenly humming with the thirst.

She did have blood on her hands. And so did he. For the short moment both his breath and arm were held, he considered telling her that.

'The state of your hands is none of my business,' he said

instead. 'This place used to be a whorehouse. That's what I meant. Funny to have a Holy Mary chattyboo here then, see?'

'This used to be a whorehouse?'

'Not so long ago too,' he conceded.

She paused.

'Dirty little bollocks,' she said, but she was looking down through the floor, so Tony knew it wasn't meant for him.

'I probably shouldn't have said that so?' he chanced.

'You probably shouldn't,' she replied. 'Not that it matters to you, my lad, because even if it wasn't my transgression you were referencing . . .' She stepped forward and he stepped back. '. . . you're still warped in thinking that a whore has no right to be religious. Haven't you heard of Mary Magdalene?'

'I didn't say that.'

'You did, boy, loud and clear. Funny thing to find a scapular in a place like this, because the only people worthy of grace are the people who've done the least to need it, hmm?'

The sun broke through outside the window, and a shaft of light appeared across the floor and opened up the room. Off the sage green walls it cast a spotlight on Maureen's head, making her, for just a second, the bulb off the Wicked Witch of the West.

'I've no problem with anyone getting religious,' he said.

'You do, and it's buried so deep inside you . . .' She poked his belly. '. . . that you can't even see yourself for the bigot you are.'

'Jesus, I was—'

'Ah, and now you're taking the Lord's name in vain.'

'Look,' he said. 'Clearly you're into all that, and I'm sorry if I offended you—'

'I'm not into any of it. I'm just pulling you up on assuming your right to religion if you're going to deny it to whores.'

'What? I'm not . . . I'm just . . . Jesus Christ.'

'And you're only saying *Sorry if I offended you* because you think the power of Christ might compel me to compel you to the next life, isn't that it?'

'Well listen, girl, whatever poor Robbie O'Donovan did to you, I want to avoid it.'

'Robbie O'Donovan,' she said.

Downstairs the door opened, and J.P. rolled his name out of his maw.

'Cusack? C'mere timme and get these tiles! Maureen? Maureen! Did that fella not get here yet at all?'

Tony looked at the gleeful old dear, and turned, and walked downstairs to J.P. like a boy moving towards a principal sworn to mete out reprimand, screaming protest in his head and yet feeling the loss of will like a punch to the gut as his feet kept inching forward.

'Nice one,' said J.P., spotting the dustpan and the bin bags, and Tony sank to his haunches and started sweeping up the broken tiles.

'I don't know how she did it,' J.P. said. 'I swear to God, that woman wrecks all around her.'

'It's coz she doesn't want to stay here,' Tony said.

'And yet here she'll stay, because she doesn't have anything to bargain with,' J.P. replied.

Tony Cusack swept the tiles into the black bag, stood up and faced Jimmy Phelan, and from his thin dry lips he said, 'C'mere, are you ever going to be ready for that piano, boy?'

The dew was heavy on the grass by the time he got home. He crossed the green towards his gate and the damp stretched from the blades to his jeans and up onto his calves.

She stood at her front door, hanging on to the jamb with a bare foot hooked round its opposite ankle.

'Evening, Tony!'

His estate was an ugly thing – near thirty houses bordering a scruffy green, a couple more rows behind each terrace. *You can't look a gift house in the mouth*, his sister once said under a wrinkled nose; he found that funny. It was home, at this stage. It wasn't perfect, nor had it been long before his family outgrew it, but it was cheap and they weren't going to be kicked out, barring his deciding to start dealing drugs out of the place or running a knocking shop in the box room.

The drawback was that there was no way of knowing what kind of degenerate would become your neighbour, seeing as the whims of the Corporation were rickety as a city of sticks and the only trait required in its tenants was a wallet full of moths. For a couple of years Tony had lived between the McDaids, who were coolly pleasant, and the Healys, who couldn't wait to get out of there. The Healys made a break for it and in their place the Corporation installed Tara Duane, who he remembered vaguely from his own schooldays. She'd gotten knocked up by some Scottish fella and her lone sprog granted her placement in a house the same size as his own.

She was frail and bug-eyed, but he knew his mother hoped that one day they'd knock through the dividing wall; a single mother and a doleful widower, sure why not, sure no one wants to die alone in a double bed. For a while Tara seemed to have subscribed to this line of thinking, and her conversations would coast between flat jokes and forced intimacy.

It was bad enough suffering this breathy plámásing, but then she took an interest in his kids.

Kelly first, because her young wan was Kelly's age and so naturally they became buddies. It wasn't such a problem with Kelly. She was like her mother: a pretty face and a vicious bitch. Ryan then, and that bothered him a lot more, because boys will be boys and this boy was easily led and, occasionally, startlingly sentimental. There were indications that she'd been playing the mammy with him. There was a flaunted familiarity with his quirks; a slight, sickening competitiveness; a proper little devil in the details.

'Nights are getting shorter,' she beamed.

He grunted. The kids hadn't closed the curtains. Every light in the house on again, and the place wide open to inspection. The idea of every biddy in the estate rubbernecking dismayed him, but there was no talking to his six; the darkening glass on the four walls didn't prompt in them self-serving instinct, not yet anyway.

Through the sitting-room window he watched a lurid parade of TV cartoons and school jumpers and various projectiles.

Laser Light

She's grand for half an hour and the next thing she is totally off her game. I'm waiting for it, so it's not a surprise.

We're out at a Junior Cert results party in town which in fairness I'd otherwise have avoided like the plague but she was mad to go; there's two floors and two DJs and kids here from every side of the city. I've been sitting by the bar all night and there's been a few people coolly wandering over because they've heard I've got yokes. They sit down beside me with their hand awkwardly curled on the seat cushion by my arse and I exchange tablets for tenners.

Karine's wearing hotpants and a tight top and a scalding pink bra and her heels are so tall they bring her right up to my height, and so she's all legs and shoulders and skin. She's sitting on my lap shouting over the music at her buddy Louise. I've got my arms around her and my mouth pressed to the back of her neck, coasting a boner that just won't go away. Not that she minds. She's figuring that if she stays sitting on my lap she'll shield me from customers' funny looks. It's her sitting on my lap in fucking hotpants that's doing the damage but no way am I telling her that.

I've popped a yoke and I've given her a half. She's never done one before.

So one minute she's talking to Louise and the next she's turning around to me saying, 'I think it's happening,' and I hold on tight as the wave hits her. I put my hand under her top, flat on her tummy, and every breath she takes is deeper than the one before.

I turn her so she's leaning against my shoulder and I put my hand between her thighs and into her ear I say, 'Y'alright?'

She nods and smiles and her eyes are flying saucers.

There's a laser show on the dance floor. Green beams chase over the ceiling and dip onto hands held high, everyone's hollering. I hold on to my girlfriend and press my cheek against her shoulder; she hooks her arm around my neck and strokes my ear and says, 'Oh God, Ryan. Oh God.'

'Is it good?'

'Oh my God, this is amaaaazing.'

She's floating. She leans her head back and though my buzz is climbing as fast as my dick is waning I catch her and push her back onto my shoulder, and she says Mmm *and I laugh and tell her to be careful, because there's stewards all over the place looking out for wasted kids.*

She kisses me then, long and slow, and doesn't open her eyes again afterwards, just smiles and sighs as if she's coming. And I just hold her and keep holding her and the lasers make a web in the air over our heads, pull it apart and build it again, make stars to fall down on us.

She's all over me.

The thing is, every girl in this place is all over some fella, so we don't look special, but we are. We're plugged into the lights and plugged into each other and I had no fucking idea it was possible to love someone as much as I love her right now.

5

So it was during a class on Newton's Laws of Motion that Ryan had an epiphany. Third Law, as it happened, and probably his third epiphany that month. Maybe even that day, if he was to scale epiphanies down to their basest elements. Small truths. Snatches of caught breath as playback skipped just enough for him to grab on to something new. Maybe that was just growing up, though no one around Ryan seemed to suffer the same sudden expansions of consciousness. He was a bright kid. A bit too fucking bright, it had been said.

There's no force in the universe, said his teacher (Mr O'Reilly, whose designer spectacles were betrayed by a face mired in 1985), which doesn't have an opposing force to balance it. Action and reaction, push and pull. That's the Law, now, kids. Sir Isaac Newton came up with that one. That's knowledge that came before you and so defines your lives without as much as a by-your-leave. Shit happens, then more shit happens.

Ah, but shit happens right up to the point where it's happening in the face of someone who doesn't want to see it. That was the truth and the truth had fuck all respect for Sir Isaac Newton and his axioms. So here, Ryan realised, was a case of the pig-headedness of people versus the Laws of Physics, and while flesh and bones have to obey the push and pull of the universe the real meat of men, their thoughts and actions and utter arrogance, ignores the processes the universe has run on for aeons.

We're all gods when we fucking feel like it.

There were a number of tiny holes on the surface of his desk, made months or years ago by students with compass points and short attention spans. Ryan jammed his biro into one, pushed down on it, circled the crater with ballpoint ink and swept an awkward black trail across to the next.

Mr O'Reilly liked to sing to the back of the room, and Ryan was right up the tippy-top, under his nose, where, it was said, he could do less damage. Ryan rested his thumb on the top of his pen, balancing it between his touch and the pre-punched holes in the desk, and looked up Mr O'Reilly's snout. There was a wedge of soft grey gunk caught in the hairs at his left nostril.

Plenty of damage Ryan could do to people's noses, directly or through encouraging lack of self-control. Did Mr O'Reilly ever take a line of coke? In his life? In college when he was learning to be a physics teacher? Between courses at dinner parties, his moustache brushing the cistern as he hunched over in the under-stairs toilet of some cunt he was only pretending to like? Before he came to work every weekday?

Ryan had a baggie in his pocket that he didn't yet have a buyer for. He wouldn't usually have brought it someplace like school, but his dad was mid-episode and hanging for trouble, so it had struck Ryan as being a better idea to take it hidden on his person than leave it where Greedyguts might get at it. And who knew, teachers might be a great market to tap into. God knows they needed an edge.

He let the biro rattle loose and Mr O'Reilly's moustache twitched.

He picked up the biro again and moved on to another little hole.

Balanced it on its tip, let it fall . . .

Mr O'Reilly leaned over his desk with his neck arched, like he was doing a push-up.

'Is there something *wrong* with you, Ryan?'

Ryan looked down at the biro. 'Gravity I'd say, sir.'

His nearest neighbour sniggered. O'Reilly glanced over and the sniggering was sucked back behind pursed lips.

'Look at your desk! School property and it's covered in black marks . . .'

There were marks on Ryan's face this week. Not black. One, kind of greening, on his cheekbone, cradling his left eye like the organic sprouting of a superhero mask. The other, purple and red-dashed, across the top of his forehead where he'd had it whacked off the lip of a step four from the bottom of the stairs. He knew that there were marks on his face because he had felt them applied and he had examined them extensively in the three days he'd spent at home convalescing under the wide eye of a father both ashamed and peevish. They were gaudy blotches, not easily missed.

More Laws there too, he reckoned. The Law of Unavoidable Contusion, where blunt force trauma drew the blood from his capillaries into the tissue around them. The Law of Here, Have a Splash of Ugly that stated that every run-in with his father had to be recorded on his face. Yeah, the Law of Fuck You, Ryan that rendered everyone around him oblivious. Like, he wanted people to see, just for fucking once, and at the same time didn't want them to notice it at all, and it was the latter that people seized on, to the extent where a moustachioed keeper of the peace could stand not six inches from him and not see the fact that his whole fucking head was bawling out for someone to say, 'Jesus, boy, whatever kind of little cunt you are I'm sure you didn't ask for that one.'

'Now that you've made that mess, what are you going to do about it?' snapped Mr O'Reilly.

Ryan rolled his tongue around his mouth and looked down at the holes and the ink and spat on them.

He looked up at O'Reilly and O'Reilly had a head on him like a salmon rolled into a hot press.

'Wipe that up,' he said.

There wasn't much moisture there to wipe. Ryan's mouth was dry. It had been for days.

He dragged his sleeve off the desk.

'Office,' said O'Reilly.

Ryan's chair clattered to the floor and he kicked it backwards and marched out of the room, carrying his classmates' stares and

O'Reilly's dogged impassiveness across his shoulders until the door slammed shut behind him.

Karine asked him all the time why he felt the need to act the maggot. Did it not exhaust him to have to explain himself to teachers? There couldn't be any peace in demanding to be thrown out of class. Even if he was in terrible form, would it not be the easier option to sit there pretending to listen than to make a show of his repulsion?

Ryan couldn't answer her. It wasn't boredom, though he'd heard teachers hypothesise that his intellect made him susceptible to impatience. It wasn't political, for he had no problem in theory with authority figures. Just . . . sometimes he was sick over it. The burden of it. Himself. All the bits of Ryan were just clumps invented by his father and moulded into an uncomfortable whole by his mother's birth exertions. Not able to get away from them, not able to get away from himself. Sometimes he thought it was driving him crazy.

A door closed further down the corridor, and there was brief adult laughter from the assembly area, but otherwise there was no sound but the duff pounding of his runners on the carpet. He was such a small thing here, like a marble rolling around in an empty bath.

He hovered outside Room 18. Annie Connelly in the front row spotted him through the glass rectangle over the door handle, and he mouthed 'Karine' at her.

She didn't have to be a lip-reader. She knew what he was saying. Any of them would.

He ducked into one of the locker alcoves.

Karine came out a couple of minutes later, hair piled onto her head in lackadaisical perfection, the sleeves of her school jumper pulled down over her fists.

'Hey,' she whispered. She was shaken still. The revelations of the week had drawn tears enough to break her boyfriend's heart, and yet she only knew the half of it.

'C'mere,' he whispered back.

'I am here.'

'More here.'

He held her and pressed his lips to her neck and she hooked her hands around the back of his head.

'Let's go away,' he told her neck. 'Deadly serious; let's take off.'

'Ah, I don't think that's going to work when I've just told Miss Fallon that I'm going to the toilet.'

'Era fuck her.'

She must have felt the heat building, because she pulled back and said, 'What's up with you, boy? You're not all right.'

One spider-leg eyelash had fallen onto her cheek. He pressed his thumb against it and the lash cushioned itself in the warmth of his skin and came away with his hand.

'You shouldn't have come back to school yet,' she said.

'The choice wasn't there this morning.'

'Even so. You could have gone somewhere else. I'd have come to you.' She paused. 'What did you do?'

'Now? Bad form. It just poured out of me. And I'm on my way to the office. For a stern talking to.'

He rested his forehead against hers.

'Everything's wrong, Karine. If I can feel it then why can't they see it?'

'You want them to see it?'

'I don't know. I honest to fuck don't know.'

She put her hand on his chest and pushed him back just enough to look into his eyes. Hers were sticky-lined with black pencil, smudged out at one corner by a stray yawn. 'I can force it, you know. I can say something.'

'And think of the trouble you'd get into. That's the thing anyway, girl. I don't want to have to instigate it. It's the same thing if I get you to do it. Fuck 'em. I don't want any of them knowing my . . . Ah fuck it.'

She winced as he dragged his knuckles off the wall. 'Don't do that,' she said, and she caught his wrist.

'I think I'm cracking up, like. They can't see it and look at you, girl, you can't see it either. Coz I'm all kinds of fucked up and you haven't noticed yet.'

'Because you're not fucked up; shit around you is fucked up. I know that coz I know you. And you know me, and we have each other, right?'

He could have cried. 'Right,' he said.

'And I'm here,' she said. 'For you, like. And I will be, too. You don't need to worry about that.'

'D'you love me?'

'More than anything.'

'It's "everything" for me. More than everything. Like the whole lot put together.'

She kissed him. A proper kiss, too, one that would have gotten her into heaps of trouble if a teacher were to come along and interrupt her. 'Maybe we *should* take off,' she told him. 'What kind of girlfriend would I be if I left you feeling shit?'

'A sensible one.' He tightened his grip on her waist and swung her around. 'Naw, it's OK. I'll face the music. I'll conduct the fucking orchestra. Whatever they've got to throw at me, I'll soak it up the way I soak up everything else.'

'I want you to be OK.'

'I will be. I'm just . . . Bad week.'

'Just don't . . .' She paused, and frowned. '. . . give them any excuse. In the office. Just say you're sorry. For once, Ryan. Please.'

'But I'm not sorry.'

'Pretend you're sorry.'

'Like they pretend my face is the right colour, yeah?'

He waited until she was back in her classroom before he continued on.

He imagined himself saying sorry. Imagined the run-up to it: the headmaster's sighs and solemn pontificating (he'd given up bawling him out long ago), the requests for clarification on motive and psychosis, and, worst of all then, the lecture on a lost future and oh, the miasma of potential he swore he could barely see Ryan through. Maybe that was the reason no one could see the clatter pattern on his face. His being too enveloped in opaque promise, choking the faculty with it. Eyes streaming and throats constricted with the noxious concentrate of Cork's great post-millennial hope. Oh God, that was it. Ryan was all tied up in nasty knots of his own smothering competence.

Don't you want to be an engineer? Or an architect? Or a scientist or a programmer or, God help us, a doctor? Don't you want to be something, Ryan? Oh go on. Fucking be something.

The apology would fit most naturally there, but Ryan knew the words wouldn't come, not even if they tried beating them out of him.

It was different with Karine. He had every reason to apologise to her, but she didn't know that. He'd mean every syllable but it wouldn't matter. Where he'd need forgiveness he wouldn't get it.

He turned into the final stretch before the principal's office.

Past the chaplain's room, and the first action in the chain.

It had started months back. One sticky, airless Saturday, dull as any clump of empty hours and charged with potential because of it.

He woke to muffled thumps and muttered direction.

He lay there for a bit, on his side, blinking at the wall, coming round to the cacophony. When he'd made sense out of it he galloped down the stairs and there was his dad and this other fella, hoisting his piano out the door.

'What are you at?' he asked, and his sister Kelly, inflated with knowledge and bobbing into sight from behind the piano case, said, 'What does it look like?'

'Dad,' he said. 'Dad, you can't. You can't take the piano.'

His father said, 'You don't need it now your practical exam's done. You don't even play anymore.'

'I play when you're not here.'

'Oh, you do, yeah.' There was a pause as they stared each other down and his father blurted, 'It's doing nobody any good having that thing here. Don't you tell me you still play!'

But he did. When there was no one around to hear him he did, even though it felt increasingly weird to sit on the piano stool and stretch his fingers and watch them fly over keys like they belonged to another boy entirely. A couple of times he'd played for Karine and that was even weirder, when they weren't his hands and his hands had done so much to her. And she'd said, *Oh my GOD Ryan, you're really good*, but he hadn't been; everything he'd played for her had been stilted, because he was so desperate for it to sound the way it did when he knew there was no one else in the house to hear it and nothing to prove even to himself because he already knew it was there, the music, in his head and in his belly and in his hands. And he'd presumed, *Well, one day I'll be able to do that for her, too, because I won't be freaking the fuck out about how she thinks of me*, but now that day wasn't going to come, was it, now that his useless cunt father had stolen his piano from him.

Oh, you fucking gom, boy, for fuck's sake, it's only a fucking piano, it wasn't your knob you lost.

Now he crossed the assembly area, taking care to plant a foot on the thin blue cushion of the nearest of the benches laid out in rows, pushing off each to land with mock jubilant grace in front of the next.

Only hours after the theft he told Karine, even though he knew what would happen once he lost the confession from his gritted teeth to her ears. He told her up in his bedroom as she lay happy and naked on top of him; he always got chatty Afterwards, in a stupid *Here's my soul, why don't you shit on it?* kind of way.

'My dad sold the piano.'

That bit was easy, but then she raised her head from his chest and he realised that none of the other things he wanted to tell her – how the piano meant this much to him and fuck all to his father, how it wasn't fair that they didn't just sell the telly if they needed the money, even though he knew the telly was worth a fraction of what his dad got for the piano, proceeds he was probably soaking in right now, having followed the piano out the door – that none of those things had to be pushed past his throat because she already knew. Instead he fought to keep his eyes unfocused and fought to not look at her and started losing the fight and feeling that horrible juddering weakness begin in his tummy and work its way up to his face. So he pulled his arm over his eyes and sucked air through his teeth.

'Aw, baby boy,' she said.

Still with his eyes screwed up, he put his arms back around her and pressed her against him so that she'd stop his heart leaping out of his mouth, and she lay there until he was able to breathe again.

She lifted her head, and said, 'I'm sorry.'

'It's all right.'

His phone was on the floor beside the bed. He reached down to get it, and started thumbing the screen, blinking at menus.

She smoothed the corners of his eyes with a fingertip.

'I want to make you feel better,' she said. 'Will I give you a blowjob?' and he thought how lucky he was, really, no matter what else kept landing on him, and he said, 'Yes please.'

He didn't bother announcing his transgression when he got to the office. He sat himself in a grey plastic chair facing the secretaries and the saggy one, Mrs Cronin, looked up at him and said, 'For God's sake, Ryan.'

He folded his arms and stretched out his legs and stared at the floor beyond his runners.

Karine had heard plenty warning about allowing a boy to keep compromising images of her on his phone, because boys are cruel and the moment any of them see your tits is the moment you lose all value in their piggy eyes. Yeah, yeah. But she trusted Ryan, and he trusted her, and the two-minute video of her looking up doe-eyed while she sucked him off was something he knew he would never show to anyone else. Never. It would have ruined it.

He watched it a couple of times late at night, with the lights off and his dad passed out and his brothers snoring. OK, a fuck of a lot more than a couple of times, but he didn't feel anyone could blame him. Even Karine was OK with it still being on his phone weeks and weeks after. Any time she'd texted him something sexy before, she insisted on nominating use-by dates, and went through his phone afterwards just to be sure. The video was different. Maybe it was that she could see the same thing in her upturned eyes that he could. Maybe it was because she knew that there was something missing from his life now, but something he chose to think of as a necessary loss as he transitioned to a better future. No piano, but who needs pianos anyway? That was something he did as a boy. At night he looked at the nymph on the screen and let his hand close tighter and his chest rise and fall and thought, *Yeah, well, she's something I do as a man, isn't she?*

The thief's guilt was manifest. There'd been more drink taken than usual; Tony Cusack clearly felt the loss of the piano in the back of his mouth. He was irritable and when he was irritable he was to be avoided – everything was everyone else's fault when he was on the skite.

The neighbours knew. Why wouldn't they know? It takes persistence and dedication to remain oblivious to violent noise in a small terrace, and if there was work in the bed Ryan was sure most of his neighbours would sleep on the floor.

Last Saturday night he got a nice black eye over something Kelly had done. God forbid his dad would ever smack Kelly – Tony didn't hit girls, oh sure girls were precious altogether – so Ryan had to take it like a good big brother, a puck into the left eye administered after closing time.

The shiner was a map left for Tony to read on the Sunday morning, and it put him in even worse form. He went out in the afternoon and Ryan stayed in his room, tripping between seething and sadness and smoke. When Tony arrived back that night his son counted his steps and paid heed to the drumbeat of cabinets and doors, and when Tony settled in the sitting room Ryan pulled his runners on and went out into the back garden and sat on the wall. He did that plenty, on the nights he knew that even a glance could nudge his father back onto the warpath. Tony would be asleep soon enough.

And then out scuttled Tara Duane.

With only a hollow wall between her house and theirs, Tara

knew the score better than anyone, and she never pretended otherwise. Sometimes Ryan sold her a bit of dope and sometimes she invited him to come in and skin up with her and sometimes if it was raining he complied, because sometimes anywhere was better than home, even if sometimes the stupid bitch tried to pay him in prescription drug leftovers and sometimes she even tried it on with him, with her dainty bone-fingers climbing up his leg to see if they could charm a hard-on.

'You don't have to go through this alone, pet,' she said.

It wasn't raining but he took her up on the offer anyway.

Afterwards he asked the mirror, *What the fuck were you thinking, boy?* His reflection suggested, Well, maybe the loss of the piano had shattered his common sense. Or maybe the video had made him cocky. Maybe this, maybe that, maybe the other. Whatever it was he was desperately sorry.

See, there was a cup of tea and a shot of whiskey in the cup of tea. Then there were a couple of joints and a couple of cans of lager and the fact that he'd been smoking earlier on made him especially susceptible to being blasted, he supposed, though wasn't hindsight twenty-twenty?

All he knew was that he'd drunk too much and smoked too much and lost control, which was the wrong thing to do because c'mon, fucking hell, he knew she had a bit of a thing for the young fellas, everyone knew she had a bit of a thing for the young fellas. He remembered her telling him the back story to the show she was watching on the telly, and he remembered her laughing at some piss-weak anecdote he couldn't give two shits for, and then he remembered . . .

He didn't feel like remembering it even now, days after the fact and not even the worst thing that had happened that week.

The principal's name was Mr Stephen Barry. He came out into the corridor, in his shirtsleeves, like he was going to have a go and all.

'I was planning on having a chat with you today, Ryan,' he sighed, 'but not like this.'

*

He remembered waking up in his own bed on Monday morning, the house mercifully still, his siblings long dragged off to school. He was sick as a small hospital. He sent Karine a text, telling her he had caught the flu or something, got up and puked his ring out, went back to bed and put his head under the pillow and watched what was left of the night before jump and fade and bleed in over his eyes.

Piss-weak anecdotes and carefully pitched laughter, and Tara Duane standing then with her arms folded as he pulled his tracksuit pants back up, saying: 'You have a girlfriend.' Putting him straight, with her knickers crumpled on the floor beside the couch.

Tony called up the stairs around midday, saying that he was heading out but that he'd be back soon, and Ryan couldn't answer except under his breath: *I don't care if you never come home, you prick; look what's after happening.* He curled into terror and tears.

Tara *fucking* Duane.

If Karine found out, she'd never forgive him.

But I'm sorry, he told her, and she a mile away in a classroom and utterly oblivious. *I'm so fucking sorry. I fucked up. I didn't mean it.*

Kelly came home at half past four and popped her head in the door and screeched, 'You must be *dying*, boy. You were a mess last night. I'd to let you in at three in the morning and you fell down twice and it was Un. Fucking. Real.'

'Yeah,' he said. He rolled onto his belly and closed his eyes; the sheet smelled of sweat and sick. 'I pulled a whitey I guess.'

'Where were you, anyway?'

'Nowhere,' he said. 'Leave me alone.'

'You've been out for three days, Ryan. Is it too much to ask that you sit quietly for three hours on your return?' said Mr Stephen Barry, Principal.

Ryan said, 'I might as well. I'm fucking invisible anyway.'

*

The penance was swift and as deserved as its supplier was ill-chosen. When his dad got back on Monday evening he let a roar out of him that ricocheted off each of the four walls in turn.

'Ryan!'

He inched into the kitchen. Tony was leaning on the sink, his lips and eyes bulging. 'Gimme your phone.'

Ryan handed it over.

He assumed his dad needed the phone to make a call, because Tony was as often lacking credit as he was lacking everything else. He stood waiting for it to be handed back; that's why he was only an outstretched arm away when the phone played out the soundtrack to Karine's salve. The floor plunged under his feet and his blood pushed through pallor; Tony said, 'What the fuck, Ryan? What the *fuck*?' and the first slap landed, on his left cheek, and he breathed in the shock and the whiskey stench and willed himself hard not to cry.

'I'm sorry.'

'You're sorry? You're fucking sorry?'

'It's just a video, Dad. Just a stupid thing.'

'You're proud of it, aren't you?'

There was nothing new in his father's intent to wreck his head inside and out; whiskey had never agreed with Tony, no matter how convincing his arguments. Ryan puckered his brow. 'What?'

'Who else has seen this?'

'No one.'

'Then why the fuck did Tara Duane just tell me to go looking for it?'

'What?' Ryan said again.

Didn't matter how many whats he managed; those bits of the night before he needed to access had been erased by shots and dope and bile. Gone. Slipped down the back of Tara Duane's couch, on which he'd spent just one too many nights getting stoned for the sake of having something to do. Had he shown her the film he was so privately proud of? Had his traitorous dick been fuelled by her reaction? There was no room for remembering in any case; he was being slapped back out into the hall, pinned to the wall by the front door, cuffed between accusations.

'How did that bitch know it was there?'
'I don't know.'
'You don't know? Is she fucking psychic, is she?'
'I don't know.'
'Ryan . . . Do you think I'm fucking stupid?'
This is how he knew he was in the biggest trouble of his life; his dad was crying. He grabbed Ryan's neck and slid two clammy thumbs up to his cheekbones. 'Where were you last night?' he howled. *Nowhere* wouldn't do; Ryan started into it by loose instinct, and Tony shook him. 'Where!'
'Next door,' Ryan whimpered.
'What were you doing next door?'
Hiding out coz you were fucking langers, you useless, bitter prick.
None of the truth for Tony Cusack. Instead Ryan blubbered, 'I'm sorry, Dad. I didn't mean to. She started it. I was really, really drunk.'
'What the fuck does that mean?'
Ryan was pushed onto the stairs. His forehead clattered the fourth step. His father continued the interrogation with one knee between his son's knees and both hands down hard on his back. *You didn't mean to what?* Ryan shut his eyes and coughed out brackish remorse. Tony wasn't happy with rescinded answers from a spineless child. And sure why would he be? Why should he be?
'What the fuck do I do with you, boy? What the fuck else can I do?'

'You are going to have to calm down,' said Barry. 'Into the office here. We'll talk over it.'
'We'll talk over it, will we, boy?' Ryan said. 'What'll we talk over?'
Mrs Cronin wasn't even bothering to hide her interest. She stood by the photocopier with her outrage hung on the set of her mouth.
'We'll talk over your behaviour,' said Barry. 'We'll talk over

what it is that's compelling you to spit in the face of your potential, Ryan. And the best place to do it is behind closed doors, don't you think?'

'Fuckton that happens behind closed doors, don't you think, sir?'

'Watch your language.'

'I will,' said Ryan. 'When you start watching. When you start opening your fucking eyes.'

'Fill me in, then. I'm on your side, Ryan. Tell me what I'm missing.'

Ryan's fingers, which had the grace for concertos so long as there was no one there to hear them, closed around the baggie in his pocket and he fucked it at his headmaster, and it fluttered to his feet, inconsequential and shining bright.

'You see that, I bet. You see that all right.'

Mr Barry looked down at the offering and said, 'What. Is that?'

'That's cocaine, sir.'

The principal looked up again, and for once in his eyes, proper fury; not disappointment, but something Ryan could deal with.

'You're a fucking stupid boy, Ryan Cusack,' he said.

The Initiate

6

The city isn't going to notice the first brave steps of a little freeman, especially one emancipated only by tearing down all around him, but all the same, Ryan Cusack walked on like he was being watched.

That was an easy strut. Chest out, shoulders back, the heavy gatch of a lad whose balls hung low. Locomotive chicanery for after the tears had dried up. Once school had finished for him he'd had one last run-in with his father, anticlimactic in that there wasn't room in his throat, past the gawks and the hot mass of babyish misery, to force the words up from his belly. Then he'd left home, followed (courtesy of his cousin Joseph) by his hobo's kerchief of personal effects: socks and jocks and a toothbrush. A brief spell of sleeping on strange couches and, twice, town centre doorways, and he conceded and approached his boss for extra work.

'I'm just saying that if you need any bit more, boy, I'm at a loose end.'

Hanging from it.

His boss's name was Dan Kane. He was a well-turned-out brute in his early thirties: mild-eyed, going grey, accent dampened, intentionally featureless up to the point his hands closed round your throat and his spit bubbled through a growl only an inch from your empty pleas. He was an anomaly in the underworld, a little monolith in a city held on blood bonds. Ryan had been selling for him indirectly before Kane copped on and decreed it hilarious; there weren't many teenagers who could move quantities. Dan had made kind of a pet of him – allowed him tick and engaged him in grinning debate on ethics and best practices – but better a pet than the leech that drew blood from Tony Cusack's knuckles.

Dan had work for him. More than he could spare. He possessed the keys to a couple of apartments which he used as walk-in safes for stashes of shifting size. He installed Ryan in one to keep an eye on things – the four walls, mostly. On the first night they sat at the bare kitchen table and talked fathers, and Dan slapped him on the back and grimaced in sympathy. He had an arctic disposition punctuated by explosions of lurid temper, but a heart too, when it suited him.

Ryan didn't bother trying to make himself at home. He knew he'd be moved on soon enough. Dan Kane's flat was a place to sleep: that would have to be sufficient.

He wasn't fond of being alone. This apartment, climate-controlled for the benefit of the stash, was as clean and as cold as the cavity in his chest. He had a telly, an Xbox and a laptop, and a fridge for beer, and a double bed with a duvet heavy enough to keep his girlfriend warm. That only helped a little. He missed home and this failing kept him up at night. He missed the terrace and the green outside it and the shortcuts and gatting spots that had marked the boundaries of his world. He missed his brothers' snoring and the banging on the bathroom door and the blaring of non-stop *Simpsons* episodes from the sitting room. A couple of times he thought he might miss his father, kind of like you'd miss a bad tooth, or a gangrenous arm.

He guessed that it was just the hangover of being from a big family. And like any hangover, he could only deal with it by getting through it and avoiding the source until he forgot how much it hurt.

Beside his father's house was the scene of the crime, tended by a treacherous curator, preserved without his collusion. One day he knew he'd want to see his dad again, and that shame would line the path home. He'd seen enough of Tara Duane to last him till perdition, in her sickly back garden come-ons, in her half-dressed admonishment, in the crippling late-night replays he conducted alone in his borrowed apartment. She had turned him on to turn him in, and though he'd folded up the memory and folded it again, it flared on dark occasion, and he couldn't get his head around it.

It was April. A surf of cloud broke grey over the streets and Ryan walked through a city where debris stuck in damp clumps in every dirty corner. He was alone, still feeling out the expanse of it. There was hint of Dan coming around later on to evaluate his reserves, which wouldn't take long with a bit of luck, because Karine had a dance class she intended to mitch from so she could come up to the flat and get naked.

They had celebrated their first anniversary in March, on his sixteenth birthday. There was another anniversary today, and he wasn't sure whether it'd be a good idea to mention it. It had been a year since they'd first had sex. Would she go for that, he wondered? Some alcohol, maybe a smidge of Dan Kane's coke, and fuck right through the everyday and into something new to make another anniversary of?

He trotted on, chest out, shoulders back, for an audience oblivious.

He was headed for a service station, which by a perverse twist would probably employ the people with the fewest fucks to give, but there was an off-licence on the way, and it was worth a shot. He ducked in out of the drizzle and stood back from the counter, behind a half-sized, snuffling woman intent on procuring a kind of liquor that neither he nor the thin-smigged clown at the till had ever heard of.

'This is the only ice wine we stock,' said the fella behind the counter. 'It's Canadian. That's probably the one.'

The woman spun her wrist like she was winding a crank.

'That's not it either,' she said. Her voice was thick and deep; she cleared her throat. 'Maybe it's like a schnapps thing? Or a brandy even.'

'What fruit?'

'I can't remember. I'll know it when I see it.'

Ryan picked a couple of bags of Taytos from a lopsided display and gawped at the ceiling. It made sense to cloak himself in the inertia of a musty shop interior if his success depended on his not looking like he was on a great adventure. No adventure to doing the shopping, was there? Grabbing a naggin, heading home, doing the washing or his taxes or whatever the fuck. Ryan Cusack was a grown-up and grown-ups were always bored.

That left just one person in the off-licence who wasn't a grown-up, and she appeared to be the dithering woman's child. A doonshie wan of no more than four stood back by the beer fridge, her baby finger in her mouth. Her mother postulated that the alcohol she sought was cherry-based. The assistant turned to the shelves behind him and the child stuck her paws into the beer fridge and picked up four tins and ran out the door of the off-licence as quick as her matchstick legs would carry her.

'D'you know what?' said the scrawny woman. 'I'll leave it. I'll check the name of it and be back to you.'

She didn't look at Ryan as she went past. Through the window he watched her join the tiny thief and a man as bony as she was, and the man picked up the cans and she picked up the child, and they darted over the wet streets like the city was being ripped out from under them.

'Can I help you?' said the guy behind the counter.

If there had been a bit more enthusiasm in his offer, Ryan might have warned him to look out for repeat visits. Instead he threw the Taytos on the counter and said, 'A naggin of Smirnoff and a naggin of Jameson.'

'Have you ID?' snapped yer man.

'Nope.'

'Well, what age are you?'

'Sixteen, boy.'

The sarcastic feigning of sarcasm proved too dense a barrier to cut through and, besides, it was during the school day, and Ryan was in civvies. The vendor twitched and turned.

'Bring some ID next time,' he said, knocking the bottles off the counter.

They had a dog at home. Nero. A mongrel with a touch of

Labrador to him and a habit, in his old age, of sleeping underneath the kitchen table, farting at intervals with such gusto that it was a wonder there was varnish left on the legs. He'd come home with Tony when Ryan was five – too young to teach his puppy any tricks. When he was old enough to have given it a shot, he no longer wanted to. It was as though in teaching the little fucker to fetch, he would have been corrupting him. Changing his lolling doggy nature to suit a movie mandate.

It was pretty fucked up to do the same to a kid.

He gathered his purchases and went in the direction the matchstick trio had taken.

Here's your trick, Junior. When Mammy's in her hour of need and the guardian's back is turned, you stick your hands into the icebox and retrieve the medicine. When Daddy needs it and he can't drag his arse out of bed to get it, you dash down to the offy with your blankest-ever face and wait till Missus Horgan's cleared her weepy eyes enough to hand over the whiskey. And maybe Matchstick Mammy will drink up and get warm and happy, and cover you with cuddles and confirmation of your preciousness, or maybe Splintered Daddy will turn on you and accuse you of judging him or having the wrong kind of face, and maybe all you'll get from it is a clatter headache. Either way just do the trick and shut up.

He found them preparing to cross the road. The man's eyes met Ryan's as he approached, but there was no flicker until Ryan said, 'C'mere, what d'you think you're doing?'

At which the man said, 'What?'

'I said what the fuck do you think you're doing?'

The man stood in front of the woman and the child – more by accident than instinct. He was wearing a baggy green hoodie. He looked like he'd shrunk in the wash. Or maybe he'd swiped the hoodie like he'd swiped the gatt; maybe he flung his little accomplice over garden walls in the sunshine so she could harvest washing lines for him. Whatever it was, he was a mismatched nothing with sticky eyes; Ryan knew his sort.

'Getting a small wan to steal your drink for you while your ould doll throws fairy stories at the shopkeeper. And you outside with your hands down your trousers. Aw stop, aren't you the fucking berries?'

'Listen—' said the man.

'You fucking listen,' said Ryan, 'because people obviously don't tell you you're a scumbag half enough.'

'Sorry, who died and made you Chief Inspector?'

'I couldn't give two shits if you went in there and cleared the gaff, boy. What you do with your grubby paws is nawthin' to me. But you get a kid to do it for you, that's low, boy. That's creepy low.'

'Here, mind your own business,' said the woman, throwing shapes from behind her fella.

'If you were doing the same we wouldn't be having this rírá,' said Ryan.

'You'd want to scoot on,' said the man.

'Or what? Or what, boy? You going to take me on, yeh little mockeeah man, yeh? You are, yeah.'

'And you're hardly going to swing for me if you're so worried about the small wan, are you?' the man sneered. 'Isn't that right? So keep walking.'

'Yeh brat, yeh,' said the woman.

Ryan grinned. It'd be all too easy to take this pair by the scruff and toss them onto the street. They wouldn't have weighed fifteen stone between them. They were right, though; he'd bound his fists on this one.

'I'm not going to bate you,' he said, 'unless I see you again, like. Though that said, I'd say you bring the small wan with you everywhere, do you? Stand behind her out of harm's way, right? Is she yours, boy? Because you're some waste of a pair of testicles.'

The child looked put out, but not as much as either of her guardians. She had a long way to go before she hit sixteen and was able to take off from home and find herself a safehouse stash to babysit. Ryan winked at her.

'Tell your mam and dad to steal their own tins. Do.'

'Don't you dare talk to my daughter,' said the woman.

'I hope she's taken off you,' Ryan said, and crossed the road ahead of them.

He tried to think of other things on the way home – whiskey, anniversaries, his girlfriend's tits – but something like that happens and it fucks up your innards, belly to brain. He sated his temper with fantasy, and beat the man in the green hoodie to a pink and cream pulp between the river and Dan Kane's flat, and when the door shut behind him he put the naggins and the Taytos on the table and sat on the leather two-seater opposite and stared at them, and then at his watch.

After a while he thought, *I'm never going to be like that.*

Too big and too bold now to be the stooge, and too smart to put his roots down in the shade of his family tree.

It was a year to the day since he'd become a man and already he'd progressed beyond Green Hoodie's sorry state.

He rolled a joint and looked at his watch again.

Maureen was seeking redemption.

Not for herself. You don't just kill someone and get forgiven; they'd hang you for a lot less. No, she was seeking redemption like a pig sniffs for truffles: rooting it out, turning it over, mad for the taste of it, resigned to giving it up.

Robbie O'Donovan, said her conscience. *Poor craitur. Had a name once, and a body, before you offered both to the worms.* How easy it was to kill someone, really, much easier than it had any right to be. One day they're occupying space in a living city and the next they're six feet under – or wherever it was Jimmy stowed his leftovers – and out of sight, out of mind. Because no one came looking for Robbie O'Donovan. No guards, no wives, no mammies. Poor craitur.

He inhabited the old brothel with her now, out of harm's way and anyone else's eye line. He watched her from the stairs. He waited to one side of the kitchen table while she ate, avoiding the spot of his ebbing. He stood at the end of the bed, right at the middle of the footboard, staring down at her when she couldn't sleep.

'Is it any wonder I can't with you here?' she used to say to him.

He didn't reply. His mouth wasn't made for it. His face shifted with her guesswork and never settled long enough to answer back. Sometimes he had blue eyes and luminescent white skin. Sometimes he had thin lips and hollow cheeks. Sometimes he smiled, or formed a wide O in belated horror. He never had teeth.

The cape of sticky crimson spread over his right shoulder and weighted his faded black jumper so it clung to him, exactly as it had in his final moments.

She sought redemption in him first. She lay awake at night and explained herself to him, first her actions, then her history, in case it would provide background against which he could shape his acceptance. But his mouth wouldn't stay put to confirm it. She told him again, fleshing it out where she thought he might want it. His sometime-face refused to engage.

'Will I tell you a story, Robbie O'Donovan?'

His blue eyes smeared across his sockets and onto his cheeks. Black substitutes flowed into position.

'When I was eighteen I met a man. He was twenty-four and from out Cobh direction, he wore a beard and beads; you wouldn't know the type, Robbie O'Donovan, because it was long before your time, but he was a catch and all the girls said so. His name was Dominic Looney, so it's a good job I didn't marry him. I was a skinny minnie – I used to wear pants up to my ears with bottoms on them wide enough to sweep the streets, and I had a head of hair on me like a mushroom cloud, so between the trousers and the fluffy *ceann* I don't know how he saw enough of me to want what he thought was on offer. But there you go: you fellas are strange. He thought I was a lasher and I didn't deny him the chance to keep telling me. So we were doing a line. We'd go out to Crosshaven for the dances and he'd get me drunk on shandy, which will tell you, Robbie O'Donovan, how small I was back then.

'We didn't go out for that long but it must have looked fairly serious because there was an assumption amongst the girls I worked with that we'd get married. And we pretended to be married enough times; we went for weekends away and told the Mary-Anns in the B&Bs that we were Mr and Mrs Looney and only married a year. And you can imagine what went on after that, can't you? Not that it'd do you any good imagining it now; I don't cut the figure I used to.

'Of course, it's different nowadays, but back then being a trollop was full of occupational hazards. No doubt the Mary-Anns would have called it my own fault and gloated at my situation – and that's what they used to call it then, Robbie O'Donovan; a situation, or a problem, oh, something vague and fateful. *What are we going to do about Maureen's problem?* Well, the first thing I did was arrange a shotgun wedding in my head. I was to wear a floating cream dress, and he'd have his beard and a suit, and we'd be in a house of our own before my belly escaped from bondage and made a whore and a charlatan out of the pair of us.

'But that wasn't to be, for as soon as Dom Looney got wind of it he was out the gap, flapping like a chicken trying to outrun a fox.

'So what do you think happened then, Robbie O'Donovan?'

The apparition's face flickered.

'Then I was sent away. For the neighbours' benefit I was gone away to work, but really I was being watched as I grew and grew and grew and the faces around me got longer and longer and longer. And then when I had the baby my mother – God rest her soul and say hello to her if you see her – fell head over heels for him and so it was decided that I give him up in atonement so that my mother and father could raise him in the stable and proper home that had given rise to the likes of me.

'So you tell me this, Robbie O'Donovan, when your face stops fading in and out and your mouth fixes in whatever shape your parents gave it: why was I asked to redeem myself for something my mother ended up coveting? Hmm? And if I've done all my redeeming, forty bleddy years of it, why in God's name do you think I should be seeking redemption for you?'

Lacking the necessary equipment to answer, the ghost of Robbie O'Donovan said nothing.

'I'll atone,' grumbled Maureen, 'but I'm not taking any more punishment. Up to me oxters in punishment I was, for doing feck all. Do you hear me?'

Her thirst for redemption unquenched by the wraith's sullen insubstantiality, Maureen was left picking through more indirect routes.

The church seemed like the obvious place to start. The clergy were self-professed experts in bestowing grace on behalf of the absentee landlord. Then there was the notion of being pre-cleared of the burden of Robbie O'Donovan's death by dint of her suffering years of penitence with no sin to show for it. Was that not a thing with the Holy Roman Empire? Didn't they tend to make up these kind of dirt-kicking assurances whenever anyone sufficiently gold-laden came to them dragging a sack of their indiscretions? If the church that condemned her to childless banishment forty years ago could offer her something in the way of a consolation prize, well, she was interested in hearing it.

The church nearest her was across the river and ten minutes down the quays. The morning after she told Robbie O'Donovan his bedtime story, she took a walk.

It had been a nasty April so far, the weather weak and wet, and bitter. She had wanted to wear white for the occasion, but the rain dissuaded her; she swapped white trousers for a black pair, and her sandals for sturdy dark shoes, and her cream cardigan and white shirt gave her the look of someone who'd only sinned from the waist down, which was generally where it manifested on nineteen-year-olds in the seventies.

It was an old church, imposing in a way they'd discourage now that the country was wide to their private flamboyances. Maureen strode up the steps and through the colossal doors and inside spied grandeur good-oh. Gold and marble and wall-mounted speakers so as to better hear the word of the Law-Di-Daw. She chortled, loud enough to upset a couple of biddies sitting in one of the end pews.

There were confession boxes in the corner. She ran her hands over the outside of the left-hand door. Hardwood, varnished over and over again; all veneer at this stage, she thought. There was a black grille on the top half. The priest's station in the middle was hung with a velvet curtain.

Maureen slipped inside and stood in the dark, remembering all that time ago, when you'd be waiting on the priest to slide the hatch open, enjoying the stuffiness, the pomp of the ritual, even the smell of the thing, rich and musty, something of the bygones . . .

The hatch slid to the side and a voice said, 'We're not scheduled for confessions now, but I saw you come in.'

'Jesus Christ!'

' "Bless me father for I have sinned" is the customary salutation.'

She shoved the door open and hurried to the exit, and behind her the priest, bespectacled and white-haired as uniform dictated, opened the door of the confessional and hung out on one foot.

'I didn't mean to startle you,' he called.

Robbie O'Donovan was waiting for her when she banged shut the door of the brothel. His face, elongated this time, mouthless and sallow, stared her down from the end of the corridor. He was standing at the kitchen door, blocking entry.

'I'll get them,' she said. 'Not today, obviously. But you'll see at the end of it: you, my lad, have no right to be here.'

She wanted a cup of tea and to sit down, and so she blinked hard, and when she opened her eyes again he was gone.

7

Maureen sat on it like a bird of prey fluffed up on an egg. She guarded it closely at first, but as soon as Jimmy gratefully consigned the deed to history the air around her turned viscous with her glee, and Jimmy watched it bubble into thick sighs and snorts and unspent exclamations until she decided it was time to tell him what she'd learned; it wasn't good.

That gowl Cusack had let slip the name of the corpse.

What harm? Dougan might have asked, if he'd been let in at all, and he hadn't. The worst of all possible outcomes had already happened; the fool was dead. What difference did it make if Maureen knew the name of the man she'd killed?

Without Dougan, though, Jimmy Phelan was a mess of what-ifs and how-dares.

The name of the corpse was a complication. Maureen made casual references to a ghost who'd popped into existence as soon as she had a name to give it, and the breeziness bothered him. No manifestation of guilt, this. Who knew what else the witch could do with a name?

It had been a season of extremes. The sun, when it shined, crisped everything it caught, but it never appeared except in a bruise of cumulus clouds. Showers kept the children indoors. The air was thick with fuming wasps.

Jimmy drove up to Cusack's house to beat out of him what in fuck's name he thought he was doing telling Maureen who the dead man was. He drove up to beat sense into him. He drove up to gauge his unruliness, and to find out whether there was more to this fuck-up than insubordination. Jimmy Phelan thought himself a great judge of character, and Cusack hadn't seemed like he knew the corpse's identity on the day they'd removed it from Maureen's floor. There was a possibility the fucker had conducted his own investigation, and carried the results back to Maureen for her to do with as she pleased. Jimmy didn't know.

He didn't know!

Tony Cusack's terrace was only one of dozens flung out in a lattice of reluctant socialism. There was always some brat lighting bonfires on the green, or a lout with a belly out to next Friday being drunkenly ejected from his home (with a measure of screaming fishwife fucked in for good luck), or squad cars or teenage squeals or gibbering dogs. Jimmy parked and grabbed a passing urchin for exactitudes.

Tony's house was in the middle of a short terrace facing the green. There was a silver Scenic in the stubby driveway, but the curtains were closed on both floors and there were no signs of life behind the frosted glass on the front door. Jimmy knocked anyway, and knocked harder when he didn't get an answer. How many children did the man say he'd sired? Six? Jimmy turned. The lawn was overgrown, the garden didn't sport anything in the way of ornamental hedges or flowerbeds, and the only indication of children was the couple of sweet wrappers caught between the corner of the lawn and the pebble-dashed front wall.

He stepped onto the drive and leaned against the car bonnet.

'Where are you, you little maggot?'

He cast his eyes to the end of the terrace, where figures shrank behind cars and walls and rosebushes, then looked the other way and caught a familiar face diving behind a curtain in the house next door.

That would do.

He began to whistle as he crossed from this driveway into the next. When he rapped on the door she opened it only a couple of inches and allowed him her eyes and her forehead.

'Can I help you?'

'For fuck's sake, Tara. You're not playing oblivious, are you?'

He slapped the door again, and it bumped off her nose.

'I'm not playing oblivious,' she said.

'Good girl. Because I don't have the patience for your play-acting. Are you going to let me in?'

'My daughter's in bed.'

'That's not an answer.'

She winced and sniffed as she stood aside and let him into her hall.

The sitting-room curtains were drawn. The room was illuminated by the glow from a laptop on the coffee table, supplemented by rolling sunlight from the sundered summer sky. Jimmy sat on the couch, spreading his arms across the back and crossing his left leg over his right and Tara Duane hovered by her own sitting-room door like a burglar made to face the music.

She was a poisonous runt, Duane. She drifted on the edges of the city's real meat, feeding on its carcasses for a kind of sustenance he couldn't get his head around. Villains he could harness, but this one . . . He'd never met a villain so convinced of its own virtue.

She'd fancied herself a madam once, and approached one of his underlings for collaboration. The ugliness of the work had stunned her, and she'd spent more time wringing her hands over the ashes of her Munster Moulin Rouge than exerting herself, so she'd been deposed, and the collaborating subordinate given a slap around the chops. Since then she'd learned conversational Russian and had assumed a position as a kind of guide for girls whose penury pointed them towards sex work. She still fancied herself a madam, only now she believed her freelance status allowed her an attractive impartiality and an air of great benevolence. A whore had once told Jimmy that Tara kept unhealthy hours online, employing sockpuppet accounts to argue with anti-prostitution campaigners and cribbing about Catholic Ireland. That had tickled him. He was happy to give her delusions free rein; his managers used her on occasion as a finder or a go-between.

Her front room was poky. There were magazines stacked on the shelves, clashing art on the walls. Beside the laptop on the coffee table was a mug with a delicate paper label hanging down the side. There was a chat window open on the laptop screen.

Of course hunni xxx Dont worry. My mom's just come home brb. Don't start without me plz luv u.

Don let her get to u baby. B strong.

'Online chat?' he said. 'I thought your daughter was in bed?'

'She was up a while ago, like.'

He grinned and leaned forward. 'Her "mom" just came home and sent her to bed, was it? Was she up all night talking to nobbers? And drinking tea with labels on it; ah, she's pure sophisticated.'

'Can I help you with something, Jimmy?'

'Probably,' he said.

She went to fold her arms and changed her mind, for one brief moment falling into the chicken dance.

'Tara,' he said.

'Yes?'

'I'm obviously looking for someone.'

'Yes.'

'Do you know where the fuck he is?'

'Tony Cusack?'

'That'd be the man. I have the right house so.'

'Why are you looking for Tony Cusack?'

'Why are you asking me?'

Her hands made fists. She tucked each into its opposite armpit.

'Seriously, Tara? Trying to ascertain what I know before choosing your best answer is only going to make me very pissy.'

She pouted. 'He's drying out.'

'He's what?'

'Drying out. You know. Some residential programme. The kids are with his sisters and he hasn't been home in weeks.'

'I didn't see Cusack as the health-conscious type,' he said.

'He's not,' she said. 'It was court-ordered.'

'Court-ordered? Fuck me – what did he do to deserve that?'

'What didn't he do to deserve it?'

'Seems a harmless sort, is all.'

She seethed. 'He's not harmless. He's a horrible man. Violent. Very violent.'

'We are talking about the right Tony Cusack, aren't we? Scruffy fella, big brown peepers, married a dago lasher with knockers out to here?'

'Some people are just bad,' she said. 'No matter how often you get lost in their eyes.'

Her peevishness tickled him. 'That doesn't sound like the bleeding-heart Tara Duane I know.'

'He's a child abuser.'

'Holy fuck, anything else?'

'Yeah, actually. He put my front window in. With a hurley. Beat the glass through. And I have to live beside him after all that and I frightened of me life of him.'

'Tony Cusack put your front window in.'

'Yeah. So I'd advise you to have nothing to do with him.'

'Why'd he put your window in?'

'Why do you care?' she said.

'I don't.' He leaned forward, elbows on knees. 'Lovers' tiff?' he asked. 'Were you fucking him, Tara?'

'Excuse me, I was not.'

'Why else would a man blow your house down? Did you put the wrong tags on the bins? Stay up too late bawling along to ABBA? Come on, Tara. Why'd you fall out with him?'

'Are you looking for him or questioning me?'

'First one, then the other.'

The light from the laptop screen dimmed as it switched to screensaver. Jimmy stretched and shifted back on the couch.

'His oldest is a boy,' Tara said. 'Sixteen. He thought I was . . .'

It was pause enough to draw out his laughter.

'Jesus Christ, Tara. You're fucking children now?'

'I am not,' she hissed. 'He's paranoid with the drink and the drugs. You'd want to be, wouldn't you, to accuse a young mum of something like that? Especially one like me.'

'One like you?'

'I'm a good person!' she snapped. 'And that man is a nutjob.'

'If he caught you with your legs round his young fella's ears I'd say he had good reason.'

'Don't be disgusting.'

He was close to paroxysms. 'Oh come on, Tara. I work at a conveyer belt of deviants and I know for a fact you failed quality control. The man knocked your window in because you've been playing Hide the Underage Sausage.'

'I didn't! I did not! I tried offering the kid a friendly ear and he obviously took it the wrong way, all right? And I had to offer that friendly ear because his father's a lunatic and living beside him has lopped years off my life.'

'If only living *with* him put years *on*, eh?'

'Yeah, getting back to it, OK? I don't know where he is,' she said. 'Drying out. Court-ordered.'

'For what?'

'Drunk and disorderly. So taking into account his unprovoked attack on my glazing, that was enough for a judge to decide he had a problem. He's got too many kids for gaol, I guess.'

'That part sounds like Cusack,' he said.

'It all sounds like Cusack. You obviously don't know him very well.'

'I don't,' Jimmy said, and clucked his tongue, and put his hands on the couch, readying himself to get up again. Tara thought to exhale. He laughed.

'Christ, Tara. You'd swear you were the one up to no good.'

She sucked her lips in.

'I'll be on my way,' he said. 'You've been useless. Still, I get you have more important things to be doing, like pretending to Mr Internet there that you're his little wet dream soulmate. Sorry I haven't been a better *mom* to you.'

She followed him to the front door.

The pavement glistened under a sky indigo and low. Jimmy rolled his shoulders.

'One more question,' he said. 'Do you know a fella by the name of Robbie O'Donovan?'

Her eyes widened. 'No.'

'Think now. He'd know Cusack.'

She shook her head.

'Maybe thirty. Foxy hair. A right hand-me-down-the-moon. You couldn't miss him, but that's of no benefit to sore eyes.'

'I guess that's what you want Tony for?'

Jimmy stepped out the door and onto the driveway.

'So much guesswork, Tara. I'll take my leave of you. Stay weird.'

He walked towards the front gate. Wasted journeys tended to put him in bad form, and he could see that mass ahead of him, maybe five minutes into his future, maybe ten, a private tantrum that would fuck the rest of his afternoon. He had things to be doing. Much bigger things than chasing Tony Cusack around the city.

Behind him, Tara Duane called 'Wait!'

He turned.

She was nodding. 'Robbie O'Donovan. A tall ginger guy, whippet-thin, no great shakes, yeah, yeah.'

'Oh, it's come to you! Tell me: what do you know about him?'

She stepped onto the driveway and closed out the door behind her. Beyond her front wall, two bickering girls played on scooters, oblivious to the building pressure above them, the carillon hum of the imminent squall.

'He's with one of the . . . working girls,' she said. 'You know.'

'One of the whores? Which whore?'

'I don't know what she calls herself but I know her as Georgie Fitzsimons.'

'Irish?'

'They do exist,' she said.

'And where does she work? What does she look like?'

'Oh, she's one of the unfortunates. She's on the streets. Not hard to miss; she's usually down the quay. She's short but, y'know, chesty.' She gestured extravagantly. 'Dark hair down her back. Skinny now, like, but she was pretty once. I think the term is "gone to shit".'

'I know the sort.'

'She used to work for you,' she said. 'In the house at the end of Bachelor's Quay.'

'Really.' Well, now the langer's being there made sense. The insignificant other of one of the whores, probably a junkie, probably thinking the house was empty, probably looking to rip the copper out of the walls or the carpet up. Probably the kind of company that eejit Tony Cusack was used to keeping. The issue of the corpse's exposed identity quickly shrivelled.

'Does he owe you money or something?' Tara asked.

'Who?'

'Robbie O'Donovan. I get the feeling he skipped town, is all.'

Jimmy chewed the air.

'You ask too many questions, Tara.'

'I'm just trying to help . . .'

'It'd be more in your line to try zipping your trap, because the day will come when someone will solder it shut for you.'

'OK. Jesus,' she said, and held on to the wall dividing her property from Cusack's, and put her other hand to her chest.

'Just a pointer.' He dismissed her with a casual wave and returned to his car.

She reappeared at her front window, peeked out from behind the curtain, disappeared as soon as she saw him watching. He snorted.

One of the squabbling girls pushed her companion off her scooter. The deposed one screamed. Tara Duane glimpsed out again. Jimmy considered another wave.

The distraught girl's screams were met and matched by a yowl from one of the gardens across the way. A man with gym-sculpted shoulders pitched towards them, snarling at Sarah or Sasha or whoever she was. Jimmy couldn't tell whether it was the victim or the perpetrator that had drawn out the yowls, but the chap was coming for them, hard, and when he reached them he picked up the screaming one with one hand and slapped the offender with the other. The one who'd been pushed was set upright. The culpable one was spun around by her wrist. She went white with shock. The judgement kept coming.

Hot day, though. Short tempers.

A woman in lilac with a stretched-out seahorse tattoo waddled towards the scene. She stood back from the spitting man, the bawling children, and threatened to call the guards. The man raised his hand.

Still there was no rain. Jimmy smiled out at the olive light and the drama and drew Tony Cusack's indiscretion from catastrophe to conspiracy to clanger.

Boyfriends

We're going out later. Nothing much happening, but we're going to get some cans and go gatting with Joseph and the lads, have a few smokes, a bit of a laugh. Karine, though, she'd get dolled up for the opening of an eye. We're up in Dan Kane's stash house and she's 'getting ready'. Getting ready, like. So that if she pulls a whitey at least she'll look gorgeous gawking all over my runners.

I'm at the bottom of the bed, rolling a joint, and she's sitting up against the pillows watching telly and painting her toenails baby-blue.

It's one of them dancing competition shows that's on. She loves them. She does hip hop twice a week and enters competitions with a proper crew and everything. She can do the splits. She can rest her calves on my shoulders. Yeah, it's fucking awesome.

'Your manno's amazing,' she says, all goo-eyed at this fella lepping around in front of the judges in a pair of leggings.

'Yeah?'

'Yeah, he's got moves like.'

She's completely gripped. She finishes her toenails and leans back, a finger in her mouth as she stares at the screen. I hold the joint up in invitation but she pays me no heed.

Her toes are splayed in case she ruins the paint job.

I take a pinch of tobacco and slowly, slowly stretch over.

She sighs as the judges give a standing ovation. She gets very wrapped up in the feelgoods.

I sprinkle some of the loose tobacco over the nails on her right foot and it sticks to the polish, flecking it baby-blue and bog-water brown.

She doesn't notice.

I do the other foot. She pulls her knees towards her just as I finish.

'He is like super talented,' she says.

I spark up.

She looks over at me, mouth open, ready to tell me something else mind-blowing about the steamer on the screen when she lamps her piebald toes.

'Oh my God! Ryan!'

I'm breaking my hole laughing.

'Ryan Cusack, you are fucking LOUSY!' She jumps up and throws a pillow at me and practically has a fit right there on the floor. 'You gowl! I don't even have varnish remover with me, like. They're ruined! What am I gonna do? Oh my God, you break my melt, d'you know that?'

She is beetroot with fury but I can't say anything, I'm choked.

She stomps into the bathroom and just before she slams the door she screams, 'I wish I was a fucking LESBIAN!'

On the screen yer man in leggings is standing with his hands joined in a silent prayer. I wipe the tears from my eyes. The judges call yer man's name and he jumps out onto the stage like he's got a wazzie down his drawers.

She comes out again a couple of minutes later.

'Your boyfriend got through,' I tell her.

She scowls. 'My boyfriend better get his jacket on coz he's going to get me nail polish remover right now. I honestly don't know why I put up with you, Ryan. You're such a child.'

8

It was beautiful down at the lakeside in the early morning. The air was cold, stripped of the fragments it had picked up the day before, though it would be stale by midday and offering mouthfuls of flies by dusk.

Georgie had made a habit out of coming down to the water before breakfast. In the great expanse of hill and sky, it stayed early for longer. Back in the city there was traffic and torment from dawn. Out here, so long as the air held that chill, the limbo between then and now stretched as far as she needed.

She sat on a flat rock by the water's edge and closed her eyes to the milky-blue sky, and the breeze that coaxed tresses onto her cheeks and over her lashes. The birds could be raucous near the water, but this morning their song was spiralling light. Beyond that, nothing. Later, when duties began, there'd be car engines and noises of cooperation as people grouped off to deny the devil idle hands.

David's voice, behind her: 'You weren't wrong.'

She neither turned nor opened her eyes. 'You're so negative, David. *You weren't wrong*. You could have said instead, *You were right*. Turn the negative into the positive, remember? Break free of sour processes. Turn that frown. Upside down.'

His shoes crunched on the shingle. When she opened her eyes, he was standing at the water's edge, his back to her, hands on his hips.

'You look like you're appraising the plantation,' she said. 'Lord and Master of all you survey.'

'Only one Lord,' he said. 'And no possessions. Isn't that right?'

She laughed, and he turned to smile. He was neatly proportioned, moulded by good fortune rather than hard work. He had a trimmed beard, which tickled, and eyes blue as the mountain sky.

'I didn't think you were one for getting up early,' she teased.

'You said it would be worth my while,' he said.

Gambling was David's vice. He used to hole himself up for entire weeks, just him and his laptop, losing shirt after shirt in landscapes of flashing lights and vivid green. You wouldn't think it to look at him. He seemed more like the lead in an IKEA ad. When his parents got divorced, his father had turned to pastors new, which was how his youngest son had ended up at a lakeside refuge run by Christian soldiers whose military tactics amounted to communal porridge pots and long walks in the woods.

Georgie's first thought had been that it was all very American, but the mission leader was Irish. William Tobin was his name and he called his organisation CAIL, which she had since discovered, with a hastily stifled snigger, stood for Christians Active In Light. Try as she might she couldn't find an ulterior motive to William's decency; he was too gentle a soul for trickery. He had a grey ponytail and a wife called Clover to whom he displayed a very noncultlike monogamous devotion. He had found Georgie in need and had given freely.

What that need had been was nobody else's business. William had told her that what she disclosed to his knot of volunteers was entirely up to her. So she'd told them she was an alcoholic, which was probably true, even if it was the least of her problems.

It wasn't rehab in the traditional sense. William Tobin's West Cork property was more drop-out than check-in. Bed and board in exchange for a little light farming and daily sermons about the loving grace of Jesus Christ. Georgie hadn't yet found the Lord – in His defence, she hadn't been looking very hard – but they seemed an honest bunch, she had always liked porridge and she loved the lakeside air.

'You're sure you're set for later?' David said.

'Oh yeah. That won't be a problem.'

'I guess it's handy they're bringing you.'

'They must trust me not to run off into the nearest pub, screaming for a Jägerbomb.'

'You think they're right to trust you?' he smiled.

'Please. Booze is so last month.'

He sat beside her on her boulder perch and as he stretched an arm around her he looked back, in the direction of the centre, just in case.

William and Clover didn't like to make rules not already enshrined in the teachings of Himself, but He probably wasn't keen on fraternisation and, if Georgie remembered her religion classes correctly, thought fallen women only handy for washing His trotters. The fact that she had embarked on a quiet affair with David would no doubt have been a deal-breaker, at the very least an incitement to proper spluttering Bible-thumping.

But there was something so perversely pure about it. Georgie hadn't told David about the career path that brought her to William's door, and his blind attraction was quite the aphrodisiac. And though she had long lost the notion that she would be dragged out of perdition by the clammy hands of a man, there was something therapeutic in the nature of their bond. The secrecy reminded her of the first few stolen kisses as a girl back at home; furtive pecks at the back of the hurling pitch, the fluttering excitement of a hand sliding under her top. So there was a kind of rebirth to it, she supposed.

She leaned into David's shoulder and they kissed.

The first time had been a revelation. They had been talking late in the common room about his converted father and her stubbornly pious mother. Without warning he'd lurched forward, an action as clumsy as its resulting kiss was tender, and as his mouth worked hers open she'd felt heat spreading, belly to hips to thighs. Like a blossoming, a poet might have said, but at the time she had linked it to the idea of an opening tomb. Something that would stir a pharaoh's wrath and unleash a plague of locusts. It had been a diversion from genuine butterflies.

That night they'd had sex on the bench Clover used to fold sheets. She thought afterwards that she probably shouldn't have, on the basis that it wasn't good for her rehabilitation, but actually wanting to was novelty enough to carry her.

If Robbie were to come home now, would he find her willing and born anew?

If Robbie were to come home now he wouldn't find her at all.

David slipped his hand down the front of her dress, teasing taut a nipple.

'D'you think we have time . . .' he said.

'I doubt it.'

But David was a gambling man.

She had leaned against a parked car and heaved.

You could never be safe, even though you'd be so careful and smart, leaning in through car windows to slyly sniff their breath for signs of riled drunkenness, reading the tics and faces pulled to gauge violent intent. A few would always get through, and the ones you couldn't interpret were the worst of the lot, the real evil bastards, the ones who hid behind stony facades the rage, the frustration, the deep-seated mammy issues they were only dying to take out on you. You, the dirty whore. You, representing in living, breathing audacity everything that was wrong with them.

This one had accepted the terms of the sale, then decided, once she was in his car, that the terms of the sale were unacceptable.

When she protested, he punched her. When she shouted, he walked around the side of the car to the passenger door, took her hair in his fist and dragged her out. He pushed her onto the bonnet and raped her. Then he punched her again and spat into her face and hair and told her that she disgusted him, and left her at the side of the road, and from there she began walking back into town, and a host of the oblivious walked and drove past until by luck or as he might have put it, divine intervention, William Tobin found her.

He was driving home from the hall he maintained in the city for prayer services and Bible study groups.

'You poor child!' he exclaimed, tearfully. 'God is here for you. You have only to let him in.'

She had been asked to return to the prayer hall in the city now with William and Clover and a couple of the converted: Saskia, a girl of near thirty who'd been raised in bohemian carelessness down in Kerry by her German parents and all of their hangers-on; and Martin, a bearded giant in his forties who had spent years in prison for some crime only darkly alluded to. William drove the minibus, and Georgie balanced her chin in her hand and watched the countryside drift by as Saskia wondered aloud if Ireland was, in its heathenism, doomed to suffer the fate of ancient Rome.

The four were to attend some public meeting about political non-compliance, or the threat of feminism, or knitting jumpers for Jesus or something. Her role was to prep the hall for their return; sweep the floor, arrange the chairs, make the sandwiches.

She had been looking forward to the excursion since William had mentioned it, three days before. It wasn't just because of the plan she'd hatched with David to bring back some goodies for a midnight feast, though that was most of it; giggling with David behind the backs of the brethren made her ache for childish pursuits. She had also been looking forward to some time away from the serenity of the lakeside. To feel something real again, and in its contact make certain that she was entitled to it this time out. Because sometimes she felt that the earnest faith of William and his disciples, the cleansing chill of the lakeside air, even the sanctified secrecy of her encounters with David – all were fragments of someone else's bedtime story, lost in the aether and erroneously granted her.

The 'hall' was a poky thing. There was a keyboard by the back wall, and a few books of sheet music, and enough faux-leather-bound Bibles to make a fort. Once she'd set up the circle of plastic chairs and the trestle tables, and pulled out the lectern from the corner, there seemed a dangerous shortage of the room necessary to keep breathing an assembly of Christians all equally afire with the faith. Still, the first part of her job was done. She locked the door behind her and walked to the Centra on the next street over. She had sliced pan to buy, and a plan to put in motion.

'I'm sorry to ask,' she said, as the girl behind the counter scanned the provisions, 'but is there a phone I could use?'

There was no provision given for call credit at the centre. Mobile phones were a distraction, William said, a link to the outside world that had chewed them up and puked them out. That had made perfect sense at the time, because Georgie had been sure that nobody needed or wanted a call from her while she was getting sober or realigning her principles or whatever you fancied calling it. She hadn't taken her phone out of the bedside table drawer in weeks.

She remembered his number, all the same. It was one of those numbers you never forgot. 999, your parents' house, your dealer.

'*What* is going on with you?' he asked, in charmed incredulity, when she opened the door.

'What, the rig out?' She twirled. 'Better than freezing your arse off in a greyhound skirt, isn't it?'

'It's a bit wholesome, like.'

'It's a long-sleeved maxi dress, not a burqa! Modesty is the whore's kryptonite. Besides, it's kind of a condition of this whole thing.' She gestured at the hall, and he stepped in and looked around and said, 'Jesus Christ, Georgie. You're hardly trying to convert me.'

'Could you be converted, Ryan?'

'Not without a skinful of acid.'

'Well *phew* for the pair of us, coz they haven't gotten me yet either.'

'Clearly not if you're calling me down. Where've you been anyway, girl?'

'Getting saved,' she said, and he smiled at her, and she was pleased to note that his smile lacked the mercantile cunning she had worried the missing months would give him. 'Down in West Cork. They have this commune.'

'A cult, like?'

'No! Unless you mean it in the Christian sense. But I bet you're a good Catholic boy so you can't really talk.'

She handed over the money she'd put together with David, and Ryan produced a couple of wraps, one of which she tucked into her bra.

'Don't get them wet,' he said.

'I'm not lactating, for God's sake.'

He looked put out. 'If they get damp they're fucked altogether.'

'I'll mind them. Anyway, they're not yours anymore, so relax.'

She sat in the circle of chairs and opened the second wrap.

'Have you got anything to chop this with?'

He was wearing combat-style jeans; folds and compartments enough for the one-man band. He reached into a pocket and produced a small knife.

'Aren't you ever worried you'll be stopped and searched? Drugs and weapons on you; it's like something out of *The Wire*.'

'That's not a weapon,' he said.

'Yeah, I'm sure the guards would see it that way. Here, pass me one of them Bibles.'

The faux leather wasn't the ideal chopping platform; she'd have to wash the cover after. She opened the wrap.

'Sit down,' she said, and he did, across from her.

'Your congregation aren't on the way back for you so?'

'They'll be a couple of hours yet,' she said. 'I told them I was going to visit my mam and dad.'

'But you're from Millstreet.'

'Exactly.'

She was glad to see him. It wasn't wise to get too fond of your dealer, and the likelihood of one of that breed gaining her approval had never come up before. It's just that Ryan was . . . well, young. And though his existence was proof that they were learning the dark arts prematurely these days, she still felt safer in his company than she had done with any other dealer.

'Is it good?' she asked as she chopped, and he said, 'It's unreal.

Seriously, Georgie, you could get ten lines out of that, especially if you've been dry this past while.'

'As a bone,' she said.

She wished she had figured out sooner that young merchants were the way to go.

Maybe, too, young punters.

It was a bad thought to come roaring in after two months of Christian healing in the arse end of nowhere; she hadn't killed off the whore, not entirely. She told herself she had yet to bring her thinking back in sync with the rest of the world. The longer she stayed out of sight in flowing garments in West Cork, the more likely the stench of sin would be obfuscated by contrition's perfume, until repentance diluted her history, until all but lupine senses were confused by her spick, span self.

But the thought was there now and the ghost of who she was an hour ago bleated its dissent.

She'd heard of fathers bringing their sons out for a taster, and wasn't Hollywood always eking out the comedic charm in golden-hearted hookers and the desperate young virgins who found more than surrender in their welcoming depths? Oh yeah, it was really noble. Popping cherries all around her, that would have been the way to go. Charging them fifty quid to bob, red and tearstained, on top of her with her sworn guarantee she wouldn't laugh at the size of their winkies. Ridding them of the burden of inexperience so they didn't make fools of themselves when their pretty little girlfriends finally granted them entry. Before they fixed on their own perversions and started getting grabby.

She bent over the Bible with a rolled-up fiver and snorted her line.

What difference would it make to get them young? They were animals soon enough.

She passed the Good Book to Ryan, and as code dictated he accepted.

'Never did one off a Bible before,' he said, pinching his nostrils and blinking.

She took the book back. 'Mass produced and made of dead trees; there's nothing special about them.'

'It's a bit mean though, isn't it?'

'What?'

'Snorting coke off your Christians' favourite book?'

'It's not like they'll ever know.' She tucked up the wrap and dotted the residue from the book's cover with a licked thumb.

'Are they not nice to you?' he asked.

'Eh?'

'The Christians, like.' He gestured at the book. 'There's a bang of vengeance off that.'

'That's not it at all,' she said. 'I didn't even think, to be honest.'

'So they're not bad to you,' he said. 'They're not asking you to change anything but your wardrobe.'

'Well, and my wanton ways.'

He pushed the chair onto its back legs, folded his arms and looked at the ceiling.

'That's it, though,' he said. 'All the judging. Doesn't that put you off?'

'They're not really judgemental,' she said. 'They're meek and mild and shapeless. They think God has a plan and that all they need to do with their lives is follow it. Live in the country and milk goats.'

'No wonder you were aching for a bump.'

'I wasn't, really. I was convalescing. Coke doesn't go with convalescing; I needed my feelings, you know?'

'You don't anymore?'

'I'm sick of having feelings.'

She was joking, and he smiled as he should have, but he said, 'Seriously though, Georgie. You're looking well, like. Don't fuck it up.'

'Oh my God. A dealer's telling me to stop doing drugs.'

'Dealing doesn't automatically make someone a cunt, is all.'

'Unlike whoring.'

The cocaine hadn't kicked in yet, of course, and the line she'd given herself was more a taster than a parade, but she had always found the ritual very encouraging of conversation.

'I don't know how judgemental they'd be,' she said. 'Truthfully.

Only the leader guy knows that I was on the game. The rest of them just think I'm a souse. But even if they knew and hated me, well, more to forgive, right?'

'I didn't mean you in particular,' he said. 'It's just judgey bollocks all round, isn't it? That's the whole point.'

'That's not very fair,' she said.

He shrugged.

'They've been really decent to me. Free accommodation and all the veggies I can eat and all I have to do is renounce bikinis and not look bored when they're going on about Jesus.'

'And they've no ulterior motive?'

'*That's* the motive. Saving my soul. And let them think they're saving my soul, because in doing that they're saving me from being abused by bastards who think they have a right to rape me.'

He winced.

'It's true,' she said. 'It's not as if Mr Punter Man's bothered whether I enjoy it. And he can't be a nasty, angry prick to his girlfriend so he hires a woman to pound his cock into instead. So if some cooperative of Jesus freaks want to give me an extended holiday that's fine, and if they're only doing it to hook me into their prayer circle that's fine, let them; it has to be better than the alternative, doesn't it?'

He looked at her.

'But what if you don't think you've done anything wrong?'

'I have done something wrong. And I suppose I'd be directed to show Christian forgiveness to you for not knowing that because a: you're male and b: you're never going to be in a situation where you're made cannon fodder for the appetites of people better off than you.'

'All right,' he said. 'All right. Leave it.'

He stood up, making, she thought, to leave, but instead of heading for the door he went the other way, towards the lectern and the keyboard and the stacks of unsullied Bibles.

'I know it's not like I should expect you to care,' she said.

'It's OK.'

'It's just, y'know, the Christians might be daft but they're trying to do the right thing.'

'Yeah, I get that.'

'They might think short skirts are slutty but at least they've come up with an alternative.'

He picked up one of the books of sheet music.

'You wouldn't use a prostitute, would you?' she asked.

It was a funny thing to ask a kid, even if he was your dealer. She chased this grown-up disquiet with ugly reminiscence: the younger men, booked in groups to sate the gang-bang fantasies unearthed by porn habits that stretched from pre-teen curiosity right up to the stoked cruelty of adulthood; the ones who were never satisfied; the ones whose displeasure reverberated in slaps and misspelt jibes.

'I have a girlfriend.'

'That's not an answer.'

'It is,' he said. 'I wouldn't because I have a girlfriend.'

'That doesn't stop your typical punter,' she said. 'Girlfriends have nothing to do with it.'

'That's as may be,' he said. 'I have a girlfriend. I'm not interested in anyone else.'

'How long have you been with her?'

'Year and a half.'

'Jesus.' And then a nasty thought, as she remembered their initial introduction. 'It's not Tara Duane, is it?'

He looked like he'd come down Christmas morning to find a box of bees under the tree.

'What?'

'The night she gave me your number, she let on that there was history between you. Which is partly why I got some fright when you rocked up in your school *geansaí*.'

'That's sick.'

'She's not your sugar mammy, then?'

'That's fucking sick, Georgie.'

'I've seen weirder.'

He placed the sheet-music book on the stand over the keys and said, 'If I'd seen weirder I would have gouged my fucking eyes out.'

'So where did she get your number?'

'She's my dad's next-door-neighbour. Happy? Seriously, Georgie, you're giving me the gawks.'

'Weren't you her dealer?'

'Once upon a time. I've gotten picky with age.'

'Couldn't be too picky, if you're coming into Christian retreats to sell me coke.'

'Maybe I don't find you half as creepy, Georgie.'

'That's a compliment, is it?'

'Statement of fact. Even with your new cult.'

She started to protest, but he hushed her with the first few notes from the keyboard; startling, in that she didn't expect it, and certainly not from him. She didn't know what it was, except that it was played with fluidity and grace, and she gawped, and tried to shout over it, but he ignored her, and by the time he got to the end of the piece she was muted but good, yes, getting there, feeling good.

'Did you play that just to shut me up?'

'It's awful,' he said. 'Lazy, simple bollocks. But it's the only instrumental in here.'

'You don't look like a musician.'

'You don't look like a God-botherer.'

He put the music book back where he had found it, and walked to the door, hands in his jeans pockets.

'What's your girlfriend's name?' Georgie asked.

For a moment he looked like he wasn't going to tell her. He narrowed his eyes, and considered her, and conceded. 'Karine.'

'What's she like?'

'Stunning.'

'So what would she say if she knew you were doing coke in a Christian prayer hall with a prostitute?'

'I've done worse.'

'So she's a saint.'

'Higher up than that, I'd say.'

'So where do I get one of those?'

'You don't,' he said. 'She's one of a kind.'

He stepped onto the path and hesitated. 'Take care of yourself,' he said. 'Seriously.'

She gave him an awkward smile. 'Don't buy prostitutes. Seriously. If I can't change any hearts in virtuous Christian chests than at least I can change yours.'

'I told you. Not going to happen.'

'Good. And Ryan?'

He looked back.

'You should probably avoid that Tara Duane, too.'

'Give me fucking strength. Anything else?'

'Go in peace?'

'Go and fuck off for yourself,' he said, and he was gone.

The day had gone without a hitch. She'd gotten to the city, she'd called a dealer who wasn't a bullying bastard to bring her blow she had both mind and money for, she'd helped her new friends conduct their Bible study without yap-yap-yapping her true colours into their Christian ears. And when she got back to the farm in the late evening, David was delighted to see her, and over tea and biscuits in the common room she demonstrated, by way of smiles and winks, that she had been successful in her quest, that their midnight feast could go ahead.

David crept to her room when the others were asleep and as she watched him snort a line in childish glee, the day's leftovers tangled in her head.

The rush in chopping up the lines, the unintended sacrilege of a hastily adapted base on which to do it. The thoughts that had come on considering her dealer's frame: that she'd been doing it wrong all those years on the street and in the back bedrooms of crumbling townhouses, that boyhood was a state on which to take pre-emptive revenge.

Then as David came over to lie beside her, murmuring tactile promises on her skin, she knew, suddenly, lucidly, that what she was doing was a curse. She was the succubus aiding his fall. He'd come here, wide-eyed and broken, to mine some life from the depths of his failure and she was bringing him coke and pretty falsehoods.

This community, this flaky citadel of do-gooders, had been poisoned by her presence. The meagre rules of William Tobin, smashed with pitiless zeal. *Respect your body*; here she was on her back again, for some man she hardly knew. *Respect your friends*; here she was, having brought cocaine into their cocoon.

'I need to get out of here,' she said to David, who shrugged it off as he spread her legs. 'I don't belong here.'

'*Ssh*, baby; can't let them hear us.'

'Get off me,' she said, and then, 'Get off me!'

She pushed him off and pulled on her dress as he spluttered disbelief, and ran through the deep shadows of a house she had just begun to know and out onto the yard, down the woodland path to the water, her feet bruised by the shingle, the hem of her ridiculous dress floating as the mud hindered her.

'Georgie!' David was behind her; she didn't turn to look. 'What are you doing, Georgie? Jesus, you'll drown!'

No fear of that; the water, cold and still as the morning air, didn't have the depth to either baptise or kill her. So she stood up to her waist in it, and cried at the shadow shore opposite, for how could good intentions so easily dishonoured ever stand a chance of saving her?

9

They held it up as a Get Out of Jail Free card when it was just another yellow star. Tony lay in the dark in a residential treatment centre in the middle of a vast nowhere. Here, he was to be crumbled to dust and put back together. Here, he was to admit his failings and submit to something of greater import and headier influence. At the end of it he would be a more humble man with drier balls. And sober! Yes, he'd be sober; the Law decreed it. Inside, he succumbed to the horrors doled out by their programme and sobriety stretched in front of him like miles of broken glass.

It had been a stipulation of his admittance that he completed detox before they began his re-education. Even so, his frailty punished him. Getting to sleep was no longer something accomplished by design, but by some Fates' trick: he lay sweating and watching shadows, harrowed over fleeting agonies until he began to dream. The dreams were vivid to the point of cruelty, and he would wake up and have to start all over again. His shell cracked and splintered. His stomach heaved; his muscles sagged; toxins oozed from every pore.

Every time he broke the bottle the period of adjustment was longer and harsher. They kept hanging him out to dry before he was ready to come out of the brine. Next time round it would probably be the DTs. Hallucinations, fever and death. But that'd suit them fine, wouldn't it? They always lumped for the option least bothersome to them. If they'd really given a fuck about his drinking they'd have asked him, *Why? Why, Mr Cusack, did you feel the need to medicate yourself into such a state? It was in effect an overdose. To what end, boy? To what fucking end?*

He turned on his side. His watch, flung onto his bedside table two days ago when it had begun to itch, flashed 3.17. He had been sleeping. He'd dreamt he was drinking again. In therapy sessions he had kept that recurrence to himself, thinking it a sign of ill intent the staff would take badly, but his fellow inmates had mentioned similar delusions. Horrors to them; they were in it for the long haul.

Well, the why is an interesting thing, Mr Bleeding Heart Bastard. Maybe not everyone in here drinks out of Neanderthal instinct.

Interesting, Mr Cusack. Do go on.

She denied it, the venomous bitch. She struck her chest and made a speech about trust and breach of trust and how she had offered his son nothing but a shoulder to cry on. 'And why the fuck would you think he'd need to cry?' Tony snapped, to which Tara cocked her head and wept through narrowed eyes, 'Oh, we both know you're struggling, Tony, there's no shame in admitting that you're struggling.'

He attempted to hound the truth out of her by demonstrating his rage on her windowpane, but all he'd ended up with was a legal obligation to reimburse her and a neighbour who spent her days by the new glass with her curtains bunched into her fist and who skittered up and down her driveway like a spider making a dash across the kitchen floor.

Ryan, then. Tony might have asked him about the night in Duane's, his half-confession, about what perversion had prompted his sharing his home-made porn with the pasty witch, but he'd been so fucked from pilfered flashbacks that the thought of holding a conference had riled him into atrophy. He stewed for days. Then he let the boy go to school in an attempt to win back breathing space. The boy threw a bag of cocaine at his headmaster.

Too much to ask for Ryan to have explained this act of self-sabotage before he took off from home. Temper. Revenge. Something foreign and intangible. When threatened, the boy went mute as Father Mathew himself.

So why did you threaten him at all, Mr Cusack? Don't you think The Demon had something to do with that?

Tony didn't ever set out to lose the rag with Ryan but in no way did the young fella ever quell the rising tide; God forbid he use the term 'asking for it' . . .

Asking for it would be entirely the wrong turn of phrase.

Well, far be it from him, then, to suggest the boy was asking for it but they certainly seemed to have locked themselves into rounds. Tony would attempt to admonish the lad, the lad would go still as a rock, and the boy's silence drove Tony like a whip.

That he was driven to drink by a taciturn child was as good a reason as being defective in spirit and in genetics, but the counsellors preferred internal triggers and vague spiritual shortcomings to logical grounds for needing the poison. In one of last week's sessions he'd explained it: the cruelty of his progeny was what had left him in this shitheap.

'I got into trouble because the woman next door was up to no good with my kid. If that wouldn't drive you to drink then I don't know what would.'

'Did you not find your drinking to be an issue before this?'

'It's not an issue at all,' Tony said. 'I'm here because the court would rather punish me than prosecute that psychotic whore.'

'Jesus, what age is your kid?' said one of his fellow losers.

'Fifteen at the time. And she's my age. And I put her window in and suddenly the problem is my relationship with alcohol and not her relationship with my bloody child.'

He could have killed her. He had practice now in getting rid of bodies, didn't he? He could have killed her and then J.P. would have been obliged to help him turn her to fertiliser, owing him a favour and all. He could have kicked her door in and bludgeoned her, literally knocked the smile off her face, smashed her to pieces. But didn't she have the devil's own luck; he wasn't that kind of man. His rage manifested in muttered oaths. He took out her window instead. He could have killed her but instead he was stuck here, gelded, talking shit in circles so that vultures with clipboards could pick over his compulsions while his children were fed and watered by better people and his son was out there alone being fucked and fucked over.

There were no locks on the windows or doors. Part of the insidiousness of this dungeon was that the only thing keeping him there was torpor. But they didn't make it easy for you; oh no. They had built their covered hellhole in the middle of a post-card vista: miles from the main road and miles from there to anywhere else.

It was boldly functional. White block walls, blue carpet, big windows which left the place airy and bright and cold and exposed. He supposed the intent was to provide a stark alternative to whatever stuffy sets they'd come from, but he was the participant with the most children – the next to him had only three – and so the contrast hurt him worst of all. He yearned for all of it: the crusts on the worktop, the empty toilet roll tubes, the plates under beds and on shelves and, one time last month, on the bathroom windowsill. The triumphant complaints from Kelly on yet another infringement of her teenage right to languor. A mound of socks tumbled onto the kitchen table for Ronan and Niamh to match into pairs. The modish disdain for schoolday outerwear. Him in the middle of it all, dazed sometimes by the whirligig colours and cacophony, but operating nonetheless, handing out lunches, putting on dinners, emptying bins. He couldn't think of home as a space that demanded his reconstruction. There was nothing wrong with it. He was not in here because once in a while he forgot to empty the washing machine or get up on time on Mondays.

He turned again and eyed his bedroom window. Where would he go, if he cranked it wide and made a run for it? Even if it was, defiantly, to one of the pubs peppered over the countryside, he'd be waiting until late morning for them to open. Even if it was back to the city, he'd be sitting in the shell of his home, taunted by echoes and prepping himself for Garda custody. The choice was no choice at all.

From the outside world he heard someone cry.

Such sounds had no right to be anomalous in the dry asylum. Tony stared at the window. The cries were faint, but tormented; this was no fellow inmate indulging themselves with a sneaky wah, but someone further afield, across the lake, in one of the bordering copses. There were other buildings viewable from his window with a daytime squint, but they were either farms or piles of stone and glass belonging to Cork's upper crust. These cries could not have belonged in those places.

No words he could make out.

He got out of the bed and stood by the window with his palms against the glass.

It had been a while since he'd had mind for ghost stories.

The wind rushed the plaintive sounds over the water toward him. He thought about closing the window. Some childhood memory warned him to put the eras between himself and the echo, to make a barrier of modern glazing, or window locks, or a set of headphones. Or was it that you were fucked altogether if you heard the banshee's wail? Maybe there was no escape; it was an omen stirred in blood.

Shrieking, then silence.

Maybe she had come for someone else and he hadn't been meant to hear it.

It was an unusual curse and he only barely had room to nestle it with all the others. He stood at the window looking into umbral immensity, waiting for the screech that confirmed his surveillance had been noted, but he heard no more after that.

'I don't think you should go in,' said Joseph, 'but that's only me, and I'm a lot less forgiving than you are. Whatever I think, I know for a cold hard fact that if you don't go in, you'll regret it.'

They were sitting in the teeming car park of Solidarity House on a Wednesday morning in August. There were vans making deliveries, official sorts carrying folders, visitors doing what Ryan was doing now – hesitating behind their windscreens and tying their fingers up in knots. Ryan's legs were leaden. His shoulders were fused to the back of the seat.

He'd been badgered into attending by his aunt Fiona, Joseph's mother. His dad's twin was as coolly insincere as her counterpart was reckless and thick; the evidence pointed towards her having requisitioned more than her share of nutrients in utero. Her having bullied him into turning up at Solidarity House's 'family day', in which loved ones were roped into the rehabilitant's long-term recovery plan, had been recognised and assuaged by Joseph, who offered to cadge a car so that Ryan wouldn't have to suffer Fiona's pontificating on the journey down. It was a small comfort.

'What d'you think is going to happen in there?' Ryan asked.

'What did they tell you? You get a chance to talk about how his drinking affects you, and then you all learn coping strategies.'

'How his drinking affected me,' Ryan grunted. He doubted they'd welcome the answer: *Physically*.

'And then you all hug or some shit and Tony goes home to resume gargling himself into the ground. Great craic.'

'If I don't show up though I'll be the biggest cunt on the planet.'

'You shouldn't care whether anyone else thinks you're a cunt. What are they going to say to you, anyway? *Oh Ryan, you're a bold, bold boy with no regard for your daddy's disease*. Fuck off. Like six weeks in the country's going to cure Tony.'

'Stranger things have happened.'

From the corner of his eye Ryan saw Joseph consider him.

'Maybe you're right, boy. He's your dad. I get it, you know. I have a dad too.' And then, 'Are you going to have that joint or what?'

Ryan had crafted a fat spliff before they had set off from the city. First, he was going to smoke it on the way down – it'd provide a nice rollover from the one he'd had at breakfast – and then he changed his mind and decided he'd smoke it when he got there. Now he didn't want it at all.

'Feels wrong,' he said. 'Can't go into a place like this stoned, can you?'

'Why not? It's not you making a hames of clean living. They'd probably spot it, mind you. Deprivation can make you very fucking perceptive.'

Ryan shook his head. 'It's just wrong.'

'It's not a church, boy.'

'It's not far off it.'

Fiona's car glinted across the gravel. It was empty, because it was five past the hour and the session had already started.

'I better go in,' Ryan said.

'You know you don't have to, boy? You know he doesn't deserve the steam off your piss?'

'I know that.'

'So why're you doing it, then? What's making you go through that door and into a meeting that's just going to wreck your head? Fifteen minutes, boy, and we could be in Clon, buying a box of beer for a day at Inchydoney. Give this a couple of hours and it'll be baking. Fucking bikini weather and all the lashers down sunning themselves. How bad?'

Ryan let the scene play through his head – the sand, the beers, the sunshine, the flat tummies and the perky arses and necks flowing into shoulders and shoulders pouring into soft curves – and was sorry for it as soon as it faded away. *No harm in perusing the goods*, Joseph might have said, if Ryan had confessed the periodic crises that turned him from red-blooded man to cowering penitent. Or maybe he'd have said, *What the fuck is wrong with you, boy? Are you that whipped?*

Once his pause weighed what reverence Joseph's suggestion demanded he gave his cousin a joyless smile and opened the car door.

Tony waited in the meeting room, chewing his knuckles. His mother was due down to catalogue her myriad disappointments. His father had been invited, of course, but wouldn't Father Mathew have made the trek before him? And then there was Fiona, who had arrived in the world seven minutes before him and so was very saddened she was so frequently dismissed as a font of knowledge. She lived in Dublin, but had driven down for the brouhaha and custard creams.

Tony's counsellor had recommended his older children attend, and so Fiona had roped in Cian and Kelly, and vowed that she'd track down Ryan. On the face of it that wouldn't have been hard; the boy and Fiona's own son were thick as thieves. In reality, Tony knew that getting Joseph to divulge such a touchy secret would have been like asking the Pope where the bodies were. And yet when the door opened there he was, the brat, bringing up the rear and then, when the door was closed, hanging by the wall as if welded to it.

His mother asked Tony how he was. Fiona positioned herself directly across from the counsellor. Cian smiled at him because he was a generous kid – always had been. Kelly smacked her arse onto the chair nearest the door. Ryan stayed by the wall, his hands behind him and his fingers flexed on the brickwork, not meeting his father's eyes, not meeting anyone's.

'Do you want to take a seat?' the counsellor chanced.

The boy said, 'I'm grand.'

'If you take a seat we can get started.'

'I'm all right a minute.'

The counsellor was stumped.

'Yeah, keep standing there,' said Kelly. 'G'wan, make everything about you.'

On any other day her barb may have been snatched mid-air and flung back in her face, but the surroundings had sucked the fight out of the lad, just as it had Tony, who late at night stood staring for *sídhe* and willing them to whip the skin from his bones.

The counsellor smiled as Ryan detached himself from the wall. There were two chairs left: one beside Tony, the other between Cian and Kelly. He took the one between his siblings, and Tony looked at them, sitting in a row as if ordered to file into the formation most likely to bother their father's conscience. When you haven't seen your children in weeks, and for so long before that only through a medicated haze, to have them organised so neatly was a bit of an eye-opener. All three had shot up like weeds.

'Our focus today isn't on mediation or family therapy,' intoned the counsellor. 'We have a specific task and that is to deal with the addiction. So what's helpful at this juncture is for each of you to tell Tony, honestly, how his drinking affected you, and that will provide a solid foundation on which to build a strategy unique to this family. Yeah? *This* family. Everyone has a different story.'

'I can start,' said Fiona.

'Oh. Yeah. Yup. Sure.'

The charade took each of them in turn. Fiona spoke about losing her connection with her twin, conveniently leaving out her globetrotting and how her resulting affectations made her as popular as a Guinness fart in a snug. His mother said something about the shame of having birthed a professional noodeenaw. Tony watched his children. Kelly feigned boredom, but she was all ears under that leonine mop. Cian kept patting his pockets. Ryan hunched over, staring at his shoes. Black rubber dollies with the thick white sole; there was a name for them, but Tony couldn't remember it. The lad was never out of them. God knows where he got them, because they weren't a brand Tony had the money for.

It could have been Tara Duane. The bitch had always maintained she didn't have a bob to her name but with only one kid and a frame that suggested she only ate on Thursdays, it was obvious she was hawking the poor mouth. She could have been spending her money on fancy footwear for his son; he wouldn't have guessed. How would he have guessed? The concept was too fucked up to take a decent run at. He cast back to see if he could hit on a time when Ryan had had anything but those fucking plimsolls on his feet but nothing came. He'd been a runt of a thing till he was fourteen. Maybe then. Tony's fingers hooked under his seat. His nails scraped off plastic.

Cian looked mortified but managed something about homework and bedtimes and proper breakfasts.

But sure what could you do about it? Fucking nothing. If you called the guards what were they going to do? Arrest her? They would in their shit. They'd have come stomping in all over him, as if he had been the one offering cause to the child to run to that bitch's flapping teabag bosom.

Kelly launched into a gleeful speech about how she had to do everything around the house, and got a dig in too at her older brother for having left her there up to her elbows in the ware and the washing, and Ryan ignored her and Tony ignored her too until it came down to it, when the counsellor turned in his chair to face the boy.

'Ryan?'

He didn't look up. 'I don't have anything to say.'

'Nothing at all?'

'No.'

'Your father's drinking didn't affect you at all?'

'I can't think of anything.'

'Oh my God,' said Kelly. 'Like, seriously, Ryan? Fucking seriously?'

Her grandmother said, 'Kelly! Watch your language.'

'Are you for real, boy? Oh, it didn't affect you at all, is it? Just the rest of us and we're all making a fuss. You're such an enabler!'

'Well,' said the counsellor, 'that may well be an avenue worth exploring when we talk tactics, but right now it's an unhelpful label.'

The girl was on a roll. 'I bet I'm not supposed to know that word, like. *Enabler*. Yeah, I couldn't possibly be able to look this shit up on the Internet before I get here. Fine, I can spill the beans on his behalf. My dad's drinking has affected my brother in the following ways: he doesn't rat him out and he doesn't hit him back and he sure as shit doesn't take responsibility when he drives my dad so crazy he smashes our neighbour's windows. Do you know . . .' She made a great show of lowering her voice. '. . . why my brother can't live—'

'How my dad's drinking affects me,' Ryan said, and he stretched back in his seat, instantly claiming his due space in the room as if by a magician's trick. 'I can't remember a time my dad wasn't drinking so I can't tell you.'

'Oh my God, such bullshit,' sang Kelly.

'So if my dad's always drinking, how am I supposed to tell you how it affects me? How would I know?'

The counsellor shrugged to concede the point, but Kelly snorted, and the cretin let her wade back in.

'He's just changing the subject,' she said, 'because he knows it's his fault Dad's here.'

Her brother snapped, 'Will you ever mind your own business?'

'This is my business, Ryan. This couldn't be more my business.'

'I don't make my dad drink.'

'You make him break Tara Duane's windows.'

'We could frame this a lot more constructively,' tried the counsellor.

Tony's mother folded her arms. 'What's all this about?'

'Ask your grandson,' Tony said.

'That's right, Dad. It's all my fault. It's always my fucking fault.'

Tony's mother made to say something but Fiona gripped her arm, and by no small miracle the damn woman shut her trap again.

'Ne'er a truer word,' Tony said. 'I'm not in here because the guards found too many empties in my bins, am I? I'm in here because I smashed Tara Duane's window. I'm in here on the tack because that's a hell of a lot easier for the State to deal with than your gallivanting.'

'I didn't ask you to put her fucking windows in, Dad!'

'I wasn't going to wait for you to fucking ask me. Don't think I don't know what went on.'

'Nothing went on.'

'Didn't you tell me yourself?'

'I told you nothing.'

'Just to interject here,' said the counsellor. 'Tony, you're not here at Solidarity House on criminal charges, only as a condition of your parole, because the judge felt that alcohol was a considerable factor in . . .'

It was drink. Oh, look, no denying that. Course it was drink, but it was drink because circumstances required saturation, and again, this bullshit chatter was only blaming the medicine instead of rooting out the tumour.

Ryan looked at his father now with an off-kilter malice Tony wasn't used to seeing from him.

'You told me half a story,' Tony said. 'Why won't you tell me the rest of it?'

'Coz you're dangerous enough with half a story, aren't you?'

'And you think telling me lies is the answer?'

'I'm not lying.' Even in the lie he offered the truth. He shook his head, then bowed it, and started on his nails.

Tony heard his mother hiss *What in the name of God?* at Fiona, who shushed her yet again as the counsellor cleared his throat and Cian folded in on himself like a paper fan.

'You're lying to me because you're a fucking liar, Ryan. Brought up in two fucking languages; of course you are. So what were you up to with her, then? Teaching her Italian? Or selling her smoke? Ah, that's it and part of it,' off his son's set jaw, 'dealing drugs at your age. You should be in here, not me. Eh? D'you want to tell your grandmother that?'

'I knew this was going to happen,' Kelly chanted at the counsellor.

'I knew it too,' Ryan said, and up he sprang, making his sister jump. 'I knew nothing would have changed and still I let them talk me into it. Like drying you out would make a blind bit of difference.'

He went for the door, and Tony would have gotten up and knocked his head clean off his shoulders if it wasn't for the fact his mother was there, and the counsellor, a right old man's arse in a skinny shirt and a nose only just long enough to look down.

'That's your answer when I say you're no angel, is it? Walk away?'

Ryan turned back. 'You didn't even ask me where I was, boy. *Where're you staying, Ryan? Who are you with? What're you up to?* Nawthin'. Is it that you couldn't give two shits or you're afraid I'll start talking about what drove me there?'

'You think I don't give two shits? I'm in here for you, you little bollocks.'

'You're in here and you're supposed to be getting better when you're still damn sure there's fuck all wrong with you.' His eyes were shining; the chin was starting to go. 'And d'you know what? I never told no one. About you. And if I had done, where would you be? Not in here complaining coz you're sober; you'd be behind the fucking high walls.'

The door rattled on its hinges as he slammed it.

'Does anyone want to go after him?' asked the counsellor.

'Oh, trust me,' said Kelly, 'he won't be part of the recovery.'

Back out into the car park, one foot after another and blinking desperately, as if every drop squeezed was poison. Ryan had just cleared his vision when he reached Joseph and the car, but he was still sniffing salt and slime back down his throat as if his life depended on their sustenance. Oh fuck, that was no good at all. Not when the very act of leaving home was meant to cure him of that childish weakness that only his father could twist out of him. He could build a customer base whose appetite for smoke, coke and yokes was matched only by their inability to keep their wallets shut; he could live on his own and trick sales assistants into giving him naggins of whiskey; he could strip his girlfriend gently and fuck her hard but for the life of him he couldn't figure out how to move his triggers so his father wouldn't know how to yank them.

'Jesus Christ,' Joseph said, as he got back into the car.

Ryan took the spliff out of the glove compartment and stuck it in his gob.

'He'll never change,' he choked. 'He'll never fucking change.'

Gold Digger

Joseph is on Paul Street, busking. That lad has balls, like. He just toddles down there with his guitar and lays the case on the ground in front of him and off he goes, belting out anything from rebel songs to shit that's in the charts. I don't know how he does it. I'd be mortified just singing in the shower.

It's Saturday lunchtime and town is jointed. I go in with Karine and we get milkshakes in Maccy D's and then slink round the corner to watch him. He's doing a cover of 'Gold Digger'. He's got a daycent voice and there are a couple of girls shaking their arses and giving the air the old sexy one-two. The sun's out. One of the girls removes her jacket and whoops, provoking the evil eye in an ould fella shuffling past. If I was being a prick I'd tell her that Joseph's ould doll has just had a baby girl and that there's no point waving her tits at him coz he's too fucking tired to notice.

Leigh, they called the baby. The christening's next month. I'm gonna be the godfather. Joseph swears he didn't just ask me because I'm half Italian.

Karine stands in front of me and backs her arse right up against me so I take my hands out of my pockets and join them round her waist.

'He gets better every time I hear him,' she says.

There's a bunch of people sitting outside the pubs and outside Tesco. Some of them are singing along. There'll be a few bob made today.

'Did y'ever think of coming down with him?' Karine says, and she twists in my arms to stare at me.

'Me?'

'No, the fella behind you. Yeah you!'

'With Joseph? Busking? G'way outta that. All I play is piano and I don't think they'd let me drag one of them out into the square.'

'You could sing. You're way better than he is.'

'I am in me shit.'

'You're really good. You're a proper musician, like. I don't know what you're doing selling dope. You could go for X Factor.*'*

'You're shaming me now,' I tell her.

'Hasn't he asked you?' she says. I slide my hands up along her arms and down again and press up against her arse in a fit of gall; I'm wearing trackies, though, so it's probably not a good idea to think too hard about her arse.

'He's said it a couple of times, like.'

'And what did you say?'

'What d'you think I said? I said what I'm saying to you now.'

'You were really good at music at school, is all.'

'Can you imagine me?' I tell her. 'Caterwauling away and lads I do business with rubbing their eyes and wondering who put what in their weed? Imagine what Dan Kane'd say to that?'

The joke flatlines. 'I like to think there's more to you than Dan Kane.'

'There is,' I tell her. 'Loads more.'

'Oh, you reckon so too, do you? For a while there I was thinking it was only me.'

'Well it's not, all right? I'm just . . .' But I can't think of what to say. Joseph finishes the song. People cheer. He catches my eye and I give him the thumbs up and then quietly I go, 'There's no choice, like. I either do a bit for Dan or I go home, and I can't go home.'

'Jesus, Ryan, d'you really think you need to explain that to me? I know that, like! That's not what I'm saying.'

'You're saying I don't fucking sing enough?'

'I'm saying *I didn't start going out with you because you could get yokes.'*

There's frost now. It's like I've said the wrong thing and it's like she's said the wrong thing and we're just a bit out of whack, just enough to notice but not enough to fight over. She folds her arms. I move my hands back down to her belly but I don't let go; there'll be a real fight now if I let go.

10

'Bless me, Father, for I have sinned. It's been decades since my last confession.'

'Decades?'

'Oh, aeons. Can you imagine what a burden it's been, Father? Carrying all that sin around, like saddlebags on the back of an ass?'

'Well . . . You're here now. It's the contrition itself that's important, after all.'

'Yes, and there's sins here I'm only dying to be rid of. Ready?'

'Go ahead.'

'I killed a man.'

'. . . Are you joking?'

'Do I sound like I'm joking? What do I sound like? A sixty-year-old woman, if your ears are sound, forgive the pun. Do you think that's how the bingo brigade get their kicks? Confessing crimes to priests?'

'When did this happen? How did this happen?'

'It was a long time ago. Didn't I tell you I hadn't been in decades?'

'But it's playing on your mind now.'

'I live on my own and one day a man broke into my flat. I crept up behind him and hit him in the head with a religious ornament. So first I suppose God would have to forgive me for killing one of his creatures and then he'd have to forgive me for defiling one of his keepsakes.'

'And did you involve the Gardaí?'

'Indeed I did not. You'll have to add another Hail Mary on for that. I didn't involve the Gardaí at all; instead I called up my son and he cleaned up the mess on my behalf.'

'He contacted the Gardaí?'

'No. He has his own ways of dealing with things, I've discovered. And that would be his sin on the face of it but unfortunately it looks like we can attribute that to me too. Another Hail Mary! Will I tell you all about it, from a mother to a Father?'

'If you are truly repentant, God is always here to hear you.'

'God is great that way. He has massive ears and a mouth sewn shut.'

'Well, that doesn't sound in the least bit contrite.'

'I've always had an attitude, Father; you'll have to forgive me for that yourself. It was my attitude that brought me all the way up to your lovely old-fashioned confessional here today. You see, I had a son. But I had him illegitimately because I had an attitude and therefore no respect for myself. He was reared by my mother and father who were very much in cahoots with the Man Above so between my bad attitude and my parents' piety the poor lad was spent, and so now he has no morals at all and he's turned to a life of crime. And you might say that's his own sin, Father, but surely his circumstances had something to do with it?'

'Well . . . Well I suppose we never act entirely alone. Our actions are informed by everything around us. And there is much temptation in the modern world.'

'Temptation that leads young girls into sin, you could say.'

'Times change. There are unique challenges for God's children in every age.'

'Oh indeed there are. And I suppose God was challenging me to deny my son's father his hole. But the Trickster was having none of it, so off my drawers came.'

'This is entirely the wrong tone for the confessional! You must be respectful . . . this is a Sacrament!'

'Is the Sacrament as revered in God's house as the miracle of birth?'

'Well, one is divine, and the other very much an earthly thing . . .'

'So do you think God could accept my contrition when all I've done is put to ground one of his earthly things? I killed a man, Father. Now surely that's a story fit to stretch the Seal of Confession?'

'Nothing can break the Seal of Confession. All I can do is encourage you to approach the authorities; it is the moral thing to do. Not doing so would only add another sin and call into question your remorse for the first.'

'So you won't absolve me unless I go to the guards.'

'I cannot put stipulations on God's grace. You will know yourself what should be done.'

'It's a funny thing that the ritual is more powerful than the killing. What's tied to the earth is less important than what's tied to the heavens. You're crosser about my language in the confessional than you are about the fact that I killed a man. An unpleasant man, a waster man at best. A man maybe as born in sin as my son was and therefore an expendable man. Who knows?'

'I sense you're struggling with guilt, and again I must tell you that while God will absolve all who repent with an honest heart, perhaps the only way for you to find peace is to tell your story to the Gardaí.'

'Ah, Jaysus, they must have you on commission or something. No, I'm not going to go to the guards. Not a condition of my telling God how sorry I am.'

'You don't sound very sorry.'

'Well look, Father. There are a lot of things I'm sorry for. Indeed, when I think about it, it feels like I've been sorry all my life. First I was supposed to be sorry for having a child out of wedlock – and if it weren't for the Magdalene Laundry being on its last, bleached-boiled legs I would have been up there scrubbing sheets for the county. Instead I was exiled. I went away to have the baby and then I gave him up as my penance and was sent away again. Your kind had my mother and father's ears; I didn't stand a chance. So if many, many years later my son has found me and brought me home, only he's turned into a thug and my hands are so shaky I accidentally kill fellas, don't the amends I've already made mean anything to the Man Above?'

'It seems you don't want to be absolved at all.'

'Of course I do. Why wouldn't I? I have a son; why wouldn't I feel bad about taking another woman's? I was a wretch; why wouldn't I feel bad about doing in one of my own?'

'Are you really asking me if the punitive measures you felt were forced on you back when you had your child exempt you from guilt now that you've done something you feel is worth God's attention? We are all born in sin; no one gets respite from the nature of their soul.'

'I found out his name, Father. The poor eejit I killed. That was accidental, too, but it was something I held on to, like rosary beads. When I got the chance to tell my son what the man's name was, I seized it, because I couldn't wait to see the look on his face. Oh, Father; he was livid. He has no mercy in him. He wasn't made to examine his actions by the fact the corpse had a name; he was furious that the name provided a complication. He doesn't want to have to deal with his mother's conscience. He's a pup, Father. And who's to say I couldn't have raised him right? Propriety did nothing for him.'

'Well, times were different—'

'Oh, they were. Times were tough and the people were harsh and the clergy were cruel – cruel, and you know it! The most natural thing in the world is giving birth; you built your whole religion around it. And yet you poured pitch on girls like me and sold us into slavery and took our humanity from us twice, a third time, as often as you could. I was lucky, Father. I was only sent away. A decade earlier and where would I have been? I might have died in your asylums, me with the smart mouth. I killed one man but you would have killed me in the name of your god, wouldn't you? How many did you kill? How many lives did you destroy with your morality and your Seal of Confession and your lies? Now. For the absolution. Once God knows you're sorry he lets you off the hook, isn't that right?'

'How can I believe that you're sorry when you're—'

'Me? Oh, Father. I know I'm sorry. What about you? *Bless me, Ireland, for I have sinned*. Go on, boy. No wonder you say Holy God is brimming with the clemency; for how else would any of you bastards sleep at night?'

The Echo

11

The weatherman said that this April had been warmer than usual, but as the charcoal canopy was wrung out over the city and the hem of her dress sucked up the residue of a hundred days' winter, no one could have convinced Georgie that it was balmier than Himself had intended. She stood on the corner of the Maltings and the Mardyke; not the first time she'd been standing on street corners in dismal weather, but this time she was accompanied by Clover, which discouraged bitter memories.

They had had a busy morning. They'd been up at the Lough going door to door to spread the Good Word, Clover with calm determination, Georgie in abject mortification. Clover had insisted on their returning to town via the university, where she managed to pass on a few leaflets outside the back gate. Most of the students who took a leaflet immediately bunched it up and carried it just as far as the next dustbin, but a few had absent-mindedly stuck them into pockets of rain jackets or baggy tracksuit bottoms. If only one of them was moved, Clover pointed out, that would be worth the whole excursion. Georgie thought that if only one of the students was moved it would be a waste of their very meagre printing budget, but she kept it to herself.

They had carried on down the Western Road and towards the Coal Quay, where William had parked up the minibus for his own mission across the river on Shandon Street – and excited he was about it too; 'So many Africans!' he'd enthused, mysteriously. It was on the Mardyke, just around the time a relieved Georgie could once again taste sweetness in the air, that Clover got the notion they should visit the few houses in and around the quay.

So they stood on the corner, Clover running over the strategy, Georgie exhausted and close to tears. She'd already been told to fuck off, to get off the doorstep before the dog was called, to get a life, to burn in hell, and to stick her propaganda up her shapely hole. She had no mind to repeat the process.

Especially not around here. The old brothel was only around the corner; she was nervous, even though it had been two years, even though the enterprise had moved on since. Jesus, it may have moved only in a loop; the building couldn't have been sold in the interim, not in that dilapidated row, not in this dilapidated economy.

'Well, look,' said Clover. 'Let's split up. That way we'll get through them faster and then we can have a well-earned rest. Hmm?'

'We haven't earned a rest yet?' Georgie despaired.

'Come on, Georgie, what would Jesus do? Besides, we can't meet William with so many flyers left.'

'Throw them in a bin then,' Georgie said. 'He'll never know.'

Clover darkened. 'William's not omnipresent. The Lord is.'

'Fine,' said Georgie. 'I'll go around the front here and meet you at the other end.'

She'd made a mistake in suggesting they dump the flyers. Clover was as rotund and twinkling as a fairy godmother, but she treated Georgie like a puppy she'd brought home from the pound for the sole reason that the authorities would otherwise have put her down.

'I should go with you,' she said, 'seeing as you're so tired.'

'I can manage. It's the shorter route, you know?'

'I'll come with you,' Clover decided, and marched on, with Georgie waddling after.

They deposited some of the flyers into the limp hands of those fretting outside the hospital, and while Clover was explaining her mission to a bemused pensioner with a Westie on a leash, Georgie desperately demonstrated intrepid spirit by dropping some of the leaflets into the communal postbox of an apartment complex.

Between that and the delay brought about by the pensioner's

heedlessness, Clover seemed more reluctant to continue her chaperoning. She stood with Georgie on the corner of the quay, only a couple of doors away from the old brothel, and relented, as if shrinking in the rain.

'Maybe it would be quicker if I went the other way,' she said.

'It would be.'

'Maybe if you continue along the quay and meet me halfway.'

'Sure.'

'Go on then,' said Clover, and pointed towards the first door.

In Georgie's day the house next door was empty. She moved towards it, doubtfully, and Clover stood where she was and watched.

'I can do this, Clover.'

'But what if they have questions?'

'But what about the time?'

Another mistake. Clover frowned.

'I'll just make sure you're grand with the first few here,' she said.

'Clover,' Georgie cried, 'let me do this. Honest, I can!'

The older woman's aversion had not come from nowhere. Georgie knew she'd let them down time and time again; they had allowed ball lightning into their nest. Breakdowns and escapes and more than one interlude where she claimed not to care about what she was doing to them, the poor, gullible eejits; any other collective would have been tested up to and over the line, but William and his disciples were either made of more resilient stuff than she'd accounted for, or they had never encountered ball lightning before and as such hadn't a clue what to do with it.

She had been sure her last blunder would have guaranteed her exile, but that wouldn't have been their style. These days there was so much more of her to save.

There was no answer at the first door.

'Just drop a couple of leaflets through the letterbox and move on,' Clover advised. 'Maybe they're apartments. Try the next one.'

'That'll probably be the same.'

'Try it anyway.'

The door had been painted; the front windows looked new. The intercom, which had once signalled appointments with gutting regularity, was gone. The building seemed to have been reassigned. Apartments now, maybe, housing underpaid professionals who ambled round ignorant to the shadows. God, maybe even young families.

She stood in the archway and tapped on the door.

'They won't have heard that,' Clover said, from the corner. 'Give it a good rap.'

'I don't think anyone's home.'

'Oh come on, Georgie,' said Clover, and moved as if to join her, so Georgie gave it another go; she rapped on the door and stood back and felt tears even under the damp on her lashes. She couldn't explain this to Clover, though there was little doubt that William had divulged her origin to his wife. There were some parts of her story that she could simply not vocalise, held to silence by shame and by expectation of judgement, and, really, William's group were accommodating but they operated entirely on judgement; who can forgive what they haven't already judged? Ryan had been right – their grace could only come from a pitying verdict.

So when the door opened she could neither bolt nor smile.

The resident was a woman in her sixties or so, too dishevelled to make an apposite gatekeeper, but healthier than the nubile corpses who'd toiled here two years ago. Her hair, still thick but hued entirely in shale and snow, came most of the way down her neck and stood out in waves. She said nothing, and scowled.

'I'm here . . .' Georgie said, and faltered, and the woman raised her eyebrows.

'Have I been expecting you?' Her voice was a tart growl.

To her right, Clover made to move.

'I'm here,' Georgie began again. 'To spread the word of . . . of Jesus Christ.'

'You'd think He'd send someone less scatty,' said the woman. 'But fine. What has He got to say for Himself?'

Georgie thrust one of the leaflets at the woman. Clover shifted her weight.

'Oh, He's written it down for you,' said the woman. 'Handy.'

'He says . . . He says: *Go unto . . . go into the world and proclaim the gospel to . . . creation. Whoever believes and is baptised will be saved, but whoever does not believe will be condemned.*'

'Harsh fecker, isn't He?'

'He's loving,' said Georgie. 'He's . . . *We love because he first loved us.*'

'What a pile of shite,' said the woman.

Georgie wilted and Clover beckoned her away, but the woman said, 'What are you doing out preaching on a day like this, anyway? And in your condition? What are you doing? Walking off your sins?'

'We have prayer meetings every week—' Georgie began.

'Era, balls to your prayer meetings,' said the woman. 'You want to convert me, you better do it now, because this missive is going in the bin as soon as I close the door. Do you want to talk to me about the Lord God Almighty or not?'

Georgie looked at Clover, who gestured towards the door.

'I'm not an expert,' Georgie admitted.

'Let me tell you this,' said the woman, 'neither is yer wanno there. Anyone who claims to be an expert in the mysterious waftings of Himself is talking through their high hoop. Are you coming in or not?'

Clover nodded.

'There's so much in the leaflet,' Georgie said.

'Are you going to deny an old lady her consultation, little preacher? Who goes door-to-door and declines the first invitation they get to pontificate?'

'I don't know what I could answer,' Georgie said.

'Give it a go.'

The woman turned and walked back into the building. Clover came to Georgie's side, and said, softly, 'I know she seems a little off but think of it as good practice, and if I don't see you by the time I've covered the rest of the houses I'll come back and get you, how's that?' She walked on before Georgie could answer, and so she went through the door and into the hall in which she used to hear her heart snap, every single time.

The place had been done up. Even from her tiptoed spot in the downstairs hall she could see that. The walls had been painted cream and there was a new floor; when she closed out the door behind her, gingerly, she noted that it had been painted on the inside, too, and the old bolts and chains removed for a single, modern lock.

'Come through,' called the woman, and Georgie followed her voice into a downstairs kitchen, a room she'd never seen when she'd worked there, as her company had only been required in the bedrooms upstairs.

The kitchen was new, too. Cream units around a sleek oven and hood, a breakfast bar, a shining sink before a window that looked into a quaint, ivy-draped yard. The design was defied in magnificent fashion by the proliferation of religious keepsakes on the windowsills, on the shelves and in the corners of the worktops: crosses, statues, rosary beads and sombre brass busts.

The woman clicked on the kettle and took two mugs from one of the presses. 'Tea, I assume?'

'Oh, I'm grand.'

'You'll have tea. And for God's sake will you sit yourself down?'

She sat at the table, and the woman stared over with one hand on the counter and the other on her hip.

'You haven't a clue about the Good Book, have you?' she said.

'I told you,' said Georgie. 'I'm not an expert.'

'You're an actress is what you are, and you haven't learned your lines. What's your name?'

'. . . Georgie.'

'Mine's Maureen,' said the woman. 'And, Georgie, what are you doing wandering around Cork trying to convert people when you haven't completed the process yourself?'

'I haven't been doing this long.'

'That's not what I asked.'

Georgie faltered. 'It's that obvious, is it?'

'I just don't know what your pudgy friend was at, letting you doorstop heathens when your words don't have a backbone. Not to mention how tired you must be.'

'They think the Lord appreciates physical labour.'

'You'll be going into labour if they're not careful. Who are they, anyway?' She turned over the leaflet. 'Christians Active In Light. Ha! Christians Active In Lumbago.'

'They've been really good to me.'

'Is that before or after you blossomed out to here,' she said, with a flamboyant gesture. 'How long are you gone, anyway?'

'Six months.'

'You're big for six months. I suppose you're very short, though. I was the same. So when did they recruit you? With sin or without?'

'Ten months or so ago.'

'Lord almighty. A sex cult, are they? Christians Active In Lovemaking? How did you manage to get into trouble if your soul had been saved? Married off already?'

'No.'

Maureen dropped teabags into the mugs. 'Milk? Sugar?'

'Yes, please. One.'

'Christians Active In Lactose,' Maureen muttered, and Georgie said, 'Are you going to keep doing that?'

'Up until it stops amusing me.'

She got a spoon and started jamming the teabags against the sides of their mugs.

'I met a man through them,' Georgie said. 'That's how.'

'One of their number? I take it they approved.'

'They didn't. He left and I had nowhere to go.'

'And does he know?'

'Yes, he knows. He's from a well-to-do background. It'd be awkward if I went with him. He'll be back to me once he sorts things out.'

'Are they still telling the girls those stories?'

'He will,' said Georgie. 'It's complicated. He's in recovery too. So . . . It was just decided it would be damaging to both of us to deal with this together. We can't focus on our recovery if we're focused on each other.'

'How practical. And what are you recovering from, if it's not virginity?'

'Drugs,' Georgie said. She was too tired to snap.

'What kind of drugs?'

'I don't mean to be rude, but what's it to you?'

Maureen placed the tea in front of her. 'Would you rather we talked about the Lord Jesus Christ, so? We can do. I fell out with Him myself.'

Georgie cupped her hands around the mug and slumped.

'I don't know much. They say you have to be open to letting Him in. They say that He makes everything clearer. That you get a purpose. That it's . . . I guess that it's a load off. I haven't found Him yet.'

'Have you checked under the bed?'

'I'm trying to take this seriously.'

'And yet something's telling you it's not worth taking seriously. Maybe that's a thing with us short women: hands too small to grasp at straws.'

'You sound like a preacher yourself.'

Maureen snorted. 'Oh, I wouldn't know a soapbox if it was bubbling. I have as much time for the Man Upstairs as he does for me. Take a breather and finish your tea; you'll do no converting here.'

The mention of the Man Upstairs made Georgie start and glance upwards, and Maureen noticed and smiled a thin smile.

'Did you know,' she said, leaning conspiratorially, 'this house was once a brothel?'

Georgie's feet were sore, her back ached, she hadn't taken a full breath in weeks. If she had been just a bit further along, just a bit more drained, she might have come clean to the supernatural quickness of her hostess. Instead she swallowed and feigned interest.

'I didn't know that,' she said. 'Like, in a historic sense?'

'Try a couple of years.'

'Oh, are you serious?'

'The lines are coming easier now, aren't they?' said Maureen, and she straightened. 'Yes, I am serious. A place of vice in twenty-first century Ireland. Have you ever heard the like?'

Georgie wanted to ask *What lines?* She took a sip of her tea and scalded out the objection.

'It might have been a brothel historically too,' Maureen continued. 'But not to my knowledge. You don't need the eras echoing to feel the weight of this place.'

Georgie rested her chin on a trembling hand. 'Did you buy it cheap, so?'

'Indeed I did not. It belongs to my son. It's belonged to my son this long time.'

'How long?'

'Long enough,' Maureen said, 'for him to direct its activities.'

Georgie stood up, prompting groans of discord from her feet, her thighs, her back. 'C'mere, thanks so much for the tea. You're really kind, but I better be going now.'

Maureen said, 'Would he even recognise you?'

Georgie sat down again. *I don't know what you mean*, she tried, but the statement struggled to leave her mouth, and what words she managed wilted in the air.

'I'm guessing he wouldn't,' Maureen said. 'He doesn't strike me as the kind who shits where he sleeps.'

Georgie said, 'I owe nobody anything,' and started to cry, quietly; she brushed the tears away with a brittle sweep. 'Don't think you've caught a runaway because you haven't. That was a long time ago.'

'There's a shadow on you,' said Maureen. 'Dripping black and miserable. It was there when I opened the door. I knew you didn't want to come in and that you hadn't a clue what you were supposed to be doing and that some sanctimonious prig had convinced you that you had something to atone for. You either need to accept the past as the building blocks that brought you right up to today, or you need to be a better liar. The world is full of girls like you.'

'You're J.P.'s mother? He puts his mother in a place like this?'

'I'd like to think your tears are for pitying me. Yes, he put me in a place like this. He's a bit too pragmatic, that boy. Hollow with it. I didn't want to stay here at first, but once I learnt the history of the place, something told me it was my duty to remain, in case he drowned it again in squalor. Now he can't get me to move. I'm sure it'll come to his barging in and wheeling me out one of the days, but for now I'm happy. It has whispers, like I said. It has ghosts.'

Georgie gulped and hung on to the tabletop. Maureen brought over a roll of kitchen paper. It was beyond Georgie to ask what the ghosts were doing.

'Do you think,' Maureen said, when Georgie had calmed, 'that this will save you?'

She gestured towards Georgie's belly, and Georgie clasped her hands over the bump and said, 'Why do you think I need saving?'

'I don't. I figured you thought it, seeing as you're in the company of zealots. Whatever way you want to look at it, I hope it works for you. Take it I have an interest. Take it that you're the anti me. Take it pregnancy's awful transformative.'

'I didn't think it was even possible,' Georgie said.

'Then you were probably in the wrong line of work.'

'I mean . . . I didn't think I was . . . entitled to this. This is my second. I lost the first.'

'I'm sorry,' Maureen said.

'You don't get it. It was my fault. I was on drugs, I was drinking . . .'

'Maybe that's so, maybe it's not. You don't know with these things. Pointless to work yourself into a lather wondering about it.'

'I keep thinking this one'll leave me as well.'

'Yeah, well it might if you don't put your feet up and stop trying to cure the lepers. You tell your Nazarenes that; their path to Heaven isn't flattened out by you shoving your boulder in front of them.'

'They're not bad people.'

'How very gracious of them.'

Maureen took Georgie's mug from the table, brought it over to the counter and refreshed it. Georgie sniffed and wiped her eyes and straightened in her seat. She looked towards the kitchen door and at the ceiling. She strained for the whispers and the ghosts.

'You can look around if you like,' Maureen said.

'I don't think I want to.'

'Maybe it'll be good for you. You can scrub the shit off absolutely anything, maybe. This can be your metaphor. Maybe.'

The endeavour to reduce a pile of bricks seeping shadow into a thimble of symbolism didn't appeal to Georgie, but neither did the idea of entering into another conversation with the seer Missus Phelan. Caught between gratitude and flesh-rucking unease, she chose gratitude, accepted the topped-up mug, smiled weakly at Maureen and skittered into the hallway, where she stood by the banister and stared up at the landing.

'Go ahead,' Maureen said, from the kitchen door.

The rooms upstairs had been gutted. Where there was once the colour of lazy decay were clean walls and restored wooden floors. The beds and furniture were gone, as was the telephone on the wall. The makeshift kitchen where the girls had stashed their inebriants had been ripped out and smoothed over.

Maureen was standing behind her. Georgie turned and said, 'Did you find things here? Were you here when they were doing the work?'

'I was in once the downstairs flat was done. They were working away up here after that. Why, what are you missing?'

'Nothing. It's just that the place looks so empty.'

'There were a couple of trinkets. I have them in a drawer downstairs. Let me go and look; you'd never know. That said, if it's a bra you lost I have them well fecked out.'

Georgie frowned, but Maureen had turned away.

She continued through the other rooms, but they were pretty much the same: their darkened corners ripped away, insignificant to the quest Maureen had given her. She tried to reconcile this shell with flashes of a past she had mind for only late at night: being shoved onto her belly, hot breath on her cheek, semen on her breasts, on her face, in her hair, like they were dogs pissing all over their territory. These flares made her shrink into herself – her nails dug into her palms and she hunched her shoulders – but they were still very far away, as if they had taken place not just in her past, but in another country. A lick of paint and she felt no connection to this place.

In one of the rooms on the second floor, there was a small pile of paper and a notebook on the window ledge. A pen made up the accoutrements of the writing space. The ledge was deep, and the room looked onto the Lee. Today the river was swollen, and cars moved either side of it like a lava of litter. But on sunny days, when the light was glinting from the water and the steel, she was sure it would have made a much more inspiring perch. She moved the papers towards the pane, carefully, and sat down with her back to the wall, looking over her shoulder and onto the street.

Two storeys down, she could hear Maureen opening drawers.

She picked up a couple of sheets of the paper on the sill. It was hardly likely that the beast Jimmy Phelan had come from a mother sharpened on art; she had had no run-ins with him, for he had directed their movements only through the pimp, but his legend was monstrous both in reach and report.

The first page appeared to be the start of a letter to a priest.

Bless me Father for I have sinned. Or is Dear Father all right with you, pitter-pater?

Georgie slid this sheet under the other, and read:

Robbie O'Donovan was here.

She should have dropped it. In doing so she'd have given the poor guy some sort of regard, after the fact. Instead she turned it over, as if on the back she'd find an explanation of how his name had scrawled its own clue into the palm of her hand, but the rest of the page was blank. She turned it over again, and reread it: *Robbie O'Donovan was here.* in the same hand as the priest letter. Her breath caught. She sat suspended in voicelessness, as if the sudden stasis of her lungs could make her float, bounce off the walls, up to the ceiling.

Maureen came back into the room with an armful of leftovers.

'Robbie O'Donovan was here,' said Georgie. The air escaped her throat.

'Oh, him?' Maureen clucked. 'Don't mind *him*. He won't touch you. He just stands around.'

'He just stands around?'

Maureen's eyes narrowed, and she smiled. 'Did you know him? He died here.'

Georgie dropped the paper and darted past the woman and down the stairs. Her shoes slipped on the last step; she grasped the banister, and cried out, and scrambled for the door. The lock wouldn't budge on her first go. She found the clasp and the bolt sprang back and she ran out onto the street, where Clover was approaching, only a few yards to her left.

'What's wrong, Georgie?'

'I'm just feeling sick, Clover, really sick. Please let's go.'

'OK,' Clover said. 'We can do that.' She put her arm around Georgie, and Georgie clung to her, sniffing and retching. They had gone only a couple of hundred metres when Georgie heard a voice behind her, calling her name, and Clover slowed but Georgie begged, 'I'll be sick, Clover, I'll be sick!', but it wasn't the matriarch Maureen closing in on them. The voice had that unmistakable ringing whine, the musicality of shattering glass. Georgie turned and Tara Duane waved at her, hurrying forwards on stiletto boots that cast her to the left and right as if she was dancing on a listing deck.

'Georgie! Wait up! Oh my God, it's so great to see you! Where have you been?'

'This one's not a good one,' Georgie said to Clover, who nodded and squeezed her arm, but stayed otherwise stupidly solid to watch the scrag advance.

12

Karine arrived over with a bag stuffed with goodies: two chicken salad rolls, four packets of Taytos, handfuls of chocolate bars, tobacco and Rizla, a two-litre bottle of Coke and, best of the lot, a bag of pick 'n' mix as big as a baby's head.

Ryan said, 'You absolute lasher, D'Arcy,' and she rolled her eyes and said, 'You better remember this when you're rich and famous.'

The curtains were closed, because there wasn't light worth letting in. It was damp and miserable and balls-shrinkingly chilly. There wasn't much to look at, in any case; Ryan was in his father's house, and all he could see from his bedroom window was other people's back gardens, sodden from the pitiless April march. Next door and almost a week ago, Tara Duane had dragged a plastic airer outside and draped a number of towels over it, either from desperation or bloated optimism.

He hadn't meant to spot her, afraid that if she looked up and saw him watching she'd take it as a favourable sign. It was anything but. He'd sunk behind the curtain and sat on his bed, elbows on knees, hands joined and eyes to the floor. There were tons of drawbacks to being home again, but none that frightened him like she did. Two years might have diluted her story to the point where it would sound, to Karine's ears, reedy and fanciful. That was the best possible scenario and even that could ruin him. Karine might not want to share him, even in secret thought, with someone like Tara Duane.

'Ew, like she was hollowed out and sewn back together,' she'd whispered one time, years back, when Duane had offered to do an offy run for the underagers.

Tara's airer had toppled and the towels had fallen to the ground. They were still there today, rumpled in the mud.

Karine slipped her shoes off, smoothed her school skirt and climbed onto the bed beside him.

'Pass me my roll there,' she said, and he retrieved the tobacco and started rolling a joint as she tucked in.

'Where'd you get the smoke?' she asked.

'Dan the Man posted it to me.'

'He *posted* it to you?'

'Swear to God. He has me spoiled.'

'Eat your roll first,' she said. 'There's warm chicken in that.'

'All right, Mammy.'

He finished rolling the joint and tucked it behind the curtain on the windowsill, and they sat together, munching into the picnic in their cobalt cave. When he was a couple of bites from the end she reached into her schoolbag and produced a pen, pad and her maths book.

'Where are you supposed to be, anyway?' he asked.

'Maths grind,' she said, and placed the things on his lap.

'You're funny.'

She buried her head in the bag again. 'Come on, Ryan,' she said, once she emerged. 'Be sensible. The sooner I get my homework done the sooner we can relax.'

'I'm already relaxed.'

'Unrelax yourself, then. Page 57, questions 11 to 20. And I'll do my French while you're doing that and if you're really, really good, you might even get a blowjob at the end of it.'

'I'll get a blowjob anyway.'

'And you're haunted, aren't you?' she said. 'You think you'd be more inclined to help your girlfriend out with her homework, so? When she's so nice to you?'

She placed her French book primly on her lap and brushed a strand back from her face and he started laughing and she said, 'What?' in mock indignation.

'It's just funny.'

'What's just funny?'

'You're just funny.'

'D'you know what's not funny?'

'What?'

'The fact that you haven't started my homework.'

He opened the book. 'You can't keep doing this to me,' he said.

'Yeah? What are you going to do about it?'

He *was* haunted; plenty of fellas would confirm it. His girlfriend liked giving him blowjobs. There was only the fact of his required passivity to sully the act. As a precursor to sex a blowjob was a hundred per cent awesome, but occasionally – only very occasionally, he wasn't a total loss – if she was going down on him just for the hell of it, there was a shade of submission that maybe knocked that hundred per cent down to ninety-five. He tried to reframe it as something which put him in the driver's seat, but it wasn't easy to claim control when he was putting his cock in someone else's mouth. There was something of la Bocca della Verità about it.

He knew what was wrong. He knew that on the occasions that last five per cent was taken from him it was because of a flashback, not to a scene – there was little of the memory left – but to a feeling of losing the run of himself, and making stupid mistakes for no good reason.

There was a time they filmed it and it was a hundred and ten per cent, fucking perfect.

Now there was a half-hour of quiet, punctuated by the odd remark about something that had happened in school, various text messages, the sounds of his father opening and shutting the living-room door, of Niamh and Cathal bickering about who had authority over the remaining Coco Pops. He finished the maths before she'd done her French and lay back on the bed, and when she'd caught up she put away the books and pens and lay with him.

As was custom in the years before, he had pushed Cian's bed in front of the door after she'd come in. It was a strange thing to be back where every second was bloated with the possibility of ambush. They kissed for a while; she was fine with removing her school jumper and letting him unbutton her shirt but when he went to remove it she hunched her shoulders and whispered, 'Oh God, Ryan, I'm so scared he's going to come up the stairs. I don't know how we ever did it like this.'

'Necessity is the mother of invention.'

'Eh, you'd want to invent something more convincing than that!'

'He won't come up,' Ryan said. 'He's been avoiding me like the fucking plague since I got here. Like he thinks I'll drive him back to drink.'

'I guess it's awkward because you were away so long.'

'It's awkward coz he doesn't know what to do with me. I came back here and I wasn't a kid anymore . . . He knows anyway.'

She winced in agreement. 'I know that video was more than a year ago, boy, but I'm still cringing.'

'Me and all, but . . . It means he knows. And that, plus the fact that he spends his days pretending there's nothing wrong from his fort in the sitting room, means he's not coming near us, girl. And even if he did come up, he can't get in.'

'I suppose not.'

'Are you gonna let *me* in then?' He kissed the spot where her neck joined her shoulder and she arched her back and sat up with him. He slid her shirt from her shoulders and she pulled his T-shirt up and off and when they were a lot less decent they dived under his duvet.

He framed her against the sheet, skin-blush to blue shadow. She kissed his neck and traced his spine but both as reactions to his actions, because that's what he wanted, today and anymore. After a while she put her hands on his shoulders, wordlessly suggesting he roll onto his back to accept the promised blowjob. He kissed her; she pushed at him again and he resisted again, and she pulled back and smiled and whispered, 'Don't you want me to go down on you?'

'It's just . . . I dunno . . . I could go down on you?'

She gave him her most pained smile, the kind she usually reserved for instances where she had to cry off on a date, or guilt him into a shopping trip, or indeed, turn down his offer of cunnilingus.

'I don't *know,*' she sighed, which generally meant *Not in a fit, but I don't want you to feel bad about it.*

'You go down on me all the time,' he said.

'I know, but you love it.'

'But you might love this.'

'I don't *know*.'

'We're two years together, like. I don't know anyone who's been together longer than we have. And I've never gone down on you.'

'You might not like it.'

'It's supposed to be about you, though.'

'Why are you so mad for it, then?'

'Coz I want to do it for you.'

She sighed again, and smiled and looked away, and he inched back the duvet and said, 'Seriously, girl, you're the most beautiful thing I've ever seen in my life,' and she tutted and he said, 'You're the most beautiful place I've ever been in my life, too.'

'Ryan!'

'It's true.'

He traced his finger from her mouth over her neck, between her breasts, down her belly, between her legs.

'You let me do that,' he said.

'That's your finger.'

'You like my finger, and my finger's all rough and I bite my nails and it's not nice, really.'

She giggled. 'It's not the same and you know it.'

'Yeah . . . I think my mouth'd be better.'

'Ryan!'

'Seriously though. Seriously. What is it about this that's putting you off?'

'I'd be embarrassed.'

'Why? With me? After two years you'd be embarrassed?'

'Look,' she said. 'You're probably thinking it's going to be a certain way and then it mightn't be and you might hate it and then I'd die.'

'What d'you mean, a certain way?'

'Like . . . you know. Like in porn.'

'You been watching porn, D'Arcy?'

She stroked his neck. 'No. You have.'

'No I haven't.'

'Have.'

'Haven't.'

'Course you have! All boys do. And you're probably thinking it'll be bland and rubbery like . . . like plastic fruit and you'll get a terrible land.'

'You must think I'm an awful gom.'

'No . . . I just think . . . I don't *know*.'

'You think this is something you're doing for me?'

She frowned. 'What?'

'Sex.'

'No. Of course not. Don't even think that.'

'It's just . . . I want you to love it, like.'

'I do.'

'Well . . . if you love it, and you're not embarrassed when I lie here and look at you, or when I kiss you or finger you or when you come or when you go down on me, why should you be embarrassed about me going down on you?'

'It's different for boys,' she said.

He felt his shoulders tighten. He said, 'No it's not. Why should it be?'

She looked away and smiled, and he watched the smile twitch at the corners of her mouth like a living thing, growing, fading, taking root.

'Haven't you ever thought about it?'

She didn't answer.

'Listen,' he said. 'We're together two years. And we'll be together two more. And another two after that and on and on and on because I'm that sure that this is it for me and you, that this is it entirely. So I don't want you to hold anything back because you're afraid of what I might think; that's just wrong, girl. I love you. That's what love is supposed to be.'

She said, 'You say the deepest things when you're trying to get your own way,' but she was teasing, and she reciprocated when he kissed her.

'Please, Karine.'

She threw the playful smile back out into the expanse of their sanctuary.

'Please?'

Still no reply. He kissed her breasts, back up to her neck, along her jaw and said, 'I'm not going to do it until you tell me yes, girl. Has to be a yes, not just a *not no*.'

'If you don't like it, it's all your own fault, though. OK?'

'Totally.'

'*Mmm* . . . Yes, then.'

She wouldn't kiss him afterwards. She made him brush his teeth. He went for a piss while he was in the bathroom and leaned one hand flat on the tiles to keep himself upright.

Weak at the knees for my girlfriend's cunt.

As an attempt at a statement of fact, it felt ridiculous, but intoxicating. It was something new. It constituted a nail in the coffin of the memory.

All on his own, he allowed himself a jagged sigh.

When he returned to the bedroom she was wearing her skirt and his Napoli jersey, rummaging through the bag of pick 'n' mix.

'D'you think your dad would twig it if I had a shower?'

He lay on the bed and put an arm around her waist. 'No. Yes. Maybe. Who cares?'

'I care.'

'I don't. It's none of his business.'

'Yeah I know, but . . . D'you wanna white mouse?'

'I've just brushed my teeth, remember?'

'All part of my diabolical plan.'

'Here, if you eat all the cola bottles I'll kill you.'

She chewed, and stuck a finger in her mouth to dislodge a jelly, and said, 'Well? Was it OK?'

He sat up with her and she gave him a stern look, one more

suited to *Did you just write with my eyeliner again?* than *Did you enjoy the act of oral pleasure, you selfless tongue champion?*

'I loved it,' he said.

'Really, though?'

'Really. You have no idea. Did you like it?'

She made a face.

'I know you did,' he said. 'I could taste it.'

'Oh my God, you're so disgusting.'

'Why is that disgusting?'

She made a big deal out of dismissing the question – clucking, rolling her eyes, giving him a playful slap – but she understood, she accepted it, she was fucking delighted.

She went off to have her shower and while he waited he opened the bedroom window and started on the joint. Beneath the clouds his estate lay still as the rain uncovered brilliant shades of green on the trees, and the ivy, and the weeds growing along the back wall.

She came back in with her hair in a towel turban and he handed her the joint. She took his place by the window and shivered dramatically, so he got one of his hoodies and she snuggled into it.

'That's tasty,' she said, exhaling.

'Yeah. It's handsome.'

'I can't believe he posted it to you.'

'Yeah. He's not such a bad guy, really.'

'And yet here you are . . .'

'You know what I mean, girl. I was bricking it. I thought he was going to kill me. And yeah, for a while he was pissy beyond, and I thought *That's it, boy, he is gonna flake into you*, but he knows I'm not going to say anything and . . . Like, he trusts me not to blab and it's not even because I know he'd slaughter me otherwise.'

'Maybe he realises you wouldn't be in this mess if it wasn't for him?'

'But I probably would be, girl. I have two previous convictions and they were before I even met Dan.'

'Yeah, but . . .' She passed the joint back. 'It was his coke. This is his mess. And you're the one in trouble for it.'

He shrugged.

'I don't know how you can be so OK with it, Ryan.'

'I'm not OK with it.'

'You are. And you don't seem to realise you don't have to be. Sometimes it really is someone else's fault.'

'It's how things go, is all. Risks and stuff. You make an educated guess as to whether you'll get away with something but at the end of the day it's just a guess. It got me out of the house for a year and it got me out from under my dad's feet, so it was worth it.'

'I don't mean to take that from you,' she said. 'I know you had to get away from your dad. But this shouldn't be the price you pay.'

'It probably won't work out all that pricey.'

'What if it does, though? I mean, who gets a twenty-four-hour curfew? That's off the wall; you said so yourself.'

'I guess coz I wasn't living at home, they thought this was the best way of keeping tabs on me. If I had been living at home I'd probably have gotten your common-or-garden bail. *Turn up on April twenty-first for your hearing, sonny Jim. And no drugging while you're waiting.*'

She plucked the joint from between his fingers.

'Well, it sucks,' she said.

'I know it sucks. Being here with him sucks. I mean, he's on the dry and he's trying not to be a prick but . . . I dunno. Too much water under the bridge. For both of us.'

'Oh my God, whatever about Dan, everything that happened with your dad is his fault only.'

'Is it, though?'

'Jesus! Yes!'

She handed back the last drag, and he turned to watch her return to the bed. She slid her legs under the duvet and pulled his hoodie across her chest.

He knocked out the joint on the sill outside and closed the window.

'Look, there's more to what went on between me and my dad than . . .'

'Abuse?'

'Don't say that.'

'Is there a better word or something?'

'Look,' he said. 'I don't want to talk about my dad. Not now. Not after what we just did. Coz that was lovely and . . . amazing and . . .'

'Yeah well, I'm scared, Ryan.'

'What are you scared of?'

'Ah, the judge? The judge doesn't know you, like.'

'It'll be grand. Honestly. The solicitor said. I'm pleading guilty, I'm not going to break the curfew, I'm being good as gold. We tell the judge that, y'know, I did OK at school and that I'm looking into going back and stuff.'

She considered him. 'Are you serious?'

'Why wouldn't I be?'

'You're gonna stop dealing.'

'If I tell the judge I'm going back to school, I'll have to go back to school, right?'

He slipped into bed beside her and she rested her head on his chest. Her towel turban scratched his cheek and flopped open on the pillow behind them.

'It'd mean more of this, though,' he whispered. 'Me living here with my dad, me and you having to do it all stuffy-quiet in the middle of the day. The last year of freedom, it'd be gone.'

'It'd be worth it in the end, wouldn't it?'

She slid a hand underneath his T-shirt and thumbed the skin around his bellybutton.

'I like the idea of Ryan going back to school,' she said. 'And Ryan going to university. And then Ryan getting a nice job and buying me lots of shoes.'

'Hey! Buy your own shoes.'

'I never said I wouldn't buy you shoes too. A pair of Cons for every day of the week.'

He stroked her shoulder, and she nestled in the crook of his arm.

'You think we'll still be together then?' she said.

'Told you that earlier, didn't I?'

'Really though?'

'Yeah. I can't imagine it any other way. If I had another joint right now I'd see the whole decade out before me and every minute would have you in it.'

'And what would we be doing?'

'The usual, I suppose. Buying a gaff. Getting married. Popping sprogs.'

'How many sprogs?'

'Dunno. Four or five?'

'Jesus, I hope you can buy them in Tesco by then or you're going to be very disappointed.'

'I won't be disappointed. There's no disappointment in it. It's all good. Every second of it.'

He raised his head. Her eyes were closed. He kissed her forehead, and stared up at the ceiling as she started dreaming, and he watched the world spread out in front of him, corner to corner, flush with colour and glowing like the sunrise.

Downstairs, there was a gentle knock on the front door, as if even the visitor was wary of interrupting them.

13

The next step was getting a job. It wasn't a step of his own design, but shaped by so many gloating well-wishers that Tony was stuck with it.

The woman at the Social was as helpful as he wanted her to be. He brought up youthful summers working on fishing boats, with pointed references to cutbacks at the Port of Cork. She passed him the details for a deli assistant position. He told her he had six children under eighteen and frying builders' rashers at 6.30 a.m. was a welcome impossibility. She recommended he try an internship. He asked her if she thought he was fucking crazy.

Springtime held another challenge when the Law, consistent as it was in its pointed cruelty, dropped Ryan back into his lap. Silly gosser had only gotten himself caught with enough cocaine on him to be done for possession with intent. Again.

He'd run from them. That was his undoing. The guards had stopped him on the street when he had a couple of baggies on him, and once he felt their questions were snowballing, he bolted. *Stupid thing to do*, Tony had groaned; the boy had responded tetchily that they would have searched him anyway, and so he had to chance flight. If one of the guards hadn't been a young muck-savage swift as he was zealous, he might well have gotten away with it.

The amount they'd caught him with wasn't enough to threaten him with gaol; he was small fry, and they were trying to squeeze names and dates out of him. Tony noted wryly that the last thing on God's green earth Ryan Cusack was likely to do was talk. The cops didn't know that. His capture had been a waste of their time and when they cottoned on to that there might well be hell to pay. Tony didn't mind that. A bit of intimidation might do the lad good. Maybe the guards would find, through spite, a way to bully him straight.

At the first hearing the judge had imposed a twenty-four-hour curfew, remanding the kid in the custody of a father newly dry and squeaky clean. Between himself and Cian there wasn't room to swing a cat, but Ryan seemed content to shut himself off in his bedroom, black buds jammed in his ears and a laptop screen as his mask.

An effervescent liar from the phone company had sold Tony a broadband subscription, which had had the effect of lobotomising his three teenagers and giving him the cold comfort of meditative silence. Once a week Kelly commandeered the laptop and went through the jobs website with her father, and between them they figured out which posts were worth procuring rejection letters from. Sometimes he got an email back that thanked him for his efforts but denied the existence of suitable positions. When he was so blessed he showed them to his probation officer. The job hunt was going well.

April had come around in a vicious funk, summoning snowstorms in Dublin and floods in Fermoy. Tony ordered home heating oil earlier than he'd presumed he'd need to, and he'd handed over the fee before it had occurred to him that he'd done, without wheedling procrastination, something of equal import and expense. It was a fine thing to be sober, sometimes. It hadn't been pointed out in rehab: *When you're sober, you'll buy home heating oil when you actually need it and it'll feel like a fucking miracle.* It was the small things.

It was the big things that threatened him, though: the loss of routine and the awkward jettison of bad habits and old pals, the boredom, the claustrophobia. Small victories he stockpiled, and yet the barricade was flimsy and dangerously stunted. Sometimes he sat halfway up the stairs when the kids were in school and watched the world warp through the frosted sidelight of the front door. On occasion he rested his head against the wall that separated his territory from the grabby púca Duane's, and listened with dour intent as one would to penance given as the world outside splintered his front door and chipped away at the plaster. Even purer than that, sometimes: he really wanted a drink. The physical addiction had been dismantled, but the compulsion grew unchecked without its frame. *I want a drink*, he thought. *I want a drink*. He would grip the armrests on his living-room furniture as the longing threw a whirlwind around him. *Just one. Just one, for Jesus's sake. I want a fucking drink.*

That's why they were so keen on jobs, the therapists and the probation officers and the mammies and the sisters. They kept telling him: a job to replace an addiction.

Cian brought the *Echo* home from school and Tony sat in the living room, in front of the telly, and went through the jobs page for opportunities for which he was underqualified. The kitchen, designated as a homework hub, shook with his squabbling brood. Young Karine had arrived over a couple of hours ago and made great haste to wall herself up with Ryan in the back bedroom, where, no doubt, they were getting into divilment, though he'd take that over Duane's insinuating guilt any day of the week.

Through a lull in the kitchen mayhem he caught the last taps of a half-hearted knock on his front door, and he rose. Too feeble for any of the kids' friends, and far too gentle a sound for anyone trying to flog a leather three-piece suite.

He opened the door to a young woman blatantly pregnant.

Without protection from the rain, her hair had sprung into a wiry halo; she clasped one hand to her forehead and squinted.

'Tony?'

'That's right.' He thought she might be a new caseworker. They had a habit of shapeshifting, though he'd never had one come to the door wearing her incompetence on her head before.

She was dressed in a denim jacket and some measure of patterned tent, befitting her fecundity if not the miserable weather.

'I'm sorry,' she said. 'I don't know how to say this but . . . Do you know Robbie O'Donovan?'

The name pushed past Tony and into his hall, wheeled around

his head, clung to and coloured his walls, a shadow for every letter.

'Who are you?' he asked. 'Sorry, what's this about?'

'My name's Georgie,' she said. 'I was told you knew Robbie O'Donovan. I'm sorry, this is . . . Do you think I could come in?'

'I don't know any Robbie O'Donovans,' he said.

'Maybe if you think back? He was my boyfriend, and he went missing a couple of years ago . . . Look, if I could come in? I'm pregnant, you see.'

'After a couple of years?'

'I'm tired. And it's raining. I'm really sorry to ambush you like this but I think maybe if I go through a few bits with you, you might remember him?'

'There's a lot of kids in the house.'

'I'm only six months gone,' she said. 'I won't be adding to them.'

Behind him, the kitchen door opened and Niamh's dark head popped out to pry. Over his shoulder, he said, 'Get back in there a minute.'

An offended tut from his nine-year-old busybody and the door was closed again.

Outside, the young woman stood, pained and wringing.

Tony moved aside and she accepted the invitation gratefully. He gestured towards the living room and she stepped in and sat at the edge of the sofa.

'D'you need a towel?' He nodded at her hair.

'Oh! That would be so great.'

He climbed the stairs and retrieved a towel from the hot press. The break didn't provide time enough to think. *Robbie O'Donovan – how do you know him?* Drinking buddy? Gambling buddy? You don't know him at all? *Jesus Christ, Cusack; pick one.*

Who'd think he knew Robbie O'Donovan? Had the lass gone sniffing out bones in the pub they used to drink in? Had Maureen Phelan sent her?

His blood fizzed. The balls of his feet found dips in the carpet beneath him.

He'd given J.P.'s mother the gift of a name and she'd accepted it like a child accepts a mound of sweets and the promise of sticky hands. Had he thought, in the months of eerie silence that followed, that she'd forget his slip-up, or clutch it jealously? No. Sure why would she?

Stupid fucker, Tony. Stupid. Stupid.

He closed the hot press as the door next to it opened and his firstborn gawped out at him.

'Who's that, Dad?'

'Just someone looking for someone. It's nothing.'

'Looking for who?'

'No one, Ryan.'

Back in the living room the sodden visitor accepted the towel and attempted a smile. Tony stood by the fireplace and said, 'Georgie who?'

'Fitzsimons. I don't think I've met you before.'

He shook his head. 'You're looking for some ex-boyfriend?'

'Robbie O'Donovan. I know this sounds very strange. He disappeared just over two years ago now. I reported him missing at the time but the guards have had no luck. He was kinda hard to miss, though. He was around six foot two, red hair, really skinny.'

'I don't know anyone like that. Someone's after telling you I do, though.'

'Yeah, there's a girl that lives up around here, she said that you might be the man to ask. Her name is Tara. Tara Duane?'

Tony bit his cheeks and rubbed his palms off his thighs. Georgie turned the towel over and ran it through her hair again.

'She's my next-door neighbour.'

'Oh. I didn't know that.'

'Why the fuck would she tell you I'd know where your ex ran off to?'

The expletive hit hard. 'I don't know . . . I met her in town the other day. She flagged me down and said if I was still in the dark as to where Robbie went that you might know.'

'She flagged you down?'

'Yeah . . .'

'I don't get along with her. Suppose she neglected to mention that. She's trying to drop me into something. She's a vindictive bitch.'

Georgie clutched the towel.

'Drop you into something? No, she just said you were a mate of his, and I thought maybe . . .'

Too late, Tony found the meagre details in the girl's few statements and concluded she had little reason to be suspicious before he'd opened his mouth. He sagged and the mantelshelf pushed into his lower back.

'Look,' stammered Georgie. 'I'm not usually in the habit of annoying strangers over something as dodgy as one of Tara Duane's notions. I wouldn't have come up here, not in a fit, but it wasn't like Robbie to run off. If I told you half of it you wouldn't believe a quarter—'

'Listen, girl, I don't know any fella called Robbie O'Donovan. I'm sorry but there you go. I do know a woman called Tara Duane and I've had my run-ins with her. I'm thinking maybe she's stitched you up to stitch me up or something but I had nothing to do with your fella going walkabout. I've enough of me own problems!'

'I just want to know where he is,' she whimpered. 'I would have been grand but only a few days ago this started up again. Someone told me he was dead . . .'

'Duane?'

'No, not Tara. Meeting Tara was a coincidence . . .'

Tony thumped his fist on the mantel. Coincidences followed Duane like rats after the piper. Once he tore through the conspiracy he'd tear through her, consequences or no consequences.

'Well ask whoever told you, then!' he barked.

'I can't. You don't understand . . .' Georgie's countenance had changed; her chin was quivering. 'I can't bring it up with them again, I can't go to the guards . . . Tara just told me you knew Robbie. I really didn't think I'd be upsetting you like this, or I'd never have come here . . . Oh God!'

'Here,' Tony said, desperate as the tears intensified and the hubbub from the kitchen died down. 'I feel for you, girl, don't get me wrong, but I don't know the fella you're on about, and I've a house full of kids and a working pair of ears on all of them. You're going to have to take this up with Duane.'

The girl wiped her cheeks with the flat of her hand. She was short and raven-haired, pudgy around the cheeks, and, it seemed, in the process of completely losing it right there on his couch. Tony endeavoured to make sense of her fit. Tara Duane's name rose a fog in him. He sank into the armchair across from the crying woman and blinked.

How the fuck would Tara Duane know he had anything to do with Robbie O'Donovan? How the fuck, how the fuck . . . He found himself mirroring Georgie's actions, pinching the corners of his eyes, running his hands over his head.

The girl's chest heaved in an exaggerated hiccup and she knotted her hands over her belly.

'You're going to have to leave,' Tony tried, but she sat up straight, mouth open under her shining eyes, and said, 'Shit, you're Ryan's dad.'

'What?'

'You're Ryan's dad! If Tara Duane lives next door to you . . . I *knew* I knew you from somewhere.'

'You don't know me at all.'

'He's the bulb off you. It's unreal. Are you trying to tell me you're not Ryan's dad?'

'I haven't a notion of talking about my children with some girl who's just accused me of burying a man I never met.'

'Look, I'm sorry. This past week has just been throwing the weirdest shit at me . . . I don't know what I'm doing here.' She started sobbing again.

'Stay here a second,' Tony snapped, and bounded up the stairs and onto the landing, where he knocked an elbow off the boy's bedroom door.

Ryan came out far too wide-eyed.

'Who the fuck is yer wan downstairs?' Tony hissed.

'Who?'

'Don't fuck with me, Ryan. That's why you came sidling out

when I was up here at the hot press; there's a fucking woman downstairs claiming to know you and flinging some serious shit at me.'

'Who's she looking for?'

'Me, for some fucking reason. Why is that?'

'I don't know.'

'Ryan, for fuck's sake. Not this now. Of all times, not now.'

The lad . . . could he even call him that anymore? He'd left the homestead in a haze of his father's regret and he'd done so as such a narrow thing. He'd come home again with a couple more inches on him and a trim muscularity his father could track most easily down his back, across his shoulders. Maria's brothers were sinewy and tall. It was disconcerting to spot that in his own son.

The lad, what was left of him, said, 'I know her from a couple of years ago but I haven't a notion why she's up here.'

'How? How'd you know her?'

'Jesus, Dad . . . How d'you think? I used to sell her a bit of dope. That's all. She's not my buddy or anything.'

'She's a grown woman, Ryan! How in Christ's name were you selling her dope?'

Ryan paused. 'She's a pal of yer wan next door.'

'Oh, fuck me. And?'

'And yer wan gave her my number.'

Tara Duane was a hex neither of them had given name to since the boy's return. 'Tara Duane,' said Tony, and Ryan looked away. 'Every time I hear that cunt's name it shaves years off my life . . . Get rid of yer wan downstairs, Ryan.'

'But what's she want with you?'

'Don't fucking talk to me, boy, just get fucking rid of her.'

He followed Ryan down the stairs and hovered then in the kitchen doorway, listening to the hum of his son's words and the shrill, to lowing, to wet return he was getting from the stranger.

'Who's that, Dad?' Ronan had gotten a slick of butter on one of his cuffs. Tony beckoned him to the sink and swiped at it with a damp J-Cloth. 'Who's that?' Ronan said again. He was only seven, friendly and guileless.

'No one,' Tony said.

'Is she sad coz she's fat?'

'Yeah.' He caught Cian's eye. The boy snorted.

After ten minutes he returned to the living room. Ryan was standing in front of the fireplace. The crying woman was holding the towel on her lap, twisting it in her hands, wringing salt out of it. From the kitchen there came a crash, then a clamour of moving chairs and giggling.

'You only need to hop the front wall,' Tony told Georgie, 'if you want to take it up with the person you really have a problem with. I told you I can't help you.'

'I'm sorry,' she said. 'I'm desperate.'

'I don't care how desperate you are; this is intimidation.'

'Dad,' Ryan winced.

'What? It is. On the behest of that crazy bitch Duane you're coming to my home and telling me ghost stories.'

'It is a ghost story,' Georgie said. 'That's exactly it. Two years on and suddenly I'm hearing his name everywhere.'

'If it's everywhere that means there's a ton of other places you can haul your lunacy. I'm a single father, for fuck's sake. Crackawlies instructed to hold seances in my sitting room while my kids are doing their homework . . . This is all wrong.'

'Georgie,' said Ryan, 'why did Tara tell you my dad would know where your fella went?'

'She just asked if I knew him and when I said I didn't she said I should speak to him. She said that he'd have known Robbie well.'

'You didn't ask her how she knew that?'

'Why would I?' Georgie cried. 'I just thought maybe they were friends or something. Ryan . . . you know I'm not crazy.'

Ryan said, 'I don't know you at all, Georgie,' whether through honest affirmation or a clumsy sidestep, his father couldn't tell.

'You know me well enough! So if I tell you that this is the second time in a week someone's mentioned Robbie to me and the first time I was told he was dead, you know I'm not making it up.'

'This is bullshit,' Tony said. 'Bullshit, and you need to get the fuck out of my house.'

He flung open the front door and clambered over the dividing wall, marking his hands with the mossy slime of a barrier unkempt for its significance. He pounded on Tara Duane's door but it stayed closed. He pounded on it so hard that it looked like giving underneath his fists. He came back into the house and the girl Georgie was standing up, still crying, with Ryan beside her looking for once in his little life like he had encyclopaedias in his gob lined up and ready to be recited.

'The bitch isn't home to shed light on this,' said Tony. 'And the last time I tried busting in there to drag her arse out for an inquisition I got done for it. In the absence of her mediation, you're going to have to jog on. And do it quick, girl. Heavy and all as you are you don't want to push me.'

Georgie said, 'I'm sorry. But you have to understand—'

'I understand you're unhinged. I understand you're only familiar with my son because you were using him to get your drugs for you, and I understand you're associated in some way with that toxic whore next door. I don't have to understand anything more than that. Leave now, stay away from me, and stay away from my kids. Do you understand?'

She left. She closed the door out gently behind her and made her way down the driveway – as he noted when he looked out to make sure of her trajectory – with shaking shoulders and a gait to match. There was a pang of sympathy, involuntary. Tony clasped his right hand around his neck to choke it down. Every time Maria had been pregnant it had built in him what her wild nature had eroded. He was a whole man when biology had required it. Six times he'd watched her blossom and it had been the making of him, as well as of his children.

The first of them, his sullen antagonist, his bravest soldier, stood waiting for his father to grill or dismiss him.

'What the fuck, Ryan?' Redundant, repetitive, and frail, and what else could he manage?

'I swear to God, Dad, I haven't a clue what that was about.'

'Never mind what it was about! Jesus!' He pushed his hands over his forehead, walked to the far wall and knocked the flat of his fist against the plaster. His son stood his ground, though even Tony wasn't sure whether this spat could escalate according to precedent.

A sober man now, he felt the months tug at him.

'Why would you have anything to do with these people?' he said, and Ryan looked away; they both knew it wasn't just the visitor he was referring to.

'I wouldn't now,' he said. 'That was years ago.'

'How many years ago?'

The pause had him well told before his son confirmed it: 'I dunno. A couple.'

'And we know what you were up to a couple of years ago.'

This was old ground, overgrown. There was more laughter from the kitchen, reminding him he could choose just as easily to push forward, to send Ryan back upstairs to the charming little tyrant to whom he was sweetly indentured.

He brought his forehead to his fist.

'Is it the mother thing?' he asked, and turned then, and said, 'Is that what drives you to people like that?'

'No, Dad . . .'

'Coz every time I think I'm making progress, something happens to remind me that I've fucked up with you. The reason you're home. The reason you knew that bloody woman.'

'Dope is the only reason I know her,' Ryan said, softly.

Tony assumed he was worried about eavesdroppers and retribution.

'Whatever it is or was,' he said, 'you'd hardly tell me. And I'm supposed to be protecting you. Isn't it desperate? Even if I wasn't shit at it, you wouldn't let me, would you? Why would you? Go back up to Karine.' He shook his head. 'I won't say anything.'

How could he tell J.P.? There was no telling with J.P.

Tony returned to his *Evening Echo* and the lies of his sobriety. Ryan went back upstairs and the rest of them trotted in and out of the kitchen in turns, losing interest as he batted away their questions. The interruption was largely forgotten by dinnertime.

He ran through a confession in his head, and forecast a bloody nose and a march on his home, threats flung at his children, and an interrogation that would expose Ryan's minor role. What then? The lad would be quizzed on Georgie's background. Maybe it'd go well. What then? J.P. would track the girl down and grill her. What then? There would be a mess to be tidied. Maybe the girl would be disposed of; maybe she'd be encouraged towards amnesia. Tony pondered taking that chance. She was pregnant. He couldn't risk it.

She might go to the guards, despite her assertions to the contrary. If someone had let slip to her that Robbie O'Donovan was dead, then chances were good that she knew better than to take it to the cops. Even so. If the cops got wind at all, he was fucked. All the more reason to tell J.P. about the visit.

But then what of Ryan? If J.P. was involved, Ryan would know there was something up. The woman had turned up talking about ghosts and suddenly the meanest cunt in the city – and it was all but guaranteed that Ryan knew who J.P. was, seeing as how he was knee-deep in the runoff – shows up on the doorstep asking after her? Tony's declarations of ignorance would be examined and judged as bollocks.

Fucking stupid kid. Fucking involved in everything he shouldn't be. If the girl had turned up on the doorstep and the boy hadn't recognised her, well, wouldn't that have been something? Wouldn't that have been too much to fucking ask?

If Tony said nothing about his afternoon visit, J.P. would remain at arm's length and maybe the bitch next door would spill sense. There was only one woman looking for Robbie, and judging by her belly she'd moved on. Maybe there was fuck all to worry about but happenstance and his shrunken city.

The rain cleared off in the evening. Tony walked down to the off-licence and stood outside it like a child with tuppence to his name outside the toy shop. If he pressed his nose to the glass, he may well have been able to smell it. The heady warmth of the thought seeped through his shell and into his bones and lifted him onto his toes and rose off him like holy water off the devil's shoulders.

The twenty-first of April was as miserable as the rest of the month had been, and it came round before Tony had made his decision. The last ninety-six hours he'd spent in airless languor. He had tried Tara Duane's door every morning and every evening, but there wasn't a peep out of her, and Kelly had eventually thought to tell him that young Linda was temporarily staying with a buddy while her mam ran up and down the garden path with some sap in Dublin; whatever the destination, it seemed that Tara Duane had thought it a good time to go on the missing list.

The courthouse was packed. Ryan's hearing was set for 2.30, along with everyone else who'd been summoned to the afternoon sitting. The newcomers mingled with the dregs of the morning's session, who had commandeered the seats in the stuffy green waiting room. Parents sat gloomy and still, like rows of turnips in a grocer's box. Their little criminals sat with them, tapping LOLs on their phones, or milled in the yard outside stinking of Lynx and taut nonchalance. Solicitors strode in and out in a twist of slacks and briefcases.

They called him shortly before four. Tony ducked out of the waiting room and found him standing with McEvoy, the solicitor. He gestured them both inside.

McEvoy was a decent chap who had taken more care with Ryan's case than they'd enjoyed with previous representatives. He hadn't taken instruction so much as informed his own brief. They were blessed with him; Tony hadn't wanted to use the same one who'd failed to save him from six weeks in Solidarity House.

They were blessed with a different judge, too. Mary Mullen. McEvoy said she was smart and thorough. *Is she OK, though?* Tony had asked, and McEvoy had replied, *You could do a lot worse.*

She spoke to the solicitor. It was a rare judge who bothered with the pleasantries. Tony leaned forward. They could be over so quickly, these hearings.

'And what do you think yourself, Mr McEvoy,' said the judge, 'about where he goes from here, if he's not in school?'

'My client intends to return to school in September. He got excellent results in his Junior Certificate and knows that was the better path to be on.'

'What kind of excellent results?'

'He shows a great aptitude for music and mathematics, both of which earned him an A grade in Higher Level. University, rather than training, is clearly the right way to go and the boy is taking steps to—'

'And, Mr McEvoy, how do you suppose he'll stay out of trouble?'

'I believe that a probation bond would be the most suitable response, Judge. Given the circumstances—'

'I've heard the circumstances.' She straightened, and looked over at Ryan, and said, 'Let me tell you something, young man. Are you listening?'

'Yes, Judge.'

'There's a very specific kind of boy I see whenever I come here. A lot of them have no family support; a lot of them have no education; a lot of them have been, most likely, led astray. But you are not like my typical young offender. Mr McEvoy has shown me that you're intelligent, that you've got a good father, that you did well in school, that when you apply yourself to something you achieve it without struggle. Would you say that's accurate, Ryan's father?'

Tony cleared his throat. 'Yes, Judge.'

She looked back again at the boy. 'And, Ryan, this is what frightens me about you. You are smart, and you do apply yourself. And you have no qualms about pointing your brains or your determination in the wrong direction entirely. When I see boys coming up here before me, there's a fair amount of them who don't know any better. Genuinely. They don't know any better. But you do. And Mr McEvoy tells me that you have learned the error of your ways and that if I apply conditions to your parole, I won't see you here again. I don't have any faith in that.

'I have to bear in mind that you refused to cooperate with the Gardaí who questioned you and that every time you've appeared in this court, it was for the same offence. And what worries me, Ryan, what really worries me, is that you don't seem to be learning anything except how to do this better.

'What is he like at home, Mr Cusack?'

Tony went to stand up, stopped, gripped the back of the seat in front of him. 'Your typical teenager, I suppose.'

'What I'm concerned about is how easily he can switch between being your typical teenager and your not-so-typical criminal. Other than the loss of his mother, are there any family circumstances that could be contributing towards this behaviour?'

Tony said, 'No.'

'Do you feel you have any measure of control over him?'

To which arose, unbidden, an image of Jimmy Phelan bellowing for answers, seizing the boy for a search of the city, sending him into drug dens and tenements to flush out the Georgie girl, having her dealt with, having him dealt with, uncovering ugly truths and dismantling whatever peace they'd forged during the curfew.

'Oh, God,' he breathed.

'Mr Cusack?'

'I don't have any control over him,' said Tony.

The boy turned in his seat and said, 'Dad . . .', and Tony looked down as the judge hushed them, and directed Ryan to look at her, and said, 'In light of the circumstances, and in light of the seriousness of this crime, something it's clear you are gravely and deliberately underestimating, I feel the best sentence is one of nine months' detention in Saint Patrick's Institution, wherein, my lad, you'll find a school to blaze a trail through.'

On the Cheap Midweek Flights

It's supposed to look like a shopping trip. My mam spins it as a pre-exam treat, in case any of the neighbours twig.

On Tuesday morning, instead of putting on my uniform, I go with her into town to the airport bus. She's trying to talk to me but I don't feel like talking. Everything she says is slapped back. I guess I'm sulking. I dunno.

We buy our tickets and walk around by the side of the station and she sees them before I do and I hear her go, 'Oh dear Jesus.'

There's four of them, two men and two women. They've set up a trestle table and they've got big signs saying 'Abortion stops a human heart from beating' and 'For unto us a child is born' and this picture of a haloed foetus and you'd think my heart would fly up my throat and out my mouth or something but instead I am just instantly raging.

My mam is horrified. Like, she doesn't know where to look. I call over at them and she grabs my arm but it's too late, the words are flowing. 'You sick bastards,' I say. 'You sick, shaming fucks. Why can't you mind your own business and keep your glorious mysteries to yourselves?'

The two fellas and one of the women are old as balls but the second girl is only in her twenties I'd say, and you'd think at that age she'd know better. She's sitting behind the trestle table. When I get close I see why. She's pregnant. Massively pregnant. She's like a blimp pregnant. So I say to her, 'You're down here shaming when you're having your own baby and you don't see anything wrong with that?'

And she's like, 'Well, we're just campaigning for—'

But I stop her because honestly, I could hop off her. 'How many girls walking past here might have had to terminate even though they don't even want to? What about the ladies whose babies have no brains and stuff? What about girls who were raped? Oh, my God, you know what you are? You're fucking evil. You're a fucking evil cow.'

The oldest guy, the one with a grey ponytail and big stupid eyes too close together, says, 'Please move along, this is a peaceful protest.'

'You should be moved along, you miserable bastards.'

But my mam is dragging me away and I'm letting her, because the rage is making me cry. I hate that: when you get so angry you start crying and then people think they've beaten you when in reality you're just so wound up you can't stop yourself. My mam stops in front of our bus; it's not boarding yet. 'Don't mind that now,' she hisses. 'Don't think about it.'

'When am I allowed to think about it? On the plane home again?'

I wished she hadn't noticed this mess in the first place but that's what mams are for, isn't it? Noticing.

They were the worst two weeks of my life. At the beginning I get a call from Ryan's phone and I answer it all, 'Oh hey, baby boy, go on, what happened?' and it's his bloody dad, not him and I'm crying even before he tells me: 'He got nine months, girl, I'm sorry, he's gone, they took him straight up.' I couldn't eat for days I was stressing so much, and everything I did eat I threw up again, till my mam came into my room one morning and shut the door behind her and said, 'I know you say you're sick from stress, hon, but . . .'

And she was right. The second she noticed she made it real. And I wish she hadn't noticed, I really wish she hadn't, because then I might have been too far gone to talk out of it, I dunno. Stupid to think that, isn't it? Ryan would do the entire time inside, away from me. Yeah, nine bloody months. And how would I cope with that? I've never been this long away from him and I cry every night because I miss him and I'm scared for him and I want to fucking kill him.

My mam said, 'Can you not see what a bad match you are? A time when you needed him and he's in prison, Karine. Prison!' My dad was way harsher but only because I've never seen him so close to bawling. 'That's the kind of waster he is, girl, gets you into trouble and fucks off. How much school and grinds did you miss for this fucker in a fucking exam year? And there you go now, isn't it a roaring lesson for you?' He's always hated Ryan.

And you know what? They're right. I did need him and look what happened. I could be here with him now, working this out, deciding how to manage because if he was around I'd be keeping this baby but he's not, is he? He's not around and if he keeps dealing he'll never be around and if I can't trust him how can I have his baby for him?

The driver opens the door and my mam and me get on.

She sits near the front but I walk a few rows back from her and sit by the window with my iPod turned all the way up.

As the bus pulls off I put my hand on my tummy. It's still flat, because what's in there is only the size of a grain of rice, it's not a baby yet and it never will be and I'm crying again, because I know this is the right thing but I'm so cross that I have to do it, cross with my mam and dad and cross with Ryan and missing him and hating him and loving him and I'm scared, above all. I'm so fucking scared.

14

Frank Cotter: they called him General Franko. He had a head of curly black hair and wind-tanned skin; he looked like a lighthouse keeper, or a shepherd, something that spent its days in the elements rather than in the back rooms of shuttered casinos, breaking fingers and cracking skulls.

He was waiting in the yard when Jimmy arrived, the waves on his head lifting with the coastline bluster, dressed in a faded jumper and jeans, dirt on his shoes and a gleam in his eye.

'Thanks for meeting me, Franko.'

'No bother, boy. You know me. I'm not afraid of hard work.'

From his jacket pocket Jimmy fished a pair of black gloves and pulled them on as he rounded the other side of the Volvo.

Though cleaned from his chin and lips and philtrum, the blood had caked around Tony Cusack's nostrils; Jimmy guessed he'd decided not to spend his last hours picking his nose. When he opened the door Cusack chanced weight on legs unable to hold it. He flopped out of the car and onto the dirt, then got to his knees, holding on to the inner fittings of the door to steady himself.

'Come on, Cusack,' Jimmy offered. 'Jellyleggedness is so unbecoming in a grown man. And father of six.'

'Why are we here?' Cusack croaked.

'Because I can't trust you. And those I can't trust I don't keep around.'

Cusack started keening his own wake. He put his hands to his face and his fingers dragged at the skin under his eyes. 'Oh God,' he said. 'Oh God.' Jimmy gestured to Franko and he came around the car and pulled Cusack upright. 'Oh God,' he said, again, and then for variety's sake, 'Oh Jesus.'

The yard was trimmed with nets and rope, the substantiation of a forsaken hobby or a career left to rust in old age. Later on, when Dougan arrived, they would take the boat out. They would wrap the body in rope and weigh it down with shale and quarry blocks. They'd drop it where it would never wash up again.

Jimmy Phelan hadn't been able to swim in the sea for many years.

'I don't know this one,' Franko said. 'What's he done on you?'

'Why would you think I'd answer that?' Jimmy said.

'Ah, I'm only asking. It'd be a rare time you wouldn't know the feen, is all.'

'You're all mouth, Franko.'

Cotter simpered.

The yard was at the bottom of a boreen bordered by overgrown hedges and divided by a thick ridge of thriving grass. Sometimes you got dog-walkers and joggers chancing the stretch; they never got close enough to worry about. Half a mile along the wild shoreline, over flaking gates and on a path beaten only by shuffling gangsters when there was an undesirable trussed up to use as pollock bait, you reached the little harbour, and the dinghy that would take you out to the fishing boat. It was a good spot. Jimmy and his boys had used it for a couple of years, longer than he was comfortable with, but the yard was a hard habit to break.

Besides, he liked getting out of the city.

'Right,' said Franko. He pulled Cusack forward, to a tearful yelp.

Jimmy shook his head. Cowardice was nobody's darling. So much of a man was stripped away when notice was given of his demise; it was no surprise to see them cry and beg and empty their bladder all over their shoes, but it was an ugly thing. What use was a man who couldn't stand up straight to face his mortality?

He saw Cusack clearly now, a prolific weakling, a creature at his peak in his teens who'd been steadily sinking since.

Franko had begun the prep. The tarpaulin was laid flat. The hose was extended to sluice the inevitable mess from the concrete; they were promised rain later, too. Jimmy raised an eyebrow, and Franko produced the prearranged weapon and handed it over.

Jimmy crooked a finger around the trigger. It had been years since he'd taken on a job himself, but he had the same good reason for keeping Cusack from his crew now as he'd had when the waster had first clawed at his patience. Dougan knew nothing about the O'Donovan corpse and the brief maternal glitch that had produced it. It followed that he couldn't be told about Cusack's flapping insurrection, his spilling the dead man's name in front of Maureen. It followed then that he couldn't be told about Cusack's reluctant reveal of yet another damned aggravation: a visit from a panicked ex-girlfriend on the direction of that ridiculous cunt Duane. For what could Jimmy tell Dougan on that cock-up? That his mother was a loon and that his attempts to provide a smokescreen had backfired and left him blind and gasping?

It was a skit of the highest fucking order.

Franko stood Cusack in the middle of the yard, shaded his eyes, and searched the skies.

'Why are you here, Cusack?' asked Jimmy, and his old friend whined, 'This isn't something that needs to happen, boy. You know I'm no danger to you. I'm a father, for fuck's sake. They're already missing a mam; don't do this to them.'

'D'you know your problem?' Jimmy brooded. 'You don't know when to stop. I asked you why you were here and you went off on a tangent. I don't know what Maureen asked you but you went off on a tangent there, too. So many angles are bound to ride your arse eventually. Why are you here, Cusack?'

'Because of a fucking accident, boy, a stupid slip-up, a name and a surname is all, dear God.'

'You'd think that'd be all, but what happened? You left it unchecked because you thought Maureen might neglect to tell me. You retreated to your hovel on the hill and quaked into a bottle and you let your slip-up grow and grow until there was a whore prying at your door for a dead man. See what happens when you think shit'll just work itself out?'

'I get it, I get it.' There were two colours a man could turn out here, apart from the pervading yellow backdrop: ashen or dribbling puce. Cusack was white from forehead to knuckles. 'But I'm not the problem, boy. All I did was make a mistake. I'm no danger to you. Why can't you see that? Why can't you . . .' Whatever force had fed his voice ran dry.

'You're a waste of space, Cusack.'

'I was there when you needed me,' Tony rasped.

'And look where that brought me.'

He'd been sniffling even when he'd come crawling to Jimmy. Panic about a mourning girl turning up on his doorstep, two years after he'd done his good deed for his old friend, compounded by the fact she'd been directed there by Tara Duane. *It might just be one of Duane's notions*, he'd said, flaccid and wheedling. *She may have only just remembered that we used to drink in the same pub, some shit like that.* Jimmy had cursed the bitch under his breath, warned Cusack to let him handle her, and assuaged his anxiety through gritted teeth.

Alone in the aftermath he'd wondered if Tim Dougan was his good-luck charm. It had been decades since he'd tried unpicking complications without his old buddy's help, and his efforts had double-knotted the thing and bound his hands with it.

This morning he'd determined to have a final lash of it, called General Franko, hounded the retching Cusack into his car and made for West Cork.

By the time Dougan showed up Cusack would be gone and Franko certainly wouldn't be talking.

Cusack got a second wind and launched into another petition he'd cobbled together on behalf of his little darlings. Jimmy held up his hand.

'Nothing you say's going to change my mind that you're a maggot and my mistake.'

'Jesus, Jimmy, do you want me to fucking beg?' Cusack sobbed.

'You are begging.'

'Six kids, Jim. Four boys and two girls. Seven to seventeen. What d'you think is going to happen to them? We're so brittle as it is. I've one in prison, I need to be around for them . . . You have kids of your own!'

Jimmy said, 'I have to show you what happens to people who I can't trust, Cusack.'

'Please! Please, for fuck's sake—'

The gunshot shut him up. The second made him wail. Jimmy stood over the little General Franko and put a final bullet in his head.

Tony was on his knees. He heaved. Saliva anchored his head to the ground.

'You see?' Jimmy said.

Cusack said nothing. He was crying.

'One mistake can bring the whole city down around me, Cusack. I take mistakes more seriously than you think. Don't for a second believe that if it had made sense to, I wouldn't have wiped you the fuck out.'

'What did he do?' Cusack blubbered.

'Him?' Jimmy waved a wrist at the former general and his fragments and fluids. 'He talked too much. More than you do, even.'

He stepped over to his old friend and caught the back of his head, twisting him on his hands and knees so he could face another future.

'Don't let what happened to him happen to you, Cusack.'

Cusack dispatched to wait in a pub five miles back, Jimmy relaxed in his car with a well-earned cigarette and half a playthrough of *Against the Grain*. On the other side of the yard, beyond the concrete wall and over the rutted sea, cloud begat cloud and the air turned damp and grey. Where Frank Cotter's blood had washed into the muck the flies danced, intoxicated.

Dougan arrived a couple of hours post-mortem. Jimmy watched from the car as he approached the tarpaulin and surveyed the glittering concrete. He was a bulldog of a man: squat, muscular, and stern. He had a stomach lined with iron and a pragmatism that extended to murder and murder's horizon.

He flopped onto the passenger seat and said, 'JimBob, you started without me.'

'I was feeling old and fat, Timothy. I thought it was time I got busy again.'

'And how was it?'

'Overrated. We should bring the boat out soon. Rain later. The water'll be choppy.'

Dougan said, 'You were down here a lot earlier than you said you'd be, boy.'

'Yeah.'

'Always your plan to do it yourself, was it?'

'Yeah. I suppose I was being a bit snakey about it.'

There was a pause. Dougan considered the tarpaulin. Jimmy watched the clouds.

'Has it happened to you yet,' Jimmy said, 'that you thought going into a job that you might feel a bit too old for this carry-on after, that you thought, *Well, this'll be the one to herald my retirement*, and yet when it came down to it you felt the same old familiar nothing?'

'Being honest, boy, I never expect to feel anything, and I remain unsurprised.'

'Twenty years ago this shit used to rise bile. You get used to it, then you wait for a time you'll lose the knack for it. I hadn't pulled a trigger in years up to today. And look at that; I'm still a killer.'

Such blunt language was exceptional, even between old friends. Dougan frowned, but raised his eyebrows nearly as quick, thought about the infraction, let it slide.

'Were you expecting ascension?'

'I was expecting to be older than I am.'

This is how it was usually done. A man would commit an unforgiveable transgression. Maybe he'd screw the wrong fella over, maybe he'd be found in a position where ratting out his betters might seem the only option, maybe his jaw was gaping and clumsy, as General Franko's had become. A decision would be made. Most of the time there was a good run-up to the action. A call would be made, a favour called in or loaned out to a contact in the UK. Someone would fly over, find the problem and snuff it out. It was all very neat. Everyone had an alibi. The assassin wouldn't be in Ireland long enough to shit and wipe his arse.

General Franko's demise might have been arranged this way, if Jimmy hadn't found himself with an extra thorn to pluck from his paw.

He doubted that there'd be harm done in having Franko sorted the traditional way. In fact, he was banking on it being constructive. He was still capable of rash decisions if his temper was so stoked; beware of the dog. And if this Robbie O'Donovan thing came to light – the whore had to be found and he didn't think Cusack capable of the task – he wanted there to be no illusion as to the boss's mental faculties. When he needed to be ruthless he was.

'Let's go fishing,' he said.

Cusack phoned him up two days after.

'She's home,' he said.

'Since when?'

'I dunno. The last half hour or so. I didn't see her come back but I can hear her moving around in there.'

Like a rat in the walls. Jimmy went straight over. He parked at the bottom of Cusack's driveway, blocking him in for the divilment of it, and hopped the wall to Duane's front door, where he knocked with polite restraint and waited, one hand resting on the sidelight.

Her bottom lip started quivering as soon as she opened. Her hair was arranged in two childish plaits hanging over her shoulders; he reached out and tugged one, and said, 'What's wrong, Tara; aren't you pleased to see me?'

'I'm only just home,' she said. 'What, I don't even get an hour's peace?'

He stepped in and she stepped back.

'How was your holiday, Tara?'

'I was only in Dublin,' she said. 'Visiting my sister. She's not well.'

'Is she not? Ah, Jesus, that's awful.'

He closed the door behind him and she said, 'I don't even have milk in the house or anything.'

'It's OK. I'm not after tea.'

'Well what do you want, then?'

'Oh, just to follow up on the last time I saw you. Remember? I asked whether you knew of a fella called Robbie O'Donovan.'

She held on to the banister and pursed her lips. 'Yeah. You said he was a buddy of Tony Cusack's.'

'Did I?'

'Yeah. And like I told you, he's on the missing list, so I—'

'You told his girlfriend and now the whore's been up here nosing around. Did I fucking ask you to befriend his fucking next-of-kin, did I? *Tara, will you ever go and tell Robbie O'Donovan's ould doll that Tony Cusack knows where he is*. Did I say that at any stage, did I? Did you hear me do it?'

'You didn't tell me I wasn't to say anything about it!'

'Well fuck me, I didn't think I'd have to spell out to you that you weren't to give the floozie the idea O'Donovan was dead!'

'He's dead?'

'The only person who seems to know for sure is the fucking call girl, and you're the only one who's been talking to her.'

'I didn't tell her he was dead!'

'Well, how'd she get the idea then?'

'Maybe because he looks the sort?'

'He looks the sort to die?'

'He looks like a junkie! Junkies die! Junkies die all the fucking time! I didn't make him overdose; it's not my fault!'

He reached for her, but she ducked and dashed into her kitchen, where she avoided his second grasp by swinging a chair between them and then diving under the table, to which he could only stand and laugh.

'Come out from under the table, Tara.'

She was bawling. 'Leave me alone! Leave me alone!'

'Do you really think I can't get in there after you?'

'I tried to help you! It's not my fault you didn't make clear it was a huge big secret!'

'It is your fault, Tara. You're a fucking cretin.'

'I have a daughter!' she shrieked.

'What is it with assholes trying to hide behind their offspring when they think they're getting a clatter?'

He sank to his haunches and made a grab for her, and she batted his hand away and cried out.

'Jesus Christ, it really is like trying to catch rats in the walls.'

He grabbed again and managed to catch one of her plaits, and he pulled her across the floor as she kicked out behind her. She ended up faceplanting in front of her fridge; he stood over her and pulled her upright, and she whined and spat like a small child throwing down in the biscuit aisle.

'Why is it so far past your grasp, Tara, that you shouldn't be sticking your nose where it isn't wanted?' he growled. 'Why are you so fucking dense that in asking you a simple question I run the risk of you summoning apocalyptic shit-storms?'

'How was I to know?' she gasped.

'Well you can forget you knew, or I'll have more than words to batter you with next time. But before you scrub your broken brain clean, tell me where I can find this whore who's so desperate to tell the city her boyfriend's dead.'

'I don't know where Georgie is! She's not around anymore. I was shocked to run into her.'

'If anyone can track the drifting bitch, it's you. You like to suckle the lifeless, don't you?'

He let her go.

'Find the whore,' he told her. 'Get an address and deliver it straight to me. Don't talk to the whore and don't talk to Cusack. Don't even talk to your fucking self if you can manage it. Does that make sense?'

'I was only trying to help,' she cried. The lasso plait had come loose into a soft kink. Her face burned red with the exertion of playing wounded.

'Sure that's you all over, Tara. Only trying to help when you stir up shit that didn't need stirring. Only trying to help when you herd the whores. Only trying to help, I bet, when you stuck your rickety claws down the front of Tony Cusack's young fella's jocks. Is he the one in prison? I assume so.'

'In prison? What?'

'Didn't he tell you he was going away, Tara? Did he not put your name down on the visitor's scroll so you could go press your tits against the Plexiglas for him every fortnight?'

'You're not funny,' she said.

'Fucking remember that,' he replied. 'I'm not.'

There was a piano recital that evening. Deirdre had phoned him twice to ensure he didn't forget, and so he showed up in the stuffy auditorium of the old community hall and sat with Deirdre and smiled encouragingly at Ellie as she spread her fingers and plodded over the keys. Ellie looked worse than her exertions sounded. She frowned all the way through the piece and then turned and faced her audience like she'd been instructed to do so by a voice in her head which intended later to encourage her to burn down an orphanage.

And how they clapped, those munificent blenchers, tucked into their bitter rows, thinking about *EastEnders* or the match or the tubby lovers whose grunts they were missing to cosset the egos of their neighbours' dumplings. They clapped like their escape depended on the rhythm. Swollen with forged pride, they jostled each other and muttered in empty approval as one bored child after another took to the stage to play out their dues. The smell was intolerable; perspiration, ancient stage curtains, slippery arse cheeks, perfume.

Jimmy Phelan was not at home in such a crowd, but who was? Some of their number looked more comfortable than others – the women, mostly, whose painted smiles hid well their boredom – but they were not happy to be here. There was no camaraderie, no real regard. Jimmy's parents had enjoyed a sense of community. The city was a smaller place then, and the people's expectations matched. Now the world had burst its banks and no one had anything in common with anyone anymore.

All day he'd had that anxiety festering again at the back of his skull: that his mother's streak of madness took him out of the society he'd built, that the lads he turned the clock with would catch wind of his genetic defects and abandon him, betray him, give tribute to a new chief. They were not tied to his character, only to the qualities they found use for.

He would give Tara Duane a chance to quietly find the whore. But he thought he'd have to make it all disappear then: the whore, Duane, and Cusack too, whether or not he wanted to.

15

When she was small, they said she liked to toy with things. That she enjoyed making babies of dogs, people of woodlice, pets of dying birds. That things existed for her amusement, whether they were lacquered wood or flesh around a beating heart.

Maureen Phelan's mother had been brainwashed beautifully. There had never been a question of her choosing her gender over her church; she pandered to the vestments as if by debasing herself she could avoid the stain of her sex. Her own daughters she saw as treacherous vixens. Puberty marked their descent. She hated the hair under their arms, their sloping waists, the blood that confirmed they were ready for sin. She was a vicious and stupid woman. Some combination. Her name was Una.

Una's parents lived just up the hill from the Industrial School and Laundry, where, she told her daughters, all the bad girls went. She seemed both deathly afraid of the place and satisfied it was there at all, in the same way she was full sure of hell and content that it wasn't for the likes of her. She announced that the Laundry's inmates would therein learn the humility they were sorely lacking. Every girl with a fashionable hemline, every girl who had notions about herself, was fit for nowhere but *behind the high walls*. Boys she had less of a problem with; they were dumb creatures whose animal whims were to be carefully managed.

Maureen was the middle child of seven; despite her efforts, Una's management of her husband's impulses hadn't followed her austere ideal.

Una Phelan was a frightened hag, comfortable in a dying Ireland and snapping feverishly at its future. For her there was no authority but the Holy Trinity: the priests, the nuns and the neighbours. Hers was the first generation of the new Republic, the crowd hand-reared on Dev and Archbishop McQuaid, the genuflectors.

When Maureen figured out that not only was she pregnant, but pregnant and abandoned by a coward, it was both horrifying and vaguely freeing, like hitting bedrock. She considered her options: the stairs, the coat hanger, the boiling baths. It didn't take her long to reject them. There was something to be said for fulfilling the destiny her mother had kept harping on about.

So she flounced into the kitchen and announced her misdeed with the bravado of scientific detachment. She watched the colour drain from her parents' cheeks, and the emotions that betrayed their humanity cross their faces like clouds on an October sky. She was nineteen but they were still the authority; she prepared for their punishment with frosty curiosity. One thing she knew: she wasn't doing her penance up to her elbows in soap and steam in the Laundry. She would have killed them both first.

She had brought the devil into the family home and so all hell broke loose. *Behind the high walls* seemed her mother's preferred choice, but in the 1970s the tide was turning. Giving up a daughter to appease sour-faced nuns no longer seemed the only thing to do, and the third leaf of Una's Holy Trinity was beginning to wilt and fall. A second cousin was found in Dublin willing to take in the slattern.

James Dominic Phelan was born in Holles Street and clutched to his mother's breast 'like a doll', according to the scowling grandmother, while the grown-ups debated what to do with him. In the end they decided the shame of raising him themselves was the lesser shame. He was taken from Maureen, whose childish wont would otherwise have been to make a plaything of him, and this was no time for games. He was installed as the baby, twelve years younger than his youngest uncle, and Maureen was sent to a hastily procured position in a London office.

She started three weeks after giving birth.

'No toys there,' Una announced, triumphantly. She was wrong.

There were plenty of things to toy with in London, but the joy had been taken right out of it.

Ten minutes walk from her front door and she was at the entrance to the old Laundry. If there was someone at the gate lodge, or the newer building near the entrance, they didn't bother her. She walked up the path. Overgrown now, the city reclaiming its darker monuments.

There were cracked stone steps leading up to the building, but the building itself was only a shell, the red brick, the arches, the iron crosses on its towers, all stained and falling down. She walked a little way along the front of the place, and spotted the space behind the facade; it had been gutted.

Statues everywhere. Some of them defaced. Here was a shepherd with a twirling black moustache, a lichened maiden with an alien name daubed on her robes. They stood in silent guard, oblivious to the unchecked march of the branches, grasses and fronds. Oblivious to Maureen. Relics of the past, swallowed by a world expanding.

Christ, it was silent. Maureen stood, her back to the barren brick, and looked out towards the river.

There were plenty of other Irish exiles in London back in the 1970s. Maureen had met her share; they rushed together like streams of the same mercurial poison. She'd known a number of women who'd spent their girlhoods in places like this, two who had been right here. Both had had baby boys. One of them had reared hers until he was twenty-one months old. The nuns had come in one day and informed her that he was being adopted, and that was it; she said her goodbyes and never saw him again. The other had only had five months with hers before he was taken away at an hour's notice; she had sat on her cot, she told Maureen, her breasts still heavy with milk, clawing at her face, rocking, sure now that this was the end, that she'd never be out of the place. There was talk of surrendering her to the asylum, but the action was abandoned when she came to her senses and her elbow grease became profitable again. Born only around the corner, Una Phelan was damn glad of the nuns' service.

To think of the babies, when they grew old enough to wonder! James Phelan had been told with dignity stiff and cold that Maureen-in-London was his real mother, and that he should think no more of it, but still he'd come after her once Una had given up her grip on the world and expired in her marital bed for an audience of effeminate printed Jesuses. So many other boys and girls grew up with holes in their chests gaping as wide as the Christian fissure that had spat them into the world. Maureen had read about it in recent years, once the tabloids had tested the value of Magdalene anguish. Hordes of Irish children – American, too; the exported generation – digging through Catholic detritus to find out who they were. Their searches were, more often than not, fruitless. Natural mothers had died, returned unto dust by the chemicals in the laundries. Documentation had been scant and useless. Women who'd moved on refused to remember and denied their flesh and blood their closure. Sometimes the mothers had just disappeared, as their country had designed.

In the shadow of the landmark, Maureen Phelan picked her way through thickets and thorns, enduring memories, even the ones that were not hers.

When she rounded the corner at the end of the building there was a man sitting in the grass, more interested in the weight of his bottle than he was in the walls before him. He spotted her but seemed indifferent, then testily, as she approached, he brought the bottle to his lips.

He was a vagrant, much younger than her, though his beard hid it well. He wore jeans and scuffed boots and was sitting on a pair of waterproofs. His baseball hat displayed the name of a Florida golf club; underneath its peak he scowled.

'D'you want something?' he said. He wasn't American.

'What do you know about this place?' she asked.

'What? G'way with you.'

'Just how you can sit here getting merry and looking up at that ruin. Admirable.'

'Do I look merry?' he said.

'No. I assumed you were giving it a lash, though.'

'Fuck off.'

'I'm about to. I didn't come up here to talk to you, sunshine.'

'Grand, so . . .' His wit failed him. He took another drink. 'Jog on.'

'D'you know this place used to be a Magdalene Laundry?'

'Course I did. Fuck off.'

'D'you know what happened to it?'

'Are you not going to fuck off?'

'When I'm good and ready.'

He considered the bottle, then frowned at her. 'It burned down. Twice. Now fuck off.'

'Twice?'

'Grudges everywhere, up here,' he said. 'One for every brick.'

'Is it possible to get in?'

'Missus, the grudges stuck because it's impossible to get out. Why the fuck would you want to get in?'

'To set another fire,' she said.

He smiled. He was missing a tooth on the top, right in the middle. 'You don't look like a woman who'd set fires, in fairness. I was reckoning you were walking a dog. A bitching-freeze or chi-wow-wow or something. The last thing I needed.'

'No dog,' she said.

He raised the bottle again, and stared at her between the peak of his cap and the vicious slope of the glass. When he'd finished, he said, 'Are you one of them?'

She looked back up at the crumbling brick. 'No.'

'So you're not going to set any fires, then.'

She grimaced.

'Me neither,' he said. 'There's not much left of it to burn. Still, though. Nothing as cleansing as a fire. This heap turned the air black but d'you know what? Everyone felt cleaner after it.'

'That so?'

'That's the job, I'm telling you.'

She found a tenner and gave it to him and he thanked her for not fucking off sooner. And even knowing he was there watching the walls for her, she felt uneasy walking away, like the heat of a pointed stare was burning up her shoulders, like the bitterness soldered to the past and to the ground the past was built on had touched her, and marked her. There were places this city wanted no one to tread.

Hidden Messages

It's Tuesday morning, the place is baking, and I'm stuck in writing you a letter. Melting, I am. Neapolitan blood will only get you so far. Only wearing prison-issue trackies and socks in my cell and I'm wringing. Tough on me, eh? S'pose next time I'll try not getting into trouble and see how far that gets me. Until then I just have to deal with it.

Prison is shit. Prison is very very shit. Of course it's supposed to be shit. Still, it's some land. Every day I get up I have to deal with the fact I'm only another day closer to getting out. Destination all the ways over there in January and January seems like a million miles away when you're stuck gasping hot in the middle of a heatwave. This is the absolute worst place you can possibly be when all you can think about is going down to Fountainstown for the day and balming out.

On top of everything else school is out for the summer, which I totally get the irony of because when I was at home I'd have done anything to not go to school. Weird what you miss. Really considering getting back into all that once I'm done here. It wouldn't be that hard. There's loads of schools in town. Except I guess Barry'd have to tell them I was expelled. There's no way I'd get away with that one.

Have a load of books taken out from the library over the past few weeks instead. It's funny how sick you get of reading when that's all you can do. Seriously, I was down there flaking through books thinking I'd never be bored again but a couple of days later I'm sick to death of them. Obvious irony is obvious.

Pretty much lost for things to tell you. Every day's the same. Nothing new happens. Least of my worries I guess.

'You like prison, Ryan?'

'Bored as fuck in there I was.'

'Eh, isn't that the point? Can't make it into a holiday camp for you, can they? Arts and crafts you're after? Ukulele? Surfing? Elephant polo? Tell me you're for real, boy. Here's a slap of reality. Eventually you'll get out and you can go surfing then. Shut up and put up in the meantime.'

Christ, I went off on one there, didn't I? Really, there's so little to tell you I'm waffling. Education through reading is noble but not the stuff of brilliant letters home. What about if I focus on the stuff I'm going to do when I get out? Seriously, here's the plan.

Ryan gets out of prison. Ecstatic, he dives into a whole new life. And he sticks to it. Determined, wiser and with a whole head full of book-learning, he finds some course to do, gets a job and even goes busking with Joseph. Eventually, he atones for fucking things up with his girlfriend and she forgives him. Very very slowly, but she gets there. Each day then is better than the day before. Ryan buys her tons and tons of shoes. Yup, he knows he said he wouldn't but he's changed his mind. There aren't enough shoes in the world for Karine D'Arcy. Heels five inches high, slipper flats, Cons, boots, whatever she wants. It's shoe central around her gaff. Now her mam can't even get through her bedroom door for shoes. 'Girl, your boyfriend must be loaded if he keeps buying you all these shoes,' she'll say. And you'll say yeah, he is, he got himself together, he's totally worthy now. Next thing Ryan knows, Jackie D'Arcy has invited him in for dinner and is telling him what a daycent son-in-law he is with daycent taste in shoes.

Does me good, that little dream.

Cian came up with Dad last time and said one of the McDaids next door to us emigrated last month. Australia. Now there's a gaff I wouldn't mind dipping my toes into. Melbourne, did he say? Adelaide? Karine, I don't remember but let's write them all down as possible destinations. Even the poison spiders would be worth it. There's more things that can kill you in Australia than anywhere else on the planet. Heard it on a documentary on the telly in the cell a few days ago but it didn't put me off.

I probably shouldn't have told you about the poison spiders, should I? Now you'll probably never go. Get over the poison spiders. Sun, sea, sand and surfing. There's no way we wouldn't love it. Of course, they're always looking for nurses there so maybe we could go once you're qualified. Until then though I guess I can cope with Fountainstown.

Guess who sent me a letter? Head-wrecker general herself, Tara Duane. I know. Freaky. The woman's actually off her game. How she'd think I'd want to hear from her I don't know. Even reading it gave me the wobblies. You know she lives in cuckoo land. There's rumours about her, like. Heard stuff like she told Con Harrington's ould doll that they were having an affair and poor Con hadn't gone next nor near her. It's insane what some people make up. No way is she to be trusted and no way do I want letters from her. Keep well away, like.

Yesterday it came. Opened it up in front of the officer because you always open letters in front of officers and he said my face could have turned milk sour. Unreal, in fairness. Restless all morning waiting for the post to come around and when it does it's a letter from a raving loon. Excitement wilting into nothing in the space of five seconds. Like you'd ask yourself if she really thinks I'm wasting one of my letters writing back to her? Obviously not.

She had nothing to say either. It's very quiet on the terrace, my dad's grand, my brothers and sisters are grand and she's sure they all miss me. No shit Sherlock, thanks for the update. God almighty like. I know I'm bored but I'm not that desperate. The silly bitch even hinted that I should stick her name down on the visitor's thing and she'd travel up to see me. Batshit! Up the walls of the cave batshit!

The thing is, I know it's not easy for you to come up and see me but your name is down as a visitor, like. I know I'm kinda clutching at straws on that one. Can't imagine your mam and dad would be too keen. And I know that I really let you down when I did what I did and ended up here. Never thought you'd even write for a while. Thought you'd be furious. But I guess you're even more amazing than I thought you were, aren't you? Really, you didn't have to be as nice about this as you've been. Every time I think about it it shames me. All I can say is that I don't deserve you.

That's the sad truth, isn't it? How I let you down. Even though the worst thing I could think of was being away from you I let it happen. When I get out I'll make it up to you.

I could do a hundred of these stints and if you read one letter for every one of those sentences I'd consider myself lucky.

That's about all for this letter I'd say. How to end these things I never know. Only to say I love you I suppose. Understand? There's nothing more true in the whole entire world.

Yeah, that's a pretty soppy ending.

Off I go.

Until January.

Ryan.

Kindling

16

Tony got the call at a most inconvenient time, halfway down his second pint with Catherine Barrett's hand halfway up his thigh, to which she'd progressed following a friendly pinch of his knee maybe ten minutes back.

He didn't get up to answer. 'Hello?' Eyes on his conquest, who smirked with easy confidence, welcoming even. She was married but on bad terms with her fella, who'd been sniping at her from England for the last four months. She had cropped dark hair, laughing eyes and a great wide mouth like a sock puppet; no looker, but she had a soft spot for Tony, and he'd learned to manage with a lot less.

'Am I speaking to Tony Cusack?'

'You are.'

'Hello, Mr Cusack; it's Michael Tynan here.'

It was the governor. The fucking governor, at whose voice Tony became immediately enfeebled. He had always been inept in his dealings with authority figures, even when they weren't his own.

'The car isn't on the road so I can't get up there,' he said, and Catherine Barrett returned to her glass of beer with the careful grace of a spurned braggart. 'But I could send my sister? My sister lives in Dublin. She could pick him up.'

'The usual arrangement would be to give him his train ticket,' said the governor, 'but with him not being eighteen yet, I'd prefer to have him picked up. If your sister is available that would do.'

'Yeah, of course, yeah. I'll get her to meet him.' He paused. 'I thought he'd be another week.'

He'd counted wrong, or they'd been messing with the dates again up there. They did that. Tony was confused by the process, but then it was made to be confusing, was it not? They were trained to make a monkey out of you. Over the past nine months he'd visited, written, received phone calls which were recorded and often, whether by design or shoddy apparatus, cut ridiculously short. Every time there was communication facilitated by these people they made Tony feel like a shit-flinger.

The visits were the worst. It was like going back to school. The same impatient courtesy, the same hot mass settling at the back of his tongue.

For the second call he made his way out to the smoking area, ignoring the woman Barrett with whom he might otherwise have enjoyed an ugly but crucial ride.

'Fiona? You'd never do me a favour, girl?'

'Jesus. What's he need now?'

'A lift to the station?'

January, and his lungs were full of fog and soot. January was a cunt at the best of times, pissing ice down upon a crowd damp to their bones. Sudden room in the shops after the Christmas eruption, cold space in the pubs and the cheer sucked back out and up the chimney.

This January reeked of vengeance. Tony had suffered a Christmas subdued for his recharged addiction and the absence of his oldest son, and then a dose that confined him to the bed for a week. In the horrors, he'd had to plead with his mother to buy him a few naggins, citing the DTs, the sickness, his weakness, his failures, until she'd angrily relented. Then he'd curled on his side under the duvet, clammy and gulping.

He deserved it, oh, he knew it well. He'd turned in the pregnant girl, he'd watched a man die, he'd broken his sobriety, he'd betrayed his son.

Now and then J.P. took his recreation at the terrace, watching him or watching Duane or neither; he didn't know. His children, oblivious, had walked past the Volvo on the way home from school. They had been in the house when J.P. had barged in for unscheduled one-to-ones. He'd even turned up on Christmas Day with a bottle of Jameson, gift-wrapped but only half full.

Tony attempted to show his belly and hoped that it would prove too pathetic for the invader's sense of pride. The rolling over stung. Late at night, between hallucinated gunshots in a concrete bay and his next nightmare, he remembered J.P.'s sneer about jellylegged dads, and the shame burned down his gullet and summoned sweat. Feeling keenly the gaps in his character, he wept alone.

He had betrayed his son but his son was the forgiving sort and Tony Cusack was deeply sorry. The rationale had stood up to scrutiny; little doubt the boy thought he could handle himself, but wandering into Jimmy Phelan's field of vision was a life-changing experience, as Tony knew too well. Even so. Seventeen was no age to be locked up. Tony's family had intimated he deserved it. Gurriers tied to you were still gurriers.

During their visits the boy had been reticent to the point of silence but that was nothing to wonder about, not when the visiting room had been so full. Roaring mammies and young fellas screeching 'HA?' down the phones; who could have a conversation in that environment? Ryan had always been soft-spoken.

Tony had a quick cigarette under the wind-rippled canopy and went back into the bar.

Catherine Barrett was sending a text. When she saw him on the way back over she smiled, and her mouth split her face in two.

'I thought you'd gone and left me!' she cawed.

He saw her plan in her twinkling eyes. They would drink up, drink up a couple more, she'd get frisky and they'd go back to her house and have a joyless fuck on her living-room couch, provided he could get it up and she didn't throw up over the edge of the armrest.

It was half an hour shy of midday. The barwoman continued with the clean-up from the night before, stretching out in the narcoleptic presence of her early drinkers: Tony; Catherine Barrett; Seamie O'Driscoll with the bent, bulbous nose; a couple of flushed ould fellas on whose pints the heads had turned the colour of straw; one crumpled ould wan whose name Tony had never learned, sitting alone at the end of the bar with a glass of crème de menthe. Tony had taken care with his disguise since his tumble from the wagon; today he was clean-shaven, fragrant and ironed. He was close to charming the knickers off Catherine Barrett, whose long coral nails and ornate necklace made a decent equivalent to his get-up. He was a morning drinker, but of a different kind to the horde. He could have been heading to a wedding, or a business meeting.

He drained his glass, and Catherine Barrett looked at him with vicious dismay.

'Have to go, Kitty Cat,' he said, and she tried a cartoonish pout and said, 'Ah, Tony. But weren't we having the craic?'

'Another time,' and he considered adding *Something's come up*, but he didn't think he could bear the innuendo.

Tony arrived home with a slab of lager and a bag of rubbish – crisps, chocolate, fags. What else would the young fella need? Nothing, sure; he'd left the place in such a State-enforced hurry that he'd not even packed himself a bag, knowledge that had hit his father like a knock to the neck when he'd returned from the court. After that first weekend he'd made the trip to Dublin with the few things the lad was allowed and the shock still hadn't rolled off him. The kid had pretty much stayed in that state for the whole nine months, as far as Tony could tell. He'd banked on it; once he'd fallen for the Demon again, he'd fretted about Ryan twigging it on visits.

Later on there'd be words, if it still mattered to the young fella. Tony was hoping to circumvent that. Share a couple of pints with him, rip away the hard feelings.

He opened a can while he cleaned the house.

Bedrooms, bathroom, hall. He cleaned out the fridge and made space for the lager. He retrieved the laptop from Kelly's room and left it back on Ryan's bed. He hoovered the stairs. He had a second can while he rang his mother; she had received word already, through Fiona, that the boy had been released. A text message confirmed that Fiona had met Ryan at the prison and was taking him for something to eat before dropping him to his train. And that was it – nine months passed in the blink of an eye, and all that could happen within.

He texted back: *Is he OK?*

Fiona's reply: *Not a bother on him. All he wants is a Big Mac.*

Tony was, like the gaff, in tip-top shape by the time Ronan, Niamh and Cathal arrived in from school, and, off their reactions, in even better form by the time Cian and Kelly wandered in an hour later. He met them in the hall. Kelly dropped her bag by the door and glared at him, giddy in the kitchen door frame with a third can snapped open in celebration.

'Your brother's on the way home.'

She curled her lip and said, 'I'm sure he's only desperate to see you.'

'Do you ever take a day off, Kelly?'

Cian waited until his sister had stalked away and cheered, 'That's pure brilliant!'

'It is, isn't it?'

Cian reflected, 'It flew.'

'Ask your brother whether it flew and I'm sure we'll get a different story.'

There were plans to be made. Dinners: there had been a quiet complaint about boiled spuds and cheap chops, so none of that muck. Should he ferry the lad over to see his grandparents? Maybe tomorrow; they'd likely nag but he might get a present of twenty quid out of it, and that'd keep him going for phone credit at least. It might have been an idea to put together a list of schools that might take him in, if he were to return to do his Leaving Cert. What else, what else? He didn't know. The drink was going down well.

The train was due at 5.30. He pulled on his coat and stood in the hall. Did Ryan have a coat with him? Had he been wearing one for court? Funny how memories you'd swear burnt tattoos on you dissolved into nothing when you needed to examine them. He remembered the judge, disastrously businesslike; the solicitor, who'd turned magenta with the indignity of having been so fucking wrong. He remembered Ryan, turning to face him, eyes like dinner plates, going, 'Dad . . .' but as to what he was wearing, his father couldn't remember.

What had Maria been wearing the night she had sworn to take her children to the other side? Those were the details he didn't wish to remember, they were of no practical purpose. Here she was though, in the hall with him, threatening to wake the lot of them up and leave him in an empty shell. She went for the stairs, he dragged her back. She kicked his shin, he made a grab for her ankle and missed, he caught her only at the bedroom door where she was heading for chubby little Ronan, he slapped her, he caught her wrists, she screamed in rage. Black jeans, a trim grey Nike T-shirt, ivory ballet slippers dirty and worn, her hair kinked from heat and fury.

He came back to himself and shook his head like a swimmer dislodging a trickle.

He hunted through the coats under the stairs and found Ryan's hooded jacket, which he balled up under his own. He left the house distended and frightened Tara Duane, who was coming out her front door at the same time.

'Tony!'

He set his jaw and started down his driveway, but she hurried to reach the gate and hopped out in front of him.

'Tony, please stop.'

He stepped off the footpath to swing around her and she babbled, 'I know we haven't spoken in months and months, Tony, but now that all that unpleasantness has died down I thought we could mend some bridges.'

He stopped. 'What's died down?' he snarled. 'Your fucking paedophilia?'

'Jesus, that is so insulting. I tried to be *pleasant* to Ryan – to all of your children – because we're neighbours. What's wrong with you that you have to twist that?'

'Get away from me, Duane.'

'You smashed my front window, Tony. You terrorised me. You embarrassed me in front of the whole terrace for giving you a friendly heads-up about Ryan's advances. And I'm the one trying to make peace; will you not even give me credit for that?'

'You're full of shit and I hope you die roaring,' he said. 'And no fucking unpleasantness has *died down*; if you think I'm ever going to forget what you did with that girl . . .'

He shoved past and she threw her arms up and marched alongside.

'What girl, Tony?'

'You know what girl,' he said. 'The pregnant girl. The one you sent up here on a watery promise that Tony Cusack would know where her boyfriend had gone. The one that came into my house and accused me of killing the prick in front of my fucking kids!'

'I had nothing to do with that, Tony, I swear.'

'If you had nothing to do with it, Duane, then why was the girl so sure that you did? Where'd she get your name? She string it out of her arse? Must be the same place she got my son's name when she was looking for a bit of dope, isn't that right?'

'I resent that. All I told Georgie, who I've known for *years*, was that you may have seen her boyfriend before he went missing. He was a drinker.'

'What's that supposed to mean?'

'You know,' she said, lowering her voice, 'like yourself.'

'The day,' he said, 'that I take lifestyle pointers from you . . .' He shook his head and dug his fingernails into his palms. 'You stay away from me, Duane. I don't know what you've done or said to that poor girl but I'm sticking to what J.P. tells me and he can deal with you.'

'How are you so cosy with J.P. anyway?' she said.

'None of your fucking business.'

'Because if you had nothing to hide you wouldn't have involved him, would you? I tell Georgie that you knew her boyfriend and the next thing I know Jimmy Phelan is at my door looking for Georgie's address. Why is that, Tony?'

He exhaled.

Shit, he thought. *Fuck. Fuck shit fuck.*

The therapist down at Solidarity House once said, in a moment of rare candour, that the problem with functioning on even low, steady levels of alcohol was that it makes you thick as shit. For J.P.

to have dealt with Duane as he'd said he did would have meant explaining to the bitch that namedropping Tony Cusack in conversation with the dead man's ex-girlfriend was inadvisable. Therefore, that there was a real connection between Tony Cusack and the dead man, forged in steel by J.P.'s insistence that Duane forget all about it. To have missed that could only be attributed to the Demon. Ta-dah. A couple in the morning and three afternoon cans made him thick as fucking shit.

Same as thinking about the night his wife's drunken stubbornness killed her off on the day their firstborn got out of juvenile detention. Same as getting involved at all with Phelan, who he'd run with as a kid, for fuck's sake, who'd dragged him as a grown-up into murder after murder and Jesus, what was Tony Cusack, only a grown-up with the cop on of a twelve-year-old?

He tried to exude menace but his voice came out croaking.

'You need to stop talking, Tara.'

'I see. The shady bully thinks I'm not good enough to be his ally.'

'Get fucked.' How he wished he hadn't said that. *Get fucked*, as she stripped off in front of his kid and worked at him till he was able for her bony thighs to straddle his. Now he jabbed both elbows backwards, on the chance that it might maim the bitch; it fucking didn't.

'I've hit a nerve,' she marvelled. 'Call Tony Cusack a lot of things, but don't call him a bully, even when the evidence stacks. Even when he's running around after Jimmy Phelan.'

She grabbed his wrist and dragged back, and he whirled around, fist in the air and ready, so close to it he could feel the air thicken between his fist and her head.

'Or running to him!' she gasped. 'Setting him on me. Is that because when Georgie got up here she said Robbie was dead? Is he dead? That's it, isn't it, Tony? Robbie O'Donovan's dead. Don't worry; I'm not going to tell. Why would I drop you in it on the day Ryan's home from prison?'

'You don't fucking mention my son!'

'Kelly just texted Melinda and said he was coming home – that's why I thought now would be the time to make peace.'

'Stay the fuck away from him.'

'It's funny, you kill someone and he goes to gaol.'

She dropped his wrist and put her face in her hands. Beneath the tresses, underneath her fingers, from the utter depths she made a gurgling sound that could have been laughter or tears or some mad chant. Tony jumped away and she came to again, smiled and said, 'Don't worry, Tony. J.P. asked me to track down the girl. See, I'm just as close to J.P. as you are. We're on the same team, for God's sake.'

What did he expect? That he wouldn't need a drink?

He arrived down at twenty past and ducked into the pub across from Kent station for a pint of Guinness – medicinal, respectable – and a short, straight Jameson.

He took a seat by the window and when the traffic in and out of the station evened he asked the barman to watch his pint and jogged across the road.

There had been one open visit, one opportunity to hold his son in nine months, and that had passed with a kind of apologetic awkwardness, the boy taciturn perhaps because of the screw sitting there all eyes and ears, or maybe because he'd decided, in the long hours of lockdown, to try holding a grudge for a change.

So it had been a while. And there was no guarantee that there would be any contact now, awkward or otherwise, with all that had gone between them, with the courtroom betrayal, and the drink, and the fact that he'd grown way up and all behind Tony's back . . .

He was standing at the door of the station with his bag on the ground beside him, wearing his court date clothes. Tony saw it now: the courtroom, the polished wood of the row ahead that he'd gripped when the judge had called him to speak, the black and white checked shirt . . . Funny how you forget shit, even when it's something like that, even when it involves your own baby.

Ryan tried a smile when he spotted his father, in fairness to him.

Tony pulled the hooded jacket out from under his coat and held it out.

'Thanks, Dad.'

'No bother. How are you, boy?'

A shrug.

'How was the . . .' Tony started, and then, by dint of that shot of whiskey, broke off and found a lump in his throat and reached out and pulled his son into an embrace, caught the back of his neck and pressed his head onto his shoulder and held on until he felt him exhale, until the rigidity across his back and down his arms melted into brief, beautiful amnesty.

He held Ryan then at arm's length, gritted his teeth and said, 'You've grown again, I'd swear.'

The boy smiled in bitter defeat. He looked over his father's shoulder and said, 'You've been drinking.'

'Only a splash. Only coz you're home. It's a celebration, isn't it? I've a pint sitting across the road; come on over, I'll get you one. Bet you were mad for one, weren't you?'

'But you're not supposed to be. I thought.'

Tony swung into step beside his son, one arm around his shoulder, and said, 'It's all under control now, though. No difference anymore between me and the next man,' and they walked together towards the entrance, back in the direction of his pint, towards an interlude in which Tony swore there'd be no thinking about J.P., none at all about Duane, not while this harmony lasted.

Homecoming

Joseph wants to cart me over to his gaff the night I come home and I'm all for it, because my dad's half cut and it's weird to see him like that after he's been dry so long. In fairness, I'm half cut too. Two pints and my knees are going like the Shaky Bridge. We leave my dad nodding in the blue glow of the telly and we swing by the bottom of Karine's road to pick her up.

I get out of the car when I see her approaching.

Nine months. She's more beautiful than she was when I left her. She's in college now so maybe that's it. She's eighteen. She's a grown-up. I dunno, she's just delicious. And I get weirdly shy, and it's as if we have to start all over again because I feel like a stranger in front of her.

'Hey girl.'

She slams into me and puts her arms around my neck and presses her head against my shoulder. I put my arms around her waist and fold over enough to bury my head against her neck, and after a few minutes she pulls away and looks up at me, and places a silk soft hand either side of my face and I kiss her, and she opens her mouth to me, and I'm so relieved I think I could cry.

'You can breathe now,' she whispers.

We go back to Joseph's. He's only just broken up with his ould doll, so the house is kind of scanty. He's got some grass and a box of Corona in the fridge. I sit on the couch, and Karine sits beside me with her legs over mine, and we listen to him blether on about his new band, and how my god-daughter's doing, and what's been on telly, and what albums have been out and on and on and on and you'd think I'd be bored off my nut but you'd be wrong. Spend nine months inside and you come out just starved for your mates, for the banter.

For your girlfriend.

It's kind of coming up to it and I don't know what to do.

In the end Joseph very mildly says he's going to hit the hay and that if we want to stay over that's grand, there's a duvet on the bed in the second bedroom.

I go all shy again. We kind of hang around for fifteen minutes after Joseph goes to bed, talking around it, and then I say, 'D'you want to stay here, like?' and she shrugs; she's shy too. So I take her hand and lead her up to the second bedroom and we sit on the bed.

There's nothing in the way of mood lighting up here; there's the overhead or the dim glow of the city outside the curtains. I move against her until she lies back and she hooks her hands around my neck and brings me with her. The bulb's like a million watts and the room is practically bare. It's not too far off a cell, I guess.

So we do it, eventually. It takes ages because we're both kind of waiting to see where the other leads; I only want to do what she seems to want me to do, and she's very quiet and very timid, and so we get undressed in fits and starts, and I've still got my jeans on when we get under the covers. All the way through I'm thinking she'll stop me and tell me she doesn't want this now that I've done time; I'm so scared I'm fingering her like I'm trying to pull a hair out of a bowl of soup.

And it's the strangest thing. Like it's probably the worst fuck we ever had because we're both so anxious, but at the same time it's the best feeling in the world, better than the first time even. Despite the pure awkwardness she's so wet I slide right in and pretty much come straight away. It's a mixture of having a nine-month horn and being overwhelmed with relief. She doesn't mind.

Once I've come it's immediately better. Like there's a weight off. She snuggles onto my chest and doesn't ask for tissue or a T-shirt or anything. I get used to the air in my lungs and she talks to me till I'm ready to go again.

17

Dan Kane might as well have carried him out of the prison on his shoulders. The day after he'd come home, Ryan had contacted him, nervous as fuck, really, coz the man might have thought he was tainted or something now, who knew? But Dan had been even more pleased to see him than his father was, and that was saying something. It was nice to get a welcome home. Blew Ryan's mind, if he was honest.

On the second night of freedom Dan brought him out to dinner. It seemed a rather formal gesture, the mere notion of it pompous and off-putting, but once they were there it was grand. Dan had lumped for a bistro filled with large, loud groups. There was nothing out of place about the pair of them. Ryan wore a T-shirt and a new pair of jeans. He had grown, only an inch or so, but enough to air his ankles in his pre-prison clothes. Funny really; he would have sworn he'd shrunk in there, hunched down to maybe half the size he should have been, homunculus to his own sentence.

Dan said, 'Order anything you want, boy. Order the fucking lot if you like.'

Ryan grinned and Dan said, 'I mean that. You did nine months for me, little man.'

'What else was I gonna do, boy?'

'Lot of things you could have done and didn't; you're a fucking lion, d'you know that? Do you drink red? I'm getting a bottle. Have the steak, for fuck's sake.'

Ryan ordered lasagne and went through it like a chainsaw through chopsticks. He'd been ravenous since he'd left St Pat's. When Fiona had collected him she'd brought him for a Big

Mac and a milkshake, which he'd been hanging for all week. When he arrived home, he'd had a couple of pints with his father that left him vexingly woozy, eaten three Tayto sandwiches and a jar of pesto, washed that down with a bottle of Coke and then almost gawked the lot out the back door. Hunger had been one prison universal; he ate everything he was given, but there was never enough. He'd thought the liberty to make a pig of himself might take some getting used to. He was wrong. Wrong and famished.

'Yeah, yeah, put it away,' said Dan. 'You'll hit my age and suddenly everything over a ham sandwich will give you a paunch.'

Ryan sat back and rubbed his belly.

'It's the odd time I remember you're only a cub,' smirked Dan.

'It's just nice to get a bit of decent grub, is all.'

Dan leaned back, arms folded, and smiled.

'So,' he said. 'How bad was it?'

Around them the hubbub continued. Birthday shout-outs slapped the air; cakes went past, sparkling; girls tugging at ambitious hemlines trooped to the toilet in twos and threes; ould fellas, their faces wrinkled with mirth, howled.

'Worse than I thought it'd be,' Ryan said. 'And I thought it was gonna be hell.'

He hadn't said this to his father when he'd been asked. He'd said, *It was grand, Dad*, or *It was doable, like, you keep your head down*. Joseph, on the doorstep as soon as Ryan had crossed it, had pried but Ryan had pleaded with him to change the subject; he wasn't ready for stories, his thoughts were fucked as far as the rafters.

'I was there myself,' said Dan. 'Just before the millennium. I did three months for nicking a car. It was shit then; I can't imagine it's changed much since the nineties.'

'I don't think it's changed since the 1890s.'

'So what was so bad? The other fellas? The screws? The boredom?'

'Everything. The whole fucking lot.'

The screws had placed him first night in one of the committal cells. He'd stood waiting for the sound of the door slamming shut behind him, expecting some significant, gut-wrenching crash. It was quieter than he'd predicted and then he stood wondering if that was it, and if he shouldn't holler out at them to do it again, because he hadn't felt it hard enough the first time. He didn't cop right away but realised eventually that he was playing out the echo in his head. The door shut behind him. And shut behind him again. It looped and looped and he was sitting on the bed staring at the wall with his hands in his pockets, retching with the bleak and absolute scale of it.

The screw who processed him in the morning had asked, 'Did you phone home?'

Ryan hadn't been given the option.

'You could have,' the screw had shrugged. 'You probably should have. Called your mam at least.'

The seventeen-year-olds had been kept separate from the older lads and the screw had said he was lucky. There were only twenty-one other seventeen-year-olds in there with him. No overcrowding in their wing, separate facilities, spoiled little bastards.

The first month they'd had him on lockdown for, they said, his own protection. He was only a couple of days clear of that when one of the Dubs had volunteered to cut his throat. Ryan had told him to just fucking try it. Back on lockdown. Three months in, and back on the wing, he'd realised that he'd done only a third of his time, and the enormity had crushed him. You didn't tell them if you were feeling in any way down, whether it was because you'd stubbed your toe or wanted to hang yourself – you just fucking didn't, not in a fit, you kept your mouth shut because you knew what was waiting for you otherwise. One morning had come around when he just couldn't get out of bed. The screws had pulled him out, dragged him to the observation cell, stripped him and left him there.

How do you tell your dad something like that?

The other prisoners were cretinous or vicious or in most cases, both. When he was on the wing he hung around with a couple of lads from Waterford. One of them was due to hit eighteen and would be transferred down to Cork, and Ryan assumed he was looking for influence to bring in there with him; Ryan being banged up for possession with intent was, yer manno hoped, a bankable connection. Ryan had little time for either of them, and less time for the Dublin jackeens, and though Dan had various connections in the capital he didn't wish to find where to plant an affiliation. The Dubs spent most of the time throwing shapes and attempting to kill one another. Ryan was too busy gasping for air to want in on that.

Now, back in the real world, Dan said, 'It's no joke, I know that.'

'It's grand.'

'We both know it's not. Shit like that you don't forget in a hurry. That's a burden you carried for me.'

'Well look . . . It's over now.'

Dan grimaced. 'Hard to say this to you now, Ryan, but it's not over until you get your head around it. It stays with you. You'll think of it when you're meant to be doing anything but thinking of it. That's what the system's for – to break you down. And it works. Believe me.'

A girl, maybe Ryan's age, maybe a bit older, came in from the smoking area. She was wearing a royal-blue dress that wrapped around her fleshy thighs and barely covered her arse. She smiled at him, and he felt an urge to jump up, follow that smile to the back of the restaurant and convince her to cross her ankles behind his waist. He supposed if you've been surrounded by nothing but smelly, dopey fellas for nine months it whet your appetite for the ould dolls.

'I'm just glad to be home,' he told Dan, who leaned forward.

'I'm just saying to you, little man, the methods they use inside are designed to control you even after you get out. They want to fuck you. They want to fuck you so hard you forget what it was like to live without a cock up your arse. Don't let them take your autonomy from you. Don't bury Pat's. Because this won't be the last time the Law will look to lube you up and remembering how they work is the first step to fighting them off.'

He sat back again, sucked his teeth and sighed.

'This is only the start of it, little man.'

Joseph had broken up with his girlfriend and she'd gone home to her mam and dad with their baby daughter and left him in need of a housemate. On Dan's promise of more lucrative employment, Ryan volunteered, so only a week after coming home he was out of there again, hobo's kerchief and all.

Tony went over for an ineffectual root around.

'I didn't think you'd leave again so soon,' he mumbled and Ryan, halfway in behind the television with the Xbox cable bunched in his fist, matched the wounded tone and said, 'I'm eighteen, Dad.'

'Not for a couple of months you're not.'

Ryan came out from behind the telly and concentrated on pointing the remote at the screen.

'So much shit you don't know yet,' Tony said.

'So much shit I do, as well. I've been to prison for fuck's sake.'

'You were too young for that, too.'

Ryan could have turned to face his father. What harm? Accept the hint and stare him down. Instead he put the remote on the couch and hunted around for something that wasn't there.

'You're still only a kid.'

'I'm not.'

'You should be at home.'

Ryan pulled out the couch and looked behind it.

'I don't want to see you making any more stupid mistakes, Rocky.'

Ryan sank to his haunches and rested his head against the back of the couch, giving himself the chance to exhale, to close his fists, to screw up his eyes.

Are you going back to school, boy?

Ryan wasn't. Not in twenty fits. Where would he be going at almost eighteen? Back into another fucking uniform to sit under the gaze of another fucking moron who knew nothing about anything? It was all bollocks anyway. They'd said he could do school in St Pat's and there was nothing even like a fucking school up there: arts and fucking crafts and fucking cooking, what good was that to anyone? He'd learned more sitting on his arse staring at the four walls. Some of the lads he'd been in with couldn't count to twenty without taking off their socks. Learning? No fucking learning in there, unless you were learning how to watch your back or how to get out of a fucking headlock.

So if he went back to school now, at almost eighteen, back into fifth year with all the sixteen-year-olds as his girlfriend danced through university, yeah, well, he'd find himself on the scrapheap before long, wouldn't he?

Oh Karine, where's your boyfriend tonight?

He couldn't come out, girl, he had homework to do.

Not a fucking hope. If he was old enough to throw in a padded cell, he was old enough to make his own way.

What could they teach him anyway? The country was fucked. If he took the straight decision it would be between the airport and the dole queue.

What hadn't they fucking taught him already? How to be fucking blind and deaf, how to apply the rules that suited them, how to deal with awkward problems: lock them the fuck away. *Oh, having trouble with your dad, Ryan? Having trouble with this jackeen scrote? Having trouble with your fucking brain, tangled up in thoughts that your girlfriend, the one fucking good thing in this whole fucking world, is out there finding a better man to fuck? Ah, we have solutions for you, boy.* Clang. Another fucking door locks behind you.

Fuck the lot of them.

Dan Kane's main man was nicknamed Shakespeare, because he was as verbose a thug as you could find. His real name was Shane O'Sullivan, though it had taken Ryan two and a half years of dealing with him to figure that out. He was absurdly wiry for an enforcer; his success stemmed from the fact that there was barely enough of him to punch back. Ryan had heard it intimated that Dan Kane kept him in a spaghetti jar.

The first time Ryan had met him, it was because the order he'd placed with his usual contact was too big to proceed without notice. Shakespeare had come to investigate. Ryan was fourteen, pre-Karine, quick-tempered and unafraid to pay the price for it. Shakespeare hadn't looked very amused but had apparently reported back that the whole thing was quite the hoot. Kane hadn't been looking for a protégé but the opportunity to take one had tickled him too much to turn down.

And of course there were parallels. Dan Kane had had a shit time with his own father. Dan Kane had been to St Pat's.

Shakespeare wouldn't tell you whether or not he'd been inside. He liked puns and proverbs, but he was as blank a professional as the archetype; you worked with Shakespeare, never with Shane.

Ryan was going on a job with him.

He hadn't received all of the details and Shakespeare certainly had no mind for filling him in. Dan had nominated him as backup for a recovery operation – some waster who owed a few bob and had a deeper mouth than pockets. This was learning. This was a practical.

Shakespeare picked him up at the end of Ryan's new road. There had been frost in the morning but now it was foggy and silent. Headlamps moved in the mist like the lanterns of the lost. The stereo played a techno set so tight as to be practically featureless. It was headphone music. Relegated to the background, its rhythm was unsettling and relentless.

'How are you in a scrap?' Shakespeare asked.

Ryan shrugged. 'I can handle myself, like.'

'And how are you initiating a scrap?'

'What d'you mean, boy?'

Shakespeare frowned. He had a precise goatee, a slender nose and narrow eyes; his face sharpened into a sparse sketch of geometric shapes.

'You can handle yourself, grand, but can you start aggro when you have to?'

'I suppose so.'

'You suppose so?'

'It's not something I do all that often. I don't go around raking up shit, like.'

'And usually I'd say life's too short but sometimes you've got to throw down, d'you know what I mean? Our troublemaker today isn't going to flake into you, but nor are they going to listen to reason. If I said, *Here, slap this cunt*, would you do it?'

They stopped at traffic lights. Ryan fixed on the red glow and said, 'Yeah. I would.'

'You're pure obedient, aren't you? You'd have made a great guard. Can you drive yet?'

'Yeah.'

'Have you a car?'

'Not yet.'

'Have you your licence?'

'Not yet.'

'I'd stick that on the To Do list if I were you,' said Shakespeare.

He followed Shakespeare's instructions with the same robotic deference that had inspired the enforcer to sneer about a vocation in An Garda Síochána; what else could he do?

He did the knocking, Shakespeare barged in. He pulled the curtains and checked the gaff for hangers-on, Shakespeare kicked his target down the darkened hallway. He found their quarry's phone and purse, Shakespeare hissed and grumbled as she expelled choked promises for deaf ears.

'C'mere!' Shakespeare snapped, and Ryan came into the hallway just as Shakespeare smashed the woman's forehead off the kitchen door sill.

'Show me that purse.'

Ryan handed it over and Shakespeare, one runner jammed over the woman's right wrist, rifled through it, pulling out cards and receipts. A couple of twenty euro notes fluttered to the floor.

Shakespeare flicked a small photo in front of her nose and said, 'What age is the small wan? Four? Five? Nearly time to collect her,

I suppose,' and Ryan's eyes flickered onto the crying debtor, a dumpy girl with a weak chin and a belly halved by an elasticated waist, whose curls plastered to the skin under her eyes, whose top lip was split and bleeding.

'I don't understand people who drag their kids into this shit,' said Shakespeare. 'You'd think if your fella was snapping tempers all over the town you'd send the child to live with someone a bit more organised. You think you wouldn't expose your smallies to your failings. One thing that drives me mental, like.'

He opened the door under the stairs, slapping it off the debtor's head.

'I'm going for a slash,' he said. 'Don't let her get up.'

His back to the wall, Ryan slipped into the living room. He shut his eyes tight and swallowed, opened them again and caught snapshots of a life scattered around him. An orange striped mug on the coffee table, the TV tuned to a chat show in which a procession of slobs tried to snarl tears out of each other, on the mantel a photograph of a doleful tot in a roomy blue and grey school uniform. The smell of fresh toast, wafting from the kitchen.

All against the steady stream of Shakespeare's piss hitting the bowl.

Ryan rolled around, forehead to the plaster.

This woman's partner could owe Dan thousands. He could have stolen from him. She could have threatened to involve the guards; they were likely to do that, he supposed, the ould dolls.

'Fucking disgusting,' Shakespeare said.

Ryan stood back into the hall. Shakespeare was in the doorway to the toilet, curling his lip.

'Smells like a wino's drawers in here. Jesus Christ, it wouldn't kill you to sluice the place out once in a fucking blue one.'

She whimpered. Shakespeare grabbed her hair at the back of the neck, dragged her onto her knees and pulled her into the bathroom.

'Lookit! Fucking bog roll and everything still in the bowl. You don't even flush, you scab.'

Louder tears now, then a scream. Ryan caught a grunt in his chest.

'Are you just going to fucking leave it there?'

'Please,' she said. 'Oh God, please . . .'

'Pick it up. Go on.'

Ryan had assumed a male target and had prepped for fists swung. Instead Shakespeare had settled for intimidating the sinner's woman, not as a consolation prize, but because the task didn't call for finesse. Perhaps Shakespeare would have claimed its ugliness was the mark of any entry-level mission. Didn't matter. It was a jolt no matter how Ryan defended it.

He sat on the stairs, facing the front door, his head in his hands.

'Put it to your nose and take a good sniff and tell me, girl, that that's any way to keep a house.'

The woman retched, and Ryan echoed her.

If there was one thing Joseph O'Donnell loved, outside of starting shouting matches with political conservatives in old-man pubs, it was launching short-lived bands. When Ryan arrived back there were three other blokes sprawling with his cousin in the living room, guitars abandoned in corners to make room for the migration of a couple of chunky joints.

'Cusack Cusack Cusack, do you have anything nice for me?'

'I might do,' Ryan said. He'd put aside an eighth for Joseph. He wasn't keen on flashing it about. Fuck knows who any of these dudes were, and open season on dealers lasted the whole twelve months with double points on bank holiday weekends. Joseph acknowledged his glare, tutted, and made his way out into the hall. 'They're all sound,' he said, 'honest to fuck. I know you're a bit . . . y'know.'

'You know the way the "sound" ones get once they get wind of a dealer. There'd be girlfriends less possessive.'

'Like you'd fucking know. You're only one step up from "virgin".'

Ryan winced and Joseph took it as confirmation.

The lads were watching *Family Guy* clips on Joseph's laptop.

Ryan sat on the armrest of the couch and was introduced – 'This is Darragh, this is Graham, this is Barry, we call him Bobo, don't ask' – but he'd left his mind back with Dan Kane, who'd been glib and jovial about the mission and who'd peeled Ryan's reluctance from his vacant answers and labelled it a temporary blip.

'It's a lesson, little man. You've got to be tough. If you're a soft touch in this game you'll get steamrollered, and you can't call the cops when you're shafted, can you?'

What the fuck was the game? The playing field expanded with every step he took; he was always at the middle of it.

Dan Kane had caught his shoulder and laughed and given him a handy hundred quid.

A hundred quid, you silly panicking fuck, and just for sitting on the stairs with the gawks while Shakespeare made a cokehead suck his piss from a handful of bog roll.

A joke went around his new front room, and he missed it. Bobo reached for the laptop and said, 'This one's my favourite,' and there was Peter Griffin, standing in the doorway of a young fella's bedroom, trying to talk to him about bullying, losing the rag altogether with the brat and lashing out with trademark brutality. The lads howled.

What was it, ten seconds? If that? Ten fucking seconds of a cartoon man punching a cartoon kid, and it stretched into a wound.

Ryan gave the congregation a swift thumbs-up and went to his bedroom.

A cartoon man beat up a cartoon boy. One pile of pixels laid into another. Same thing as blasting through bots on the Xbox, and you didn't see Ryan Cusack falling to pieces over virtual casualties for the sake of a couple of overwound heartstrings. Nor should you see him seizing the corners of his mattress and gulping back the sniffles over something as fucking stupid as seeing Peter Griffin fly into a rage.

Ryan pulled out his own stash, found the book he'd requisitioned for the task – one of Joseph's, a hardback boasting a hundred essential chords – and rolled a spliff. He sparked it, opened the window and leant against the sill staring into the silver evening fog; he breathed deep, willing the thoughts drowned, but they persisted. Of course they did. The weight of his psychosis dwarfed a piddling fucking eighth.

As contrite as Tony was there was history in his fists and a thirst on him that couldn't be quelled by God or son. Peter Griffin had straddled that cartoon boy and knocked a string of pucks into his jaw; that's the position you needed to be in to be broken, prone on the floor while a row of knuckles knocked red-flecked spit out of the side of your mouth and onto the carpet beside you. Prone again while the screws barged into your cell for your own fucking good, took an arm each and dragged when the enforced crouch failed your legs, three of them, big fucking men weren't they, cutting every stitch off you if you so much as kicked out, and sure why wouldn't you? Of course you'd kick out, for fuck's sake, mechanically if anything, out of fear and shame and what pride you had left.

Who didn't like a good fight now and again? Who didn't like to stretch their muscles and throw their body into the fray? It made you feel alive, wasn't that it? Ah, just the job. Go beat up some young mammy somewhere because you could do with the exercise and after all, she owes you a few bob.

You had to get off on it. They all got off on it. That's why your shelves were full of *Call of Duty* games and box sets of *The Sopranos*. That's why you could crowd around picking out your favourite bits from *Family Guy*, because you hadn't been fucked irrevocably by shit that isn't even supposed to upset you.

Karine was at home finishing an essay. He was of the conviction that she could have finished her essay just as easily in his gaff, but he'd let it slide. She had stayed with him nearly every other night this week, and they were making up for lost time. He couldn't get enough of her. Shoulders, breasts, navel, cunt. Everything else too: laugh, smile, voice, breath. Funny thing then that he hadn't yet given it to her hard. When they'd done it in the past couple of weeks it had been slow and gentle. He'd wanted to savour it, fuck her like a princess should be fucked. Now he worried that his laziness had been born of anxiety, not generosity.

The spark of a brief connection was enough to freak him out. He grabbed his laptop, opened PornHub, and went for everything on the front page: threesomes, cumshots, gangbangs, anal, whatever. The fellas had donkey dicks and dead eyes; the girls glared. Any other day there would have been a ton of shit he would have gotten into, and here he was after nine months of celibacy with barely a semi for the lot of them. Every pounded ass, every rough hand grasping blonde extensions, every 'bitch' and 'whore' was a weight on his chest. He opened his jeans and coaxed a hard-on but he couldn't come, didn't know why either, except that everything looked like humiliation, everything looked like plunder.

In the end he snapped the laptop shut and lay staring at the ceiling. How he managed to start crying with his dick still in his hand he didn't know, but there you go.

This was only the start of it.

He felt a lot better in the morning. Miles better. Fucktons. Dan phoned and told him to come over for a slice of a delivery. The coke had been cut and divided into grams, and Dan was generous with a payment plan. 'Get shot of it and pay me then,' he said. 'No rush. Don't I know you're good for it?'

That evening he and Karine went down to the local, The Relic, which was, converse to its name, one of the lively pubs his dad chose not to frequent. She, eighteen since November, went in ahead of him, so by the time he reached the table she'd procured him a pint and herself a vodka and Coke.

'Told you you'd come in handy one day,' he said, and she replied with tart grace, 'Fuck off.'

It was Friday night and he was two weeks out of St Pat's. Karine was all dolled up in a white dress and towering sequinned heels, smoky eyes, pale pink lips. Tresses of her hair, styled into loose curls, fell over her shoulders; he teased one around his first finger and said, 'You look so fucking hot.'

'I know that.'

'Grand so. How do I look?'

'Tall! When did you get so tall, like? I'm wearing five-inch heels and you're still all the ways up there.'

'I'm five eleven, Karine, not the BF fucking G.'

'You couldn't be,' she mused. 'Coz I'm five five.'

'You are in your shit five five.'

'My mam's five five and I'm the height of my mam.'

'Your mam's a munchkin.'

'Yeah well at least I have a mam.'

He choked on his pint, swallowed, coughed, wiped his mouth and then his eyes.

'You're some bitch, D'Arcy.'

She bit down on her smile and when he'd recovered she rested her head on his chest; he put an arm around her and kissed her forehead, and she said, 'I can hear your heart.'

'How's it sound?'

'Steady.'

The plan was to have Joseph and his sometime band meet them in a couple of hours, do some shots, neck some pills, and go into town to meet Karine's posse. For the time being they shared a stillness. The staff played R&B over the PA system for a sparse crowd too sober to sway. Karine sat up and stretched, and checked his shirt for the powdered residue of her affection.

He thought about asking her to set aside her plans for the night and head back to bed with him, though he knew what the answer would be. Being allowed into nightclubs was a novelty to her, three months legal and only out of school. He felt a twinge for the partying he'd already missed.

'Karine?'

'What?' She was playing with her curls, fluffing them carefully before letting them tumble through her fingers.

'Can I tell you something?'

'Only if it follows "You're amazing and I love you."'

Pfft. 'Obviously.'

'Go on so.'

'When you're inside,' he said, 'you feel like your life is over. Like even though you know you're only doing so many months or whatever, it stretches out beyond all logic, and you're so smothered by all that you forget what's going on outside. And I missed stuff for you, y'know? Birthday and Christmas and your Leaving and your Debs. I've been an asshole. I know it, like. I'll make it up to you.'

She touched his arm. 'Ryan . . .'

'Y'know, Dan thanked me for it. Doing the time for him. But while I was doing time for Dan you were out here waiting for me and I reckon that deserves thanks too.'

'That's just silly,' she said. 'Let's just get on with living, like. Gimme a tenner; I'll get a couple more drinks.'

He watched her walk to the bar on her killer heels and let his eyes travel from her calves to her thighs and then over the curve of her arse, running into the small of her back . . . The same way, he thought with a turn, that he'd been looking at the girl in the restaurant, except this time it was right that he wanted to slide his hands between her legs, push out her thighs.

He wasn't the only one. At the bar, a fella walking past grabbed a handful of her arse, and she started and yelped. The guy put his arm around her waist and that was as much as Ryan saw before he landed over beside them, going, 'Ah, what the fuck?'

It was a fella they'd gone to school with, a bloke Ryan had barely seen since. Niall Something. Coen? Vaughan. One of the hurlers. One of the sort that was never found hiding behind the fence at the back of the pitch, so stoned he could barely stand up.

'Fuck me,' said Niall Vaughan. 'Is that Ryan Cusack?'

'Is that my girlfriend's arse in your hand?'

'When did they let you out?' Vaughan asked.

'Fuck off and mind your own business.'

'Everyone was talking about it, is all. Y'know, you look at your Leaving Cert class and you remember who's missing and why.'

'You'd want to say sorry to Karine,' Ryan said, stepping right up to Vaughan, chest to chest, and in fairness, the other didn't back away. There was a grin dancing on his face.

'Karine doesn't mind,' he said.

'Karine does,' snapped Karine.

'Oh God, sorry I grabbed your arse, your ladyship.'

Karine took her vodka from the bar counter, gestured towards Ryan's pint, and tugged at his arm. Ryan didn't move.

'You don't sound very fucking sorry,' he said.

Vaughan rolled his eyes. 'Jesus Christ, get over yourself.'

'Ryan,' Karine whinged, 'come *on*.'

'Come on, come on!' Vaughan echoed, pressing his hands together.

'I'm not convinced he's that bothered about being called on his bullshit,' Ryan said.

'Yeah, he's drunk? Can we leave it please?'

'I'm not drunk,' said Vaughan. 'I didn't know you were back together, did I? Y'know, grabbing your ex's arse shouldn't bother you.'

'She's not my ex,' Ryan said, moving close enough that he could snarl into Vaughan's ear. 'And if you touch her again I'll take you apart, yeah?'

'Sorry, Mr Breaking fucking Bad. Far be it from me to go back for seconds with you gawping at me. She's all yours.'

'Ryan!' snapped Karine. 'Come. On!'

Ryan frowned. 'What d'you mean, go back for seconds?'

'Seconds of her arse, like. Seconds of the rest of her.'

'What's he on about, Karine?'

'He's pissed and he's disgusting,' she said. 'Pick up your pint and get back to the table. Now.'

Niall Vaughan mimed a cracking whip.

'Ryan, honestly, if you're going to spend any more of tonight spatting with clowns . . .'

'Ah, Karine,' said Vaughan. 'Ah now. That's not nice.'

'Dickhead,' she muttered, turning away.

Ryan looked back at Vaughan, who pushed his bottom lip out.

'You don't have to be so aggressive, like,' he said. 'Or is that what happens in there? No, seriously? Like after a few dozen rapes in the shower?'

Ryan said, 'Whatever problem you have, d'you wanna take it outside?'

Vaughan held up his hands. 'Ah no. No, I couldn't do that to you.'

'Yeah,' said Ryan. 'I didn't think so.'

When he turned around Vaughan said, 'Not after I fucked your girlfriend.'

Ryan turned back.

'What'd you say to me?'

'I fucked your girlfriend. After the Debs. In fairness, boy, she was in fucking heat. If it hadn't been me it would have been someone else.'

Ryan would have punched him. Not a bother; he would have levelled the fucker. What contest? The lad was barely able to stand up straight and he was asking for it, howling for it, taking out billboards up and down the motorway advertising his need for it.

But he wasn't lying. Ryan Cusack stared at his girlfriend of three years and the look on her face, her glistening eyes and her parted lips, told him that this was the rawest truth he was ever likely to hear.

On Cheating

She's sitting on the bed, mascara smudged under her eyes, and I stand as far away from her as I can get, over by the door, my hand hovering onto the handle every so often as instinct tells me to get away, get the fuck out, just run, boy, keep running. I have to make myself stay. Every molecule is screaming against me being this close to her and it's a feeling so alien I've already thrown up. I just can't believe it, like. I can't fucking believe it. I just . . .

She's crying and I'm crying.

'C'mere,' she implores, for the seventh or eighth time.

I shake my head. I can't look at her. 'No,' I say. I fix on the corner of the ceiling. My head is sliding left to right. I'm like Churchill the fucking dog.

She's sniffing. My head feels like it's been scooped hollow. Then the next minute it feels like my brain's been jammed up right behind my eyeballs. Then the next it feels like the brain's dripping down my throat and choking me.

You've no idea. You've just no idea. Like that's it. I'm done. I'm finished.

'Ryan, please, just talk to me.'

She's already spilled her side of the story. It's the end of August, I'm away in prison, she's got her Debs coming up, yer man asks her, her mam and dad and sisters tell her she'll regret it someday if she doesn't accept, she remembers what a prick I am for leaving her, she drinks the bar dry and he fucks her in the car park. There you go. I lost my girlfriend up the side of a fucking Ford Focus.

'You have no idea what I went through,' she blubs.

'You, girl? You? What about me? All I fucking had in there was

the knowing I'd come home to you and you were spending your nights out whoring with fucking Niall fucking Vaughan!'

'You did come home to me, Ryan! I'm still here for you!'

'No. No you're not.'

'I am! One mistake, for God's sake. And where were you? In prison! You weren't thinking about me when you got yourself caught with someone else's cocaine, were you?'

'It's my fault, is it?'

'It's both our faults! Ryan, for fuck's sake. I love you.'

I cough out a laugh and drag my hand across my eyes.

'I do, Ryan.'

'No, you fucking don't.'

'I do. Oh for God's sake, I do!'

I'm fucking proper bawling now and I can't get the words out at all. Jesus fucking Christ. Jesus fucking Christ. I wheel around and kick the wall. I kick it again, and again, and knock my head off the plaster and she jumps up and hugs my back. I don't even push her away. I'm too exhausted. I don't know what I am.

A few minutes later I get the words out: 'Did he come inside you?'

I shake her off and she sits back on the bed and folds up like a poked slug.

'Did he, Karine?'

'He wore a condom, if that's what you mean.'

'How would you know if you were that fucking drunk?'

'Coz I made sure. Fuck you, Ryan. Because he wasn't you.'

'Did you go down on him?'

'Of course I didn't.'

'Why "of course you didn't," Karine? I'd have said up to two hours ago that of course you wouldn't cheat on me and here we fucking are.'

She puts her head in her hands. 'I didn't go down on him. I swear. It was just an ugly stupid fuck in a fucking car park.'

'Did you come?'

She says no and I really want to believe her. If the Lord God appeared right now and said, 'Here, Cusack, you can have either the promise of eternal life or the promise that your girlfriend didn't show her O-face to Niall Vaughan,' I'd take the second with both fucking hands.

So we sleep somehow. Both in our clothes, beside each other on the bed, fucking bate. And when we wake up, she starts kissing me, and saying sorry, and touching me and I'm getting hard despite myself and there's this sudden forked road and a signpost telling me if I don't fuck Karine D'Arcy right now I'll never fuck her again.

So I do. I have to. I can't lose her. I'm not able. I hold her down and fuck her like I'm exorcising her. An ugly fuck. That's how she wants it, isn't it?

And after I come I roll over and listen to her crying again, until I can't stand it anymore. I get up and go for a slash and when I come back to bed she looks at me all red-eyed and says, 'That's how it is now, is it? That's just how we're going to fuck from here on in?' and I can't answer her. I lie on my side with my back to her and stare instead at the fucking floor.

18

'You don't have the money to take this to a courtroom. You'll drag it out, you'll hurt everyone, and you know you'll fail well before the end. So let's be sensible and settle this now. For God's sake, isn't that the only thing we can do?'

Georgie was sitting on the couch in the living room of the CAIL centre. Flanking her, William and Clover Tobin. Across from her, elbows on his knees and staring at the floor, was David. His mother, a glacial thing in a thin cardigan, sat on the armrest of his chair, rubbing his back. Opposite and to Georgie's left sat David's father, Patrick Coughlan, CEO-turned-cultist. He had plump jowls so clean-shaven they seemed artificial. He looked like a melted bucket.

In Georgie's arms slept Harmony Faye Fitzsimons. Born on a Monday afternoon with a student midwife holding her mother's hand in her father's stead, she was, as all babies were, perfect. Her primitive demands invoked something similarly primal in her mother, but Georgie was careful not to indulge instinct. Though Clover said that Harmony should be breastfed and allowed to share the bed with her mother, Georgie chose bottles and a Moses basket. It had been ages since Georgie had done cocaine or touched a drop; being with child had proved a better deterrent than being with Christians. Still, the notion that she was contaminated by her past was a tough one to get shot of. Harmony was too beautiful to risk blemishing.

Patrick Coughlan sighed.

'This isn't how we wanted things to go either,' he said.

'How did you want things to go?' asked Georgie. 'Did you hope

David would find a paragon of virtue so tolerant she wouldn't be turned off by his drugging and gambling?'

'Well, I tell you what we didn't want. Him to impregnate an addict when he was supposed to be tackling his own demons.'

William delivered a wobbly interjection. 'Is this going to resolve anything? This mud-flinging? This is a place of mercy.'

'It's a place of bloody vice!' snapped Coughlan. 'I'd hoped your adherence to the gospel would be enough to direct David, and look what happens! This woman is a damned vagrant. How did you even accept such a person? I sent David to you, William, because I thought he would be protected. And instead you fed his weaknesses.'

'All we can do is ask for your forgiveness,' said William.

Georgie shifted the weight in her arms and leaned forwards. She'd cried all her tears, and was left with a dull headache and stained cheeks.

David kept his eyes on the floor. He had spoken only to confirm his father's assertion that this takeover was his wish. They were at the centre because they wanted to take Harmony with them, and their logic was watertight.

William and Clover were anxious about the idea of raising a child on their land. They explained that they couldn't provide structure but were too spineless to admit the fear that Georgie would drag them into ignominy with her once again. In David's bid for custody he had complained how Georgie introduced him to cocaine, which she'd procured and brought to the centre under pretext of conversion during a city break. William and Clover were upset, but more again, they were frightened. Their lakeside retreat had crumbled into a mess of responsibility and risk. Their notion of bringing the world together under the Jesus banner hinted now at effort without recompense, and they hated it.

'It's clearly in the baby's best interests to be with her father,' Coughlan said. 'We can support him. She'll be safe with us. What has she otherwise?'

'She has her mother,' Georgie said.

'A "mother". Why do women think that word alone is enough?

Why should my granddaughter suffer while her "mother" gets her act together? Grand, you're clean, whatever. That's no guarantee that you won't relapse.'

'David could relapse just as fast!'

'If he does, he has his family there to stick him back on the straight and narrow. If you relapse, who's here for you?'

'I'm not alone down here.'

William sighed and sat forward off his wife's silence.

'We're not set up for looking after a baby,' he said. 'I'm sixty-two, Georgie.'

'You wouldn't have to look after her,' Georgie cried. 'I'm just saying it's not as if I don't have support. You know. For if things . . . If things don't . . .' She stood and turned to face William. He looked away. 'Things will be fine, actually,' said Georgie. 'Why wouldn't they be?'

'We can't support you both, Georgie,' said Clover.

'I'm not asking for charity.'

Coughlan said, 'Then what are you going to do, ha? Move out? Get a job? Go to college?'

'Other women manage. I'm not the only single mother on the planet. I've been fine up to now, haven't I? I never starved.'

William said, 'Georgie, the state you were in when I found you, how much worse would that have been if you'd had a baby at home?'

Harmony Faye pursed her lips. Georgie crooked her first finger and stroked her cheek and the little mouth opened.

'I didn't though,' said Georgie. 'Did I? I was looking after myself.'

'And you were failing.'

'I've grown up since.'

'Have you?' asked William. 'Look, Georgie, I know your heart's in the right place—'

'I thought that was enough? Belief and good nature and all that shit, am I right?'

'For God's sake this isn't a game, Georgie. You were a prostitute! You could have been killed and you didn't care!'

Forced to listen to her saviour's well-intentioned treachery as the faces around them turned white, Georgie fixed her gaze on her daughter, her perfect face, the even features yet to display allegiance to one parent or another. There was nothing she could say. William stammered and David's mother gasped.

Georgie had not yet been saved. The baby had to be given up. David looked up at last with round eyes and lips pulled back. Georgie managed a tear. It slid down her face and hung on her jawline; when she cuddled Harmony the tear fell and landed on her cheek.

She tried for a while, chasing salvation in hard work, except it was hard work in rounds and circles, and it never got her anywhere. She arranged a cut of the profits from the farmers' markets in return for her tending shoots and weeding, so that she could put some money away for a training course. But what was she left with, only pennies? William told her not to worry about funds while she was at CAIL; her leaving was no longer a priority, now that the baby was safely away.

David had left her an address and phone number. Whenever she called he would run through Harmony's development as if he kept milestones noted on a pad by the phone. Should she wish, at any stage, to acknowledge his selfless hard work he was available for praise and appreciation. Should she wish to revisit their arrangement, he warned, she would have to get herself a house, a job and a lawyer.

William and Clover and her fellow spiritual halfmen continued as normal. They got as far as pitying Georgie, for pity was easy enough.

'I don't know how you could have done that to me,' Georgie bawled to William, after the community indicated they'd wring their hands for her behind turned backs.

'You forced my hand, Georgie. What else could I do?'

'Oh, I don't know. What would Jesus have done?'

'The very same thing,' William frowned. 'You'll see that someday.'

Georgie left CAIL nine months after they'd given her daughter away.

'Left', like it was some proud stand? No. 'Stole away', months later, like it was a last resort. She went through her stuff in the witching hour and plucked out what remained of her old life, which was sweet fuck all after William had tried shaming the devil out of her wardrobe. She stuffed her world into a stolen knapsack and slipped out the back door, clambered over the fence at the back of the vegetable gardens, and tripped through wet grass in the black night until she had room to skirt around and come back to the road. From there she trudged, the bottom of her dress wringing, a deserter from Christ's army.

The road was bordered with brambles. She pushed into the hedgerow and dragged her arm along the thorns, and after seven miles of penance she found a bus stop and sat on the other side of the wall propping it up until morning.

Was there a more miserable month than February? Was there a less welcoming time to return to the streets?

Once off the bus at Parnell Place, Georgie realised she had nowhere to go. Her escape had been fuelled on the assumption that some way would open up as soon as she arrived, but she left the bag on the ground by her feet, bunched her hair behind her head, looked out over the Lee and that was as much as she got.

She had accumulated enough to rent a cheap hotel room. The receptionist directed her to the nearest Internet cafe, which was full of Spanish students attempting to stave off the damp by flailing loudly at one another from computers placed inconvenient yards apart. Georgie searched for one-bedroom flats and calculated deposits.

She got a takeaway for dinner and felt sick afterwards. In her hotel room, she fought a losing battle with the air conditioning and made herself a cup of instant coffee that twitched in her veins for an hour afterwards.

At eight thirty she got a phone call.

'William said you'd run off.'

It was David. He was peevish.

'I'm back in the city,' Georgie said. 'I'm going to get my life together and I'm going to come for Harmony then.'

'You're going to get your life together with what, Georgie?'

'Something more concrete than prayer.'

'Yeah? Well, if you think you can battle with me using ill-gotten gains, you're mistaken.'

'Ill-gotten gains? What the hell are you talking about, David?'

'You know what I'm talking about.'

Quivering with the effort of indirect accusation, he berated her for vague intent as she sat on the hotel bed and cried.

'I never said I was going back to that, David. I've moved on. I'm only sorry that William Tobin didn't have the decency to see that and keep his stupid hippy mouth shut.'

'See, that's what's poisonous about you, Georgie. After all he did for you, you're insulting him. If it wasn't for William Tobin you'd probably be dead in a ditch somewhere.'

'If it wasn't for William Tobin I wouldn't have met you, you mean.'

'If you cared about Harmony you'd never have said that.'

'I meant it for you! *You* think it would have been best if you'd never met me. Your parents think it!'

'I accept my trials,' he said.

'You're turning into one of Them, David. Is that how you're going to raise my daughter? As a judgemental little prig?'

'Something tells me you won't be around to find out.'

She paid for two nights in the hotel and for two nights she lay awake and fancied ways out of the rut. One time she was passing out CVs and getting called for interviews. In the next vision she was awarded an emergency payment from the social welfare, enough to put down a deposit on a flat. Each dream slid with the encroaching midnight stupor into stark prophesies of straddling punters in the back seats of their cars, and Robbie O'Donovan was a shroud over it all.

She had tried to put his insinuated demise out of her head, she really had. It was difficult to draw up murder mysteries in the last trimester, and after that she'd been distracted, wholly, by David's invasion and conquest. Robbie's ghost hadn't followed her down to the West Cork lakeside. Now she was back in the city and his memory jabbed at her.

She left the hotel on the third morning.

Her sums were sound and they told her that if she chose another night in a rented bed she'd be cutting her newfound sovereignty short. She had no wish to rush back to William and Clover's awkward embrace and, really, what were the odds they'd even want her to? She'd burnt bridges in dashing off under moonlight. In the daytime this shore was inhospitable, but she was stuck here.

What she was about to do frightened her. She walked through the mist, the knapsack dragging on her shoulders and her dress hanging limp, and considered running away blindly, or going to the Gardaí with her hazy lead or even jumping off a bridge and into the river, where the water might make a balloon from her skirt and take her out to sea. Her feet pushed her forward. From the mist before her loomed the footbridge. She walked over it, tracing her fingers against the steel, and stopped halfway to stare downriver at the choking white and the city that rose from the murk in blocks and sharp angles. She could clamber onto the parapet and no one would see her. She could flutter below and no one would stop her. It was a fine day for drowning and a fine bridge for jumping from.

What rest would Robbie have then, if the only one around to remember him dashed instead to meet him?

Across the bridge, she stood at the door to the old brothel and raised her hand.

A beat, a deep breath, and she rapped on the door.

She had felt the same fluttering terror when she'd knocked at the man Tony's door, back before Harmony, when she was closer to a whole person. What an experience that had been. Anger and accusation welded together in punch-drunk avowal and a stern direction to take complaints to the liar Duane. And then for her little dealer to arrive down the stairs and act as buffer between the noxious allegation and his father's declarations! It might well have proved the weirdest day of Georgie's life, if she'd followed the lead back to Tara Duane's front door and demanded an explanation. As it was she got out of there and hurried back to William and Clover, flushed at having fallen for Duane's ploy and equally so at disturbing her dealer in his own home and seeing how young he really was. There with a daddy and baby pictures on the mantelpiece and toys scattered on the living-room floor. Domesticity wrapped around a boy she'd done lines with in the middle of the day.

There was no answer now from the old brothel door. She breathed.

She stood back and watched the windows, and on getting no glimpse of life walked around and tried the back gate. It was locked, but there was a foothold on the brickwork beside it, and the lakeside air had made her agile. She climbed.

There were plenty of bits in the back yard to assist her return to the top of the wall: builders' rubbish in the process of being reclaimed by the ivy, a wheelie bin on the other side of the gate. She was about to drop down to check the back door when she noticed a toplight left open on a first-floor window.

No doubt she could be seen, easily too, if anyone were to take this moment to gaze out of their bedroom window. She reminded herself that no burglar went around wearing maxi dresses. She'd look more like a granddaughter attempting to help out after the doddering dear left her keys on the dresser. She padded along the top of the wall and reached the window, grabbed the toplight and hauled herself onto the sill. The room had no curtains, and it was as bare now as it had been the day she'd been told of the ghost.

She lifted the skirt of her dress, tucked it around her legs, kneeled on the sill holding on to the toplight and reached inside to open the casement.

Maureen still lived here. The downstairs apartment was warm and messy; she had gone out, and Georgie estimated it wouldn't be for very long. She went to the top floor and to the sill on which she'd spotted Robbie's name. The writing implements were gone, the pages missing. The rooms on the two upper floors were completely bare.

She returned to the ground-floor apartment. There was a bedroom at the front of the house, and she stood in its doorway and thought about ransacking it for a slip of paper that was likely scrapped or burned. It might have been the dregs of Christian charity clinging to sinner skin or the fact that Georgie felt deeply stupid considering looting an older woman's nest, but she knew she wouldn't be tearing the place asunder. She looked into the bathroom, in case she'd find a horror message written in steam on the mirror, and then in the kitchen, where she drummed her nails on the breakfast bar.

What now, after engaging in some light breaking and entering for the memory of a missing swain?

Georgie pulled out the kitchen drawers. In the first, cutlery, string, scissors, candles, all in a heap. In the second, tea towels and a roll of kitchen paper.

In the third, a tangle of relics.

A couple of pens, a couple of notebooks with faded names on the pages. The old phone from the desk upstairs. A necklace. A foundation compact. Two lipsticks. An old business card, blank except for a mobile number and a busty silhouette. A scapular.

Georgie closed her fingers around the brown cloth. A lipstick, wound in its bands, dropped back into the drawer as she lifted it; she bunched the scapular in her fist, shut the drawer, and leaned against the breakfast bar with her hand held against her breastbone.

Robbie O'Donovan. Did you know him? He died here.

Georgie sat upstairs in the middle of the old brothel floor.

On the ground floor, Maureen moved about, clinking cups, rustling newspaper.

Outside, the fog had lifted from the Lee in time for the night to fall down upon it.

Georgie thought, *Did he come back for this?*

It was contentious in its absurdity, but when she spread it flat it made a kind of sense. She had pinned too much meaning to the scapular. She had complained about its loss. He was useless in almost every conceivable way, Robbie, but it would have been just like him to throw his weight into something as maudlin and pointless as recovering the bloody thing.

He died here.

He'd broken in. He'd arrived in the middle of the night and surprised Maureen, who had only just been installed by her wicked son, and she had called the gangster Phelan and he'd done away with Robbie because frightening his mother was a much bigger crime than stealing away a scrap of cloth.

Such a simple story. Alongside it, Tara Duane's tip-offs knotted into sinister futility. Knowing that Georgie had misplaced her dud boyfriend she'd taken the opportunity to implicate her neighbour in a crime predicted on an educated guess. Tara Duane had almost certainly seen shit like this before, and she wasn't the kind of person you could trust with an opportunity. Even alone, Georgie flushed. That she had played her part and upset her dealer's father for Duane's smirking benefit was its own ugly burden.

Downstairs, the front door opened and she heard a deep voice call out to its mother's low answer.

'Where?'

And then there were footsteps on the stairs.

Georgie didn't have time to make for the window. On Maureen's return she had chosen to stay still and wait for the woman's bedtime; she had nowhere else to go. Logic had intimated that no one would make for the bare rooms above. She had thought herself safe so long as she stayed silent.

Panicked, she slid behind the door, and when it opened it was with such force that the door slammed against her and rebounded on the intruder. She cried out as Jimmy Phelan rounded on her. He caught her arm and dragged her upright, and hit her, with an open palm, so hard it spun her almost out of his grasp.

'You're the whore,' he said. 'Aren't you? There I was sending the whole of the city out hunting for you when all I had to do was wait for you to crawl back to me. What a fucking stupid bitch you are.'

His palm came round again and caught her between her jaw and throat. She spluttered and as her knees went from under her Phelan closed his fist around her neck and snarled, 'You know, I get a hard-on from offing bitch messes and you, my girl, have caused me no end of trouble in the past year.'

Georgie choked and he slapped her again, and Maureen came into the room and said, 'You'd want to stop that, Jimmy, or you'll regret it.'

'Stay the fuck out of this, Maureen.'

'This house has killed before and it's generally the stronger of the pairing that gets it. I'm only warning you.'

Georgie was allowed to crumple.

Through tears she saw her subjugators: Phelan, puce, wet-lipped and oh, so massive, taking up the whole middle of the floor, the span from shoulder to shoulder packing muscle and wrath. Beside him stood Maureen, only half his size, cold-eyed and calm. She crouched and plucked the scapular from the floor.

'I thought you were born again, my dear?'

Phelan pulled a phone from his pocket, but Maureen held her hand over it. 'Who are you calling?'

'I'm getting rid of this whore, Maureen.'

'That's no way to speak about a woman, especially one that used to make you money.' She stared down at Georgie and said, 'She's only looking for Robbie O'Donovan, aren't you?'

'Shut your mouth, Maureen.'

'You don't talk to your mother like that either.'

Phelan scoffed. 'That's not likely to work on me, girl.'

'Ah, sure you were brought up by Una Phelan; no wonder you're the way you are. I'd not be happy to see you hurt this girl, Jimmy.'

'Your happiness, Maureen, is exactly why she needs to be gotten rid of.'

'I'll never be happy again, so.' To Georgie, she said, 'You're not going to say anything, are you? Sure all you want to know is where Robbie O'Donovan went. And if I tell you, you won't breathe a word, will you?'

'Maureen, this is not how this is going to go,' stated Phelan, but his mother shushed him, and said, 'Of course it is. There's one dead already because of me and I don't want that number added to.'

'She's going to die,' said Phelan.

'She won't die,' said Maureen. 'And she won't disappear again either. Isn't that right, Georgie? Haven't you enough to be worrying about without telling great big secrets?' And she laid a kindly hand on Georgie's flat stomach, and smiled.

19

Oh, he wasn't an easy man to bargain with, James Dominic Phelan. He took after his stand-in mama in that sense – ignorant as the day was long and stubborn as an ass. Maureen worked a way around him, but only just. One ghost, she explained, was bad enough. Two? She'd never sleep again. Especially if they were thick as thieves. Robbie O'Donovan nodded mournfully from the corner. He didn't want Georgie's company.

Jimmy was all, *Oh Maureen, Oh Maureen, you don't understand.* The world was an orgy of disquiet once you'd killed someone. Those who might suspect you needed to be controlled. The penalties for lenience were harsh and so lenience was no option.

Era go on outta that, said Maureen. What harm in the sparrow? She was hardly going to tell anyone. She had no influence in Jimmy's world; what was she, only a pisawn whore? Who would believe her? Was she not an addict and a victim? Did she not have a history of joining cults?

Was she not a mother?

'Where's the baby?' Jimmy asked. The girl cried and said the child was in care.

'No one', said Maureen, 'steps out of line once you're holding that over them.' Hadn't Jimmy been only a baby when she'd been banished? Maureen knew what Georgie would and wouldn't do, and she wouldn't be telling tales, no she wouldn't.

'If you step out of line,' Jimmy told the weeping slip, 'I will kill you. And I'll take what I'm owed from the child.'

He made sure the windows were jammed tight and left the girl in the room, asked Maureen to join him in the kitchen, stood on Robbie O'Donovan's ebbing place and snarled, 'Now, Maureen, d'you want to tell me how that whore knows your ould buddy Robbie is dead?'

Serendipity. Coincidence. Religious intercession.

One day, Maureen told James Dominic Phelan, when she was feeling the presence of Robbie O'Donovan with oh, very particular keenness, a fallen angel came to the door, looking to earn back her wings by paying strident homage to the Good Lord Almighty.

'What the fuck does that mean?'

It meant that she'd taken the form of a little Magdalene, with a bellyful of sins. The trickster God had directed her exactly where she needed to be. She came into the brothel, and she was right at home and in great misery because of it. Maureen had at first been taken by her mangling of the gospels and she'd invited her past the threshold for larks. Then she was charmed by the stench of the girl's past. It had been pushed beyond doubt when Maureen had mentioned her son the brothel keeper and the fallen angel had stood as if to bolt.

'Why the fuck would you tell her such a thing, Maureen? Jesus, are you in the habit of telling all your visitors that I'm so fucking specific a disappointment?'

That wasn't all Maureen had told her. The Magdalene had started to cry out the truth. She hadn't wanted to cross the threshold because she'd been a whore in that very building. She'd been plucked from grace by Maureen's bastard son. Maureen had invited her to retread the shadows and the girl had reluctantly complied. On the way up the stairs she'd met the ghost. He whispered in her ear and suddenly she was all-knowing. 'Robbie O'Donovan was here!' she exclaimed. 'Ah, it's true,' said Maureen. 'He died here.' And the Magdalene had flown out the door, wings latched on to her by a truth bigger than either of them.

'Jesus Christ,' said Jimmy. He paced the floor of the kitchen and stabbed the air above his head. 'You mean *you* told the whore

O'Donovan was dead? Jesus Christ, Maureen. Why didn't you take a stroll down to the sty and tell the Law you'd knocked some junkie's block off while you were at it?'

Maureen said, 'I'm not a fool, you know.'

'Oh, you're not, naw. Jesus, Maureen. I thought Cusack telling you the name of the corpse was a slip-up I could forgive but you soaked it up only to spit it out. Who else have you confessed your sins to?'

'I hope you're not going to barney with that nice Cusack man, Jimmy.'

'I'll rip his spine out his arse is what I'll do!'

'You probably wouldn't have known them, but he's John and Noreen's boy. She's a thundering bitch and he's a drunk but I wouldn't deprive either of them of their only son. That can do terrible things to a person.'

'You think,' said Jimmy, 'you can punt at me all sly-like, but you don't have room to swing from, not this time. Have you told anyone else?'

Maureen said, 'Indeed I have not.'

'Don't you understand what would happen? Not only would you be carted off to the loony bin, but I'd be done for disposing of your rubbish and my whole life here, Maureen, this whole fucking city, runs on a cowboy's foundation. I'd be ruined.'

'Do you not think it'd be time for you?'

Jimmy stopped pacing. He welded his fingers round the corner of the breakfast bar.

'Do you think', said Maureen, 'it was wrong of you to bring me home?'

'Was it a mistake, you mean? Clearly it fucking was.'

'Not just a mistake, Jimmy. Wrong. A boundary broken. An action taken that you can never claw back from.'

'To take you home from London . . .'

'What's home, though?'

'This is home, Maureen. This is your city. To take you home again was the least I could do and I waited forty years to do it.'

'But who said I wanted to come home?'

'Isn't that how we sort anything out, Maureen? We come home?'

Maureen smiled. 'What have I to sort out, Jimmy? Whether I die here or there makes no odds to me. You brought me home because you thought it'd make you feel better.'

'I brought you home because I thought it'd be one right in a history of wrongs.'

He leaned against the breakfast bar and his head lolled forwards. He sighed. Maureen studied his shape cut rough from the air. He was broad, grown-up James. There was nothing of Dominic Looney to him. He was instead the spit of her own father, in his bullish weight and the grey stubble creeping over the folds on the back of his neck . . . grey to pink in a strange soft frailty, like his baby head as she held him to her breast.

See how the world turns?

'What do I do with you, Maureen?'

It amazed her that he was talking at all. He'd popped out sticky and cribbing, and in the next instant he was a giant in a leather jacket with his very own lifetime of words learned. She picked up a cardigan from the back of the dining chair and pulled it over her shoulders. From the back window she said, 'I don't want you to hurt the girl. It's my fault. I told her.'

'I know it's your fault. That's another cross for you to bear, you and your massive trap.'

'Would you do that to me, Jimmy?'

'I owe you nothing,' he said, 'except my existence, but if I was missing that I wouldn't know it. You don't get a say, Maureen. All you did was squeeze me out.'

'A life for a life,' she said. 'All she did was listen.'

'See how the world turns?' Maureen said to Georgie later that same evening. 'All you wanted was your religious die-dee back. And now you owe Jimmy your life simply because he could be convinced not to take it from you.'

Georgie was still sitting in the middle of the floor. She had a fine purple blotch rising on her cheek and eyes swollen pink.

Maureen had given her the cardigan and a blanket but she was still quaking like a bowl of jelly. Her hair matted down her back.

'Would you like a hairbrush?' Maureen offered.

The girl gulped.

'You can calm down,' said Maureen. 'He's not going to kill you. I told him not to and you know, I'm his mother.'

Georgie said, 'I didn't mean to frighten you.'

'Frighten me? It'd take something a bit bigger and bolder to bother me, girl.'

'I just wanted to know what had happened to Robbie.'

'You wanted your wee scapular back, sure.'

Maureen crossed the floor and sat facing Georgie, and leaned out and grasped her ankle, gave it a little shake.

'Why would a whore care about the Church?'

'It was my mother's . . .'

'Ah for feck's sake altogether. Another religious mother. You'd have to ask yourself what's wrong with this country at all that it can't stop birthing virtuous ould bags. And what would your mammy say, Miss Georgie, if she knew you'd done your time here?'

'I haven't seen her in years.'

'How many years?'

'Almost ten.'

'Almost ten? Sure if you landed home now it'd be like you'd never been away. The Holy Ghost would have carted you back again. She could take a rest on the novenas. I didn't see Jimmy for two decades before I came back to this hole. Can you imagine that? I came home one Christmas when he was twenty and he bought me a brandy. The next time I saw him he was forty and the size of a small shed.'

Georgie squeaked, brushed tears from her cheeks and wiped her hands on her dress. 'Why didn't you see him in twenty years?' she asked. 'What happened?'

Maureen paused. The bleached room provided nothing in the way of prop or inspiration, and it was such a massive story, a story too big for four walls.

'We'll go for a walk,' she said. 'I have something I could do with showing you.'

'There were girls I knew in London,' Maureen said. 'Girls like yourself. Strumpets with scarlet smiles.'

They were walking the night streets past students on the tear, eighteen-year-olds laughing in drainpipe jeans and wispy beards, crying revolution from phone screens, through bottles of beer. Dominic Looney could well have been among them, in his beads, his head full of mutiny and lust. Fashion came round in cycles. Shitehawks, she guessed, stayed the same.

Georgie stared at the ground. Maureen felt her fear as keenly as the chill. She guessed the girl would stay docile through dread of vengeance, as if Maureen might turn around and snap her neck on bad-blood whim, and it irked her. She needed engagement for the lesson to work.

Ah, but could she blame her? The girl was a shell. The only thing left in her was fear.

'I'm not judging you,' Maureen said. 'I know what made you.'

A laughing girl reeled round the corner and straight into Georgie. They both stumbled. The girl apologised. Her friends, following thick, shrieked in glee. The girl tottered on, bellowing her mortification to her posse. *Did you see her face*, one of them gasped.

'Most of them,' Maureen said, as one of the girls, yards away now, lurched on her heels and grabbed the arm of the dolly next to her, 'most of them got out of the game, but only one I remember did so intact. The rest of them were hags after their stint. They trusted no one. They drank like sluts. They beat their children.'

'I'd have made a good mother,' Georgie said, but there was no conviction behind the proclamation.

'Well you might have,' Maureen said. 'And I hope you get to find out. Me, it's not like I could have done a worse job, so they should have let me try. Look at the state of him!'

'Where are we going?'

Maureen clucked. 'I told you. I need to show you something.'

'I can't face him again tonight.'

'Who? Jimmy? I'm not taking you back to Jimmy. Or back to anywhere. I'm taking you forward. Lookit.'

They turned the corner to face the church, and Maureen flicked a thumb at it and pressed forward locked arm in arm with her fellow pilgrim.

'You're taking me to Mass?'

'Mass? I am not.'

The church was hewn from rock and the city around it built from twigs. Maureen brought Georgie along the side of the building. Above them stained-glass windows dripped dark and the hush of consecrated ground heavied their steps and made prowlers of the pair of them.

'I've always hated these places,' said Maureen.

They went round the back of the church to the priest's house, a two-storey block for a celibate man and his ghosts. Maureen didn't approve. She had never approved. She had never understood, as a child, why the priest had a bigger house than she did. Surely Holy Intangible God left room enough to walk around?

She and her brothers and sisters often played in the grounds of churches after Masses, celebrations, funerals, the litany of a faithful life. You could stretch your legs as the adults congratulated or commiserated or condemned, but every so often you'd run round the corner and get collared by the holy man white-lipped with rage over your impudence. It seemed a shame to grant such a pretty garden to the whims of a miserable old goat. It seemed a shame to tend such a pretty garden in the shadow of a grim theatre. There were always tidy lawns, flower beds, maybe even a grotto if you were lucky. It was the one green spot she'd never seen the tinkers graze their horses.

Now she brought Georgie to the shrubbery which looked onto the priest's side door. Georgie murmured protest but Maureen shushed her, and tucked her between plants with confident hands. Georgie was confused. In the weak orange light from the side door, she seemed ready, again, to cry.

'See the cars?' Maureen pointed.

'Yeah . . .'

'There are people meeting with the priest. Every night. They're always working, the priests.'

'What kind of people?'

Maureen studied her.

'Boys and girls getting married. Mammies getting Mass cards. Daddies looking for validation. Just the flock.'

'Why are we here? I don't get it.'

Maureen crouched and turned. Behind her, Georgie's eyes, downcast, searched the dirt for sense. She wouldn't find it there, but it wasn't a bad start. Born of dust and raised in stony soil, wasn't that it? The girls had no more changed than the beaded boys, one enabling the other.

'It was a wheyface by the name of Dominic Looney that led me into sin and left me there,' Maureen said. 'I had Jimmy when I was nineteen. My parents wouldn't let me keep him. It was far too shameful, you see. Those were the days. I lived in England and he grew up here. I worked in offices for a while, but I could no more hold a job than a hot poker. Did a bit of housekeeping. Worked in kitchens. Drank in the clubs with the rest of the Irish, made a few friends and stepped out with a few fellas but I wouldn't settle down. Couldn't, I think sometimes. What was the point? How do you build a life from bones? I only came home when Jimmy got the whim to bring me. There's too much passed now for us to be anything but strangers. That's why I know what's bothering you, and you having lost your little baby.'

Georgie let out a sob. She left her hands on the dirt to steady herself.

'Your Robbie O'Donovan,' Maureen said, soft as the light from the door, 'wasn't meant to die. It was an accident.'

'He meant something, you know. He might not have looked it but he did. And you had no right . . . You had no right to take him and no right to hide him then.'

'I know that,' said Maureen.

'What did you do with him?'

'Because it was an accident, Jimmy made it go away. And so Robbie's body was taken from the brothel floor, but there's the rest of him still there. I guess I'm stuck with him. You don't believe in ghosts, do you?'

Georgie said nothing.

'I wouldn't blame you,' Maureen said. 'I wouldn't believe in them but they've been following me around all my life. He came for your mother's scapular, wasn't that it? What if I told you you're not all that different to your mother?'

'What, because we're standing in a shrubbery outside a church? Is that going to cleanse me, is it?'

Maureen said, 'Do you like being a prostitute?'

Georgie stiffened. A flash of umbrage crossed her broken face, just a flash, but enough for Maureen to grasp.

'Do you think I'd do it if I didn't have to?' Georgie said. 'Do you think anyone would?'

'So why do girls do it?'

'Money.'

'They're fond of money?'

'They need money.'

'Exactly. They're in need of something and so they'll fold up under a spoiled man to stay alive, isn't that it?'

Georgie dabbed her eyes with the inside of her wrist.

'So they divide up the women into categories,' said Maureen. 'The mammies. The bitches. The wives. The girlfriends. The whores. Women are all for it too, so long as they fall into the right class. They all look down on the whores. There but for the grace of God.'

'God had nothing to do with it.'

'The point is there's a class of women put aside for the basest of man's instincts. That's your type and by Jesus you better play to it.'

'All men? Are they all like that?'

'Ha! They're divided up just as neatly, didn't you know? Saints and sinners. Masters and slaves. The good guys and the bad guys. Like my Jimmy. Hasn't he a role too? No one gets to the top if he hasn't a mound of bodies to climb.'

'What's that got to do with my mother?'

'She's religious, isn't she? They don't sell scapulars in Tesco.'

'Yeah . . .'

'She's on her knees for the higher power. The Church craves power above all things, power above all of the living. The Church has an ideal and it'll raze all in its way to achieve it. The Church needs its blind devout. Your mother, my mother, the people in there plumping Father Fiddler's ego, they're all for it. They've been given a class and they're clutching it. The Church creates its sinners so it has something to save. Your mother's a Magdalene for her Christ.'

The door opened. Maureen placed a hand on Georgie's back, willing her still.

A young couple came out into the yard, turned back and shook the priest's hand. There was laughter. The hall glow spilled onto the steps and cast an amber circle on the ground beneath the disciples and, from the shadows, the Magdalenes watched their heaving backs.

'Look at him,' spat Maureen. 'Look close. Handing out indoctrination, keeping them faithful, keeping them hooked.'

20

She had hair black as outer space and eyes startling and dark blue. The only thing about her that wasn't magazine perfect was her long nose, of which she was ashamed, but he loved that too, and the flashes of humility it provoked in front of mirrors; he used to kiss it when he thought he could get away with it.

She was supposed to get a white shirt for work but was too vain for anything functional. Instead she wore one that hugged her waist and barely covered her midriff and had to be held together with safety pins if she didn't want a button taking anyone's eye out halfway through her shift. She'd told him to meet her at the cafe. She made him a BLT when he arrived and as he munched she poked at a salad and made faces.

'I have something to tell you,' she said.

He thought she was getting shot of him. She said she loved his eyes and his up-and-down accent – 'Just like the hills at home,' he told her – but there was only so far you could go on that, and he didn't have much to offer otherwise. He had been labouring on a site off White Hart Lane but everything he earned he spent on Ecstasy and booze. She was supposed to be putting herself through Goldsmiths but still seemed to be spending the GNP of an island nation on weekend parties and shopping trips. If they made a good couple it was gauged entirely on lack of financial cop on.

The BLT stopped two inches from his mouth.

'This is such a surprise to me,' she shrugged.

It was the middle of August and sweltering. London hadn't slept in days and it showed. Small children poked about in patches of melting tar. Old women slumped on park benches as their Scottish terriers panted beneath the slats. There were two fans going in the cafe with the door wide open. Everyone was sticky and sluggish.

'You're surprised why?' he asked.

Behind them, an enormous man in a wifebeater dropped his teaspoon onto his newspaper and swore.

'You see,' she said, 'it turns out . . . I . . . am pregnant.'

The man in the wifebeater hadn't noticed but Tony Cusack had just been turned inside out.

'You're what?'

She shrugged again.

A wasp drifted towards them and he batted it away. It persisted. Tony grabbed a discarded *Sun* from the table closest the door and crushed the insect against the windowpane. Maria Cattaneo cocked her head and ran her fingers through her hair and when he came back to the table she raised her eyebrows as if to say *Your move, bucko*.

He looked down at the half-eaten BLT.

'Well,' he said. 'That's . . . ah . . . What d'you want to do about it?'

She raised eyes to heaven. 'God, you're romantic,' she said.

When Tony was eighteen a girl he'd been with said she thought she was pregnant, but it turned out she wasn't, news so good it knocked his knees from under him because she'd been his first, he'd pulled out and he didn't really like the beour in the first place. This was different. He was four years older. He was crazy about Maria Cattaneo. He prodded at the toast with studied indifference but in his head there was a brass band and a parade of tumbling cheerleaders.

'Just making sure you're OK with it, like,' he said.

'I love babies. You're handsome . . .' She made a popping sound with her mouth. '. . . handsome babies.'

'OK then.'

'OK.'

'Have you been to the doctor?'

She nodded. 'It looks like March. Springtime. Like the lambs.'

He jumped up and leaned across the table and kissed her and the man in the wifebeater said, 'Steady on, son, I'm trying to eat here.'

Nineteen years later Tony Cusack occupied himself in sluggish reminiscence. There was sunlight snaking through the curtains in his sitting room, showing up a carpet flecked with loose tobacco and cracker crumbs. The hoover was on the blink.

He was out of booze and in no shape to get more; he was logey from the heat and too caught in the kaleidoscope of memories to want to leave the house. The kids had scattered in the sunshine. The small ones were out on the green playing. Cian had headed off in high spirits and would no doubt return trying to hide his drunkenness behind his mobile phone. Kelly had folded up a couple of towels and said she was heading to Myrtleville with her buddies. They had lives, the little Cusacks, more than he'd given them. They left their father sifting through scenes beginning to wilt around the edges.

He'd come back to Cork with a pregnant nineteen-year-old whose desire to isolate herself from her middle-class lineage had spotted her vision. Friends and family alike had asked *How in fuck's name did you get your paws on her?* and he couldn't answer them, because he sure as shit didn't know.

They lived with his mam and dad for a while and when they got the house they got married and once they got married they started killing each other in earnest and the casualties – oh! the fucking casualties – they were piled high but it was worth every last bruise.

He had proved shit at absolutely everything except giving her beautiful children. She was no different. They both drank. Neither worked with any regularity. They had matching tempers. They lived in a fleapit and fought on the street. But at the end of the day he had six children out of it, six dark-haired, dark-eyed wonders with his blood in their veins and maybe that was enough.

He watched the minutes die on the Sky menu and the thirst spread until he could bear it no more.

He kept his head down in the off-licence, aware, just below the surface of his single-mindedness, that he was one of the idiots who kept the place open seven days a week. He grabbed a six-pack from the display at the back, where they stocked the cheap shit. The shop interior was lit by strip fluorescents and fridges; on display, he blinked and hurried. He made for the till, a tenner bunched damp in his fist.

His name snaked after him.

'Tony! Tony, stop a sec!'

The sunshine had brought out the slapper in Tara Duane. She was in a yellow bolero and black shorts so small they'd have scarcely made underwear. She'd piled her hair on her head and off her neck. From there down it was all bones. No tits at all. She was a mother and she couldn't have looked less like one. She'd starved herself back to her teens.

His having holed himself up while his children ran out into the world meant he'd escaped seeing too much of Duane. Occasionally he'd spotted her from the windows. A couple of times they'd narrowly missed each other hanging out clothes in the back garden. She seemed to have lost interest in orchestrating encounters since Ryan had come home only to move straight out again; Tony grasped the correlation, substantiated it and then hoped his logic was faulty. The last time she'd collared him, in the driveway, months ago now, had been to tell him that J.P. had enlisted her to conduct the hunt for the doomed girl. Tara Duane was made an ally without his consent. You'd think that'd be a thing worth challenging. It wasn't. It was a thing to be accepted and shelved.

Sure what could he do about it? Confront the bastard?

Two days after Maria Cattaneo had changed his life, Tony sat in a pub with Jimmy Phelan. Surrounded by wood panelling and echoing football commentary, he was getting congratulated and smashed with equal aplomb.

'You couldn't have done much better for yourself without a hanky soaked in chloroform,' said Jimmy. 'Are you going to shack up with her?'

'I'm going home with her.'

'Home to Italy? With your pasty Irish arse?'

'No, boy. Home to Cork.'

'Home to *Cork*? Jesus Christ, Cusack, you're only just out of it!'

'My son's gonna be born in Cork, boy. Wouldn't be mine otherwise.'

Jimmy laughed. 'When are you heading, so?'

'Dunno. A couple of months, probably. It's early yet.'

'And have you told your mam?'

'Eh, I'll arrive home "for a visit" and I'll tell her then.'

'One cute hoor, aren't you?' Jimmy beckoned a barmaid and said, 'A couple more there, love. And a couple shorts too. What's your best Scotch? This fella here is going to be a daddy in the spring.'

'Oh wow!' she said. She was carrying a tower of glasses that reached from her belly to her chin. She shifted its weight and tilted her head round it and smiled. Her eyes were heavily made up and the colours coagulated in the heat. 'Congratulations!'

Tony smiled back and she gave him an extra shot in his Scotch.

'It's a boy so, is it?' asked Jimmy, his nose in the tumbler.

Tony shrugged. 'Too early to tell officially, like, but it's a small fella, of course it is.'

'What the fuck do you want now?'

Tara Duane was momentarily and lavishly upset. Her eyes swung toward the ceiling. Her jaw dropped. 'Is that any way to greet your next-door neighbour?' she gasped.

'That's not a connection by choice,' Tony snapped.

'You think I like living beside you when every kindness I brought to your door was met with scorn and fury?'

'I don't give a fuck what you like or don't like,' he said. 'If that's why you stopped me, let's cut this short. I have better things to be doing.'

'Oh I know you do.' She gestured. 'They come in cans.'

He turned away, but there were a couple of young men at the till, holding slabs and pointing at naggins. He was captive.

'I didn't stop you just to insult you,' she said, alongside.

'Oh, brilliant.'

'I stopped you because I've been doing a lot of thinking. About J.P., and how he's made pawns of the pair of us, and how we both need to move on.'

'You think we need fucking counselling?'

She grabbed his arm with a hand that had made shit of his relationship with his son, and he shook her off with an energy reserved for pests he chased around the kitchen to crush between the tiles and the sole of his shoe.

'Don't touch me, Duane!'

'Why not? What do you think you could possibly catch?'

'It's not about catching something,' he said. 'It's about not wanting to give you the satisfaction—'

'What, of laying my hands on a nasty, violent drunk? You have a swollen opinion of yourself, don't you?'

'What did you call me?'

'I know,' she whispered, 'that you beat your kids.'

One of the men at the till broke into raucous laughter. Oblivious to the conversation that had winded Tony, he slapped the top of his lager slab.

Tara said, 'It's a skit, isn't it? You're full sure I had something with Ryan and you go on about it and on about it as if you actually cared about him. When the reality is you beat him. You humiliated him. He used to sit out on the back garden wall in the cold and the dark waiting for you to go to bed so he'd be safe in his own home. You're obsessed with the idea that I might have slept with him. Why's that, Tony? Would that make you jealous, Tony?'

He said, 'You're crazy. Fuck you, fuck J.P.—'

'Fuck Ryan.'

He inhaled, let his body go still, pushed the poison out through his lips in a cool, wordless stream.

'Cards on the table, Tony. I think you're a piece of shit. I tried and tried with you but the only way you deal with people is abuse them. I know you hate me, because you think there was more to my asking your little boy black-and-blue into my home so he could sleep off the pain of your discipline. Whatever way you used to dole it out.'

The jovial men cleared the counter and walked out of the shop, their arms full. The assistant looked towards Tony and Tara, then down at a clipboard by her till. She started marking words off with a black pen. There was an ink smudge marking her thumbprint, and another smear across two of her knuckles.

'Remember Georgie?' Tara said.

Tony swapped the cans to his other hand. He didn't reply.

'Of course you do,' Tara said. 'I couldn't find her for love nor money—'

'That's nothing to do with me.'

'Please. It's everything to do with you.'

The girl at the till began to sing a song. In an uneven jumble of breath and flat melody she forced on Tony a broken musical accompaniment.

'I couldn't find her,' Tara went on, 'but she turned up of her own accord. A few months back. J.P.'s done whatever he had to do—'

'What's that mean?'

She scoffed. 'She's fine. I'm not. Do you realise how useless we look to J.P. now?'

'I don't look like anything to J.P. I've got nothing to do with him.'

'Oh Jesus, give it up! I do a bit for him myself. I know the score.'

'You know nothing, Duane.'

'Fine. I know nothing, you know nothing.' She rolled her eyes and mimed chattering jaws with her hands. 'But while you're convincing me of your ignorance, J.P. is realising what a pair of losers we are. If there's one thing worse than being the go-to for favours, it's becoming the go-to for framing. I need to get out of the city. Go down West Cork or something, start again.'

'Go then.'

'You might not have noticed, Tony, but I'm not exactly rolling in it.'

'If you're trying to convince me that that's my problem—'

She cut him off. 'I went to the Council. Told them I was sick from stress. I asked them to move me. They wouldn't. My issues with you weren't serious enough, even though you smashed my window and intimidated me. It's classed as antisocial behaviour and the Council would be playing rounds of musical chairs all day and night if they gave a shit about that.'

She looked away, adjusted her jacket and exhaled.

'Don't think I'm not aware of how dangerous you are. You beat your son and you kill your drinking buddies.'

'You're crazy, I said.'

'Save it, she can't hear us.' She brushed hair from her face. 'I don't want to live beside you anymore, Tony. I don't want J.P. knowing my address. Help me get out of here. That way we're both happy. Pay for your medicine. I'll meet you outside. I want to tell you something and you will hear it.'

In the early afternoon brilliance of high summer, on a day earmarked for fond reminiscence, she relayed to him the details of a plan concocted over high and white spirits. She wanted him to burn her out.

This was the plan, pulled from the addled head of the lunatic, imparted on the path outside the off-licence in matter-of-fact tones broken of emotion and repellent to passing snoops. She had determined that the best way for the Corporation to take her seriously would be to demonstrate a serious problem. She wanted Tony the Drunk to serve up a Molotov cocktail and throw it through her back door some prearranged night. The authorities would move her on. As for Tony Cusack, she'd vouch for him. He'd hardly try and smoke her out when his house joined hers.

'You're fucking serious,' Tony said, and Duane joined her hands and said, 'I know it sounds mad, but I've thought about it and thought about it and it really does seem like the right solution for both of us. I'll say I've had trouble with Jimmy Phelan and the cops will drop it fierce fast. They're scared of him.'

Tony said, 'I left school when I was sixteen and I haven't read a book since, but I know a stupid notion when I hear one. You're warped, Duane. You're either trying to trick me because you think I'm thick as the hairs on a gorilla's hole or you actually think that I'll commit arson to get you a country cottage.'

'Right.' She fell back. 'So you're not going to help me.'

'Will I put my kids in danger because you've lost the plot? Let me think now. No.'

'I'll do it anyway,' she said. 'I'll do it without your input and how are you going to know when to get out then?'

'You think I'm not going to go right to the guards about this?'

'No. Because if you do I'll tell them you killed Robbie O'Donovan. And then when my house goes up in flames I'll tell them Ryan did it. Spurned lovers at that age. You just don't know what they're capable of.'

He reached for her but she leapt back and wagged her finger, gasping, 'Ah ah ah!' Tony pushed back against the wall. The streets were alive, even in the heat. Across the road, a girl pushing a bare-legged toddler in a buggy stared.

Tony said, 'I'll have to bring this back to J.P. then, won't I?'

'But you won't,' said Tara Duane. 'Even if he cared enough to do something about it, you know if anything happens to me he'll just pin it back on you, because that's what dopes like you are there for.'

In her shorts pocket, her phone trilled.

'Have a think about it,' she said, taking out the handset. 'I wouldn't want to move on it for a while yet, anyway. Melinda's going off to live with her dad soon. No date set but she can't stay in Ireland much longer, sitting on her bum. The country's banjaxed, sure she's as well off out of it.'

On Cheating II

Joseph goes into the bedroom with the other wan so I'm left in the kitchen with the green-eyed girl and she's approaching like a tsunami.

Look, don't get me wrong. She's unreal. She's wearing this black and gold patterned dress that sets off her olive skin, she's got long wavy hair just made for bunching in your hand while you shift her, she's got the absolute lot. We've been cordoned off in a corner talking all night because I'm that starved of Italian I'd wear a wire for la Guardia di Finanza if all they were promising was stammered conversation with camorristi. *Her name's Elena. She's from Salerno. She keeps finishing my sentences. It's the fucking berries.*

But I know she's expecting something in return. She's dead right, of course. I mean, me and Joseph came all the way back to their apartment to do more than admire a pair of living dictionaries. The other wan, Sofia, started mauling the face off Joe as soon as he got in the door; they're heading home in couple of days and I guess she's mad to go out on a high. The bedroom door closes. So there's me and Elena and she's giving me eyes and stroking her cleavage and here she comes, across the tiled floor, and I'm gonna have to, you know.

First girl I ever kissed was Lauren Sheehan. I was eleven. She was twelve. It was two days before my mam died.

I haven't kissed anyone but Karine in years, and I hadn't planned this.

Elena flicks her tongue against mine and all the blood rushes out of my face and down.

She pulls back with her hands on my chest, and says she won't tell my girlfriend if I don't.

Only last night me and Karine were out for a munch and then to one of her fancy pubs so she could drink cocktails and tell me how hot I am as I screwed up my eyes and tried to drink Niall Vaughan out of my head. She tells me there's nothing to forgive so I have to focus on forgetting. Her actions beg my pardon, though. She's so attentive. She's so fucking into me. She wants to spoil me and the truth is she's wasting her energy. I'm carrying anger around like a sack of wailing kittens; I'm not able to drown it. Like, this thing we have is so deep, and so brittle because of my mistakes, and my mistakes are so massive and glowing so bright I'm scared to set them down. And it turns out Karine's a reprobate too. I can't get my head around it. I'm angry, and relieved, and angry again because I'm relieved, and it's in my head, fucking pulsating, day and night, no matter what I do and I've room only for that and for nothing else so I don't even feel like me anymore. And I'm putting myself through that because I love Karine D'Arcy and it's no good, I can't bear to be without her.

Elena kisses me again, longer, softer, and my hands move down over the hill of her arse to the hem of her dress.

It's like . . . I dunno. Like something's pulling me forwards but it's splitting me in two doing it because there's a part of me completely unwilling to go with it. My fingers push her dress up and reach in and there's just this damp piece of fabric between me and her cunt. I'm pushing against her with my cock and she moans and goes for the top button of my jeans and I can hear bone splintering and wind howling and my whole entire soul shouting at me to stop, stop, two wrongs don't make a right, boy, stoppit! *but I'm gonna do it, I'm gonna fuck her, why shouldn't I fuck her? That's how it goes, isn't it? I'm out with friends and I got drunk and I'm coked up nicely and my dick's gonna do whatever it wants to do. What's the point fighting it if Karine won't bother either?*

Elena backs onto the table, pulls her dress over her head, clasps her heels around my waist and pulls me over. She slides her hands over my shoulders and I wince because she's gone straight onto the scar.

There's a brushstoke dragon across my shoulders, flicking down onto my arms. It's a week old. It hurt like hell for seven days and now it's a burning ache. Probably because it was inked on bone but maybe too because I got the artist to add an extra stroke, a K at the bottom of my dragon's tail, right on my spine.

It hurt, but it didn't stop me.

All the Stones Turned

21

Across the skyline of his city, the modest heights other men's ambitions had carved from the marshy hamlet, Tony tracked his losses and kept watch for his damnation.

Sobriety became a memory that glimmered only in his children's disappointment. Ronan and Niamh stretched past the point of coddling. Cathal turned thirteen and moody. Cian talked of pursuing an apprenticeship. Kelly entered her Leaving Cert year. Their father's failures weighed on them less and less as they fixed on their own futures. His home was peopled by the shades of the one life he had worth living. His one-time assertion that he was a father above all things burned in Tara Duane's fluorescent vision. He hid in his front room and conjured resolutions; they crisped up and withered into ash with the first lungful breathed into them.

He watched the boy Ryan burn himself out. From a distant plain he tried calling armistice but whatever it was that Ryan had become didn't need it.

One dank November morning he arrived up in a ten-year-old Golf and Tony went out to kick tyres and mutter approvingly. He didn't know from whom Ryan had learned to drive. It wasn't lost on him that the teaching was a task for a boy's father.

'Are you set for Christmas?' Ryan asked, one hand clasped to the back of his neck and wincing like he'd cupped a wasp. 'D'you need a few quid, like.'

Tony barely jibbed. His son gave him a roll of notes. He closed his hands around the gift and said, 'Where did you get this?' and his son stared into the distance like a mariner mourning the fleet and said, 'A bit of work, that's all,' and Tony knew then what he'd birthed.

Briefly, he considered asking this new Ryan what to do about Tara Duane, but wouldn't that give wings to an ugly truth? The conversation turned back to the car. Tony thought of histories etched on his son's skin and felt sick. He watched Duane's house, imagining her peeking from behind the sitting-room curtains, plotting how she was going to stitch them both up. Ryan said, 'I'm saving for a GTI but this'll do for getting Karine to and from the shops in the meantime,' and his father patted the bonnet and laughed weakly.

As Christmas rushed him he thought of Jimmy Phelan's visit the year before, the half-drained bottle of whiskey he'd brought as a fuck you. Three December evenings in a row he contemplated picking up the phone and asking J.P. for help. Each time he stopped himself with bitter rationale. Jimmy Phelan wasn't his friend. He had slung his sins around Tony's neck and Tony had bowed and let him.

Two days before Christmas, the house from which he and Jimmy had removed poor Robbie O'Donovan went up in flames.

He only realised when he saw the photos on the front of the *Echo*. Two engines blocking the quay, the dampened smoke smothering the river, the sky above, stained. He read the report and was relieved to find there had been no one in the house at the time and no one hurt in the buildings around it. Preliminary investigations suggested faulty wiring – the property was ancient, after all – so the guards had ruled out foul play. Tony knew better. He had grown cynical enough to assume that the guards knew better too.

He supposed the fire turned the page on a black chapter of his life.

But he wasn't the same man who had stumbled onto J.P.'s path nearly four years before. The tidy removal of the crime scene couldn't draw a line under what had happened. Robbie O'Donovan was still dead. Tony Cusack had still washed his blood off the floor. Tara Duane had still used the wound as leverage.

On Christmas Day young Linda came over to compare presents with Kelly. Can in hand, Tony asked after her plans for the new year. She said she'd organised to continue her training in a salon in Glasgow, where her dad lived. She said she'd be leaving in the second week of January.

Kelly said, 'Think of all your mam can get up to with you out from under her feet,' and Linda shuddered treacherously.

Pallid in the glow of the Christmas tree lights, Ryan stared straight at the telly, feigning apathy.

Tony made up his mind.

The day before the scheduled blaze Tara Duane was all zest and merriment, as if she was relaying instructions for a supermarket sweep.

'So what'll happen,' she said, placing a mug of milky tea on the table in front of him, 'is that I'll leave the house at six o'clock, and take care to be seen here and there in town, and I won't come home until you phone me to tell me that there's been a terrible incident, or . . .' and she winked, 'that the job is done.'

Tony hooked his fingers around the handle of the mug. He'd watched her make the tea and was satisfied she'd neither drugged nor spat in it. Still didn't make it any way appetising.

They were sitting in her kitchen. Efforts had been made to emphasise its owner's nonconformity – colourful, mismatched crockery, tea towels with cheeky slogans, holiday knick-knacks arranged on the windowsill – but the baubles didn't mask the decay. Piles of clothes had been set on the table and left for so long they'd become musty. The wall behind the dustbin was streaked brown and grey. The top of the cooker was thick with old grease. It was as if the resident had died months ago. Tony watched Tara Duane prep her own tea. She could easily have been a shade, remembering nothing but the most twisted flashes of what she once was.

'You don't need to worry at all,' she enthused, sitting across from him. 'I've thought of absolutely everything. I've sold off some valuables because Melinda's just left and I've taken that opportunity to sort my stuff out. See? Makes total sense. You're going to throw the bottle into the kitchen leaving the key in the door behind you – I'll give it to you now, so we won't be seen together tomorrow – and it'll be like I simply forgot to lock it before going out. You know what a bad idea that is in a neighbourhood like this. You call me straight away because we're neighbours and you noticed the smell of smoke. And if anyone sees you leaving by my back door it's really easy to say, *Well yeah, I stuck my head in and realised the fire was out of control and I immediately called Tara and then the fire brigade*, yeah? And then I tell the Council I was right all along and they move me out of here. And that's that!'

No bother on her at all that she was explaining an elaborate ruse to a man only involved because of his incurable hatred.

'Best for all of us, I think you'll agree,' she said. 'This house has always been too big for me and Melinda. There are families who need it more than I do. So! Any questions?'

Tony remembered the banshee by the lake. He shook his head.

'Great!' she said. 'Oh, have a biscuit, for God's sake. Do me a favour. I'm watching my figure!'

He hadn't planned to have a couple beforehand but he was no more able to stop himself drinking than he was to stop the act itself.

He lay in his bed and wept the poison out in preparatory ritual. Thought, *Am I even able to see this through? Will I get caught?* and then, *What will my kids think of me?* They wouldn't understand. What's a father to them, except someone who makes their dinners and ensures the house doesn't fall down around their ears? *Not even that, Tony Cusack*. What's a father to them, except someone who boozes and stumbles and fights and spews? They wouldn't understand that this was something he had to do, and he could never make them.

Every now and then he picked up his mobile and checked the hour and at 3 a.m. he slid out of the bed and stood by the front window and looked out at the estate.

It was raining. Wind shook the shrubs and hedges in neighbouring gardens, banged a gate somewhere across the way, slapped the windowpane. There were no lights on in the houses directly across the green. Nothing stirred but the night's own breath.

He stood there for ten, maybe fifteen minutes, then found his feet.

Even if one of his children woke up they would pay no mind to his nocturnal roving; it wouldn't be the first time insomnia had tortured him. He dressed and went downstairs to the kitchen, opened the back door, and looked out. No lights in the houses backing onto his, either, except the usual glow from some of the neighbours' bathrooms.

It was the kind of night that could go on forever.

The key turned in Duane's back door. He stood for a moment in her kitchen, inhaling the scent of air freshener coiled through stale smoke and grease. Then he picked his way through the darkness into her hall, the layout identical to his own heap, checked the sitting room for signs of life, and crept up the stairs. The bathroom light was on and its door left ajar.

A creak on the step third from the top. He wondered what he'd say if she woke and caught him. If he claimed to have been overcome by night-time fervours and desperate for the loving touch of a spindly bitch, would she believe him? Would she cast him aside, his being all grown up and therefore way too fucking old for her?

He tried the door to the front bedroom and was momentarily bewildered by the decor, fittings and fragrances. His eyes tuned into the dark and he made sense of the shapes around him. Posters, perfumes on the dressing table, the Playboy bunny on the bedclothes. The bed was empty. This was the daughter's room.

He stepped back out into the landing and considered the mistake as a lifeline. How easy it would be to skulk back down the stairs and return to his own home without having left anything but his uneven breath.

But what of tomorrow? What of her rage once he backed out of her plan? What of her informant's mouth?

He slipped into the back bedroom and closed the door out

silently behind him as quickly as he could, and Duane stirred in the bed, sighed and turned onto her back.

He wiped his mouth with his sleeve and stepped over to stand by her body, and bit down on his lip so that the pain would chase away thoughts of this bedroom having hosted his boy, and crossed himself for a god he didn't really believe was there, and straddled her and put his hands to her neck and leaned down and closed his eyes. She thrashed and gurgled. Her hands flapped against his. Her knee curled behind him, he felt her thigh against his back and then nothing, but he kept pushing down and kept his eyes closed and afterwards told himself she'd barely been conscious at all.

He remembered the way more from his journey home than his own death march, so he had to navigate in reverse.

He had no torch in the car but he told himself he'd be better off, not wanting to be noticed from land or from sea. It was an awkward task. He found a sheet of tarpaulin and tucked her up tight. She looked light as a feather but dead weight was dead weight.

The walk along the overgrown path to the old quay, pointed out by J.P. on Tony's first visit, was harder than he had imagined. The ground was wet, the flora overgrown, the light non-existent and his burden enormous. He imagined himself losing footing and sliding into the black water below to be found alongside his enemy's body three or four days later. He imagined what his children would think. He imagined the traitor Jimmy Phelan, livid as the scandal threw light on his butcher's yard. He imagined his investigation. He imagined him coming face-to-face with Ryan and trying to bleed out the boy's ignorance.

The water churned as he rowed out to J.P.'s fishing boat. He didn't think he'd make it. It was dark, the wind was vicious, his arms sang as soon as he set them to work, and he thought he might not deserve to make it either, no matter his reasons, no matter how far he was backed into the corner . . . But he got there. He sat for ten minutes in the bobbing dinghy wondering how in Christ's name he was going to get her into the boat. He managed it through the devil's favour. He found rope and trussed the dinghy tight to the stern and dragged her into the fishing boat through strength of desperation. And then he left the rowing boat to its buoy and set sail, believing with every passing second that he was heading to his doom, to the unforgiving open sea, to the end maybe, but at least he was taking her with him.

Spinning

This is what it boils down to: image. And not like wearing designer sunglasses and jeans so tight they melt your balls. Just in general. What you give out, what people see in you when they first meet you.

I don't play piano.

I haven't forgotten it; you don't forget something you've been doing since you were three years of age. No, it's like . . . I started dealing and I fucked it up. Doing what I do for a living in and around playing the piano would be fucking ridiculous; I'd either be seen as a precious cunt or worse again, I'd be transparent. So I don't play piano. Not so's you'd notice, anyway.

The music won't go away, though. You learn that language and you're pretty much stuck shouting in it. So I fake it. I put my fingers to a set of decks and I learned to mix. That image works. People are comfortable with stereotypes; they want to think they have a handle on their merchant. You gift them an image so you can keep earning and you jettison whatever bit of yourself doesn't fit. That's just how it is.

Me and Karine go off to a gig on Saturday night and when it wraps up we get invited back to a party. I get to talking technique with one of the DJs and he tells me to throw a couple of tunes together. So I do. And he goes a bit googly-eyed because he thought I was talking out my hole.

Mixing's easy to me. I'm a bit nerdy about the science of sound, and those few months of Leaving Cert Physics and Maths stood to me, I suppose. 'Let the dealer DJ,' the partygoers think, and then it shifts to 'Why's that DJ dealing?' I don't stay on that long. I want a bump.

Karine comes over before I've even taken the headphones off and she says, 'I'm bursting.*'*

'I'm sure they have a toilet, like.'

'They do, but they don't have a lock.'

I go with her and keep the door shut and she hitches up the dress and sits down.

'D'you need another yoke?' I ask her.

She makes a face. 'I don't want to be dying Monday morning.'

'Have half a one.'

She makes another face.

'Go on,' I tell her. 'I need a top up anyway.'

I take a pill from my pocket and bite it in two and suck my half down. I wait for her to get up again. She washes her hands and takes her half from me.

I take a piss while she checks her fake eyelashes.

When we leave the bathroom there's another girl standing waiting and she smiles at me and says, 'Do I know you from somewhere?'

Karine steps past to retrieve her drink and so I get to smile back. 'I don't think so,' I say.

'I'm sure I do.' The other girl is tall, athletic, you know the type. She's wearing a tight, short dress and spike heels and she has a dark bob that swings when she cocks her head. She steams into a cascade of places she thinks she might know me from and you know what? They're all gig-related. Like, she sees me as the DJ, not as the dealer. She's wrong on every geographical guess and she's wrong about my professional position too but her attention is light and warm and, all right, a bit touchy-feely because she's fuckerooed but I could do with it, I'm swelling up in it, it's fucking lovely.

And of course she makes the mistake of touching my chest and Karine is catapulted back over.

'D'you mind?' she says to the athletic girl.

'Sorry?'

'D'you mind keeping your big orangutan hands to yourself?'

There's a quarrel that fizzles like a damp match because the athletic girl is too high to want to respond, apart from a short, 'Girls like you give us all a bad name,' and because I'm catching Karine's wrists and pushing her gently backwards out the front door, catching each spat accusation with a headshake and a smile. There's a car parked outside and I keep walking her backwards until her arse bumps against it, and she's protesting but I push up against her and put her wrists around my neck and then my hands on her thighs and ask her what in God's name she's doing.

'Oh, you know that Mister DJ,' she says. 'All the girls love him.'

'Let's not do this now,' I say. I'm conscious of the top-up yoke, and the mood inside so essential to its success.

'Am I wrecking your buzz?' she says, accusingly.

'You are *my fucking buzz, D'Arcy.'*

'So on that basis I'm not supposed to mind you flirting Bigfoot's knickers off?'

'I'm not flirting.'

'You are flirting. And they all know in there that I'm your girlfriend and it's making me look, like, so tragic.'

'Bollocks,' I tell her. I slide my hands around under her arse cheeks and push harder against her. 'Besides, wouldn't you rather be going out with Mister DJ than Mister Dealer?'

'I'd rather be going out with a fella who could keep his eyes on his girlfriend.'

It's funny, because I can actually hear a voice, ringing clear and true, as if it was someone else's trapped inside my own head, saying Don't do it, Ryan, You'll only make things worse, *but it's too late, my mouth is opening and I'm saying 'I'd rather be going out with an ould doll who could keep her knickers on at her Debs' and she slaps me, she fucking clatters me, and starts marching off down the footpath in her tiny dress and her wobbly heels and when I readjust my jaw and follow she spins around and screeches, 'Oh my God, OH MY GOD, you have no right to say that to me after you fucked that tourist, Oh my God I had AN EXCUSE, you were IN PRISON' and well, that's shattered the shit, hasn't it? And I walk behind her and tell her I'm sorry, sorry, fucking sorry and the top-up comes up on me and catches her shortly afterwards and we end up shifting the faces off each other by a pebble-dashed wall at the side of the road at five o'clock in the morning, and whether that's something a dealer or a DJ does I don't fucking know.*

'Ryan,' she says, 'Ryan.'

'Mmm?'

'You know this is like, "it" for me?' Her jaw is going ninety.

'Mmm.' My teeth have Velcroed.

'Let's have a baby,' she says.

I go, 'Ha?' but all of a sudden she's teared up, and where I thought I'd laugh and tell her to come down off her yoke before making any life-changing decisions, I end up pulling her onto my shoulder and rocking her back and forth and telling her, Whatever you want and whenever you want it, *and usually I'd chalk this silliness down to the night, the shots and the Ecstasy, but there's something different this time, and even in my wastedness I can feel it. I hold on to her and tell her I love her and tell her I'll do anything she wants me to do but beyond my words and her weight in my arms there's the knowing we fucked this up. There was something beautiful here once.*

22

Easier get a taste for arson than murder.

Maureen accidentally-on-purpose left the candles by the curtains and burned her house down. It had, at the time, been a means to an end but she'd really enjoyed the spectacle once it got going.

With murder she found a definite crossed line, and it was hair-breadth. One second there was life, the next it was gone. The ultimate in finality. Once you cross over you can never go back.

Arson was a different thing and a glorious thing. It was a monument to its own ritual. Once the fire caught it etched a statement into the sky. There was time to savour it and time, too, to quench it, if second thoughts were your thing.

She watched the brothel burn from a broken doorstep across the river. The fire brigade was almost as punctual as the amateur photographers. There was a reverent hush and she longed to cross the bridge to tell the rubberneckers that there was no one inside, no one had died, no one would die, but she had to stay still and discreet. Modest, even. It was her handiwork but there would be no medals.

She watched as Jimmy turned up in his car – even across the river he was conspicuous as an invading army – and sprinted towards the firemen, and felt a little warmth herself, from a safe distance. There was something in the way of regard for her, then. Maybe it wasn't fondness but the idea of her dying of smoke inhalation clearly perturbed him. It was either that or he was stricken at the loss of the kitchen tiles.

Of course, he was rather heated in his own way, once he

realised she wasn't dead. He called her every name under the sun and nearly combusted listing all of the ways her insanity had inconvenienced him. To which she coolly replied, 'Don't you have insurance?' and sent him spitting out the door.

He swore to her that she wouldn't get away with trying the same trick twice, but her new dwelling, a ground-floor apartment in a gated city centre development called Larne Court, didn't deserve the punishment meted out to its antecedent. It was a modest place and she slept better without all that history weighing her down.

Robbie O'Donovan hadn't come with her. She didn't like to think of him being trapped where he'd fallen by thick black smoke but sure, he was dead already and she could hardly kill him again. She did wonder where he had taken himself, but she didn't miss him.

The vagrant up at the Laundry, a year and a half ago now, had told her there was nothing as cleansing as a good fire. Maureen had assumed to test the hypothesis, but while ridding the city of the brothel had made her feel better, it hadn't resonated, at least not in the chords she was attuned to. She had done it for Robbie and for young Georgie, but, she realised, nine months afterwards and analysing her failings, she hadn't done it for herself.

So in the sunny September, she rectified that.

You couldn't go wrong with hippies. Their philosophy hinged on their empathy and Maureen had tried sons and priests and whores and had come away without a dash of castigation. Maybe her sinless exile really had depleted the universe's urge to shit on her. She wanted to be sure.

Out of her new gate and a hundred yards to the right there was a newsagent's, and outside of the newsagent's on most mornings sat a pasty beggar in baggy jeans and plastic runners. She usually bought him a cup of tea and a sandwich and stopped to ask how he was, because he fascinated her. He was young enough to have a mammy somewhere. There was a two-week period in August when he was missing from his pew, but he'd returned before anyone's worry could be moved to action, and told Maureen he'd gone to stay with some kindly dropouts outside Mitchelstown. It had been a bid to cleanse himself of smack and it hadn't worked. Still, he was appreciative of the dropouts' conviction.

'Mitchelstown,' she mused.

'Yeah. There's this girl called Ruby Dea. She's got a farm above and she has the gates open to any ould gowl she takes pity on. Place is full of caravans and wigwams. She used to be in one of those cults.'

Maureen sniffed. 'The Catholic Church?'

He enunciated carefully. 'No. A cult. She doesn't talk much about it, but she has more than a few ex-believers up there. Ex-believers of all sorts.'

And sure how could Maureen Phelan resist that? Only hours after gorging on the beggar's tale she converted, and became Mo Looney, wife to the man Dominic Looney would have been. She draped herself in sorrow and headed up to Mitchelstown to find the girl called Ruby Dea, who turned out to be less of a girl and more of a matron, all skirts and woolly cardigans.

At first Ruby Dea thought Maureen was an irate mammy coming to claim back a loafer and blanched accordingly, but it wasn't long before she accepted Mo Looney as another casualty of faith, and lent her a two-man tent to knock out a space in a fallow field.

There were, as the beggar had promised, others. There was one twentysomething with a couple of small children and a ramshackle mobile home, who kept to herself in the bottom corner of the same field. 'Hiding from a husband,' Ruby Dea confided. There was a jittery youth whom Maureen was sure couldn't last the night from whatever longing had leached into his marrow. But the rest of the residents were friendly. Maureen was the oldest and they treated her as some Biddy Early come to set them straight. She took advantage, getting a man named Peadar to put up her tent and a girl named Saskia to make her some dinner.

It was her intent to stay only for the weekend, but come Sunday evening the hippies had spilled nothing but tobacco leaf and quinoa down their fronts, and Maureen wasn't in the mood for holding it against them.

She sat on the grass outside her borrowed tent and watched the sun set. Across the way, Saskia waved and eventually came to sit beside her, and Maureen gave her a beatific smile and patted her knee. As the dew formed they got to talking. Saskia told Maureen about her upbringing down in Kerry – 'Not too different to this, if you can believe it' – and Maureen listened with polite patience as crane flies skimmed the blades in front of them and faraway engines swept the roads.

'It was so unstructured, so *sloppy*, my childhood,' said Saskia. 'No rules, no pressure, and I rebelled in all sorts of oddly conservative ways. Everything my parents believed in, I condemned. Consider they believed in personal freedom and you get a snapshot of a real buttoned-up brat. I studied hard and went to university to spite them, not to suit myself. Graduated a virgin and found myself at a loose end because I had absolutely no interest in my law degree. So what did I do? Ran off and joined a cult.'

'A cult?'

There was something more on Saskia's face now, threaded through sun-darkened freckles and crows' feet. Disgust. It lit her up the way a smile should. Maureen winced in solidarity as the younger woman's voice continued, cracked, 'Well, when you look at Christianity that's essentially what it is, isn't it? Sorry, Mo. I hope you're not offended by that, but it's what I really think.'

'I'm not offended,' Maureen said, mildly.

'I was baptised by a real shower of freaks. The kind that hate absolutely everything: men are masters to be obeyed, women are dangerous sluts, sexuality has to be controlled to the nth. I lived with them for a couple of years until I remembered that Jesus wasn't supposed to be a subjugating bastard. I ran, and ended up with another bunch of Christians, but the doddering, smiley kind. But they had money and they had space, so I stayed with them and tried to live the life and be a decent disciple. Five years. Would you believe that?'

'So what happened?'

'Sudden disillusionment. A whole life swept away in the blink of an eye. We're pretty fragile, you know?'

She was staring straight ahead. Maureen mimicked her. They divided the washed-out evening light between them. On the other side of the field, the hermit mother held one of the children at arm's length to brush burs off its back and legs.

'There was another girl down there with us for the last couple of years,' Saskia continued. 'Had problems with alcohol, wandered into the light pissed. She had a relationship with one of the men and she got pregnant. All that Christian love just melted away. The guy's family muscled in and insisted on custody of the baby. Poor girl, she was distraught. The Christians refused to back her up. Told the guy's family that they were right to assume guardianship because the girl had been on the game before she'd turned to Jesus. They waited for their opportunity to stitch her up and by God, did they take it. She ran off; who knows where she is now? About a week later I took off too.'

Small world, thought Maureen, but she said nothing.

'I hope she's OK,' said Saskia.

'And are you OK?'

'I'm getting there.'

'I thought I needed a confessor,' said Maureen. 'One time. Took me a while to realise but in the end it came to me . . .' And she paused, let the thought permeate, like a bead of brilliant colour dropped into a glass of water. 'There's nothing there. No confessor, no penitent, no sin, no sacrament. Just actions to be burned away.'

'Burned? Strong word.'

'Nothing as cleansing as a fire,' Maureen said.

Ryan knew it was going to be a disaster before they'd even packed the car. He stood in the sitting room with Joseph and stared down at the provisions with despair and affection; Karine, in the bathroom at the top of the stairs checking her festival braids, had stacked her life's effects in the middle of the floor. Two bags of clothes. An inflatable mattress. Three pillows. A mirror. A toiletries case in which you could fit half-a-dozen small appliances. A pair of pink wellington boots with a faux fur trim, her knock-off Uggs and two pairs of flats. A duvet.

'A fucking duvet, Cusack.'

'I know.'

'You're going to have to talk to her.'

'I know.'

She hadn't wanted to go in the first place, so the notion of having to chastise her before they'd even left the house struck him as counter-productive. Karine loved music but Ryan could imagine occasional furniture more outdoorsy. Joseph had demanded a wingman for Electric Picnic and Ryan had been more than happy to oblige, but Karine would be damned if she was letting him go drinking for a weekend without a chaperone. She didn't trust him. And he was glad she was coming with him because he didn't fucking trust her either.

She'd tried to persuade him to select one of the 'glamping' options – some colossal wigwam that cost a grand to rent for the three days and came with its own monkey butler, he assumed – but he'd told her it wasn't right to two-tier their party. They'd camp in the main grounds with Joseph and his buddies. She had pouted. He had told her she didn't have to come at all. They had had an almighty row about it that had lasted a whole week.

'A fucking duvet,' Joseph said again.

Karine came down the stairs rooting in her bag and started when she saw them.

'What's the matter?' she said, brightly, but her eyes were steel-set. Half past eight in the morning and she was raring for round two.

Joseph said, 'We're going to look like we've been looting.'

'What?'

'Seriously, Karine. There's less shit in the Argos catalogue.'

'What do you propose I leave behind?' she said, folding her arms.

Ryan raised his eyebrows at Joseph, who met the challenge and scowled back.

‘Tell her,’ he said.

‘Tell her what, boy?’

‘Tell her this is too much stuff.’

Ryan sat back onto the couch and ran his hands over his head. Joseph took the car keys from the coffee table and bumbled around the installation and out of the room, tutting. Karine’s nails, specially painted black with neon rainbow stripes, drummed against her upper arms.

‘There’s got to be some stuff you don’t need,’ Ryan said.

‘What,’ she enunciated, ‘do you. Propose. I leave behind?’

‘I don’t know. Most of the shoes? A metric tonne of the make-up? We’re going to a festival, girl, not searching for Doctor fucking Livingstone.’

‘You’re being mean to me already,’ was her reply.

‘I’m not being mean to you already.’

‘You are,’ she said. ‘You never wanted me to come.’

‘Don’t be daft.’

‘It’s true. You’ve been trying to put me off for weeks. You’d much rather be up there on your own, wouldn’t you? You could fuck whatever slut you liked then.’

The words were caustic and he deserved them; Elena from Salerno had been the kick-off of a really bad habit. He looked up at Karine and she stared back at him, flushed, and maybe it was just because it was early morning or the start of a potentially great weekend or maybe even because he was a bit hungover, but he didn’t want to fight with her, couldn’t see the justification tucked into that pile of superfluous wossnames.

She identified the change in him and reeled back the tantrum.

‘I just don’t want to be uncomfortable, Ryan.’

‘But you won’t be, girl.’

‘I will be! I hate being mucky and I hate not having anywhere to shower and . . . and you know the girls he’ll have around him. Joseph. You know his mates. They’ll be all these ripped tights rocker bitches and that’s not me at all and . . .’ She exhaled. ‘They’re all gonna hate me.’

‘It’s not even possible to hate you, girl.’

'They'll think I'm a slut and I just want to be pretty for you.'

He got up, stepped over two of the pillows and the make-up case and held her.

'You don't need to be anything for me,' he said, and she shied away from his kisses and flexed her shoulders and said, 'I do, though, Ryan. I'm not good enough.'

'Oh God, please don't say that. Please.'

'It's true, isn't it?'

'None of it is your fault. None of it. I'm a dickhead who can't believe his luck.'

'Are you only saying that because you want me to leave half this stuff behind, though?'

'No.' He wrapped his arms tighter around her. 'Bring all of it. Bring your whole fucking bedroom in a trailer if you like.'

She rubbed her cheek against his chest like a cat and said, 'Tell Joseph.'

Elena. Sasha Carey who was friends with Joseph's ex-girlfriend. Rachel O'Riordan; she worked behind the bar in Room, a night-club in town. Christina whatever-the-fuck-her-surname was, at that party in Ballincollig; she of the lacklustre blowjobs. Triona Neville who booked session musicians down in the Union studios; she was at least twenty-three but what the fuck. Kasia . . . yeah, he didn't know her surname either, back at Bobo's gaff, and that was only last week. Was he finished yet? He didn't know. He hoped so.

Betrayal was a miserable salve and he was not at all cut out for it. It had started with a beautiful tourist, a goddess come to his sphere specifically to grant him justice; it should have ended there too. Beautiful as Elena was, she wasn't what he wanted. What he wanted was to go back in time and stop himself getting caught with Dan Kane's coke so that Karine would never have cheated on him. Even if he could only go as far back as the night he met Niall Vaughan in The Relic, just to walk the fuck away when Karine told him to. What he wanted, Ryan Cusack, was Karine D'Arcy, all of her: body, soul and intent.

That denied to him, he tried revenge, and the more he pushed it the harder it punished him. The ease at which he coaxed opportunity was a gilded curse. His life had become a gauntlet run of parties, negotiations, car parks, VIP rooms. He'd done more cocaine in the last year and a half than he was comfortable thinking about, and that's what it had come to: cocaine, money, pills, women.

Oh, very fucking glamorous. It wasn't glamour that kept him sleepless and dry-mouthed, or prompted the big deals and the big reprisals. And what had he become, in his travels through the underworld? Just another cheating cunt in a city of cheating cunts. It had started when he was fifteen and he was stupid for thinking he could hold it back. The predictability of his transformation hurt him terribly. He hated it. He hated the girls who came on to him at parties and his inability to say no to a nice smile and a fresh slice. He hated it all, he hated himself, he hated Dan, he hated Karine; it was all just hate hate hate, a cacophony, a blizzard, line after line after line.

The first night was a dream, more than just figuratively. Having pitched tents and torn open slabs of lager, they dropped a few yokes and crowded around each other at the backs of the big tops that housed the star performances, dancing and drinking, shouting and wading chin-deep into conversations of a hazy and numinous quality.

The day after had been stuffed into a timetable and suffered for it. Ryan had acts he wanted to see and a girlfriend who wanted placating. They walked the breadth of the arena, their tempers slipping. Twice there was a proper, thunderous row which made shit of the moods of the people around them. Once, Joseph took him aside and told him to rein it the fuck in, but though Ryan took the words as wise and heartfelt, they weren't gospel, and he couldn't heed them. After the second row Karine said fuck it, she was going home, and had gotten halfway to the main gates before he caved in and dashed after her. But sure what could he do? They were now as they would always be: splintered but desperate, in love and worn out.

Karine retired just after midnight but he was nowhere near ready for sleep, thanks to the double-drop he'd sneaked only an hour back. There was a discussion at the door of Joseph's tent. Joseph was mucky-stoned – 'I couldn't get up if I climbed your fucking leg, Cusack' – but Ryan was itching for a distraction, and in the end he wandered off to the rave in the woods with Joseph's friend Izzy, who played lead guitar in a punk outfit called Scruffy The Janitor and taught a contemporary dance class on Thursdays. She wore lots of eyeliner, but never any lipstick. Joseph was desperately in love with her, and proved it by pretending very badly that he wasn't.

There was no dancing. Ryan blamed himself because the pills were the best he'd had all year and he'd known before he'd even arrived at the Picnic that he'd be blasted. He sat instead on the grass, back from the dancers, with his arms hooked round his shins and, from time to time, his forehead on his knees.

Izzy bounced over. 'You're no craic.'

'I am usually. I'm just *fffffucked*.'

'You're no craic all day. You or Carly.'

'Karine.'

'That's right,' she said. She pulled her hair over her shoulders and started plaiting it. Around them the tree trunks blazed neon green and pink, and the beats crashed.

'Why are you guys even together if you don't like each other?' she shouted.

Ryan was getting rushes up the inside of his arms, so he stretched, and put his hands flat on the ground behind him, and let his head loll backwards. Izzy sat beside him.

'How long are you going out, like?'

'Years and years. Since the night of my fifteenth.'

'Oh right. So it's a bad habit, hard to break.'

'No, no.'

'Look,' yelled Izzy. 'It's kind of obvious. You keep her all the ways up here . . .' She stretched an arm over her head and walked her fingers along the underside of the canopy far above. 'And she doesn't deserve it. I mean that with kindness and love, by the way.

It's a shit thing to be someone else's religion. And you know, even you've got issues with it and it's coming out in all sorts of shitty little ways. Like, Joseph was telling me the story. First she did the dirt on you and now you can't stop doing the dirt on her. And still you're wearing her like a hair shirt. It's fucking tragic. As in, it's sad *and* it's pathetic.'

'She didn't.'

'She didn't what?'

'She didn't do the dirt on me first. I did it first.' He didn't leave Izzy time enough to soak it in. He turned to her and said, 'Joe doesn't know that and neither does she.'

'Shit,' she said.

As the beats ebbed into a breakdown, the voices around them came back to a roar. There was a chorus of whistles and cheers. Izzy moved closer.

'You're not to tell either of them,' he said.

'Obviously.'

'Because it'd end me.'

'Cross my heart and all that.'

He rolled out the confession. The yokes swam through him. He could see himself: sitting on the ground beside his nodding acquaintance, eyes perfect circles and jaw slipping in and out of alignment. He got to the end of his story and it meant nothing. No weight off. He still felt like a cunt.

'You know what it is?' shouted Izzy. 'You set up this whole relationship as this picture-perfect penance for something stupid you did when you were fifteen and you're pissed off now that Carly . . . Karine . . .' She raised her eyes to the lights. '. . . didn't follow the script.'

'No. I love her. That's all.'

'So why'd you keep cheating on her?'

'Because. I dunno.' An epiphany. God, he remembered epiphanies. 'Because I can.'

'Oh man. That's such a shitty thing to say.'

'No, I mean . . . Because I didn't want to the first time. Or I didn't mean to, and so now at least . . . Fuck. You know.'

'You didn't mean to, like, you feel Missus MILF had all the power or something?'

'I don't even fucking remember. It's just . . . Yeah. Probably. I dunno. I don't know why I did it and it kills me.'

'Ever think you're being too hard on yourself? We all did stupid shit when we were kids, like. I was into shoplifting and I only got caught once and I'm still morto. And fifteen-year-old boys are just . . . all dick, like. So, maybe it was just hormonal. Adolescent craziness. Maybe fucking *own* it. Face up to it, own it, and let it go.'

'How do I own it? I didn't want it. Hence the last few ould dolls I fucked. If I'm going to be hung for it, it might as well be for shit I actually wanted to do. Every fuck improves the ratio.'

A girl walking behind them stood on his fingers. He examined them as she came down to his level, put her arm around his shoulder and bawled an apology into his ear. Ryan smiled forgiveness. The girl kissed his cheek.

'That is seriously fucked up!' Izzy shouted, once the clumsy girl had barrelled on. 'Dude, I love you wholly right now, but you have issues. Like I think you need to see someone.'

Ryan stared at his muddy fingers.

'But you're not going to do that, are you?' Izzy went on. 'Because you're too fucking male or something. Well, you know what I think you should do? I think you should go talk to Missus MILF. Ask her for the gory details. This is a part of your story you can't even remember and it's turned you into a control freak.'

'I can't do that either,' Ryan said. 'She took off a few months back. Left a ton of debt behind her, locked the doors and high-tailed it. Even her daughter doesn't know where she is.'

'This is insane!' Saskia hissed. 'Mo, I am totally on your team in terms of philosophy, absolutely, one hundred per cent, you are right and I should know, I've been looking for truth long enough. But this? This is morally wrong. *Criminally* wrong. I can't be part of it. I can't *blah blah blah blah blah*.'

Maureen stood at the gable end of the church, her back to

rolling, sightless countryside. She had already broken a stained-glass window, partly to take the first step and partly to check whether the place was alarmed. It wasn't. It was probably too small. This was the thing with the countryside parishes; you were attacking something of minor import and massive sentimental value.

'Mo, listen . . .' reasoned Saskia; she did not make as good a pupil as her ex cult-mate. 'You have a bone to pick with the Catholic Church; I get that. I'm Irish as well, you know. We all harbour resentment. But this is criminal damage! You'll spend the rest of your life in prison!'

'Jesus, how old do you think I am?'

'I can't be a part of this. The Gardaí will follow this back to the commune. Think of the others. Everyone's trying to deal with their own issues. Causing havoc will impinge on them.'

'Era, it's not like we're family.'

'You can't come back, then. This kind of mischief is at total odds with how we're trying to live!'

'Mischief me arse,' cried Maureen. 'How you're trying to live . . . don't make me cough up a lung! Wasters and dropouts and dregs, hiding in fields in the arse end of Ireland, oh! don't stick your heads out of the trenches anyway, for fear, for fear.'

'Oh right! Right! So we're just not being active enough. And what in God's name is this going to achieve? D'you think this is anarchy? This isn't anarchy!'

'It's what you make of it.' Maureen turned, her back to the stone, and held the night sky in her outstretched arms. 'And you should run with it, because they can't catch me, you know. I've done my time. Everything after that is my bonus to spend as I wish. Take advantage if you want to make your mark.'

'What, and follow you? Mo, this is insane because *you* are insane, and I've copped preachers a lot more cunning than you.'

'Grand,' said Maureen. 'Off you go. Tell Scooby Doo thanks for everything.'

'Oh my God. You have no respect.'

'Scoot along, Saskia. And for Jesus's sake will you learn to stand on your own pair? Commune to commune – get a fecking job!'

Well, that had done it. Maureen had banked on having an ally, and Shattered Saskia had seemed a damn good candidate, in the absence of tried-and-tested serfs. It certainly looked as if she was going to tell tales, which was probably to be expected in an off-the-wagon born-again. She hadn't even waited long enough to hear blinding reason: the smoke would belch into the air but everyone would feel cleaner after it. It had worked for the Laundry, it had worked for Jimmy's brothel, and it would work for the Catholic Church.

As Saskia stalked away, Maureen lifted onto tiptoes and peered in through the splintered glass. Not much to see but varnished shadows, and varnish likes to burn.

Three days of Carling cans, dropping nodges, woodland confessions and curry cheese chips left Ryan in a haze bordering incoherence, but Joseph was working on the Monday evening and so he'd promised to drive him home immediately after the closing gigs. They packed up their gear on the Sunday afternoon and Ryan and Joseph carried it back to the car park, twenty minutes away, in two trips, while Karine went gatting in the dell with a bunch of college friends. They all met up again, Joseph got off with one of the college girls, Karine had a minor meltdown over having left her facial wipes in the wrong bag, and Ryan popped his final yoke from the stash tucked down his balls and lay back on the grass and tried, gamely but unsuccessfully, to let the lot float off and pop in the sticky autumn air.

They made for the arena a couple of hours later to catch the last of the big-hitters. Joseph had some experimental guitarist he wanted to see; he brought Karine's college friend with him. Ryan and Karine headed to the main stage. They found a patch of grass near the back and away from the main thoroughfare, and sat down, and she positioned herself in front of him so as to secure rueful cuddles without having to speak to him. He put his arms around her, pulled her back against his chest, put his nose against her bare shoulder and closed his eyes as the sediment of his last pill settled onto the pit of his stomach.

How they had managed to barney away the sweet evenings of the dying summer he didn't know. It felt like they'd been fighting forever. Stuff he'd said, stuff she'd said, wound upon wound ripped of their stitches. He remembered something of Niall Vaughan, and something of Elena from Salerno whose scent Karine had identified on her boyfriend's body after he'd laid stammered clues at her feet, like a cat bringing corpses to its mistress. He remembered his conversation with Izzy.

'I'm sorry,' he said.

She turned her head. 'What are you sorry for?'

'Everything.'

Directly across from him a mammy wearing face paint and fairy wings held a joggling toddler at arm's length and brushed unseen contaminants off its back and legs.

Karine waited until he took his head from her shoulder and let him kiss her. A quarter of a mile away, a figure lost on a mammoth stage invited a thunderstorm of approval. Karine took a sip from her drink. 'Is it sad that I just wanna go home now?' she asked, and he kissed her again and told her no, course it wasn't, it had been a crazy weekend, he was just as keen for a shower and his bed.

They set off from the car park at two in the morning, with Joseph's new squeeze in tow. Ryan had a fag coming back through Stradbally, another when he hit the motorway. In the back seat the girls nodded. Joseph, still buzzing, blethered on about the experimental guitarist, the inspiration he was bringing home with him, the whole experience. 'We're *definitely* coming back next year,' he said. In the rear-view mirror Ryan watched Karine's nose twitch and her mouth fall open. Mist dashed the window behind her and for a moment it felt like there was something in pursuit. His luck catching up with him, maybe. The moment washed over him and dissipated before he could get a handle on it. Maybe the only thing following him was a mighty hangover. He shook his head.

He stopped at Urlingford for a coffee and a Moro and pulled

off the motorway again just outside Mitchelstown for a slash and it was there, pissing onto the ditch off the hard shoulder, that he noticed the fire.

He went back to the car and said to Joseph, 'D'you see that?'

They climbed the ditch and stared into the dark. It was a fire, no doubt about it. Maybe five, six miles in.

'It must have been called already,' said Joseph. 'I'll ring them just to be sure.' He phoned 999 with one finger in his ear and relayed vague coordinates to the person at the other end as cars slid past them from one acre of pitch to another.

'D'you reckon we could find it?' Ryan said.

He did wonder why, as he exited the motorway and drove down winding regional roads, but what answer could he conjure, except he was curious and oddly loath to return home, tired and all as he was? Neither girl in the backseat stirred. Joseph went quiet and furrowed his brow, as invested in the mystery now as his cousin, though out of jovial drunken recklessness beside Ryan's bitter focus. There was no Internet to get maps up and what were they marching towards anyway? They kept spotting the flare, losing it behind copses, twisting away from it as the road tangled like a knotted snake. As the clock crept to four, they shared a glance and silently agreed to let it go.

Ryan pulled over and got out. A gate led into a wide, thin field, bordered by a line of trees, then a low hill and beyond that, they could see the orange glow of the relinquished beacon and smell its acrid smoke.

'If we made off now,' joked Joseph, 'over the hill there, like the intrepid bastards we are, we'd pin that gaff down in fifteen minutes. But who'd mind the women?'

'I hope it's not a house,' Ryan said.

'Nah.' Joseph caught his shoulder. 'It's probably some barn or something.'

'So fucking quiet here.'

'It'd drive me mental living in a place like this. Sensory deprivation. No wonder the boggers are always seeing ghosts.'

'Are they?'

'Yeah. Shades of dead people on the sides of the road, lads there since the Rising. The devil picking his teeth at the crossroads. Weird shit. We've more history than we're able for.'

Joseph turned to go back to the car but Ryan stayed where he was, watching the fire. His cousin came back, caught his shoulder again, knocked his head against his back and said, 'What's up with you, Cuse?'

'Just coming down, is all.'

'Dunno about that. Told you you shouldn't have brought her, man. You need room to breathe, the pair of you.'

'That's not it.'

'No? Coz it's obvious you're crumbling, you and her.'

'Going up in flames, you mean.'

'Maybe,' said Joseph. 'Maybe.'

'And nothing grows from ashes.'

'You're going ending it?'

More lights now, more smoke. Wherever it was, someone was tackling it.

'No,' Ryan said. 'I can't.'

Unsettled by ghosts and confession, he went back to the car.

23

Georgie liked to compose letters to David she was never going to write.

Dear priggish David mama's boy Coughlan,
How is my daughter? You don't need to answer, so unzip your prissy mouth and let yourself breathe. I'm coming for her. I'm nearly there. I have more money now than you'd be able to fathom. How did I get it? Oh, nefarious ways. I was wicked as the wickedest woman, and you know how we are, David, wicked as wicked can be. But it's all your fault. You made me a whore, so what harm charging premium rates for others to do the same? At least they won't knock me up then condemn me for it. All the shuffling horns of the city are better than your limp prick. I hope your Christian girlfriend chokes on it.

Enjoy your never-ending poker tournament/wanking cycle, you bearded creep.

Your pal, Georgie.

She didn't have half as much money as she wanted him to think she did, but it wasn't as if he'd find out either way, if she never got round to writing those letters. She hoped the strength of her bitterness was enough to carry it back to him as an edge to the wind, or a nagging pain that kept him up at night. Fuck the letters. Fuck David. She owed him nothing. He owed her a universe.

The notion of debt had been pressed on her and she learned to open her hands and allow its weight to pull her down. J.P. had put her earning after the debacle with his mother; he said she owed him a favour. She did six months' penance in a house where she was the only Irish girl. She reckoned she'd been brought in as a substitute for some unfortunate who'd run off or been offed. When there were better girls to choose from he let her go again. 'Don't get any ideas about telling tall tales, either,' he said. 'Coz in this world, girl, you're just a scrapheap bit, and no one's going to believe you.'

Scrapheap or not, she was the sergeant at last and this was the drill: she got up, made tea, sat around thinking of the money she'd made and lost and the money she'd make again, and did a bit of work, when she was able to.

In order to get Harmony back she needed money. In order to make money she needed to continue doing the only thing she was good for. In order to continue doing the only thing she was good for she needed medication. Living expenses, taken from her nest egg. She used the brothel contacts, even after they'd let her leave; the path of least resistance would do fine now that she had a destination. In her head she told David she was wiping her arse with fifty euro notes but the real world bled her. She was doing far too much, but she had to be muddled for the graft or the graft would never get done. She tried alternatives but nothing worked as well. There was reason in it, no matter how unpleasant the logic.

Night was when the trouble started. She didn't sleep. She didn't feel threatened as such, just restless, stuck in some cosmic halfway house, just a little out of whack and waiting for her number to be called and the process explained anew. Twenty-six was just like being twenty-one. It was nothing like being twenty-three. Georgie felt the dichotomy and it confused her. How could you be two people in five years? How could you undergo such a metamorphosis – whore to saint – and paint the slattern back over the scar tissue only a few short years later?

She lost interest in her detective novels. They were long-winded and she didn't have the time for cheesy gasbaggery. Instead she sat up reading true crime files on the Internet, nauseous and lost, following link after link until the morning came and it was time to start over. Sometimes she went to the

Missing Persons site because Robbie's picture was still there, staring out of a photograph she hadn't provided. Must have been his mother, if he had one. She'd pay her a visit one day. Tell her to quench the home fires.

'You think you'd notify *someone*,' Robbie chastised. 'After you telling the old woman I mattered, and all.'

'Oh, you mattered,' Georgie replied. 'It's your fault I'm in this mess. Bad habits you taught me. Bad habits from a bad man.'

'Yeah, blame a man and not yourself, Georgie.'

'Men are all the fucking same! Maybe you *didn't* matter, Robbie O'Donovan. There's a million more out there just like you.'

She never lost focus on the goal, even when her strategies shrivelled to husks of ideas, the residue of forgotten escape plans.

Though Maureen's words circled, she kept the scapular knotted around her wrist.

One Saturday night in April, Georgie turned a trick with a bloke who dropped her at the wrong end of the city centre. She made her way back to her usual spot slowly, shaken – he had seemed like an OK chap until he'd finished and then his disgust was tangible. She swung into an off-licence that was just shutting and bought a naggin of vodka and drank a third of it in the toilets at McDonald's before continuing on her way. The alcohol kicked in and circled the fear, gave it warmth and made it greater.

Alcohol was not going to fix this, but God never closed a door without opening a window.

For a moment she couldn't think who he was. Plenty of familiar faces crossed her path, of course. All day and night she spotted ones who'd paid for her, and for a moment she assumed he was another; punters were as likely to be tall and dark and good-looking as they were to be sweaty, squat clichés. He was walking down the street with a couple of other guys, all in their early twenties or so, jostling, lively types. Ryan. She hadn't seen him in such a long time. He was a grown-up now, all legs and cheekbones. She called after him and one of his companions jogged his arm and gestured backwards and he waited, God bless him, as she hurried over.

'Ryan. It's been a while.'

'Jesus fucking Christ, Georgie.'

She flushed. She had lost weight, she knew. It might have been what she was wearing: a mini dress, black heels, but in that there was no difference between her and the chattering girls out dancing tonight, except intent. Maybe not even that.

'It's good to see you,' she offered.

It was cold for April. There was frost settling while the city partied; it clarified the air, outlined the orange street lights, the glow from pub windows, the neon signs outside of the nightclubs. He was wearing a heavy jacket, dark jeans and thick white skate shoes, and even so he had rammed his hands into his pockets and was throwing his weight from foot to foot.

'I wish I could say the same thing,' he said. 'What the fuck happened to you?'

There was no point in pretending she'd simply found her thighs again after a few years of Christian body-policing. She shook her head.

'Really?' she joked, feebly. 'I got that old-looking?'

'Have you even been eating?'

'You're not a bit saucy! Of course I've been eating.'

'When? Last fucking summer? Jesus.'

She was needled. *What if I'd had an eating disorder*, she thought. *Or cancer? Or lost a parent and was wasting away with grief?* She chose to ignore his tetchiness. 'How are you keeping?' she said. 'I think the last time I saw you was . . .'

Up at his father's house. When she was pregnant with Harmony, and searching for Robbie, hormones backed into her brain, making her brave and crazy. Up in that poky council house, only a paper wall between them and Tara Duane, with Ryan's father asserting his ignorance and exposing the frailty of the lead with statements she only understood months afterwards; his anger that she'd disturbed his children, and threatened his status. She tried to put it out of her mind, and Ryan picked up on the pitch and cut her off: 'Did you find your fella?'

'No,' Georgie said. 'He died.'

She might have expected commiseration under different circumstances. Instead she got exactly what she expected; he flinched, and changed the subject.

'You had your kid, then.'

'Yeah,' said Georgie. 'A little girl. Harmony. Isn't that pretty?'

He nodded and looked over her shoulder and down the street.

Off his discomfort she conceded, 'I didn't just stop you to say hello.'

'No?'

'No.' She asked his shoes, 'Are you still dealing?'

'Are you still on the game?'

'Why?' she snapped; the force of his rejoinder had surprised her. 'Are you up for doing a swap?'

'Funny,' he said. He slouched and there was an echo of compromise to the action, but she wasn't finished, freewheeling on the vodka burn and the echoes of their last meeting. 'What business is it of yours?' she said. 'Are you going to save me?'

He neither answered nor moved.

'*Judgey bollocks*,' she quoted. 'Isn't that what you said?'

'What d'you want, Georgie?'

'I need something,' she said. 'I just wanted to know if you're still in the habit of selling.'

'Not on the fucking street I'm not.'

She felt the statement for an edge, but couldn't determine if he meant to cut her. 'What's that mean?'

'It means I've moved up in the world, girl. I don't carry shit around with me.'

'You don't deal anymore?'

He paused. 'Just what I said, girl. I don't carry shit around with me.'

'Oh.' The chance of instant gratification faded into another night of hurried phone calls and bitten nails. 'I'm kinda hanging, like.'

A group of girls skirted around them. Ryan moved back against the wall and Georgie stepped towards him; he put his hand up.

'Hanging,' he said. 'Back fucking hanging again.'

'It's just a turn of phrase, for God's sake. Fine, I'm not hanging. It's Saturday. I'm just a bit bored, OK?'

He gestured tersely at the moving streets. 'That's Saturday boredom, Georgie. You're wasting away. You're not asking me for help with your night out.'

'I'm not wasting away!'

'Fucking look in a fucking mirror!'

'What's it to you? It's not like you know me at all, is it?'

He remembered the words. 'I don't know you from Adam,' he said, head back against the wall, staring again over her shoulder, like a bouncer, she thought, or a guard. 'That doesn't mean I'm stockpiling the crazy shit just to spite you.'

'A dealer with a conscience,' she said. 'That's rich. You weren't so bothered about selling me shit when I was supposed to be in recovery.'

'You weren't doing such a good impression of a corpse at the time.'

'Judgey bollocks,' she said, stepping away, backwards for a few beats to watch for signs of concession, turning when she saw nothing of the sort. 'You've changed,' she said, over her shoulder. 'What happened to you? What happened to that decent kid?'

'You killed him off with your custom,' he barked. 'Get your fucking act together, Georgie.'

She marched between groups of revellers and strolling couples, holding her arms tight against the chill. Then he was beside her again. He caught her arm, she yelped, and it must have looked bad, it must have, he was bearing over her, one fist bunched around her arm and the other at an angle as if he was going to swing for her, but she knew that even on the street on a Saturday night he wouldn't be challenged on it, no one wants to interfere, never fucking interfere . . .

'Where's your kid?' he said.

Her lips moved to whimper and he snapped, 'Where's your kid, Georgie?' and she didn't dare snap back, she cried, 'I don't have her, she doesn't live with me, OK?'

'Who has her then?'

'Her dad. All right?'

He dropped her arm and stood chewing air and she took a chance on his new demeanour and pleaded, 'Look, I'm gagging, Ryan, if you can even give me a number . . .'

'I told you, that's not me anymore.'

'Like, even someone in your network or whatever, even someone from another crew, I don't mind.'

'Can't help you,' he said, and then, softer, 'Jesus, Georgie, you had your shit together.'

'What, hanging out with Cork's slackest cult?'

'Yeah, and now? It's like an episode of *The Walking Dead*, Georgie!'

'Look, I know I've slimmed down a bit . . .'

'It's not that. You look like shit.'

'This coming from a guy who makes people look like shit for a living?'

It wasn't a worthy comeback but it seemed to have done the trick. He fell back. 'There's a difference,' he said, and she replied, 'You'd hardly do what I do sober.'

'I'd hardly do what you do full stop.'

'And aren't you lucky you were born a boy, then? All you have to do is sell drugs.'

He looked down at the footpath, shaking his head.

'It's not like I want this,' Georgie said.

'Remember . . .' he said, slowly, and then he took her arm again, and escorted her to the edge of the path and the cold stone walls of their city centre. 'Remember the time I came down to you in that weird chapel place?'

The prayer hall. 'Yeah.'

'Remember you told me never to buy a prostitute?'

She remembered.

'But if I ask you to stop buying coke it wouldn't work.'

'That's sweet,' she said. Her voice cracked.

'If I told you that lads like me end up inside over shit you buy, would that stop you?'

There was nothing earnest to his expression. He seemed pained, impatient and resentful, all in one oddly beautiful tic.

She faltered. 'You don't know my life . . .'

'You don't give a fuck for mine,' he said, and took his hand away. She pushed her fingers over the spot he'd held, instinctively. And for the beat before he wordlessly left her she grasped something of what he was trying to say. And that it might have been nice to have someone like him, someone on the outside too, someone who got it, someone who might have stood by her and bawled her out of it when she stepped out of line.

When she made it home, two tricks later, she went online and deleted the bookmark for Robbie's Missing Person page, but found herself visiting him again later that night, and again, three times in total as the clock ticked on and she sat in her rented room, looking deep into Robbie's frozen eyes for something they might once have shared, but all she found was resentment, coming from inside her, rising up her throat.

24

'You are fucking joking me,' Jimmy choked, one day in the coldest April the city had seen in decades.

Maureen was like a lunatic. Not 'like', he thought. *Was* a lunatic. Right now, in her kitchen in the new apartment at Larne Court, she was doing a very passable impression of a maniacal beast, spitting, tutting, pacing.

'I'm not joking you,' she said.

Beside them, on the polished pine table, lay a copy of the *Echo*. Its front-page headline read 'Repairs Completed On North Cork Church' and underneath, '*No arrests made in nightmare arson attack*'.

'Well then why the fuck aren't you joking me?'

She stopped pacing and crinkled her nose as if she'd caught a whiff of decay. 'It was a statement,' she said.

'What kind of statement? "I'm off my fucking meds?" "I don't think my son's suffered enough?" "I'm suffering delusions of demonic grandeur?"'

'That's the problem with your generation,' she said. 'You're politically apathetic.'

'Oh? And what damn purpose does this kind of madness serve, Maureen? You burn a country church down? Up in fucking Mitchelstown, of all places?'

She slapped the table. 'It's a pyre, isn't it? For *that* Ireland. For *their* nonsense. For the yoke they stuck round our necks.'

'Jesus Christ, what are you on about? What, you wanted to make a metaphor of the horizon, was it? And you expected the buffers above to get that? Jesus, Maureen, have you any idea what they could have done over this? You're damn lucky they didn't root out some black-pantsed fourteen-year-old twerp and nail him to a fucking cross!'

'Well they didn't, did they?' she said. 'They did nothing. Why would they, sure? They've taken so much from me there's nothing left of me to see. I can do what I like and go where I like and all I get is a blind eye turned. It's ridiculous.'

'You want to get caught, Maureen? You want to spend a few years above in Limerick?'

'I can't get caught,' she said. 'Churches and brothels and Robbie O'Donovan, and not a climbing wisp of fault for any of them.'

'Oh, mother of Jesus.' He hung on to the back of the nearest kitchen chair and pinched his forehead. 'Maureen. Listen to yourself. You're not nine years old. You know this shit. Nothing goes unnoticed. You might think you got away with this and that, but people paid, and paid fucking dearly, for your messing.'

'Your insurance premium went up, I suppose.'

'You think you can burn buildings and kill gawky bayturs with impunity? Oh fuck me. Just because you don't see the stains doesn't mean you didn't make shit of things!'

There wasn't much more he could say. She refused to be moved. He couldn't tell whether anything was getting through, and in her madness he saw his city snap and tumble down and in the long years of his complicity he saw his weakness, as man and monster.

She felt she could do what she liked now. That much was clear to him. In burning down the brothel he had thought she'd made her decisive point and once he'd exhibited his rage he'd decided he could stand to grant her that last folly. He had stupidly assumed that was that. But the headline proved he couldn't trust her around loose ends. If a name lost from the lips of Tony Cusack could catch fire, then what could Maureen do with a living whore and a dented know-all like Duane?

Jimmy had watched the city long enough to know that it would right itself, sooner or later, and that the silence following Robbie O'Donovan's death was just a long, caught breath.

He extracted her promise that she wasn't going to get up to divilment as soon as the door shut behind him, and hurried to reinforce what he could before she got mind to break it.

Months back he'd been brought a mystery.

He hadn't had reason to bring the boat out in a while, but at the end of the summer he'd taken a day down at the yard, where he'd rolled up his sleeves and engaged in some therapeutic maintenance.

There was an ould fella who lived a couple of miles from the opposite end of the quay – Mike Costello, a gentleman bachelor, whose face was scored from coastline winds and disapproval at the unremitting advance of 'feckin' Japanese' technology. He had his own boat, though Jimmy rarely saw him do anything with it. More often he engaged in the lightly infuriating habit of sitting around on the quay with his Border Collie, smoking Players and offering unsolicited advice on the sea and sky. On this day, with the sun making sheets of blinding light from the puddles on the concrete, he approached Jimmy with customary solemnity, and asked after his plans for the vessel.

'I'll dock it this winter,' Jimmy said. 'It took a bit of a hammering last year.'

'Of course it did,' said Mike. 'And bringing it out in all weather, too. What you were at in January I don't know. Lucky you weren't mangled.'

'When was that?'

'January. In the rake of bad weather. Only the one time I saw you, in the early morning, but wasn't once enough? Ah sure, you do it for pleasure and you don't know what you're at; aren't you only a city boy? Dock it this winter and don't go making a widow of your good lady.'

Jimmy took this first exactly as he was tempted: he assumed Mike was mistaken. Hallucinating, even. Poking the ashes out of boredom and the malice boredom can call up. The image wouldn't leave him, though, and Jimmy wouldn't be where he was and who he was if he wasn't open-minded to cloaked dangers. He made delicate enquiries amongst his own, and no one had taken the boat out. He checked the dinghy and the boat itself for signs of mischief, and concluded there was no one tapping him for fuel and kicks on the high seas.

He didn't immediately suspect Tony Cusack, because suspicious as Jimmy was, he wasn't bloody insane. But there was an inkling, one day, driving into the wretch's terrace on unrelated business. Alongside Cusack's pile was Tara Duane's, boarded up. Jimmy asked his boys: *Did Duane take off?* It got back to him that she'd gone wandering, and that no one had any clue where; cops, drifters or the motherless chicks that lay for their sins under him.

You'd want to be stupid, he told himself, as he unwound the mystery. Tony Cusack knew where the boat was kept and where he'd been promised a watery grave. Tony Cusack had a set on Tara Duane. But Tara was a flighty fuck-up and Cusack a weeping fool. Most likely one of Jimmy's own had been moonlighting, and lying to him.

Still, though.

Still.

Jimmy did his sums.

Good clean murder was art, and that was reflected in its price. He could do the done thing and call in a professional, but even with favours recalled there'd be a cash penalty, and he baulked at the notion of spending five-figure sums tying loose ends on what was essentially a domestic spat. Five damn years he'd been taming this cock-up.

You're getting old, sneered the city. *Old and fat and soft and soft-headed.*

With Duane's disappearance he was left with two superfluous players.

Oh, far from soft-headed, he snapped.

With Duane's disappearance he wondered if he could line up his targets.

One to fall and take the other.

Against this backdrop, he re-examined the mystery of his borrowed boat and went with his gut.

He drove up to the estates on the hill and tried the handle of Cusack's front door. It opened. He let himself in.

Cusack was sitting at his kitchen table, a torn white envelope in one hand and a bill of some sort in the other. In granting himself access, Jimmy had not been quiet. But that was the thing, up where they had nothing worth stealing and five or six kids apiece. Privacy was neither granted nor expected.

Tony looked up and Jimmy watched his expression change.

'Afternoon, Anthony.'

He walked to the kitchen table and pressed his knuckles against its surface. Cusack gawped. The possibility that he thought their acquaintance suspended once more suggested itself to Jimmy, but he didn't derive the amusement from it he would otherwise have made use of. Cusack looked . . . fucking old.

'I need you to do something for me,' Jimmy said.

Cusack laid the bill on the table, and made a mask of his left hand. Jimmy looked over his head. The kitchen window was weather-splashed and smeared by little fingers writing lines in condensation, little palms wiping them off. The sill held the miscellanea of the poor bugger's life: coins and phone chargers and birthday cards soiled by the wet glass.

'You remember the whore,' Jimmy said.

Cusack said nothing, but looked down at the table and then back at Jimmy when his silence was matched. Jimmy took the eye contact as affirmation.

'She never stopped asking questions. Time's up on that bullshit. I want her gone.'

'Gone,' echoed Cusack. He took his hand from his mouth and said, 'What d'you mean, asking questions?'

'What d'you think I mean, Cusack? Come on, the ould brain isn't that mushed, is it? Asking fucking questions. Making fucking noise.'

'It's been years.'

'Years enough for your brood to grow up? No.'

Cusack came round to it. 'So you need what from me?'

'I need you to make her disappear.'

Jimmy pushed himself off the table and paced. Over at the sink, he flicked through forks drip-drying in a grey plastic caddy. Over at the drawers, he rifled through tea towels and school timetables. 'I need you to clean up another mess,' he said, evenly. 'I need you to do me one last turn. That's not so hard, is it, Cusack? For your own sake? For your kids'? I need you to end the whore so we can finally draw a line under this.'

Cusack said, 'I'm sure you have lads better qualified for this kind of craic' in a voice no match for his meaning.

'How would that be, Cusack? How would I have lads better qualified? This is our issue, and one I'm not keen on compounding. I'm not offering it up to anyone else. What do I look like? Fuck's sake.'

'Isn't this compounding it?'

'No. It's drawing a line under it. I told you already.'

Cusack managed to get to his feet. 'Jimmy,' he said. 'Jimmy', and his old friend stopped thumbing through the dregs and raised his eyebrows. 'What are you trying to do to me?' Cusack said. His voice was a testament to conviction lost. 'Jimmy . . . I helped. That's all I'm good for. Being given directions. Even then I get lost. You saw it yourself. This isn't something I'm even capable of doing. Think about what you're asking me.'

'Capable,' said Jimmy, and laughed. 'Oh, Tony. What's that they say? "You don't know your own strength till you're pushed?"'

Cusack shook his head. 'No point pushing. I can't do this.'

'You did Duane, didn't you?'

Tony sat down again. He put his face in his hands.

Jimmy waited.

'I don't know where Duane is,' Tony said.

'I can't imagine you do. It's been a long time since you sank her.'

'I had nothing to do with her taking off.'

'You did,' Jimmy said.

He returned to the side of the kitchen table and grasped Cusack's shoulder.

'She's no loss,' he said, mildly. 'And men do what they have to do, don't they? Bit of a vampire to that wan. She wasn't very good at masking it. And sure, didn't she fuck your young fella?'

'Where the fuck did you get that idea?'

'Aw, come off it. Straight from the gee-gee's mouth. That's why you put her window in. That's why you've been holding a grudge. Shattered glass, shattered bones . . . it's a slippery slope.'

It was a good fifteen seconds before Cusack responded.

'If you thought I had something to do with her running off, you'd hardly be saying shit like that to me.'

'What, because you think I'd be afraid of you? Oh Christ, you're hardly that naive.'

He let go of Cusack's shoulder and leaned back onto the table. It wouldn't matter what was said now. The man looked like a child in a dentist's chair. Jimmy shook his head. A spark was a complication, but out of deference to a shared past he wanted Cusack to show him something. Even a raised vein. A twitch, or narrowed eyes. Not this watery supplication.

'I don't blame you,' he said. 'My young fella is thirteen in the summer. If anyone interfered with him I'd rain down fire and fucking brimstone. So it was your right, Cusack.'

He leaned closer.

'And it was my fucking boat.'

'So you're saying I owe you?'

'So you're admitting you did it?' Jimmy straightened. 'I'm not saying you owe me, Cusack, not at all. This is your mess as much as it's mine. One of us has to get this sorted. It can't be me. You're a nobody. That's why it's you. You got away with the last one, didn't you?'

'I don't know where Duane went,' Tony said.

'Yeah, you said.' Jimmy went for the kitchen door. 'Let's say till Friday to find the girl and do the deed. If you need to go boating

I'll let you off one more time. Give me a buzz when you're finished and I swear to the Lord Above that we'll be done with this.'

'How do I know that?'

'What? You don't believe me?'

Cusack stood up. He leaned on the table, lost his nerve and looked down. 'How do I know you won't pin this on me? Isn't that why you roped me into the Robbie O'Donovan thing? That's what dopes like me are there for.'

Jimmy smiled, and jovially slapped his hands off the worktop. 'Putting two and two together, are we? And what fucking ridiculous number are we coming up with?'

'What would you want with this,' Tony said, 'except a place to pin the blame?'

Jimmy paused to weigh the violation.

'That could be it,' he said. 'And so what if it is?'

Cusack looked up.

'Just like that, Jimmy?'

'Just like that.'

'I did you a good turn, boy.'

'And what d'you want? A fucking medal? Cusack, if we lived in a world where good deeds meant anything I'd have played along, but this isn't that kind of world, and this isn't that kind of fuck-up.'

'You dragged me into this.'

'I did.'

'And how do I know I'm going to get out of it at all?'

'Coz I fucking said so. We're going round in circles, Cusack.'

He moved back towards his old friend, and felt – and was astonished at it; it was something he'd taken for granted for far too long – the sickly satisfaction at seeing the other flinch and then cower. His guts twisted. He caught Tony's shoulder again. Half a man, halved.

Jimmy spat, 'Don't think I'm completely black-hearted, Cusack. We have history. I respect that. Do this and we're square. Don't do this, and . . . Well. You know you're going to do it because you don't have a choice, do you? Father-of-how-many, knock-kneed killer.'

The front door slammed.

Jimmy turned, hand still on Tony's shoulder, and into the kitchen came, he guessed, the little prince.

'What's going on?'

Jimmy pinched Tony's shoulder and said, 'Well, fuck me. They grow up so fast.'

The kid was the spit of his ould lad. A touch taller and missing the gut, the benefit of his mother's genes in these and other refinements; a good-looking lad, Jimmy thought, not your typical scut. He was out of the scut's uniform, too, in a smart jacket and black jeans instead of the tracksuit and sovereigns combo. 'Ryan,' Jimmy said. 'I'm right, amn't I? The heir to the Cusack fortune. Well, how are you today?'

'Can I help you with something?'

'That's not a very helpful tone.'

'Well let me re-fucking-calibrate. D'you want something?'

Jimmy whistled.

'Not so much a chip-off-the-ould-block as he looks, is he?' he said to Tony. 'Fire in him, though this town'll have something to say about that eventually.' Back at Ryan he said, 'I do want something, and I got it. Don't worry your pretty little head about it.'

He released Tony.

'Friday,' he said. 'I'll talk to you then.'

The son moved out of the way as he walked past and back into the cluttered hallway, back out through the grubby door, back down the driveway lined with ragwort and dandelion, back onto the street outside and its concrete footpaths dashed with gum and bird shit.

He wondered, as he walked, about the sprained turns that made a man a murderer. Jimmy didn't consider himself a member of that family; no, there was something sicker to murder than pragmatic judgement, which is all he ever engaged in. Tony Cusack was one kind of man: shuffling from one weak comfort to the next. What darkness was in him had been so well buried Tony himself likely didn't know it was there to call on, when his position as man and father and household god was threatened.

But then maybe he did. And maybe the boat was a tool seized to carry out another task in a long schedule. You just don't know, do you?

He unlocked his car door and as his fingers closed around the handle a voice caught him and spun him back again.

'Hey!'

It was the young lad. Murderer or not, Tony Cusack wasn't bold enough to bellow dissent.

Ryan Cusack strode right up and stopped just short enough to leave room for swinging fists.

'What the fuck was that about?' he said.

Jimmy laughed. 'Excuse me?'

'You. My dad. In my dad's house. Just now. What the fuck was that about?'

Jimmy closed the gap between them.

'None of your fucking business, pup.'

There was a height difference. Jimmy thought: *A good gut-punch will sort that out if necessary.*

'Watch me make it my fucking business,' said the boy.

'Aw, stop,' sneered Jimmy. 'I know what you're at and I appreciate it, I do. Showing off your baby claws is how you little fuckers learn. But you don't practise your play-acting on me, because I will put you in the ground. And your daddy after you.'

He meant to turn away. He didn't. There was, all of a stark sudden, too much there to turn away from.

Beyond Ryan's shoulder was a heavy stone sky and the dark, thick green of overgrown grass, and between both the reds and greys and browns of the suburban terraces. The boy was dark as his father, but lacking the ruddy palate of these hills and their rusted air. Here was a changeling who'd laid claim to the landscape and the place had grown up around him. Jimmy curled his lip.

Ryan said, 'You don't come into my house, and threaten my father, without giving me the chance to put you back in your box.'

Jimmy pushed against him; Ryan stood solid.

'If you had any idea who you were talking to,' Jimmy said, 'you'd be cleaving out your tongue on your fucking knees. Boy.'

'I know full well who I'm talking to. Phelan.'

Jimmy bared his teeth.

'Well, look at the fucking balls on you. That must be the Neapolitan talking, because it sure as shit isn't your father.'

'Funny that, isn't it?'

'Fucking hilarious. All I had left to know about you was how you spoke to your betters. Part-time half-grown dealer scum, Ryan Cusack. Kicked out of school, time under your belt already and a future bright as a bruise.'

'Spot on, boy. And your problem with my dad is what?'

'Hoho! Like a dog with a bone. Why don't you ask him?'

'Because I'm asking you.'

'The question is, Ryan, would you like it if I told you?'

Jimmy stepped back again, leaned against the Volvo and folded his arms. The boy's fingers curled into fists. Fifty feet away, Tony Cusack hovered at his hall door. Jimmy nodded towards him.

'He's afraid for you, Ryan, but more afraid for himself. Watch him.'

'Maybe he's not afraid for me at all.'

'No, he is. Always thinking about you. Oh, you've no fucking idea. But he won't come out here after you, because you've gone and gotten yourself into deep, deep shit. Didn't he warn you, when you went rushing out the door after me?'

Ryan snorted. 'There's a problem, I sort it.'

'What, you think getting banged up in borstal qualifies you to butt heads with me?'

'You bothering my father in my kitchen qualifies me to butt heads with you. You want something, talk to me about it. My dad's no good to you. And you fucking know it.'

'Oh, hark at this! Are you falling on your sword, kid?'

'Maybe.'

Jimmy nodded at the house again.

'What did he tell you?'

'Nothing.'

'And you don't reckon that's because he doesn't want you sticking your oar in?'

'I doubt it.'

'Does he normally get you to do his dirty work, Ryan?'

'If there's dirty work needs doing.'

In the doorway, Tony Cusack pushed his hand over his forehead.

Aloud, Jimmy wondered, 'After all he's done, the man throws his boy to the fucking wolves.'

Ryan said, 'So. What the fuck was that about?'

Jimmy swiftly measured outcomes. In front of him, the young avenger waited, a sharp twist to the corner of his mouth. Tony Cusack never once looked like coming over the threshold to reclaim him.

'All right,' said Jimmy.

Underneath logic and strategy, he was burning. Anger, more than was reasonable, caught his breath and quickened his pulse. He had no time to put a name to it, but he recognised its tincture from the same processes that had fucked his place in the world he'd made since he'd brought Maureen home from London. There were more out there like Ryan Cusack, boys half Jimmy's age for whom reputation was a thing to be taken from someone else.

'There's a problem your father and I share. I want it gone. It has a name: Georgie Fitzsimons. It shouldn't be hard to find because it circles this town like a bad penny. Take the thing out of circulation and I'm square with your piece-of-shit father. Let this go one step further and I'll make orphans of your siblings and hang you over the Lee in a fucking gibbet. You got that?'

He smiled.

'Bet you're sorry you asked now, aren't you?'

The boy said, 'Is that it?'

'It's in the smart mouth you betray yourself, kid. You have till Friday.'

He got back into his car unimpeded and drove out of the estate.

Mission accomplished, he supposed.

The nights were getting shorter, and once the weather cleared they'd see the sky, the lot of them, and feel the vastness above the city; the air, the wind and the world. They just had the April to suffer first. The walls of Jimmy's city inched towards the sides of his car as he drove. The lamp posts bent over him.

It would right itself, sooner or later. He just needed to be prepared.

25

Tony was at the kitchen sink, one hand on the draining board, the other in a tight fist by his side, bled out from his forehead to his knuckles, but still standing.

His father used to be a giant but as Ryan had stretched he'd shrunk to frailty, and his stature was only part of the story. All those rages, distilled by time down to petty tantrums. The good moods Ryan used to pray for, reclassified as desperate shows of learned affection. And that fucking strength, ha? Where was the bruiser now? Ryan could take him. He could do more than take him. He could kill him. Even with his bare hands. Catch him by his mop, knock his head off the wall, slam his face off the draining board, run him onto the stairs, slip his belt off, whip the old fucker.

Instead he walked over to the table and picked up the electricity bill.

'Ouch,' he said.

He counted out the fee, then a fifty on top of it, and put it on the table. He'd brought an eighth of grass too, a good poky smoke, and as such one he was considering leaving in his pocket and laying into with extreme prejudice once he got home. He left the baggie by the bill.

'Better for you,' he said.

He looked back at his father and Tony swallowed and looked at the floor.

'Rocky . . .'

'And you say I make stupid mistakes, Dad.'

'You don't understand.'

'No.' For a moment his stance matched his father's, and then he tossed his head and looked up again and said, 'Make me understand.'

Tony came over to the table. He sat down, awkwardly pulled a packet of cigarettes from his jeans pocket, and slit one open. Ryan put his Rizla on the table. Tony rolled a joint. His hands were shaking.

'What did he say to you?' he mumbled, once he'd sparked up.

Ryan sat down. 'Nothing that made any sense.'

Tony exhaled and rested his forehead on his wrist. His fingers scratched at his hairline.

'He wants that girl killed,' Ryan said. He coughed out a laugh. 'Like, fucking hell.'

'That's the long and short of it,' Tony said.

'Eh, no it fucking isn't, Dad. That's the bare bones. The girl who came up here asking after her fella is a problem you share with Jimmy Phelan. And somehow he thinks you're capable of pulling shit like that and you're not, Dad. How could you be? What the fuck is he on?'

Tony looked up. 'I couldn't,' he said. 'You know that. See? You know that but he doesn't. Or he does and he doesn't care. But you're right, Rocky – I couldn't be like that and I'm not.' There were tears in his eyes.

'How's Georgie a problem you share with Jimmy Phelan?'

'I didn't mean for any of this to happen. I was walked into it. That young wan's fella . . . he was killed.'

'Oh, fuck me.' Ryan leaned back in his chair.

Georgie had said as much the previous Saturday. *Did you find your fella? No. He died.*

There were threads of dusted web drifting gently round the shade above him.

'I met her in town, last Saturday,' he said. 'First time since she was here in your sitting room, Dad. She looked like shit, y'know. Like a skeleton in a dress. She said the feen was dead. I guess that's why Jimmy Phelan's taking out contracts on her.'

'She's a buddy of yours—'

'No. I fucking told you she wasn't. She's someone I used to sell dope to.' He gestured at the baggie in front of his father. 'See? Just like that. Aw, fuck me!'

He pushed the chair back and paced over to the worktop, and brought a fist to the surface between the hob and the dirty mugs.

It needed saying.

'Did you kill him, Dad?'

'No,' Tony said.

He was staring at the table. 'Phelan crossed my path one day, five years ago now. He said he needed a favour. I had no clue what it was until I was landed in front of it – the fella, dead on the floor up in one of Phelan's gaffs. A total accident, he said. I was to help him clean it up. And I did it. You don't say no to Jimmy and at that stage . . . I couldn't have said no. That's Jimmy. He shoves you off the cliff and as you're falling he shouts after you: *No way back now, boy!* I didn't know the girl'd come looking for him and I didn't know she'd come up here. I don't know why she never learned to shut her mouth. Whatever madness drove her to piss him off, it's done now. And because I'm the only one who knew about the first one, he says I have to . . . to do the second.'

'How do you even know Jimmy bloody Phelan?'

'From years back. Before you were born. Before I was your age, even. We went to London together.'

'That's how he knew about my mam, so.'

'What did he say about your mam?'

'Oh, fuck all, for Jesus's sake.'

Ryan's phone beeped. He took it out of his pocket and stared down at the screen. It was a text from Karine. She'd be on her lunch break by now, back there in the real world. He turned the phone over in his palm and closed his fingers round it.

'So what did Tara Duane know about all this?'

Tony inhaled, sharply, making a sound somewhere between a hiccup and a bleat.

'What d'you mean, boy?' he said.

'She sent Georgie up here, didn't she? Telling her you'd know where her fella went?'

'Twist of fate, I suppose. She was late remembering that I knew the poor fella.'

'So you did know him.'

Tony closed his eyes. 'Yeah.'

'How'd you know him?'

'Pub. That's all. I couldn't tell her that, though, not after what had happened.'

'And Tara just landed on that one, did she?'

'Why couldn't she? We both know, don't we? The world marked that wan for divilment. Why else would she have . . .' He flinched. '. . . With you.'

'Are you still going on about that?' Ryan snapped.

'You were fifteen, Ryan.'

'Yeah, well. Fifteen-year-olds are all dick, aren't they?'

He put his phone on the worktop, placed both hands flat on either side, then sank onto his elbows and covered his head with his hands.

'I didn't have a choice,' his father stressed feebly, from behind him.

'There's always a choice,' Ryan said.

'If it makes you feel better to believe that.'

Ryan straightened.

'Right,' he said.

He put his hands on his head and moved to the window, and let his eyes drift from clothesline to back wall to lawn.

'Rocky, listen—'

'Don't fucking talk to me a minute!'

He'd seen it splashed and screaming on her face: Georgie was fucked anyway. Her cheeks, sunken; her eyes like holes punched in paper; fated to expire in a gutter after ODing or being choked out by the wrong punter and there was nothing Ryan Cusack could do about that. Child already taken off her. Slipping from salvation to the street. Hanging.

'Aw, fuck,' he breathed.

Tony tried again.

'Ryan, I—'

'I'll sort this,' Ryan said. He went back to the worktop and picked up his phone. Tony shook his head. His mouth warped and changed his grimace into something faintly ludicrous, like the painted melancholy of an old clown.

'How "sort it", boy? What's that mean?'

'It means I'm going to fucking sort it, Dad.'

'Ryan, you can't bargain with Jimmy Phelan—'

'I'm not going to bargain with him.'

'Aw Jesus Christ—'

'Aw Jesus Christ what, Dad? What? It has to be sorted, doesn't it?'

Tony got to his feet.

'Ryan . . . I can't let you do this.'

'That's grand coz I amn't asking your permission, am I?'

He turned back at the hall door.

'Don't bring this up with me again,' he said.

He watched his father's pallor wash out against the smudged eggshell blue of the kitchen walls, and couldn't decide whether it was the right tone at last that had done it, or the right words or the right height or the right criminal trajectory. Or the right emergency. What the name of the magic trick was that turned Tony Cusack from one kind of man to no man at all.

He made the decision but it sat with him for a while, and he ended up driving from one end of the city to the other, smoking, and asking himself who the fuck he was.

He picked up Karine at the hospital at clocking-off time and she jumped into the passenger seat with the post-work high she denied and he was addicted to.

'Hey, baby boy!'

There was an even blanket of mist over the city. Karine shivered. 'So dark,' she complained, turning up the heat. 'It's like December.' Out of the corner of his eye he noticed her narrow hers and smile. 'You're cranky, are you?'

'Not really,' he said.

'You OK?'

'Course I am.' They were at the car park exit; he leaned over the steering wheel and stared into the traffic. 'How was work?' he said.

'Mental. Like, we're supposed to be learning and the only thing they're teaching us is how not to explode with stress. I swear to God, that's the number one nursing skill.'

'Someone's got to do it,' he said.

She shimmied in her seat. 'Yeah! Someone's gotta patch 'em all up.'

It wasn't a dig at him. It might have looked perverse to the uninitiated, him doing what he did for money and her being nearly-a-nurse, but they both knew, well, you've got to be realistic. Someone's got to do it: the mantra applied to both paths. He was glad of that shared pragmatism, though when he was hungover he worried that it was as down to rebelling against her parents, who hated him, as it was to her urban ethics.

He dropped her home to her parents' terrace, and she leaned over and into a slow kiss.

'Will you come and get me later?' she whispered.

'Yeah.'

'Don't be too long.'

Before she pulled away he framed her face in an open hand.

'Tell me you love me,' he said.

'Duh. I love you.'

'Really, though?'

'Oh my God, is my word not good enough?' She smiled, then the smile faded, and she cocked her head. 'Have you done something?'

'No.'

'You're talking like you've done something.'

'I haven't.'

'Coz I'm all done forgiving you, Ryan.'

'I know.'

She let him kiss her again. 'I'm just a bit off,' he said. 'I was up with my dad earlier. You know how it goes. He gives me the emos.'

'I should have guessed.'

'I've a small job to do. I'll be back later for you. We'll go to mine. Watch a film or something. Listen to some tunes. I dunno. Have fucking tea and Jaffa Cakes.'

'OK,' she said, soft as the rain.

'And you can tell me about work,' he said. 'Tell me plans, and tell me stories.'

He crossed the river for the fifth time and turned onto the quay, and traffic lights quivered through the mist on the windscreen.

She was there. He pulled up alongside her and rolled down the window. *If I'm caught doing this*, he thought, *how the fuck will I ever explain it?*

'Get in, Georgie.'

She looked at him like a cornered teenager, slid towards the passenger door, and slouched in.

'What?' she said.

The mist had teased her hair into a tangle, and its volume made her face even more gaunt. She pulled her jacket sleeves over her fists. Her skirt was short and her legs bare; he'd had the GTI only a month, and was still obsessively odd about anything dirtying the seats. He recognised his revulsion to her naked skin as irrational. Possibly essential, if he was going to be smart about it. He pulled back onto the road and drove towards the Mall. 'How the mighty have fallen,' Georgie muttered.

Over her right wrist she was wearing a piece of brown cloth, wound and knotted; it kept catching as she yanked at her sleeve.

'That's the best you can come up with?' he said. 'Mumbling something snippy to shame me? Fucking hell, Georgie. You've no fight in you.'

'I'm supposed to fight you?'

'You think I'm a hypocrite, don't you? You think I've some nerve picking you up after what happened Saturday. You think it all boils down to whether or not I'm horny.' He snorted. 'And you get in anyway, and you'd let me, wouldn't you? After everything.'

'See, that's what happened to the decent kid,' she said. 'He turned into a man.'

'But you'd let him fuck you, though.'
'It's a job, Ryan. It's not personal.'
'No,' he said. 'It's not.'

He had to contact his father afterwards for Jimmy Phelan's number, and he could only do so via text; he didn't want to talk to Tony. He didn't want to talk to anyone, but he managed it with Phelan. A quick introduction and a quick confirmation. Phelan wasn't satisfied.

'Come meet with me,' he said.

So Ryan did, down in the cellar of a Barrack Street pub with a facade that had not so much seen better days as decayed the street on which it stood. They weren't alone down there, though he doubted a man like Jimmy Phelan was used to being alone. There were a number of lads in the far corner playing cards, one of them Tim Dougan, whose legend had long served Ryan both as warning and inspiration. Though Phelan kept him standing near the door and talking to the floor, he had no doubt the men around them were all ears. They glanced up at intervals, sniffing, scowling, sucking their teeth.

The room was lit by two low, bare bulbs. This was for function and for show, and Ryan was just as scared as he should have been.

'You had two days,' said Phelan.

'Couldn't put something like that off,' Ryan said.

'No? Plenty who would. Though I don't recommend it myself.'

Phelan's words, low, smooth and cold, crept up on him like a trippy pill. He flushed, felt the sweat break on his forehead, and the butterflies push against the walls of his stomach. Two of the card players turned to stare. Ryan looked away. There was a point of pain, suddenly, on each side of his nose. He pinched the bridge.

'Am I supposed to just take for granted that you came through for me?' Phelan said.

'Pretty much.'

'What if I ask you for proof?'

'What d'you want, a fucking photograph? Are you assuming I

wasn't taking you seriously in the first place? With my father's neck on the line?'

Phelan smiled thinly. 'Did you ever ask yourself, Ryan, if he doesn't deserve you?'

Ryan said, 'Are we done here?'

Phelan looked away. 'I did my research a long time back, of course. How's the apprenticeship going? How's Dan Kane treating you?'

'Am I supposed to answer that?'

'I heard he's pure fond of you,' said Phelan.

Ryan's phone started buzzing in his jeans pocket. He assumed it was Karine. He was late. Very late. It was bedtime-late. There was the doghouse, and there was the cellar. He exhaled, quietly. Having practised now for years he knew his face was hard as the stone walls around him, and almost as blank as the man he was standing in front of. But behind it all he was crumbling, and desperate to get out of here, and mad to crawl back to the doghouse on his belly and wait for her to forgive him yet again. He didn't think that edginess could break through. No. No, he knew it couldn't. And that was nearly as bad.

Phelan said, 'I hardly need to tell you that what happened between me and you and that broken fool who fucked your mother is no one's business but ours. Dan Kane is not to hear of this.'

'It isn't my proudest moment,' Ryan said.

'Ah, but you're a good boy. Dan Kane knows it. I know it. Let's say I'm done with Tony Cusack. I am not done with you. Not by a long shot.'

'You are,' Ryan said.

Phelan smiled and caught his shoulders. 'You don't get to decide that, boy,' he said.

Beneath the powder-blue sky of a new Sunday morning, Ryan sat smoking on someone else's balcony. Behind the sliding door Joseph and a couple of other lads sat around a table, doing lines and drinking beer. Karine had gone for a snooze in one of the bedrooms. Ryan needed lungfuls of sharp air and a break from boisterous conversation. He had a head full of coke and thoughts as cold and clear and even as the new sky above him.

It wasn't his fault. He knew it wasn't his fault. It was something bigger.

His 'job' – nothing personal – entailed purchasing quantities of intoxicants, cutting them and selling them at a profit to people who were, as Georgie's terminology stated, 'dealing'. Taking precedent over how he made his money was how he proved his loyalty to Dan Kane: stepping in as his representative in cases where he deemed it necessary. Negotiations with fellas further down the chain. Retribution against those same fellas if the negotiations didn't pan out. He'd gotten his fists bruised. He'd gotten his head around it. This was his part in the story. This was what he boiled down to, flesh, guts and bones.

'I'm the bad guy,' he said.

The city didn't heed him. He looked down on rooftops, the corrugated shell of thousands of lives, all with their own part to play, fitting together like cogs, keeping the wheels turning. Doctors, dockers, dancers and dealers.

He'd been twenty years coming to this point. There probably hadn't ever been another way.

From his back pocket, his business mobile rang. He shifted his weight and dug it out. He changed the SIM every few weeks. He had authority, at least, over which people he sold to. If there were any clients he needed to drop he simply didn't give them his new contact. They faded from his life without protesting their relegation. Such things weren't questioned. Ryan Cusack had that much autonomy.

He answered the phone. 'Yeah?'

Donnelly's voice. 'I got that.'

'Oh, good stuff.'

'Yeah, hassle free. I'll see you later so. What are we looking at?'

Ryan narrowed his eyes and took another drag. His mind was racing. He snapped it back. 'Six G,' he said.

'No problemo.'

Ryan hung up. He opened the browser, screencapped a map

and sent it on. Later he'd meet Donnelly at the mapped address, once he'd had a medicated snooze. He wasn't coming down for a while. He'd been flying fucked for two days straight.

Hereditary

'You're a prick is all you are!'

She's sitting on my bed in her knickers, and I'm standing at the foot with my jeans still unbuttoned, and the room's saturated with the sweat and musk of what we've just done . . . How do we manage to fight in something that heady? This is how it ends? We've become so allergic, the smell of each other's bodies is raising welts and driving us insane?

'Yeah, I'm a prick, that's what it is, Karine, I'm a fucking prick.'

We've been out since midday, had a couple of glasses of wine with the lunch, and pints after that. We came home for a snooze before heading out for the night, and when we woke there was murmuring and giggles and her turning round and pushing against me and asking me for it, and all of a sudden we have the spitting start of World War fucking III.

It's Halloween, so that's an excuse for her to go out wearing a ladybird costume that amounts to a spotty mini dress and black thigh-high stockings and a pair of glittery wings. The female population of the city will be baring their legs and their tummies and the very tops of their thighs and I'm not supposed to look at any of them because she knows I'm a pathetic twisted cheat. She can go out in a dress right up to her arse and just fucking ask to be groped but I'm to blind myself in case I accidentally exchange a look with one of her number. This is the kind of shit Karine can dredge up without even having to think about it: vicious hypocrisy dressed up in timidity and thrown back in my face if I dare question her. I'm so close now to walking out of here and getting my nose into a mound of coke and my cock up the first girl that smiles at me.

My shirt is on the floor beside her and I don't want to lean over her to pick it up.

'You don't get to tell me what to do, Ryan. You're a liar and you're a cheat and you do not get the high ground here.'

'I haven't touched another girl in fucking God knows how long.'

'Oh, yeah. God knows how long. Never mind all of them that you touched before God started keeping tabs, they're not supposed to count.'

'They don't count any more than Niall Vaughan counts.'

She stomps over and jabs a finger on my chest.

'Bring up Niall again,' she says. 'Go on, dig deeper. Because one minute you're all "Oh, when I cheat it doesn't matter but when you cheat it's because you were infatuated," so if you're equating Niall Vaughan, who you believe I was madly in lust with, with your gamut of sluts, then you're admitting that you were infatuated with all of them, aren't you?'

She's hurting my head.

Alongside the ugly little hangover, warming up for the relay as my lunchtime drunkenness collapses.

'Are you for fucking real?' I ask her.

'Are you, boy? Are you for fucking real?'

I don't know how this happened. One minute we're coming together and the next she's accusing me of emotional infidelity, and OK, listen, I've fucked other girls and I'm not proud of it. But it's not like I loved any of them. It's not like it's even possible for me to love anyone else. It's a deficiency and I know it. I feel it. It wrecks my head, it ties my tongue, it hobbles me.

'Do you have to keep pulling me inside out with this shit, Karine? You know full well you're the only one who's ever meant anything to me and what did it matter when I couldn't trust you as far as I could throw you?'

'Oh my God,' she says. 'You're so full of shit.'

'How is that full of shit? You fucked Niall Vaughan when I was—'

'In prison! You have no idea what that was like for me! You

weren't there and I needed you. I couldn't trust you not to get banged up and you're still doing the same thing, aren't you? Yeah, talking shit about Australia and you and me leaving this dump and making something of ourselves when you know full well that's not going to happen with your record. We're stuck here and it's all your fault.'

'Aw yeah, see, I'm your prison, am I?'

'Something like that, Ryan. You cheat on me and lie to me and I'm stupid for letting you . . . and the absolute kicker? You haven't a notion of ever quitting. I've never been as important to you as Dan Kane. The next time you get caught you'll get ten years and where will I be then?'

'I'm not going to get fucking caught.'

'How do you know? You were stupid enough to get caught in the first place.'

'All right, so I'm a cheat and a liar and I'm a cage and I'm fucking stupid. Anything else you want to say?'

'Oh,' she hisses, 'there's plenty else I could say.'

'Fucking say it, then!'

I can see the poison rising, filling her out as it climbs, a wave of hatred coming from her belly to her jaw. 'You have no idea what you put me through when you got caught with Dan Kane's coke,' she says. 'And I am going to make you suffer for it.'

'Fucking Niall Vaughan wasn't revenge enough, then? In a fucking car park? Like a fucking whore?'

She thumps my chest so I push her, all the way back to the wall. I stand over her and she struggles and kicks out and gets my shin with her bare foot and this is the thing, it doesn't even hurt, but it doesn't have to hurt because this is just a reflex: I lift my fist to her.

I lift my fist to her.

And she shrieks, 'Oh my God! Oh my God, you were going to hit me! You pig, you were going to hit me!' and I can't stop it, I lash out and knock my fist off the wall beside her head and then again, and again, and I've got my hand on her throat beating the fuck out of the wall and her legs go from under her.

I let her fall and she crumples to the floor and I stagger backwards and end up on my arse.

'Oh my God,' she says.

'I didn't touch you,' I say, but whatever it was has been knocked out of me; all I can do is whisper.

'I knew this would happen someday,' she sobs. 'I've been watching this coming for months.'

My chest's hammering. 'I'm sorry,' I say. 'I'm really sorry. I didn't mean to scare you, girl. I fucking love you; I'd never hurt you.'

'No?' Her eyes are red, her hair teased rough from sweat and sex and now this, oh Jesus Christ, where did this come from? 'Then what the fuck was that?'

26

It was the worst time to be in the A&E – Saturday drinking time, when the city's youth drowned standing up. It was compounded by the coming bank holiday, and the place was predictably jointed. Pale girls in their weekend finery sat dumb with swollen knees, drunks bellowed at nurses who carried the scars of their vocation on their faces . . . ould fellas, ould wans, stern mammies holding teenage boys who looked like they might burst into tears, trolleys, coffee cups, televisions no one could hear . . . Jimmy took it all in with the astonishment of a child who'd pulled a rock off the soil to see the woodlice scatter underneath.

He had other things to be doing, but – the realisation was made luminescent by the white lights of the waiting room – Maureen didn't have anyone else to accompany her. It was late in his life to feel a son's duty. His stand-in siblings had been so much older than him that he'd never felt pressure to obey, tend to or bolster. This was new, and what positive novelty did he expect to find in life at his age? From here on in it should be nothing but challengers and traitors.

Maureen sat on the plastic chair beside his, surly under the lights and the pain of her injured wrist. She had climbed up on the worktop in her apartment that afternoon to clean cupboard shelves, and had fallen. After two cups of tea and a few hours grumbling didn't cure her, she called the doctor, who sent her into A&E for an X-ray. She didn't appear to have wanted to call Jimmy. She did anyway. And so they sat together.

He tried, though where the compulsion came from he wasn't sure. 'D'you want a cup of tea?' he said. 'D'you want a newspaper?' In between staring at the weekend casualties and fantasising about getting head from that one good-looking nurse, he provided what his mother needed.

'How the A&E in this piddling hole is slower than the ones in London I'll never figure out,' Maureen groused. She had given up on her newspaper, having found it difficult to turn pages with only one hand. Now she sat with her legs crossed, holding on to her paper cup, making evil eyes at the opposite wall. A man who'd taken the seat below the spot she was directing her attention squirmed.

'Every A&E is the same on Saturday nights,' Jimmy offered.

'Bloody government,' she responded.

Jimmy smiled.

'D'you need to go out for a cigarette or anything?' he asked.

'And what if they call me? And what if I miss it and they end up sticking me back on the arse of the queue?'

'Sure I'll go out and get you.'

'Oh, stop fussing.'

To this he couldn't help but laugh. 'Fussing? Me? You're off your fucking game if you think that's fussing.'

'You're like an old hen,' she said.

Here in the vivid light, he was exposed and wrong-footed. On a Saturday night he might otherwise have been holding court in the *síbín* he ran on Barrack Street. Shadows might have cloaked him and kept him on his track.

'This is odd,' he told Maureen.

'What's odd?'

'This place, and me in it. This isn't usually my scene.'

'What? D'you think it's out jiving you are? This isn't anyone's scene.'

'That's not what I meant,' he said, and he cast his eye round again, and caught jaded porters, and threadbare corners, and footage of county floods scrolling on the TV screen on the wall. He meant normality. This was outside of his usual trajectory and yet home to all of these lifeforms who snapped and bled and shattered and had nothing but their country to fix them again. He got a sudden vision of a doppelgänger walking around, shaking hands, accepting their welcomes, like one of America's rock star presidents come to grace the spud-gobblers with his urbane presence.

His guide said, impatiently, 'Well, what did you mean?'

A nurse stood at the corridor and called, 'Maureen Phelan?'

'They'd shame you,' Maureen muttered. She rose and Jimmy alongside her. 'Are you coming too?' she asked, surprised, and he said, 'Why wouldn't I, Maureen? Is that not what I'm here for?'

They sat outside of the X-ray room and what he'd said obviously nagged at her, because she came out with, 'I'm probably not what you expected in a mother.'

He shrugged. 'I'm probably not what you expected in a son,' he said, but only because he felt he had to. That he wasn't what anyone would expect in a son was not a revelation. She was right, though. Maybe you get the mother you deserve.

He examined his hands and looked from there down the length of his legs. Alien or not, he was most certainly here, and he wouldn't have been if it wasn't for her youthful indiscretion. He glanced at Maureen and wondered how it was even possible to have come from her body and to have grown up into . . . whatever he was. It was an unpleasant sensation. His just being alive had ruined her life.

Well, he'd been called the Antichrist more than once.

She got her wrist X-rayed and was directed back to the waiting room. Their seats had been taken, so they walked around to find another pair.

Tony sat in the shadow of an enormous doctor as an exhausted climber with half a mountain yet to go. The doctor was young, calm and distracted. He had the chart in his hand but even as he spoke he was looking around at other notes, at his computer screen, at some diagnosis he had yet to make a call on. Tony felt light-headed. He held on tight.

'You'll keep him in, then?' he asked.

'Oh God, yeah,' said the doctor. 'For observation, first of all.

We've cleaned him out but, y'know, we're still talking alcohol intoxication, cocaine intoxication . . .' He squinted down at the chart. Tony flinched. 'Preliminary bloods suggest he didn't get as much paracetamol into him as we feared, but hepatotoxicity is still a concern. We'll do bloods again in two, three hours. When he's back with us I'd like someone from Psychiatry to speak to him.'

'Psychiatry?'

'Yes, Mr . . . ah. Cusack?'

'Cusack,' said Tony, miserably.

'Combined drug intoxication is usually accidental but both you and his . . . ah, housemate have indicated that this was deliberate. Better safe than sorry, eh? We don't want him in here again.'

'No.'

'So we'll move him to the unit in a bit and you can see him then, all right? I'll send a porter out to you.'

The doctor rose, and as he turned to hold the door open Tony took his hand and squeezed it. *Jesus*, he thought. *I'm like those gobshites who clap when the plane lands.*

'Thank you,' he said. 'I know these young fellas must break your melt. I know you have better things to be doing.'

The doctor furrowed his brow and smiled. 'It's what we're here for. Don't worry about it.' He allowed Tony to hold his hand for another second. 'He'll be fine,' he said.

Tony went back out to the waiting room. Kelly, Joseph and Karine were where he had left them. Joseph had draped an arm around Karine, who'd folded herself into a ball. There had been a fight earlier, apparently. She'd left Ryan and had gone into town to her friends. He'd followed, and it had culminated in a screaming match on the Grand Parade, '. . . but there's no way I thought he'd do something like this,' she wept. 'I'd never have fought with him if I'd have known . . . Oh God, this is all my fault.'

She'd confessed a variety of incidents and run-ins in the hours they'd sat in the waiting room. The past six months had exhausted her. She'd told Ryan three times that she couldn't do it anymore and each warning had developed into nothing more than a short detox: they spent a week apart and faltered, and after the second time their friends stopped remarking on it. In the meantime there were parties. 'He's DJing more,' she said and, almost as if it wasn't his father she was talking to, blurted, 'and you know what that means. Coke isn't as forgiving as we are.'

She'd stopped crying. Tony stood in front of her and she looked up, red around the nose and panda-eyed. She was a beautiful thing, still, and he thought that Ryan must be fucked altogether if he could hurt her time and time over.

He relayed the doctor's update. 'He'll be fine,' he said. None of them believed it.

'How could he be fine,' Karine squeaked, 'when I don't know who he is anymore?'

Joseph squeezed her arm. 'Hey,' he said. 'This is where it starts getting better, OK? You'll see.'

Tony went outside for a cigarette. He curled his hand around the flame of the lighter; the wind got at it anyway. He turned to the wall and tried again. An ambulance pulled into the bay to his left and paramedics removed a creature on a stretcher. They were joking. Just another night for them. Just another fucking casualty.

Jimmy Phelan stepped up beside him and said, 'Jesus, the whole of Cork City must be in A&E tonight.'

Tony's cigarette caught. He had little mind for running.

'What do you want?' he asked.

J.P. scowled. 'Is that any way to greet an old friend?' he said.

It had been months. J.P. was as good as his word. It had been months between visits before, too, but this time was different, and Tony felt it in his son's distance. The girl was gone and his association with Jimmy Phelan consigned once more to history, but the cost was all around him tonight, in white faces and Karine's tears.

'Probably not,' he said, 'but we haven't been close in a while, have we, Jimmy?'

And yet the fucker had jumbled Tony into junk.

'I suppose we haven't,' J.P. conceded. He lit his own cigarette and raised his eyebrows. *Continue*, he invited. Tony did.

'You didn't have to involve my young fella,' he said. The cigarette smoke was noxious as his very first lungful; he was nauseated, dizzy. 'Whatever he said to you. He's only a boy.'

J.P. said, 'He involved himself, Tony.'

'Are you trying to tell me he knew what he was doing? He's twenty years of age, Jimmy.'

J.P. took a drag and shook his head. 'You're dredging up some old shit there, Cusack,' he warned.

'So what?' said Tony. 'We're old shit. Aren't we?'

'Meaning?'

'Meaning we were buddies one time. Meaning you were the first person to buy me a drink when I found out he was on the way.'

Tony finished his cigarette and stood with the butt between his fingers. In front of them, the car park hosted a drowsy light show as vehicles inched in and out, swung around tight corners, searched for space in the cramped dark. Crises from one end of the county to another. What was Tony's, only another one?

'Who told you I was the sentimental type?' said J.P., mildly.

'Yeah. That's a mistake I made, for thinking there was still a man in there underneath the bullshit.'

Phelan turned. He backed Tony up against the wall.

'No one talks to me like that, Cusack.'

'I fucking know that,' Tony snapped. 'I know it better than most! Bear that in mind, will you, boy? I know what you're capable of. I've seen it and I've fucking felt it. You took my son from me. You've nothing left to take.'

'I'm sure I could find something.'

'Let me save you the trouble of looking – you couldn't. If you're going to kill me, fucking kill me. I've had enough. It's all coming away under me.'

'Why would I want to kill you, Cusack? You're not dangerous.'

Tony thought, *I didn't used to be.*

J.P. said, 'Are you finished?'

Tony exhaled.

J.P. said, 'Our friend Robbie . . . Well, it wasn't you I was worried about talking, Cusack.'

The automatic doors opened to their right and a couple came out. They stood at the other side of the doors and lit up. J.P. looked over, gauged intent and spoke again, so quietly that Tony had to strain to hear him over the autumn wind and the car park hum and the living, breathing, dying moments playing out in the building behind them.

'Consider yourself told only because we are old shit, Cusack, very old shit indeed. If it had come out about our friend Robbie, what d'you think would have happened? She's an old woman. She keeps putting herself in harm's way and it's my job to keep pulling her back again. You do what you have to for family. Absorb that one, and let the old shit go.'

'You ruined my family while you were saving your own.'

'No,' said J.P. 'I didn't. The state of you, Tony. I didn't do that to you, and you know it. You can stand here in the dark harping on about your family and your boy and your badly faked innocence, but it's just me and you here, and I see right through you. You can whinge about what needed doing, but it was nothing new to your young fella.'

'You don't know that,' said Tony.

'Yeah I do. Open your eyes, Cusack. Your young lad was well able for it. He's already twice the man you are.'

'Good news,' said the doctor. 'It's just a sprain. You'll be hurling again before you know it, Maureen.'

'Oh, mighty,' she sniffed. 'And I here all night.'

The doctor brushed off the gibe. 'Could be worse,' he said, looking over his glasses at the waiting room. He presented her with a prescription. 'Painkillers,' he said. 'Three a day, with food. Look after yourself.'

'And that's your lot,' grumbled Maureen. She stood by their seats as Jimmy retrieved the newspaper and their coats. 'What are you giving out about?' he said. 'You get to go home to bed now. If it had been broken they'd be setting it and you'd be here another four hours.'

'Sure amn't I institutionalised at this stage?'

'Well what did you expect with your messing?'

'Last time I try to clean anything, so,' she said. 'You can get me a housekeeper.'

They moved towards the doors. Across the room, Maureen spotted a familiar dark mop, and she paused.

'Everyone's in this place tonight,' she said.

'That's just what I thought,' said Jimmy.

Tony Cusack looked up at them. Maureen raised her good hand, but he didn't acknowledge it.

'What's wrong with him?' she said.

Jimmy touched her arm and shrugged towards the door.

His world wasn't something his mother had a great interest in sharing, but across from Tony Cusack she felt a connection to Jimmy's deeds. 'What's he in for?' she asked Jimmy, to another shrug. 'What?' she said. 'You didn't ask?'

'Why would I ask?'

'That's a kind of sad way to be,' she mused.

'You don't mix business and pleasure,' Jimmy said. 'It's as simple as that.'

Maureen frowned. 'I'm going to ask him,' she said.

'Do no such thing, Maureen.'

She snorted. 'Are you going to stop me? The man did a lot for us, Jimmy.'

'As I'm sure he's keen to forget.' He took her by the arm. 'I get what you're saying, Maureen. Honest to God I do. But just because you have a tie to someone doesn't mean you have to double-knot it.'

The parallel was enough to render her pliant. She let him lead her into the car park.

He opened the car door for her. She settled in and took a deep breath; the interior smelled so very like him, the grown-up him, a long way travelled between the soft perfume of his baby head and the smoke and cologne and metal and leather she associated with him now.

He relented. 'Tony Cusack was a decent sort,' he admitted,

sitting in beside her. 'Bit of a langer as a kid; I grew up with him. Sank into a bottle in his teens and never came out again. He's exactly the kind of person you'd use for such an awkward task as the one you set me, Maureen. In need of a few bob, innate mistrust of guards, too much to lose to consider talking.'

'What's "too much to lose?"'

'Kids,' he said. 'A hape of them. He met an Italian girl in London, brought her home and had six smallies with her. Then she went off and died on him. Fucking car accident. His oldest is twenty now. Young fella, criminal record acquired already. Ryan. Tony was a Man United man.' He laughed. 'His kids mustn't be so laddish, mind. I bought Ellie's piano from him. He had a house of little musicians. No wonder he didn't know what to do with them.'

'You threaten a man's kids?'

'No. The implication is enough. You ask how many he has. No more needs to be said.'

'It's a nasty way of holding someone,' she chided.

'It's a nasty world,' Jimmy said. 'What else was I going to do? You went on a rampage with your Holy Stone. Someone had to clean it up. If you don't want to hear truths like that don't go around forcing them.'

She was silent. The city slid around them and Jimmy navigated as a bright-eyed captain on a sleeping sea.

Tony sent Kelly home with Joseph but Karine refused to leave, even after the doctor had insisted that Ryan was in no danger. It took her mother, arriving down bleary-eyed at four in the morning, to drag her away, and even then it was a slog.

'You don't understand,' she bawled. 'It's my fault.'

'It's not your fault,' Tony offered, and Jackie D'Arcy glared at him, as if his input was detrimental to her daughter's return to sanity. He knew what the mother was thinking. She was a nurse herself. *Histrionic bully boy making a point with a packet of painkillers*. Maybe she was right, but here wasn't the time or the place.

'Am I upsetting you?' Tony snapped, and she jumped. 'She's crying but he's unconscious, so maybe just keep the high and mightiness to a minimum, all right?'

'I wasn't being high and mighty,' said Mrs D'Arcy, feigning injury.

'It's all right, Mam,' said Karine. 'We're just all a bit tired and stressed out.'

Jackie coaxed her down the corridor and out into the car, and that left Tony, alone in a thinning crowd, with no son yet to show for it.

Once they'd moved Ryan into the unit, he was allowed to go in. He hung back for just a moment before taking his place in the chair by the bedside.

He seemed fine. It would have made Tony feel a lot better if a nurse had popped her head around to say 'He's only sleeping it off' or 'He'll have some head in the morning' but they weren't treating this with comforting levity. He'd complicated everything, apparently. The alcohol was one thing, the cocaine another, the paracetamol a further. The treatment was a problem to be worked out. And then at the end of it they'd whistle and a psychiatrist would swoop down from the rafters with a prescription book and a big red stamp with which to brand Tony Cusack Cork's greatest fuck-up.

'What did you do that for, Rocky?' Tony whispered.

He rested his head against the mattress.

'What am I gonna do with you?'

Still with his forehead to the bed, he reached for his son's hand. His skin was warm. Tony ran his thumb over his knuckles and in his sleep Ryan took a deep breath.

'You're not going to die on me anyway.'

There was room and time to talk. Mouth pressed against hospital sheets in case anyone heard him, Tony confessed to his sleeping son. 'I didn't mean it,' he said. 'I didn't mean any of it. They said down in Solidarity House you lash out at the ones you love the most, you know? If you'd just talked to me more often . . .' He paused. Medical staff drifted past the cubicle. Murmured diagnoses were met with shaky questions.

'I know this is my fault,' he said. 'I know I fucked up. I know you stepped in and I know I should have stopped you. So if this is a point you wanted to make, you've made it. You frightened me. Whatever about me; you frightened Karine. Karine doesn't know who you are anymore. D'you hear that, boy? Are you listening to me?'

He sat up straight and looked at his son. Dark lashes rested on dark circles. The bulb off his ould fella.

'And yet with all your mam's faults, yeah. It's not enough for you to feel, boy, no. You have to feel everything ten times harder.'

Time had smoothed out the chubby cheeks, straightened the curls, sharpened the jaw line, but he could see the baby still in his son's face.

'Your mam would never have let you do this.'

Tony was tired. He could do with a bottle of water, a couple of Solpadeine and his bed.

'I shouldn't have let you, either. It wasn't right. But fuck, Ryan. None of it was right. This city's fucking rotten, falling down around us.'

The dark pool around Robbie O'Donovan's head spread on the floor of the cubicle. The tiles he'd replaced for Maureen Phelan ran patterns through his vision. The deep throb of the boat engine under his seat made him gag.

'I killed her, Ryan. Oh God help me. I killed her.'

The tears were falling and his son was blind to them.

'You need to understand,' Tony said. 'Whatever punishment comes for me I'll take it as long as you know . . . I did it for you. For the very same reason you did what you did: you do what you have to for family. How can I be sorry, then? How can I be sorry when I did it for you?'

Elegy

There's a piano in the lobby. I spot it when we're walking in and then it grows and grows until it's all I can think about. I'm not usually waylaid by pianos on nights out. I don't spend every second social occasion fantasising about enormous inanimate objects that one time used to mean something to me. But I've been fucked these past three weeks. I've been sick, and tired, and dizzy, and dead. And so that fucking piano is taunting parts of me I kept well covered until temporary madness stripped back the skin and left me beaten and bleeding. You couldn't play me now, *it says.* Your fingers have fused, your mind's gone grey, you're deaf, you're blind, you're dumb. You're nothing.

It's Karine's twenty-first birthday.

Her mam and dad have organised this serious shindig. Hotel, bar extension, DJ, canapés, cocktails, everyone she's ever met in her fucking life, this cake with white chocolate flowers all over it that I swear to God would kill someone if it fell on them. She's got everyone dressed in either black or white so she's the only one wearing colour. She's flitting about in this turquoise dress, making sure everyone's all right, that they're all having fun, that they know everyone they're supposed to know. And what am I doing? I'm stuck to the railing of the terrace outside, smoking over the river, dead to it all but that piano in the lobby and the dirge it's playing for everything I'm not.

I don't want to be here. Today is the first day I left the house since they discharged me from the hospital, three weeks ago. Karine had to cry to get me moving and even then I registered the tears with . . . I don't know. I don't want to make her cry. I'm sick of making her cry. But it's like I don't have any real will to stop it. I can hear her and I want to reach for her and hold her in my arms and tell her I'm sorry and that I'll snap out of it but I can't, because I'm a million miles away, lost in the dark, and I can't get to her.

But I can breathe. I can move around. I can eat and sleep and watch telly. Sometimes I can't believe it. I'll be three spoons into a bowl of Weetabix and suddenly I'll ask myself, Well, how'd you do that, boy? How'd you get here?

Y'know how many times I've fucked Karine since that night? Twice. In three fucking weeks. And only because she insisted that making me hard would cure me. She stripped for me, she sucked me, she whispered I could have it any way I wanted it . . . and it was grand, once I got going. But once it was done I was back underground. Like, Oh, that was nice, but it's not for the likes of me. I don't deserve it. *Worse,* I don't want it.

Maybe it's guilt, for Georgie. Slow-burn kind of guilt. Maybe the adrenalin was always supposed to take six months to bleed me out.

Maybe it's just that I did so much coke I wasted all my feelings. A whole lifetime of emotion honked through in a couple of years.

Maybe it's just that I'm so wrapped up in replaying the day I nearly hit my girlfriend that I can't feel anything else, like I've been rolled up in a bit of old carpet and dropped into the sea.

But then surely all she'd need to do to cure me is forgive me? And she has. She has because she thinks I tried to kill myself at Halloween, with a bottle of tablets and a bottle of Jameson, like an ould hag.

No. Coz if I'd wanted to kill myself I would have just shot myself.

Joseph comes out to me on the terrace.

'It's pussy central in there,' he gasps.

I might be a corpse but I've noticed him chatting up one of the other nurses for the past hour. Karine's best mate Louise is usually Joseph's fuckbuddy. There'll be drama there before long.

All I can say is 'Yeah.'

'You all right, boy?'

'Yeah.'

'You don't look all right.'

'I'm OK,' I tell him, but he's hovering, so after I finish my smoke I go inside with him, and the place is hopping, really hopping. I go to the bar and order a beer.

Karine is back over beside me. 'I thought you weren't drinking?'

I'm not supposed to be. I told her I'd knock it on the head for a while and see if that helps me stop making a total arse of myself in front of the entire city. I don't particularly want a drink, as it happens, but the whole place is staring at me. The whole fucking place.

'It's only one,' I tell her.

'Yeah, I know, but . . .' She's fixing the collar of my suit jacket, and I know there's nothing wrong with it. 'Y'know, maybe you shouldn't. Maybe you should give yourself a chance to . . . I dunno, come back to yourself.'

Yeah, maybe. And in the meantime the vultures are circling and the eyes on Mammy and Daddy D'Arcy are turning into pinpricks of hate and the room is whispering Poor Ryan, poor poor Ryan, don't you know he tried to top himself? Para-fucking-cetamol, like an amateur. But you know about him, don't you? You know his mother drove drunk into a ditch. Vehicular suicide. Imagine. Poor Ryan. Look at him not drinking, he can't drink anymore, like, can't be trusted with it, neither his dad nor his mam could be trusted with it.

'It's all under control now, though,' I tell Karine. 'No difference anymore between me and the next man.'

'OK,' says Karine. 'Just be careful, though.'

I take a sip and walk away. Careful, *like. I know what she means. Don't lose the temper and don't lose hope. No chance of that now. It's lost and gone and her boyfriend's empty.*

By the door I turn back. The dance floor is full. Joseph's shifting the nurse. Someone's rubbing Louise's back. Gary D'Arcy is watching me over his pint. Karine is twirling in her turquoise dress and her subjects are moving around her like dancers in formation, like snowflakes in the sky, like shitty little bangers around a falling star. And I don't deserve her. I can't feel sad about that, because I've broken myself, but I know it because it's that sharp and true.

I put the beer on the ledge behind me and walk out of the function room and down to the lobby and approach that vicious fuck of a piano as it goads me, You couldn't do it, boy, the music's stopped, *and I walk past it as my throat closes up, as the last of the fight goes out of me,* You waster, Cusack, you piece of shit, your girlfriend's twenty-first and you're walking out, she'll never forgive you for this, *I get to the door and out into the winter,* Pathetic, fucking pathetic, why'd you even bother trying to kill yourself, don't you know you killed yourself years and years ago, when you stopped hearing the music and started listening to the city . . .

I'm nearly home by the time she calls me.

'Where'd you go, boy?' She's worried.

'I just had to go, girl. I shouldn't have come at all. I can't do this.'

'But I need you here. Don't do this to me tonight, Ryan. Please!'

I could be back there in half an hour, at her side, holding her up when she got tipsy, giving her the first and the last of her twenty-one kisses. I could be there for her but I won't be. I can't. It's done. My city stretches in the dark, and I can no more go back than go forward.

What Ryan Did

It's a shithole, but of course it is, because it's cheap and Georgie doesn't work long enough or hard enough to afford anything else. Not since the first landlord, in her illustrious career as fucker and fuckee, has she had someone back to her own space, but she has already thought it through and accepted that Ryan's different. And besides, he's intimated that there will be cocaine, and a little party, and as weird as the whole thing is – and it is weird, because she's known him since he was a boy – she reckons he'll make it worth her while. Look, she should have known better than to try to shame morals into him. She thinks that a few decent lines will cushion the blow of reality winning out, yet again.

Ryan looks around him and notes that reality: ugly floral curtains; a coffee table stained with grey rings and round black burns; cream-coloured walls on which shadows have been made permanent through her negligence. There's a low, olive-green couch with wooden armrests; he sits down and clears crumbs and ash off the tabletop with an open palm.

'It's not like I was expecting anyone,' Georgie says.

'Don't worry about it.'

'You know, no one is ever let back here, Ryan.'

'Lucky me then.'

He takes a baggie out of his pocket and starts lining up.

'D'you want a drink or something?' she says.

'No.'

'I want a drink.'

She comes back as he finishes raking out, holding a glass of vodka or gin or whatever it is.

'OK, well, there's no point being coy,' she says. 'What are you after?'

He continues staring at the lines. There's a beat in his head, echoing loud. He feels as if the control he has over his own body is about to give in, and that he'll puke, or cry, or snap or faint or fucking something; he's afraid of that, first of all. He can be afraid of consequences later.

'I don't know what I'm after,' he says.

'They usually know.' She takes a sip. 'Did you fight with your girlfriend or something? Is that why you're here? You know, without your judge's wig on?'

'Don't,' he says.

'It's just that . . . *something's* changed.'

And she's just going to accept that, isn't she? Something's changed but she's not going to rethink her complicity. He's angry now, on top of everything else. It's beyond him how Georgie had the nerve to march up to his dad's front door barking questions, but not the nerve to find her way home again.

'I'm sure you have a price list,' he says. 'You tell me.'

'Am I still allowed to think it's weird?' she says.

'I thought you said it was just a job?'

'It is. Still, though. We have history, you and me.'

She's sorry she said it as soon as it's out of her mouth. He looks up from the bars he's drawn on her table, and his top lip twitches at the corner as a snarl is caught and turned inwards. *He's going to be one of them*, she thinks. For a moment she considers telling him she's changed her mind, and that he's going to have to leave. She wants to preserve what she thinks he showed her on Saturday last. But she decides it's worth taking a chance on and even then she knows she's wrong, deep down, buried with the rest of her cunning.

She finishes her vodka.

'OK,' she says. 'Well, when I go somewhere with a guy it's fifty for the hour. And that's, like, oral and whatever position. Not anal though.'

'That's extra, is it?'

She looks back down at the lines. 'Yeah, I guess.'

'Fuck's sake,' he says.

He's glowering, and she's surprised it turned so soon. 'If you're going to be a dick about it,' she says, 'it's going to be horrible for both of us. You know? I mean, you're the one asking for it, you don't get to judge.'

'Take your line,' he says. 'Before the fucking eyes fall out of your head.'

She kneels in front of the table. 'I'm just saying,' she says. 'I'm disappointed in you too, Ryan.'

She closes her eyes and as she snorts she hears the gentle clunk of something being placed on the table beside her.

She sits on her haunches, staring at the gun out of the corner of her eye, as he leans back on the couch and grinds out noises of disbelief and regret.

It's a while before he accepts she hasn't got a damn thing to say, so he says it for her.

'I'm not here to fuck you, Georgie.'

He leans forward.

'Why would I be? Didn't you tell me before I was never to buy a prostitute? If you really think your words are that weak, I suppose it explains why you couldn't stop asking Jimmy Phelan questions.'

'I don't work for J.P. anymore,' she whispers.

'He wants you dead,' Ryan says.

She twists her hands on her lap and looks at him with sinkhole eyes.

'How does he want me dead, Ryan? I've done everything he asked me to do. I haven't said anything. I haven't asked questions in years.'

'I don't know, Georgie.'

'J.P. told me the whole story. I accepted it. I let it go. I did! I did what he told me . . . It's been years, Ryan.'

Ryan shakes his head.

Georgie says, 'Why you?'

'It's just a job.'

She says nothing for a long time and he has no more mind for leading her. He watches her quake and he hates her for it. He watches his gun on the table in front of her and he hates himself for having it. Most of all he hates what he's about to do but he knows there's no way around it.

He bows his head and sighs.

Georgie is in the horrors.

She sits on her haunches on the floor of her rented one-bed, crying, and distracting herself on and off with the stupidest of notions. *Sniff. Sob. That's it, it ends here. Gulp. Cough. Look how dirty the carpet is. I wish I had a hoover. I should have bought a hoover. Bit late for thinking this now but Oh! To have a hoover! Vacuuming used to be my favourite chore, back when I had a mam and dad and not just old pieces of cloth holding my memories together. Sniff. I'm going to die.*

The fear-sweat leaves her shaking cold. She pulls her arms around herself.

She's sick knowing it won't work but still she tries. 'But me and you, Ryan . . . We're friends. Aren't we?'

He picks up the gun.

'What makes you think I have friends?'

'I saw you with them, on Saturday. All walking down the street, going out or whatever. You have friends because you're a normal guy. You're not . . . this.'

He's standing up. She doesn't move. She cries onto her lap and he moves around the table and over to the window.

'This is normality,' he snaps. The volume makes her jump. She blinks and he comes back into focus; he's staring, hard, his brow furrowed and his lips trembling. 'People do what they have to do. But not me. Fuck this, not me!'

He doesn't raise the gun. He cradles it against his right thigh. With his left hand he covers his eyes.

*

Ryan's failed and he knows he's not going to get away with it, even here where God fucking damn it, it could still be fixed, if he had the balls for it.

She's weeping with fright, and he feeds off it, pacing so he takes up as much air as he can, here in her dingy set.

He's pushed her into her bedroom and she stands with a bag and her passport. He's booked a flight. The next one out of Cork is to London Stansted. It'll do.

'Ryan,' she blubs. 'I can't. My daughter's here. All of this is so that I can get her back. You telling me I can't see her again is just insanity—'

'Me leaving you live is fucking insanity!'

He's right. He's giving her his life instead of taking her worthless one. He's offering his father to her whims. His gaudy rage stops him crying. He really wants to cry.

'I'm a mother,' Georgie insists. 'What about my daughter?'

'What about her!' He points at her, his mobile clutched tight in his hand like another useless weapon. 'She's better off, isn't she? You're no mother, Georgie. Mothers don't go around getting fucked for coke money!'

'That's not fair, Ryan; how else am I going to get by? There are no jobs out there, there's no way I can go to college . . . Be realistic! This is all I'm able to do right now. I'll get it together!'

'You haven't a notion of getting it together! Don't try this one on me, girl. My mam was taken off me so I know what that's like and I wouldn't wish it on anyone so don't for a second think this is because I'm being sentimental about you and your kid; she's better off without you and I don't say that lightly.'

'What if I go home? Back to my mam and dad's. It's in the middle of nowhere, Ryan. No one'll ever see me again. I won't ever come to the city, I swear it!'

'Only now you're thinking of going home, girl? You couldn't go home before you fucked my life up, no? Fuck you. You're going. You're gone.'

Georgie crumples.

'You're not saving me, Ryan. You're killing me.'

'I'm counting on it,' he says. 'And if you come back here, fucking ever, *ever* Georgie, you'll find me a lot less cowardly about putting one in your brain. And your daughter's. And your mam and dad in Millstreet. D'you hear me?'

She holds a hand over her mouth and the tears fall onto it and over her knuckles and slide onto the brown cloth over her wrist.

'I will do it,' he says. 'The only thing wrong with me can be fixed by growing up a bit. You're just damn lucky you caught me when I was too stupid to pull the trigger. You're just damn lucky Jimmy Phelan got me to do the job.'

'I'm not lucky,' she cries. 'This isn't fair—'

'I know it's not fair, girl. But that's the way of things in this rotten city. I barely know what this fuck-up is about, but it's going to take someone. And it's gonna have to be you.'

Ryan has to contact his father afterwards for Jimmy Phelan's number, and he can only do so via text; he realises, up in his old estate, parked thirty feet from his old driveway, that he doesn't want to talk to Tony.

When the reply comes through he puts his hand back on the key in the ignition and freezes.

He's not sure why he didn't notice it – perhaps because he's not been around enough for the alternative to become the norm – but there are lights on in Tara Duane's house, and Tara hasn't been there in ages. She took off the Christmas before last. Someone said she was seeing this Indian guy so she probably ran off to become a Hindu. Tara was flighty that way, and she's done shit like that before, so even her daughter Linda can't call bullshit on the theory.

For a moment he thinks: *She's back.*

After a while the facts begin to settle. The car in the driveway isn't Tara's. There are no curtains or blinds up in the front room, and he can see people, none of whom he recognises, walking past the window. He realises that someone's moving in.

It's been months since Joseph's friend Izzy recommended he seek answers from Tara.

He's conducted the conversation in his head a dozen times but it's made a poor substitute. In fairness, he hasn't cheated on Karine since that neon-lit conversation in the living woods, so it hasn't escaped him that Izzy was right. He's been trying to own it, trying hard, reclassifying it as an indulgent mistake made by a new man driven temporarily mad with the possibilities.

He tells himself, sitting in his car down from his father's house with worse deeds now to his name, that what happened in Tara Duane's house five years ago doesn't matter, not in the grand, fucking dark scheme of things.

He imagines it now again anyway, seeing as she's never coming back.

In her sitting room she hands him a mug of tea and sits there with her vacant smile as he tells her *Hey, I fucked you. I did it. I wanted to. That's what happened, OK?*

It kills him, though. He knows it shouldn't but he feels it like a kick to the gut now that he realises she's gone and his chance for making sense of it's gone with her.

I just want her to confirm it, he thinks; his lips move with it. *Tell me I went for it, that I wanted it, let me have this one, oh God, please, give me this one.*

He starts the car. He has Jimmy Phelan to lie to yet.

Georgie finds her feet. She doesn't know how. It just kind of happens.

She just kind of happens now. From one end of the street to the next. She exists.

London is a massive place and she's frequently lost, and even thinking of it as a collection of towns all jumbled together doesn't help. She is lucky, in that she's happened upon almost straight away by an Irish couple who offer to help her find where she's going. Of course she has no destination. She tells them, tearing up, that she had to leave Cork because of an abusive boyfriend. She tells the Irish couple that she has friends in London but she hasn't seen them in years and claims that the address she has for them is out of date, oh, what is she to do? They find her a guesthouse. She thinks that's about it but the next day the woman from the couple comes to the guesthouse to see her. She gives her the name of a friend in Islington who's got a downstairs flat to rent. It turns out to be no great shakes but no one pays any attention, least of all Georgie. Her desperation is a potent scent and though she never sees the Irish do-gooders again, just that stroke of luck is enough.

She finds an agency. It's not difficult; her ground-floor flat is surrounded by the domiciles of shuffling addicts and weird bachelors, and they know where the action is. She meets a bright-eyed Russian woman in a cafe on Holloway Road. She tells her she's older than is usually asked for, unless she goes into specialised stuff. More lucrative, she says. Georgie shakes her head. Whoring isn't her calling, for fuck's sake. The woman gives her the number of another agency, which provides much cheaper lays.

She has found a place in which to exist, outside of reality, as a glitch in someone else's world.

She thinks about exacting her revenge, but it's too soon, and she's not sure where to direct it. Concocting plans around Jimmy Phelan strikes her as futile, like marching on Heaven and demanding God's resignation.

She thinks about Ryan, and one day making him see what he did to her.

One day, she thinks, *God willing*.

She might die in the meantime. She hasn't made up her mind yet.

While she's waiting she posts the scapular back to whatever's left standing on Bachelor's Quay. She addresses the envelope to Robbie O'Donovan.

What Tara Did

Young Ryan is out on the back wall. Tara spots him from her kitchen window. It's a quarter to eleven and it's a Sunday night. He really shouldn't be there at this hour. She figures he's been driven out again. She determines to offer her sympathies. No harm; Melinda's away. Her dad has taken her to Dublin for a few days, to see the sights. Tara would like to be lonely without her, but she's glad of the peace and quiet. Melinda is very demanding.

Boys are demanding too. Ryan, like all boys, is usually cheeky and funny but tonight he's quiet as a mouse. There's a nasty bruise around his left eye. 'Oh, darling,' Tara says. She sits beside him on the wall and presses up against him; he's shivering. No one in their right mind would sit out in the cold without good reason. The night is damp to its very breath. Ryan has problems with his father. Tara knows because she hears the boor's convulsions. There's no privacy on this terrace. Quite rightly. If there was then the poor boy would have to suffer alone.

'Come inside,' she coaxes, 'and we'll have a lovely cup of tea.'

At first he resists because he doesn't want to trouble her. She assures him that she wants to look after him. She rests a friendly hand on his knee and when he doesn't flinch she skims gently up to his thigh and squeezes. 'You don't have to go through this alone,' she says.

If he was any other boy on this terrace she wouldn't be so insistent because some of them are only brutes in the making. They follow her down the street and whoop obscenities. They make loud remarks on the bus. Ryan is different. He has grown up very fast, the one positive from his father's cruelty. He has wrested some independence by doing a little bit of dealing to his friends. It's naughty, but sometimes Tara enjoys smoking with him. He's getting taller and broader by the day. He's almost sixteen.

She leads him inside and puts the kettle on.

'Tell you what I'll do,' she says. 'I'll put a drop of whiskey into your tea for you. It's beautiful stuff; I got it at Christmas and I've been saving it for a special occasion. Aged. Have you ever had aged whiskey?'

The boy says he's fine.

'Don't be silly,' Tara blusters. 'It'll warm you right up!'

The whiskey she has isn't old at all but she thinks it's best if he gets a good drop down him and she doesn't want him complaining about the taste in the tea. She makes it fairly strong. It is very cold outside.

'Come into the sitting room,' she says. 'And we'll have a chat. And you know what? If you don't want to talk about your dad we don't have to. We can just watch telly and talk about that instead. Do you like *True Blood*? I have a few of them lined up in the Sky Box.'

When Ryan gets into the sitting room he sheepishly produces a baggie of grass and asks if she wants some. He knows the propriety of barter. She smiles. She lets him skin up and sits cross-legged beside him on the couch and shares the joint with him.

'You roll another,' she tells him, after they finish, 'and I'll make another cuppa.'

She doesn't have a second drop herself; she doesn't need it.

He sits on the couch only half watching Bill and Sookie and messing with his phone. He's as taut as a guitar string; she thinks if she touched him now he'd sing for her. They can be so jittery at his age.

'What are you going to do later?' she asks.

'Go home, I suppose.' His voice is so very low; he probably doesn't want his father to know he's next door. Perhaps it's not allowed. Perhaps his father knows the damage a boy can do, especially when the woman next door is on her own. *Ryan knows he's being bold*, she thinks.

'Don't worry,' she soothes. 'You can stay here on the couch. I'll bring you down a blanket and pillow.'

On the way back to the sitting room she grabs a couple of cans from the fridge.

'Here,' she says. 'I've already given you my loveliest whiskey, so we might as well keep going.'

He drinks up as he's told.

Still so quiet. She tries to get him to talk but he's brooding. She sits back beside him on the couch and tells him if there's anything he needs to get off his chest, she's here for him. He says he's fine, but, mouth a bit more liberated now, he expresses thanks for giving him somewhere to sit while he waits for his dad to calm down. 'Calm down?' says Tara, eyes wide. Ryan shrugs. Tara says, 'Oh, sweetheart.' She holds him. He doesn't know how to handle that. He freezes. She puts a hand on the back of his neck and guides him to her breast. 'It's OK,' she says. 'It's going to be OK.'

He pulls away and tells her he needs to use the bathroom. While he's gone she dashes into the kitchen and gets him another can. He doesn't seem so keen when he returns. 'I kinda shouldn't,' he says. 'Oh, darling,' she replies. 'When life gives you lemons, make a gin and tonic. How much worse could tonight possibly get?'

Well, he is langers altogether once he gets to the end of the can and she laughs and gets him another. He's chattier but he's starting to slur. She wonders if he's had a few joints already tonight. By the end of the next can she's able to hug him a lot easier. 'Poor baby,' she says, and kisses the top of his head. She can feel his breath on her chest.

One more and he's done altogether. He lies back on the couch and she continues talking to him, telling him that he's worth more than his father knows and that the world is full of good friends if you only learn how to open the door. She realises halfway through one of her favourite anecdotes that he's asleep. She leans over him. 'Ryan?' she murmurs. He doesn't move. She sits at the end of the couch and puts his head in her lap and strokes his hair while she watches the end of her episodes.

He starts to snore.

Tara reaches for his phone and goes through it. She makes sure her number is in his contacts. It's saved under 'T.D.'. Maybe he's worried his dad will see but it's too impersonal, so she changes it to 'Tara x'. She opens the Facebook app and considers writing a jokey status update but concludes that it would be inappropriate. She goes through his photos. They're mostly of him and his little girlfriend. Tara rolls her eyes.

There's a video in the library. It's frozen on blurred skin tones. She presses play and holds her hand tight over the speakers.

It's the girlfriend. For a moment Tara doesn't recognise her because she's sucking on a cock and the angle shows only her lips and her downturned eyes, but when the trollop looks up she realises. The girl is naked. The camera occasionally glides the length of her body. Tara figures it's Ryan holding the camera.

'Well,' she says, softly.

The video stops when he comes. Tara watches it a couple more times.

She gets up carefully and leaves Ryan's head back on the couch.

'You're even naughtier than I thought you were,' she tells him. He doesn't stir.

She crouches by the couch and looks at him. He's wearing a pair of grey cotton tracksuit bottoms and a stripy polo shirt in lemon and grey. He's got a stud in one ear and – she gently tugs his collar down – one of those leather necklace things. He doesn't move when she touches his collar so she traces her fingers down his chest slowly.

'You're so fucked I better sit with you,' she tells him, 'in case you throw up, and then where would we be?'

She starts at his neck again.

'So fucked,' she says. There's a song to it. 'You're so, so fucked.'

This time she works a little way into the waistband of his pants, just to see. Black underwear. 'Classy,' she tells him. She strokes his tummy, under his shirt. She touches the thin dark ridge below his bellybutton and slides her finger down. His dick twitches.

'Are you even asleep?' she teases.

She touches his crotch on the outside of his tracksuit bottoms and says, 'Ryan? Ryan?' but he doesn't answer. She strokes until his dick is hard enough for her to close her hand around it.

She makes a decision. She straddles him, very gently, and leans down so her head is on his chest, and she listens to his heart beating. 'Ryan?' she tries again. His dick is still hard against her. 'You might be asleep but your body's wide awake,' she tells him. 'Don't you think that's odd?'

No response. She brushes her middle finger against his bottom lip.

'A girl told me recently,' she confides, 'that I should take what I can get. Which I thought sounded a bit ugly, but now I wonder if she just wasn't well-read enough to have heard the term "*carpe diem*". And *clearly* . . .' She laughs. 'Clearly you don't mind.'

She gets up again. She slides her knickers off, kneels by the couch, works his clothes down to his thighs and nuzzles against him for a while, eyes fixed on his face. Then she opens her mouth and holds his dick between her lips and licks and sucks him till she's ready to get back on top. She's wet and it's stupidly easy. She holds his dick and slides over him and starts to ride and eventually he blinks and groans and she's too far gone to want his input or to want to start all over so she cuddles against his chest again, still rocking, almost there, and says 'Sssh, baby, go back to sleep' and he does, how easy, how well his mind knows to stay out of this and just let his body have its fun, how fucking easy . . .

But his hands are grasping her arms, and then there's a rude tumble and she's on the floor, and she skins her elbow on the carpet and clutches it and allows her eyes to water with the shock.

'Ryan, that really hurt!'

He's curled up at one end of the couch, gasping and swallowing like he's had a desperate nightmare.

'That was not very nice,' she chides, back on her feet and fixing her dress.

He stands up, and she feels too wounded to offer an arm as he wobbles and pulls his tracksuit pants back up and peeps like a baby bird.

She folds her arms. 'What's wrong?'

And sure he can barely speak, the stupid boy. 'No,' he says. 'Coz it's not . . . I have a girlfriend.'

'Well, you better not tell her, so!'

He's very, very drunk, because he starts crying.

'Oh for God's sake,' says Tara. She's careful to look stern because in his foolish, showy blubbering she sees trouble enough to catch in her throat.

'You can't tell her,' Ryan says.

Tara moves towards him but he backs away, and knocks against the sitting-room door frame, and has to grab the banister to keep himself upright. 'Why would I tell her?' Tara says, carefully, trying out a smile, finding a foothold. 'She wouldn't understand. It's OK, I get what you're telling me. This'll be our secret, I promise.'

She watches him fumble with the front door lock.

She frets about it the next day. She really likes Ryan. He's a pleasant young man. She doesn't want to fall out with him. But she can't be so complacent as to trust his perception of the previous night's events; he drank too much, and he'd clearly been stoned before he'd even come onto her property. No, she'll have to do a little damage limitation. She can't risk him broadcasting his half-remembered misgivings, not with her history. People are far too quick to judge these days.

In the early evening she spots his father walking up the driveway and she steels herself and runs out to catch him.

Tony Cusack hates her. She doesn't mind that; he's pathetic, the kind of man whose favoured publican lives for Children's Allowance day. 'What?' he says. Tara's not at all bothered by his tone. Weak-kneed malingerers don't frighten her.

'Just a quick word,' she says. 'Ryan was around at mine last night. I don't think he was entirely sober.'

'What was he doing at yours?'

'He says he came by to see Melinda, but . . . Well look, Tony. I really don't like to get him into trouble, but his behaviour was inappropriate. It became rather clear that he has . . . well, fixated on me. He seems to think there's something between us.'

'Does he now? And where would he get that idea?'

She bristles. 'I'm hardly leading him on!'

'So you're telling me that my fifteen-year-old, who can't go ten fucking minutes without texting his girlfriend, is suddenly infatuated with you? What the fuck are you getting at?'

She scowls. He's pronounced it 'infactuated'.

'You're being needlessly hostile,' she says. 'I'm only trying to help. I'm so aware of the fact that he lost his mother and so it's hardly surprising that he's acting out with older girls, is it? He showed me a video, on his phone. I think you need to watch it,' she smiles, 'and just inform yourself as to what he's up to.'

26

The frame around which one builds one's life is a brittle thing, and in a city of souls connected one snapped beam can threaten the spikes and shadows of the skyline.

Robbie O'Donovan died hunting for sentiment to bring home to a girl he refused to save and in his expiration made shit of structures he'd never seen. Small houses. Small sanctuaries. Small lives. The city runs on the macro, but what's that, except the breathing, beating, swallowing, sweating agonies and ecstasies of a hundred thousand little lives?

Cork City isn't going to notice the last faltering steps of a lost little man. All those lives, all those beams, crisscrossed into the grandest of structures . . . the city won't see the snapping sticks, or feel the first sparks.

So scale it down. Zoom in. Look closer.

Fighting cats in the courtyard outside woke Maureen at 4 a.m. She couldn't get back to sleep so she travelled through time.

She was well aware that she lived in the past but, she decided, it was because she'd been left there. Decisions taken on her behalf forty years ago had anchored her to a moment doomed to repeat itself, over and over. Here's the piss-licking face of Una Phelan. Here's her husband, a sheep in wolf's clothing. Here are the clergy, gathered outside the maternity ward like an unkindness of ravens, grasping every perch they were and weren't entitled to. Ireland, the clouds outside. *And shame on you, Ireland*, thought Maureen, four full decades later. *You think you'd at least look after your own?*

She got out of bed and stood at the window. The cats were well gone. In the apartment directly across from hers, a Christmas tree twinkled between heavy curtains. *Bad idea*, she thought idly. *The place could go up in flames.*

Her own vengeance lay festering under piles of sodden ash in Mitchelstown, and what use was it, at the end of the day? Without a perpetrator the Gardaí had no motive and without the platform of culpability Maureen had no audience at which to shout it. The papers had said the Gardaí were looking for a woman to assist with their enquiries, so that hoyden Saskia had obviously blabbed. They hadn't found this woman because she'd never existed. In the meantime people blamed unruly youths and assumed no political motivation.

She wrote a letter to the *Indo* hinting that the person who'd set fire to the church up in Mitchelstown had, perhaps, been making a bold statement, and that maybe Ireland should expect more in the way of this kind of carry-on if it wasn't going to learn its history lessons. The *Indo* hadn't published it. What kind of Ireland had she inherited at all, when the *Indo* wouldn't even publish crackpot woe-betides?

She put the kettle on.

In Holles Street four decades past a midwife lay a wriggling mound on her stomach.

And that was all she got.

She didn't miss Robbie O'Donovan and though at the time she'd been sure it had been the flames that had taken him, she wondered now, wringing out a teabag in the middle of the winter dark, if it hadn't simply been time for him to feck off. Hadn't his demise been his own fault? He had crept in through a window on the latch and skulked though her home looking for relics, and had been knocked into his grave by the kind of woman no one thought still worthy of blame.

She sat at her kitchen table. Around her the debris stacked. She hadn't done any housework in the six weeks since she'd sprained her wrist. That was Jimmy's job and he'd failed to provide a decent solution. She assumed his interest in his mother had waned now that she was no longer causing him trouble. The girl Georgie had disappeared off the face of the earth, her lips sealed and her mind at last honed by Maureen's generous wisdom. The man Tony had been threatened to keep his mouth shut. Robbie had gone up in smoke. Maureen had been left redundant and Jimmy had other things to worry about, in his line of work.

Spraining her wrist had slowed her down, and she'd stopped hunting for redemption, or what measure of it the charlatans sold wrapped in hymn and waffle. She was finished toying with swindlers, either by laughing at their convictions or burning down their temples. She had no energy left for divilment, not now she knew how much her son got up to on her behalf, behind her back.

She went for a walk.

It was just before five when she left the house and the city was a pyre too damp to take the flame. She wandered towards the Lee. Its forked tongue was probably the reason the place wouldn't burn.

What keeps this bloody city alive at all? she wondered.

It wasn't Jimmy; wasn't he too busy ruining it?

There was no stopping him now, and even if she found a way to vocalise it, to explain that he'd done his bit but her revenge was ultimately an empty thing, so he could stop now, and rest . . . Well, someone else would take his place. Some other scoundrel bent out of shape by the twisted streets of this pirate's city. Jimmy's fall would birth another, and another, and another, and Maureen would be matriarch of all.

Too late for Jimmy. That's why she time-travelled. If she could have caught him that Christmas he bought her a brandy, when he was twenty and she was dismissed as no longer threatening by the baseless piety of her stupid parents, who's to say what she could have done?

She walked along the Lee and towards the old brothel. On the water the reflections of street lights shimmered like sinking lanterns, golden and red on the black, and beautiful.

On the iron bridge across from the gutted brick there was a figure on the parapet, standing still and staring down.

Maureen wondered first, *Robbie O'Donovan?*, because the figure was tall and skinny and definitely male, and more again, because it was so frozen and so quiet that it seemed otherworldly. She managed to walk all the way onto the bridge without disturbing him.

The likeness was startling. For a moment she fancied she had time-travelled, but had managed to land beside the wrong son, John and Noreen's, the one whose fragility had been shaped to fit under her own boy's turpitude. But the fancy dissipated; this wasn't Tony. This one was taller and thinner, quite the wrong shape, but the dark hair, the jaw, the chin, the mouth, the bloody everything else was just the same. She whistled under her breath. Another boy who wasn't his mother's son.

Now that she was this much closer she realised he wasn't so silent. He was singing something in tuneful whispers, something to which he didn't know the words. He was quite lost in it, and lost in the will-o-the-wisp colours in the black water beneath them. No light to his song. She realised with a sickening start that he was set to jump, and so she snapped,

'What do you think you're doing?'

And he turned, and her breath caught as she saw him lose his balance, but he fell the right way, just a few feet away from her, whacking his head off the concrete.

She stood over him. His eyes met hers. Big black pools, as much as the river was below them.

He sat up, suddenly, against the parapet, and she sighed and repeated, 'What do you think you're doing?'

He pushed himself upright, dragging his back against the parapet, and when he was on his own two feet he dug into his pockets and produced a lighter and a cigarette, and three goes later he managed to drag deep enough to keep it lit.

'Well?' she snapped.

'Well what?'

'Well, what do you think you're doing?'

'Nothing.'

'Oh yes. Great times we're having, when you meet young fellas making eyes at the Lee in the early hours. Doing *nothing*. What would your mother say?'

The Italian girl, the prematurely departed. Maureen wondered how happy she could have been in this city, surrounded by the insular and the suspicious, and their faith, and their fallen.

Her son stood with one hand clasped to the back of his head. His jaw rolled. Maureen assumed that he'd knocked it on his graceless descent, but moments passed and he didn't speak up, so she peered closer, though the night, through the ancestry fixed on his features, and wondered if it wasn't half out of his tree he was, and if his balancing act hadn't been born of synthetic bravado rather than the despair she thought she could spot in his stance. She didn't know the ins and outs of inebriation, outside of being able to diagnose every stage of drunkenness as dictated by her nationality; he was inebriated, though, and not pissed. It was in the size of his eyes, and she'd mistaken it for character.

'What's your name?' she asked.

He complied. 'Ryan,' he said, after a while gnawing the air in what seemed to her to be terror churned with a slight concussion, and she waited for him to elaborate until he followed up with 'Cusack.'

Of course it is, she wanted to say. *Isn't it nearly dripping off you?*

'What in God's name are you at, Ryan Cusack?'

Again, silence. He blew out his cheeks and looked over her shoulder. She cocked her head.

Under his breath, she thought she heard, 'Grandmaw, what big teeth you have . . .'

She scowled.

'Come on,' she said, turning around and walking back towards the city centre, away from the hollowed landmark, along by the indolent water, and she looked back twice and he was following her, as she knew he would, as she knew his father would too, once given a command voiced with appropriate authority, and she thought that this was how it should be. The parents cast the mould for the little ones and the little ones curved to fit.

Between the opera house and the gallery she found a stone block bench and waited for him to approach, and when he got close enough for her to see the fear and the loss she directed him to sit beside her and said,

'What are you on, then?'

He folded up and laid his head on his crossed arms. 'I dunno,' he said.

'You don't know? And what d'you think your mother would say to that? Winking at the river, having gobbled goodness knows what. Is that so you'll drown easier? Your poor father, Ryan Cusack.'

'Fuck him.' He rubbed his forehead off his forearm and raised his head.

'You look tired,' she said.

'I am tired.'

'How could you be tired? Fine lad like you. What must you be, twenty?'

'Yeah,' he said. 'Twenty-one in March.'

'Are you that afraid of twenty-one?'

'Maybe I just wanted to go swimming.'

'Aw, shite.' She leaned closer. 'Why are you afraid of twenty-one?'

'I'm not,' he said, and stared over the square, and she gave him time to figure out his mouth, and after a while he said, 'I am. I dunno. I dunno.'

'All these young fellas,' Maureen chided. She looked across the river. The Northside rose dotted in white and yellow lights, and she wondered how many of those lights denoted a young life yet to be dammed and diverted? How many of them could be another Jimmy?

She looked back at Tony's son and furrowed her brow.

'I think it's sad,' she said. 'You have a child and your child is the whole world. What did your father ever do that you'd want to take that from him?'

Ryan mumbled, 'Why does it have to be about him?'

'He made you, didn't he?'

'You don't know him. He doesn't give a fuck.'

'Of course he does.' If he didn't, Jimmy wouldn't have spun his noose so easily.

'He doesn't,' said Ryan. He leaned back and looked up at the sky. 'If you knew him you'd know that. He's a prick and that's where I got it from.'

'Ah. You're suffering from something inherited, is it? Something that makes you want to take to the Lee only days before Christmas?'

Decades ago, a twenty-year-old Jimmy Phelan offered his mother a Christmas brandy and she took it and closed her hand briefly around his and smiled.

'What if I cured you?' she said, but Ryan didn't answer. She shuffled closer to him and held her hand out and he looked at it, blinked, and frowned. There was a light sheen on his face, even in the chill. She jerked her hand, and he sat up and held out his own and she grabbed it.

'Yours aren't workers' hands,' she said.

She turned his hand over in hers and traced from the tip of his index finger to his wrist.

'What do you do, Ryan? Are you in college?'

He shook his head.

'Well, what then?'

'A bit of this and that,' he said.

'A bit of this and that? Shady little fecker, aren't you?'

He put his head back onto his free arm.

'Pup,' she said.

He looked at her, his nose and mouth hidden in the crook of his arm.

'Easy know what you are,' she said.

'That easy?'

'Oh yes. And yet don't you have complicated eyes? Very dark. But then, your mother wasn't Irish.'

He closed his eyes and for a moment she wondered if he hadn't done so in self-preservation, but then he opened them again, and she watched them focus until he was ready to say, 'How'd you know that?'

'I know things,' she said, confidently; more than the priests, more than the idiot savants down at Ruby Dea's ramshackle commune. 'You're the musician,' she stated. 'But you're not playing, are you?'

He sat straight and stared at her and his hand in hers turned heavy.

'Fuck,' he said. 'How'd you know that?'

'Coz I can see right through you,' she said. 'Coz you're as blatant as a burning church. Don't you think I know what's wrong with you? It's easy see what you're able for, and not able for, and despite what he tells me I know you're not able to play the little gangster.'

'What the fuck did you call me?'

'A little gangster. Isn't that all you are? Don't you think how you make your money has plenty to do with wanting to drown yourself?'

She'd hit the spot. He made to pull away, but she held on tight and he had neither the foundation nor the spite to drag her with him. He stopped pulling and she said, 'That river doesn't care who or what you are, but it will take you, boy, if you dare it to. Don't you know that?'

He wasn't able to answer.

'I should know. This city ruined me,' she confided. 'But the odd thing is, while it was ruining me I was ruining it, and I only figured that out when it was too late to stop it. What I did to this city, me and Dominic Looney, is something immeasurable and I see it in the faces of people I never should have met. And yet . . . maybe I can make it up to one man, at least. The city doesn't see me, but maybe I'm aiming too high.'

She rubbed her thumb over his skin again, taking him in, his father's face, his father's eyes, and a future all of his own to burn.

'Don't let the river take you,' she said. 'Promise me!'

She put her arms around him and his pulse leapt as she pressed the palms of her hands against his neck.

'Promise me, I said!'

She let him sit up and took his face in her hands.

'You don't understand,' he said. 'I'm a bad guy. Worse than you could fucking imagine.' His voice was choked with woozy torment; she rubbed her thumbs over his cheekbones, delirious. 'I've already done the damage. I had something good and I wrecked it, and ruined it and lost it. What am I without her? I'm turning into Him.'

'Not if I can help it.'

She tilted her head towards the city and smiled.

'Of course this place can pull you apart,' she said. 'But this country's done punishing me, and I can do what I like now, and so I choose to fix you, and by God this pile will let me. Don't mind that river, Ryan Cusack. Whatever's bad we'll burn it out; that's how it's done. If you want to take the fuckers with you, that can be arranged.'

Beyond them turned the world and the land and its sleeping city. Maureen felt giddy. Robbie O'Donovan had been a mistake Cork hadn't even noticed, but this one, this one she'd substitute, a life for a life, and she'd make damn sure the city knew it.

'I will put you right,' she said. 'Sure haven't I already saved your life?'

Acknowledgements

Heartfelt thanks are owed to Mark Richards for the advice and the tweaks and his patience with terrible jokes. And to Caro Westmore, Becky Walsh, Rosie Gailer and everyone at John Murray.

To the lion Ivan Mulcahy, to Sallyanne Sweeney and Stephanie Cohen for all of their help, and to the tirelessly wonderful Sinéad Gleeson.

To the brave souls who read and steered and bolstered me without ever realising how much it meant: John Green, Richard Fish, Arlene Hunt, Liam Daly, Damien Mulley, Julian Gough, Conor O'Neill, Haydn Shaughnessy and Sinéad Keogh.

To Kevin Barry, for shoving me where I needed to be, and to Sami Zahringer, for her immense generosity.

To my sprawling, intimidating, brilliant family, and to the friends who continue to put up with me, particularly to Ellen Brohan, Louise Lynskey, Kevin Lehane and his exceptional brain, and my partner-in-crime Caroline Naughton.

And most especially to Róisín, who has a writer instead of a mother and doesn't seem to mind, and to John, because there'd be nothing without John.